BERSERKER!

With maniacal fury Michael cut his way through the crowd. Casting aside his shield, he grasped the giant's head and held it aloft. Then he screamed savagely and slashed at the man before him. The lifeless eyes of their leader looked out at the Ezrians—and they fell back before his gaze.

Michael was the instrument of war now, and the backs of his enemies so enraged him that he drove after them, hurling the head at their retreating forms. Along the length of the wall they ran, while the sound of gunfire swelled in the distance. Suddenly a shadow fell from above and crashed into him. Michael's thoughts fled and he tumbled into darkness . . .

Also by William R. Forstchen
Published by Ballantine Books:

THE FLAME UPON THE ICE

ICE
PROPHET

WILLIAM R.
FORSTCHEN

A Del Rey Book

BALLANTINE BOOKS • NEW YORK

A Del Rey Book
Published by Ballantine Books

Copyright © 1983 by William R. Forstchen

Library of Congress Catalog Car Number: 82-91204

ISBN 0-345-30790-9

Printed in Canada

First Edition: August 1983
Third Printing: September 1984

Cover art by Darrell K. Sweet

Maps and illustrations by Tom Hudson

To Marilyn, who was always there
And for Tappy, who was there in spirit

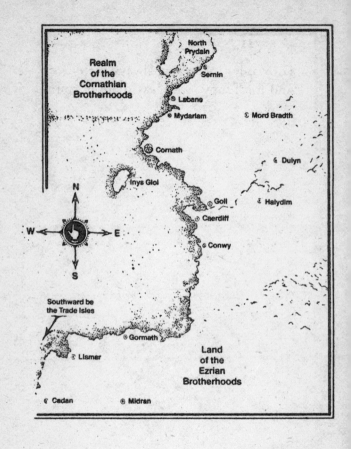

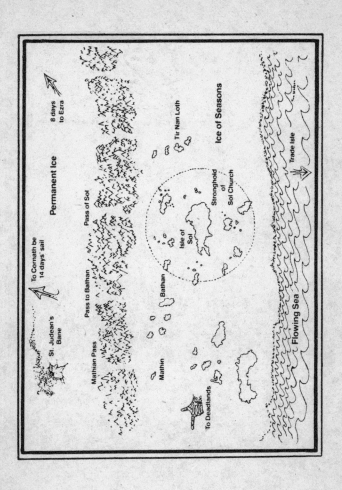

BOOK I

Ice Cruiser

CHAPTER 1

It HAD BEEN A QUIET MOMENT THERE UPON THE PINNACLE OF watching, but the time had passed all too quickly with the setting of the sun beyond the Frozen Sea. Already the first lights of the evening sky were appearing. Removing his mask for a moment, Archbishop Rifton of St. Awstin turned his gaze heavenward to watch the first dim traces of the Holy Arch appear. He knew he was resisting what had to be done, but he let the icy fingers of the night air tingle and then numb his cheeks until the polite whisper recalled him to his duty.

."Yes, Brother Niall. I know, damn it, I know," he whispered as he turned and left the evening sky of peace behind.

The fetid warmth of the caverns was a shock, but he paid little heed to the stench of home, of the cloisters, of the thousands of men living beneath the mountains in the dead of winter's night. Downward he walked, barely acknowledging the bows and mumbled blessings of the brothers, who were lining up in rank for the procession. He swiftly entered the antechamber of his apartments, where his archdeacons awaited him.

3

"Yes, brothers, I know I'm late," he growled, and with a wave he beckoned to Brother Niall, who began to dress him in the ceremonial robes.

"Your Holiness, all is ready for the procession," Brother Ceadac said in his soft lisping voice.

"Thank you, Ceadac. How are things with you, Brother Mather? Is all prepared?"

Mather smiled his usual demonic grin but merely nodded. Rifton found something distasteful about Mather; nevertheless, it was useful to have a renegade priest of Mor on one's side.

Within a few moments Niall had completed his task, and Rifton was robed in the white and golden cassock proper for the Night of Supplication. Niall stepped aside humbly and bowed as Rifton made the sign of blessing.

"Niall, could you please fetch him for me?" Rifton said softly.

"Of course, your Excellency. He is waiting down the hall."

"Fine, give me a couple of minutes, though." Rifton turned from his archdeacons and they knew they were dismissed. The door closed softly behind him.

The book lay upon his desk, where he had studied and wrestled with its words often enough. Its soft black leather was worn around the edges from years of use. He looked briefly at the cover's gold-leaf characters, which read *The Book of Prophecies*, then turned to the pages that had tormented him for so long.

"Chapter three, verse one through four," he whispered, and then started to read aloud.

"And behold there shall come a night of fire when the heavens shall cast out all those of the Saints that do not believe, and upon that night he shall come when the great light hovers in the sky, neither to the north nor the south of the Arch.

"His light shall be one with the light of his fire. And it shall search into the souls of men. And all that shall see him shall come to follow him, or in their fear shall spurn him and curse him. Yet with his coming shall be an end to all and the dawning of the new age."

Rifton stopped for a moment, then read on: "And at this

time, there shall be two above all others. And one shall be of the light and the other shall be of the darkness, and long they shall wrestle. The one of darkness shall lead his people into sin. But the one of light shall bring about the final days, when the Choosing of the First shall be complete and a new light shall dawn upon the Ice. Then the Father shall return. Then shall the power of old be shaken and revealed. But in this time of darkness even shall father strike down his son and the son his family as well."

A knock sounded at the door. He pushed the book aside and looked up, the only sign of his pain the nervous movement of his fingers at the edge of his robe.

"Come in, Michael."

The door swung open and, bending low, a young man dressed in the garb of an ice runner made his way into the plainly furnished room of the Archbishop of St. Awstin.

"I see that Niall has prepared you," Rifton said evenly.

"Yes, your Excellency." The young man lifted his head and looked into Rifton's eyes. His expression was one of confusion and anxiety.

Rifton studied him for several seconds but stoically ignored the fear in the young man's eyes. "Do you have the equipment that you need?"

"Yes, Niall even gave me a cloak that you wore long ago."

"Do you understand what is expected of you, Michael?"

"Yes."

"Beware the brothers of Mor. Most likely they have their own orders concerning you. There are no guards, so keep a close watch. Remember that you are really nothing more than a hostage of the Morians now, so take care and you should be here safely in the spring."

"Couldn't you just say no to Zimri and let me remain? I have no desire for the Ice. I would much rather stay in the monastery with you."

"Michael, you are Ormson. Take the responsibility of it."

Michael sensed the rebuke in his tone.

"It was a good maneuver on Zimri's part to ask for you personally in front of all the other archbishops. To refuse,

Michael, would have shown favoritism and brought a loss of face to our family. Besides, you're on the admiral's ship and Halvin is a close friend; he'll help you when he can. To be a ship's chart reader and keeper of the log is something a man your age should find exciting. Why, Michael, you'll see the Southward Isles and a thousand other sights as well."

Michael stood quietly.

"Michael, you must go. The others are waiting. Now take my blessing."

Michael knelt silently and Rifton made the sign of the Arch over him.

"May all the Saints watch over thee upon the Ice and return you safely to our brotherhood. Amen."

Michael rose and managed a wan smile. "Good-bye, Uncle," he said softly through his tears.

Rifton's control broke and he threw his arms around the only one in the world whom he could trust and love. The last of his family alive after the forty years of war and plague.

"Good-bye, my boy, and the Saints bless you."

Michael turned and left the room and each man hid his tears from the other.

Darkness spread across the city as the columns of monks issued from their cloistered halls and made their way to the central square, where the procession would begin.

The alleyways were barely wide enough for two men to pass abreast and they were thick with the fetid stench of thousands who lived in tiny one-room hovels during the winter's freezing night. Half the rooms were carved into the limestone hill that squatted beneath Cornath, while the rest were of quarried stone or, occasionally, of precious wood. The alleyways seemed dark tunnels, as the second and third floors of the surrounding buildings rose over and leaned against their neighbors across the way. The monks waded through dirty snow, refuse, and offal tossed from the windows above. When spring thaw arrived in late May, only the poorest stayed in Cornath, for the streets became stagnant rivers of filth.

Rifton rode at the head of his five hundred monks as they

approached the Great Square, which faced out over the harbor. From other alleyways converged the different brotherhoods of the Church. Rifton halted his column to let them pass. Some grumbling arose from the rear but this was quickly stilled as his shadowy figure turned to look down upon them.

First came the good friars of Braith de Borth, the brothers of poverty, their long rough robes scant protection in the night's cold. Each carried the traditional bowl of life that the pious filled with coin or bread. Behind came twenty brothers of the Braith de Creidman, the brothers of salvation, who would sail upon the venture as missionaries to the followers of the false prophet. At a gap in the passing of the brothers, Rifton turned quickly to Brother Mather, and Mather merely smiled. Long minutes passed and the men stamped their feet impatiently as the various orders of the fourteen brotherhoods passed before them.

The Braith de Narn, the silent ones, came in ghostly quiet, followed by the Braith de Dochas, the healing order. A cold stillness fell over all as the Mord Rinn passed. As always, they walked in groups of three, and their burgundy robes shone in the glow of the torches they carried. Their cowls completely concealed any human feature. They were the Inquisitioners, the seekers of Orthodoxy; their word could sustain life or bring death.

The various contingents appeared, then were swallowed up by the night as they descended to the harbor. Several of the orders had monasteries at Cornath but most only visited for the yearly sailing and the Supplication. St. Awstin's monastery, their home abbey, was the largest in the city, but tonight one order would have far more present.

From the distance Rifton could hear their chanting, a deep dissonant bass that reached into the very bones to send shivers down the spine. The soft whispers around Rifton grew silent. At first their procession was a shadow in the darkness, then without warning it burst forth with a blazing light as eight hundred torches flared and were held aloft at once at the end of the shadowy square. The Brotherhood of Mor was coming.

The chanting swelled as the dissonant bass called out the

rhythm of "To the Saints and Mor," the minor-key Gregorian chant that had been the sign of their brotherhood for a thousand years. The first chant ended as the head of the column came abreast of Rifton, and the drum called out the rhythm of "To the Return of the Father." Clouds of incense wafted from the column, the yellow-green smoke bearing the foul stench of sulfur. Six monks dressed in the dark-blue robes of the brotherhood led the column. Before them they carried the icon of St. Mor of Baileth, behind rode a cloaked figure who turned aside and came up to Rifton. The brothers of Mor slowly passed by.

"My brother Rifton," a low, almost melodic voice whispered, "the blessings of the Saints be upon you."

"And also on you, Zimri," Rifton said coldly.

Rifton turned and looked at the Archbishop of Mor. In the torchlight he could barely see the features of the man. The cowl was pulled up, but Zimri wore no mask against the cold and his soft, doelike eyes were mirrors of piety. The thin, bloodless lips and the high, arching cheekbones were pale in the cold light, as if Zimri's once handsome features had been carved from lifeless marble. The right side of Zimri's face was torn and scarred from temple to jaw. As he looked at Zimri in the torchlight, Rifton could almost feel pity for him. He could almost understand. With a mumbled curse he turned away. No, no pity for Zimri.

"It's a good night for a sailing," Zimri said, and a faint smile curled the edge of his mouth.

Rifton did not answer.

"Tell me, good brother, do you think the Supplication will succeed this year?" With that Zimri laughed softly.

"Of course, Brother Zimri," Rifton replied so that all could hear. "Of course, I believe the Supplication will succeed. Why, do you doubt Holy Writ?"

The monks around them stopped their conversation and turned to stare. Zimri glared at Rifton for a moment then silently galloped off to the head of his column.

"That was dangerous, your Holiness," Niall murmured from the darkness, "especially now."

Rifton waved the advice aside. He watched his enemy disappear into the dark. Rifton, the Archbishop of St. Awstin, the order of scribes, chartmakers, and knowledge-keepers, was locked in a death struggle with the young Archbishop of Mor, of the warrior order, and he had to attack whenever possible. By tradition, as head of the oldest brotherhood, St. Awstin's Archbishop would rise to the seat of Holy Father, and so it had been for a thousand years. But all was changed. With the plague years and the Forty Years' War, Mor's warrior brethren had risen in power until now Zimri was making inroads with the council. He had just been appointed Secretary to the Holy Father and his next target was obvious.

The attack had taken a new turn only the week before at the close of the council of bishops. The archbishops and the fifty brothers of the hidden image were at the closing meeting when Zimri made his move.

"By the way, Rifton, Halvin's chart reader and scribe has fallen ill and cannot sail. Can you help me with this?"

Rifton sensed a trap; assignment of personnel was a job for a secretary, not an archbishop. "I shall look into it."

"Fine, fine," Zimri said, turning away as if the matter were dropped. He turned back suddenly and added, "By the way I understand you have a nephew of sailing age."

The archbishops now looked toward Rifton. None of them had known.

"Yes," Rifton said coldly.

"Funny, I've never seen him."

Rifton cursed silently. What traitor had told Zimri? "Yes. You see, he is in the cloistered life."

"Well, then," Zimri said with a cold smile, "a voyage in service to our Church would be a fine change for him. Don't you think?" Thus was Michael's fate sealed.

Niall nudged Rifton's leg and brought him back from his thoughts. "It's time," Niall whispered.

Rifton looked up to find that the procession of Mor was long past. He signaled to the archdeacons, and the five hundred brothers of St. Awstin filed across the square and out onto the harbor plain.

At harbor's edge, the bare masts of twenty ships cut a patchwork of lines that were silhouetted by the flickering lights of the aurora that shimmered in the northern sky. Overhead the Arch was unusually bright, rising in the east and passing straight overhead to set on the western Ice.

The ships, whose sleek lines and sharp blades seemed to speak of speed and grace, were motionless; their decks empty; the crews drawn up before them by rank and house. In the bundled garb of the ice runners, the crews appeared to be long lines of faceless bearlike creatures. Only the family crest sewed over the right breast or the guild or brotherhood sign embossed upon the fur helmets identified any man.

There was an air of excitement about them as they stood in ordered ranks and awaited the coming of the holy brothers. True, it was the Night of Supplication, but it was also the night of sailing, the start of another campaign that would leave some of them rich, and many others buried beneath the Frozen Sea. For a few, though, there was another reason—it was the night that had long been foretold, the night that they had waited and plotted over for years.

From the city the gentle wind carried the sound of chanting, and gradually the men grew silent. The age-old ritual set down in the *Books of the Saints* was about to take place, in this the two thousand and twenty-first year of the Ice.

At first the men could just see the glimmering light of the torches, then gradually the forms became visible as the orders shuffled across the ice. Onward the column came, with the brotherhoods forming a great arch facing the ships and crews. Those who would sail stepped forward from the various orders to join their crews.

The Brotherhood of Mor now marched into view, and from that column almost half the brothers stepped forward and went to the twenty ships of the fleet. They were the gundeacons, the powder handlers, the warrior brothers who comprised the gun crews of the fleet. The dark blue robes mingled with the great mass of men and all then stood silent.

Finally the brothers of Saint Awstin walked upon the ice. The tenors started the chant to St. Awstin. With the first chilling note, the column exploded with light, the brothers held their torches aloft, and with their chant echoing across the ice, they marched to the great pulpit that had been prepared in the center of the harbor.

Upon his mare, Rifton looked out at the people and laughed quietly with pleasure. Mather's little trick with the torches had impressed the crowd. Zimri would be wondering how St. Awstin had learned the Morian secret of lighting without flint.

The holy procession soon ended as the chant to St. Awstin came to its peaceful conclusion. Removing his hood and face mask, Rifton looked upward to the Arch. It was shining so brightly that he felt he could reach up and touch it. During the year the shining band of light had shifted back and forth across the heavens, but for the Night of Supplication it divided the sky evenly into two. For several moments he sat in silent thought, oblivious to those awaiting him.

The old feeling of awe and wonder washed over him, driving out the cynicism that lately took hold all too often.

Slowly and painfully he dismounted, then walked alone to the pulpit of clearest ice, which rose over forty feet into the night sky. The ice carvers had spent the better part of a week embellishing it with scenes from Holy Writ. He slowly climbed the circular staircase. As he reached the top, he could see the shadowy host in a great circle around him. He gazed heavenward again, to the cold black sky. The anger slowly welled up, the suppressed anger of a race lost upon the frozen sea of winter's night. The Night of Supplication, the Night of Anger began.

"Oh, Angry Father of the Universe," he suddenly shouted, raising his arms to the heavens, "our time is short and we cry aloud to thee. Why have you forsaken us? Why have you forsaken those who are innocent of the crime committed so long ago? Oh Father, we renounce the sins of *our* fathers. Their sin was great, their punishment just. But why must you now punish us? Have we not already suffered enough? Oh Father, we beseech thee, return unto us the Garden of the Before Time."

He was silent for a moment as the aurora flared up in a great twisting coil of light that illuminated the northern sky behind him. He looked at it and wanted so desperately to believe, but the cold wind drew him away, its icy fingers reaching into his very soul.

"Lord God of Hosts, do you hear our prayers?"

It was a question torn from his soul. He was afraid, he was afraid of what he knew. That he truly stood alone in an empty universe. He continued the ritual while all those of Cornath were on their knees below him.

"You ask for our faith, yet you turn from us. You ask us to wait and to believe in your return, yet you do not now believe in us, oh Father. Why then must we show our faith to you, oh Father? Why must we show our faith, when you have abandoned us upon this frozen world?"

Rifton now fell to his knees and began the reading from the third book of Mihangel, which told of the Before Time, which told of the Garden and how the Father did watch over it and how his Son was the guardian of the night. "Great was the sin of man until he committed the greatest sin—the striking down of the Son." The prayer went on to tell of the Creator's curse upon man, that his desire was to destroy man but the Saints interceded and begged him not to.

"And thus the Lord did curse man by saying, 'I shall take the Garden from man so that he may sin in it no more and I shall leave man and be with him no more, until the end of time when all are one and the atonement of the sins is complete in fire and blood.'

"And thus were heard the last words of the Lord, for so saying He turned away from man who had wronged Him, and He went far away where none may dare to tread. And the light of His countenance waned and the Son was no more, so that a great darkness came over the land. The earth shook and fire came down from the heavens for three times forty days. And thus the shape of the world was changed forever, and the Garden was destroyed and over it all the Saints placed the Arch as a sign to man of his sin. And the Ice came." So the prayer ended.

Now would come the half-hour of silence as all awaited the sign that this year, at last, the Father would return.

Rifton was alone and his emptiness was a burden that seemed to crush him.

Suddenly a shout rose from the crowd and Rifton looked heavenward. For a brief moment he thought he would faint.

In the sky overhead a blinding light had appeared, and it arched from north to south with an orange trail of fire. Up over the Arch it crossed, and the people upon the Ice cried aloud in terror. For an instant he believed, but faith quickly faded as he realized what was happening. The light disappeared over the southern horizon and after several long minutes Rifton could feel a slight rolling tremor.

In frustration he turned away. It was only another Saint who had fallen from the Arch. The brothers of Inys Gloi would be busy tonight casting their charts and trying to figure out which Saint had fallen from favor at the Long Table. It was a common enough occurrence, but many would take it as another sign.

Only half paying attention to the shouts and cries of the people below, he started the closing prayers of the ritual.

"Father, forgive us for what we have said here tonight. We are children, lost and afraid, and we ask for your guidance. In your wisdom you have heard us not. If you wish to leave us alone forever, then such is the will of the Lord. For who are we, Father, that we should judge thy word? For who are we to abandon Him who has already turned His face from us? For what is man, oh Father, to judge his God and the just punishment that He has set for us? Amen I now say, for the Night of Supplication has ended."

"Such is the will of the Father and all the Saints," the crowd intoned in response.

One last ceremony was to be faced, and rising again, Rifton leaned from the pulpit and beckoned to the archdeacons below. In the shadows he could make out Mather unbundling fresh torches, which were quickly lit and carried up the stairs of the pulpit. Every few feet the ice carvers had chiseled a socket. These were now filled by flaming torches, so that the shadows were driven away and the ice was flooded with a blaze of shimmering color. Around the base of the tower more torches were placed. In great bowls that hung from the side, sweet incense was lit so that coils of smoke soon wrapped the crystalline tower of light.

The ships' companies turned and shuffled to their vessels. Within a few minutes Rifton could hear the chanties ring out as the crews prepared to make sail. He listened to the old hypnotic songs and to the creaking of the yards as the sailing masters cursed and roared at the straining men.

How long ago, Rifton thought. Forty, it must be forty years since I rode first with Halvin, I a young master and he a captain of the foretop. Now he goes as admiral and I remain here to wrestle with Zimri.

Suddenly, with a report like that of a cannon, the first sail unfurled. Within seconds a thundering volley echoed across the ice as the frozen sheets of canvas caught and filled with the night air. By the light of the running lanterns, all could see the ghostly forms slide forward, their skates rumbling across the glasslike sea, while the timbers creaked with the strain.

Rifton watched. And as they skimmed past his pulpit, the crews fell silent, pulling back their hoods to receive his blessing before they disappeared into the darkness. One after another they passed, first the light schooners and cutters that were the scout ships of the fleet. Next came the corsairs with four to six guns each, the fifty-man crews crowding the narrow decks. Behind them came the merchants of war, ships owned by guilds whose men sailed for trade or war, whichever would fetch the higher return.

Behind the merchants came the fighting backbone of the fleet, the four frigates of Cornath. Each was one hundred fifty feet in length, the masts towering above the pulpit. The riggings were aswarm with men, some passing so close to Rifton that from his pulpit he could have stepped over to the main yard.

Finally from out of the shadows it came, its massive bulk bearing down upon him like some giant out of a forgotten age. Its great sails seemed to reach to the very heavens and as it drew nigh it blotted out the sky. The *Thunderwind* of Cornath, the mightest of all the ships of the Confederation, came astride the pulpit. He raised his hands in blessing as the giant glided past, its skates making a bone-shaking rumble that seemed to tear into his soul. He could plainly see Halvin standing by the wheel, red beard and hair sticking out from his hood like a great circle of fire. Halvin looked straight ahead without a nod or even a friendly look to his oldest friend. Rifton stared at him briefly; since Gormath, Halvin had not been the same. Rifton then gazed across the torchlit deck until finally the light-blue robe was visible. The robe turned and swayed, and with uncovered head the young man looked up to Rifton.

"Oh Saints above," Rifton whispered, "why was he forced to leave?"

Rifton quickly raised his hands in a special blessing and the young monk nodded in acknowledgment. Their eyes held each other until the darkness washed over them and the great ship disappeared into the night.

"Go with the Saints, Michael Ormson. Go with the Saints, my son." Like a son he had been to Rifton. Fifteen years before, the plague had come to Cornath and in a day Rifton lost all his family, except for one small, terrified boy.

Rifton watched the ships' lanterns as the fleet cleared the harbor gate and heeled over with the wind. He watched with a sense of foreboding. He loved Michael, but of late he had come to fear him as well; *The Book of Prophecies* whispered to him from the darkness.

For fifteen years Rifton had isolated his nephew in the inner cloister, where only a handful were permitted to know of him. Now he was out, he was upon the Ice, and no one could watch over him. Rifton was afraid.

"Go with the Saints, Michael Ormson. And may my nightmares be false." The ships' lanterns grew ever dimmer and eventually disappeared beyond the Western Sea. Long he watched, until finally Brother Niall ascended the pulpit and with loving hands guided his friend and master down. Gently he helped Rifton to his mount and then, chanting the prayers of the middle night, the brothers returned to their monastery beneath the mountain of Cornath.

The city was quiet. All were asleep, except for the cold and lonely sentries, and an archbishop who sat and read from a book that now was a source of fear.

* * *

"Is it time yet, Brother Ioan?"

"Yes, your Holiness, the moment of passing has come."

Some of the brothers were still excited about the Saint who had fallen earlier in the evening, yet to Riadent of Inys Gloi that was but a minor sign of prophecy. True, it would be quoted later and the brothers would spread the word, but there were other matters to attend to.

"I see them, your Grace," Ioan said softly. "There, north by northeast, on the horizon." Riadent strained his eyes but couldn't make them out. Ioan was good for that type of thing; his eyes were still young, and Riadent felt passing envy for the ambitious young monk beside him.

Ah, but there were too many fires within, he mused philosophically. Far too many fires to distract and interfere. And he remembered the years of torture and anguish necessary to conquer the desires.

He looked to Ioan and smiled.

Riadent drew a long slender tube from the folds of his robe and, uncapping both ends, prepared the Eye of St. Soldim for use. As he adjusted the focus he wondered at the miracle that had created such a device. Often had he been tempted to open it up, yet he was afraid of the dreadful calamity that might result. Anyhow, why bother to learn of a mere physical toy? he reasoned. After all, he was the Select of his Order. He could read the signs, he could travel far without leaving his body, and at times he could even see into the souls of men. Curiosity of the physical was dangerous. He slowly adjusted the tube. "Yes, Brother Ioan," he whispered, "your eyes serve you well tonight."

For long minutes he watched as the fleet passed, their sails silhouetted against the dawning sky. From atop his high perch he looked out to them, and the desire once again to ride upon the Ice was overwhelming. He tracked the largest vessel as it made its way southward. His breath quickened as the vessel suddenly seemed to explode into flames as the rising fire of dawn soared behind it. Riadent heard the shouts of the brothers far below as the dawn's light finally reached them.

"You are sure that all is as planned?" Riadent asked.

"Yes," Ioan responded with a smile. "It was difficult to plant the idea with Zimri, but in the end we were successful."

Riadent looked to his assistant. A capable man, Riadent thought. I should watch out for him. "What about the others?"

"All are in their places."

Riadent turned away. For years, the brothers of Inys Gloi had prepared for the coming of the Promised One who would lead their secret brotherhood to supreme power over all the churches, but now at the most important moment they would have to leave a very big part of their dream to chance.

"Let us report to our Father that they are on their way."

"May our Brother Seth du Facinn be guided from Above," Ioan said softly.

Riadent looked again to the sea, and with a nod of agreement they turned and descended to the chambers hidden below.

CHAPTER 2

As THE DAY PASSED AWAY, EVENING WAS BORN WITH A SOFT
flow of reds and golden yellows that arched across the western
sky. In quiet enthrallment Michael stood upon the bowsprit
and watched as the cold sun touched the western horizon. For
a moment, it seemed as if the sea and the sky had become one;
the clear black ice of early winter suddenly took on the coloring
of the evening air and reflected the rainbow of colors from
above.

Removing his goggles and face mask, he let the frigid evening wind numb his skin as he watched the fleet in the last
moment of its first day of sail.

The other nineteen ships of the fleet were approaching from
the various points of the compass, each making full speed under
all its sail. To Michael they appeared to be riding upon a sea
of flame, their blades kicking up torches of shimmering light
behind them. Since leaving Cornath the night before, the fleet
had sailed in open-search order with only their top sails visible
from the deck of the flagship. For the first time, Michael Ormson was watching a fleet under full sail assembling across the
Frozen Sea.

They seemed toys as their hulls became visible on the horizon, but after several minutes he was able to distinguish the designs of hull and sails as he compared them with the diagrams in the log's battle charts. Coming down before the wind were the twin frigates The *St. Ioan* and the *St. Regis* of Caerdiff. Their masters turned them in gentle arcs as they ran a broad reach across the breeze. As the ships turned back and forth, Michael could clearly see the dark-blue stars upon their white canvas, the symbol of their home port. They had once been known as the three sisters, but their sibling, the *St. Faelowson*, had been lost at Gormath the year before. To the men aboard the two ships, the voyage had become more than a raid to the Southward Isles, it was a quest to avenge brothers and friends lost beneath the cursed walls of the city now called Macth du Wone, the city of woe.

A point to the starboard bow, like two knife edges on the horizon, were the *Snow Wind* and the *St. Almarth* of Conwy. The frigates' masts cut across the evening sky as they rode abeam the wind on their return to the center of the fleet. The crew of the *Snow Wind* boasted their vessel could do four and a half times the wind when running abeam and all in the fleet agreed that she could outsail anything upon the Frozen Sea.

To the southeast, and tacking handsomely across the wind, were the four armed merchantmen led by the *Mawr Thone, The Great Fire*. Weaving in and out among the fleet's elements were the light schooners and corsairs that had once looked so big to Michael but now were dwarfed by the great bulk of the fighting ships of the Cornathian fleet.

Largest of them all, though, was the *Thunderwind*, and Michael now turned to examine her. She was over three hundred feet in length and almost forty abeam, with a mainmast that soared over two hundred feet into the evening sky. Running her length on either side were thick oak outriggers that gave her stability and also acted as a belt of armor against attack. Beneath her massive streamlined bulk were four great sets of skates, each almost twenty feet in length, and matching them were four more skates on each outrigger. Upon the mast and booms hung more than fifty thousand square feet of sail, which could drive her across the ice at speeds greater than twenty leagues an hour when the wind was fresh and the ice was glazed and clear.

It was what stood beneath her deck, though, that made the *Thunderwind* the pride of the Cornathian Church. On the enclosed gun deck below, the brothers of Mor served forty-four great guns—the largest of which would throw a ball of forty-eight pounds. Upon the main deck were fifty catapults and giant ballistae that would throw a hundred-pound shot or shoot bolts as thick as a man's arm. She was the most powerful ship the Brotherhood of Mor had ever sailed.

To that brotherhood she was yet another symbol of their rise to power. Her forty-four guns could range for a league in any direction and a single broadside could turn a frigate into a shattered wreck. Her master builders claimed that a third of her blades could be carried away and still she would sail on. Three more like the *Thunderwind* had been built and another six were planned. With such power the Church of Cornath had finally started to turn the war in her favor.

For over forty years, since the start of the Great Death, the three churches had struggled for power upon the Ice. It had started with the coming of the plague. Rifton had often spoken to Michael of the terror of that first outbreak.

"It came in my twentieth year," he would say. "For Cornath it was bad, but for the Southward Isles it was worse. Far worse. Men who laughed in the morning by nightfall would twist in agony as the plague ate their lungs. Aye, Michael, I remember the screams, the carts of death, the stricken piled in the alleyways. It came in 981 and again in 992. We thought then that it was over, but it came again, Michael. The worst one when you were five."

Michael remembered and he shut out the pain. His mother, his father, and his younger sister dead, while he sat terrified in a corner until Rifton came to take him to the darkened monastery.

Some say that a merchant from the Church of Sol had dared to visit the forbidden lands and that the Saints had punished man. No matter the origin, the cities of Sol were left mere shadows of their former strength and the balance of power that had lasted for hundreds of years fell apart. Ezra and Cornath were soon locked in mortal strife to pick up the pieces of the dying church.

With an unrelenting fury they fought, as raid turned to skirmish and then to full-scale slaughter. An entire generation had been lost to the plague and then another to the wars that followed.

From the spectre of that struggle a new power arose, the warrior monks, the Brothers of Mor. The keepers of the gun had been only a minor order before, but in the forty years of war their power came to rival that of the traditional founders of the Church. Michael's order was said by some to be in eclipse. He realized he was but a pawn in the game as he looked across that ship of Mor. Michael wondered what the winter would hold for him as he rode to battle with the brotherhood.

A horn suddenly echoed from the fighting maintop. As the signal was picked up by the other ships to end the first day of sail, Michael was stirred from his examination of the ship. The *Thunderwind* hiked up on her downwind outriggers as the helmsman turned the wheel over, sending the ship straight into the eye of the wind. Dozens of men streamed up from below decks and scurried aloft to take in the sails. Booms were loosened to take the tension off the canvas and soon the frozen sea echoed to the flapping and snapping of sails luffed in the wind. Quickly and with practiced skill, the sails were drawn in and furled for the night.

The ships of the fleet glided to a halt in their assigned positions, forming a great circle a quarter mile across with the flagship at the center. Even before the ships had come to a stop, anchoring teams were over the sides and running out anchor ropes and the ice resounded to the driving of anchor spikes. From the stern of the frigates and the *Thunderwind*, hatches were flung open and man-size ice blocks were disgorged. The schooners swung in and hooked cables to them and dragged them astern of the fleet.

The passing of an ice boat left a frozen wake that could stretch for a thousand miles. Long after the ship had disappeared over the horizon her marks could still be seen, a spoor that any curious ship could follow. A practiced eye could quickly tell when the ship had passed and her size, and some could even judge the weight. An enemy could easily pursue and in the night sweep down to surprise the unsuspecting prey. Therefore a good ice runner prepared a welcome.

The schooners dragged the blocks several miles astern and quickly laid out a pattern of ice barriers that would turn an enemy into a splintered wreck. Around the rest of the fleet, men randomly drove great steel-tipped wooden spikes into the ice, and finally, five or six miles away, the schooners laid out track marks which they would follow as they patrolled during the night.

To sail at night was usually a risk. When close to home, with ice that was known, it was an acceptable one, but beyond a hundred leagues the ice could offer a surprise, such as a double shelving, a fissure, or a jagged buckle. In seconds a fleet could be destroyed. But stopping held its risk as well. A generation before, an Ezrian flag fleet of ten major and a dozen minor ships anchored for the night on seas they thought safe. For three days they had been shadowed by a single frigate and two merchantmen. An unusually bright aurora had outlined them from several leagues out and a reckless young captain had decided to attack. Abandoning his ships, the attacker led his party in on skates and with one-man sails. Luck was with them as they managed to sneak past the patrolling schooners. Before the enemy had time to react and cut anchor, the Cornathians had smashed barrels of oil against the sides of the ships and set all but one afire. The attackers lost half their party, but the Ezrians lost an entire fleet. The captain was Halvin, his assistant and lieutenant was Rifton. The lesson was remembered and the defense was laid out by his command.

The horns blew three low, full notes. Having finished their mundane tasks, the men turned their attention to their souls; the summons to prayer had sounded. Michael reluctantly left his perch on the bowsprit and, with the rest of the crew, quickly made his way astern. From the sides of the ship came the anchor and defense crews, while from overhead the rigging men slid down to the deck. All were dressed in heavy fur leggings and short fur jackets with hoods and leather face masks. Most had taken off their wind goggles, their exposed eyes the only sign of humanness beneath a mountain of fur.

The crew massed upon the main deck and faced the quarter deck, which covered the last fifth of the ship and rose ten feet above the main. In the middle of the massive structure were two doors that rested on the main deck and rose to the full height of the sterncastle. The doors had been the labor of years for a master carver of the Mor brotherhood. It bore the image of a lush garden that shimmered with brilliant greens and glowed with flowers the colors of the rainbow. Standing in the garden was a towering man dressed in flowing white robes, his back turned, his head bowed, as if he was wrapped in gloomy meditation.

From someplace hidden deep within the ship, the horn sounded again. All fell silent at its call. Several minutes passed as the shadows deepened around the men. Then, silently, the doors glided open. From the deeper darkness within came a procession of priests.

As the doors swung open, the Icon of St. Mor was visible. Six priests carried the massive relic, which barely cleared the doorway. The drawn face of St. Mor was almost skeletal, its blazing eyes lit with a strange green fire. The image was wreathed in fire and his mouth was drawn in a mocking grimace of agony.

Behind the image, two priests in full robes of dark blue with high peaked hoods swung censers that spewed rolling clouds of yellow-green smoke. Next came four monks, each carrying the sacred symbol of the Church—a silver staff atop which was a hand pointing heavenward, and above the hand the half-circle of the Arch. Finally almost one hundred brothers followed in two columns of long swirling robes while they chanted the hymn, "To Mor in War." The two lines turned and climbed the stairs that flanked both sides of the door.

At the end of the procession were the three priests of Mord

Rinn in robes of dark burgundy, their faces concealed beneath their hoods. They stepped forward and flanked the holy icon that was held before the door. The crew kept their eyes lowered in fear. The chant reached its climax then drifted away, and Michael could hear similar prayers from the other ships of the fleet.

All stood in silence with eyes lowered as the Essob Ulthane, the High Priest of Mor, walked solemnly from the darkened hall within. He turned to the right, and with a slow even pace mounted the ladder and entered the small pulpit above the carved image of the lost Garden.

A small bell was sounded and the men looked up as the high priest swept them with his gaze.

His hood was pulled back, revealing the shaven head of a Morian priest, the pale skin shimmering in the light of the torches that flanked him. His face was long and narrow, reminiscent of Mor's skull-like image. He held them with his gaze, and Michael suddenly realized that the priest was examining him, as well. They stared at one another and then Gareth, the high priest, lowered his head and started the evening prayers.

"My children," he intoned with a full rich voice, "I need not speak to you of our holy mission. For forty long years our coast has been harried, our cities laid waste, our mines ruined, our women raped, our children slain; all this at the hands of the Ezrians and the followers of false prophets. Now we sail forth with sword in hand to seek our revenge against the unbelievers."

The wind softly moaned around them, while overhead the Arch began to appear.

"Remember, my children, the Garden shall not return until all the world has heard the word of the one true faith and all mankind together begs the intercession of all the Blessed Saints. This is our sacred trust. This is the holy duty passed down to us by our fathers' fathers. When it is complete, upon that blessed day, the Ice shall part and the face of our Father shall show forth again in all His radiance and we shall bask in the warmth of the Garden forever."

He bowed his head and the priests and monks behind him

softly responded: "By the intercession of all the Saints shall it be done."

Gareth began again, his voice booming as he invoked Holy Writ. "A reading from the book of St. Ioan, chapter three, verses five through eight."

Michael looked up while all the others stood with bowed heads and he saw that the priest was looking straight at him.

So he has been told, Michael thought, already the attack is beginning.

"Amen I say unto thee," Gareth began, "'for there shall come a time of darkness when pestilence shall walketh the land and the Ice shall be torn by war and strife. And at that time shall come forth the false prophets who shall lead men into the snares set by the evil one, so that many will be lost forever into the freezing torment of hell, and the Long Table of the Saints shall be denied them. The Saints, in their infinite wisdom, shall set upon them a sign so that all may know of them and drive them out into the darkness of night and death.' Thus is a reading from St. Ioan. Fear his words, all ye believers, and pray. Amen."

Silently Gareth pulled up his hood. The service had ended. His gaze turned from Michael and he stepped from the pulpit, while below him the brothers with the Icon returned to the darkness of the sterncastle. The procession re-formed, and silently retracing their steps, the priests and monks disappeared below.

As soon as the doors had closed, the crew swarmed to the hatchways amidships. A fierce numbing cold was settling over the ice, and Michael could feel its frigid hands on his flesh.

Suddenly a lumbering giant pushed ahead of Michael and all but knocked him over. The blow was bad enough, but the giant stank like a carcass exposed too long to the midday sun. What with his expansive, shaggy black beard and a truly impressive head of hair that tumbled past his shoulders, it was impossible to tell where the giant's hair ended and his coat of black fur began.

A badly disfigured nose was the only flesh that showed at all; obviously the fellow had caught the bad end of at least one fight, though from his bulk it was hard to imagine a foe that could beat him. The giant leaned over Michael and then his dark-brown eyes seemed to twinkle with laughter and his mouth yawned wide in a gap-toothed grin.

"He's a right good one with those prayers, he is; like to have scared me half to death with that devil talk, he did." With that the giant broke into a thundering roar of laughter.

Michael tried to ignore him and made as if to push on to the warmth of the hatchway, but a hairy paw clamped onto his shoulder and turned him gently but firmly around.

"And who might you be?" the giant continued. "I ain't got a memory of seeing your shaven scalp."

Michael looked into his eyes and said coldly, "Michael Ormson of St. Awstin and log keeper to Lord Halvin." He held the giant's gaze.

For several seconds they stared at each other and the giant hesitated, his expression twisted up in concentration as if to recall a half-forgotten thought. Suddenly, with an explosive slap on Michael's back, he exclaimed, "Saints damn my eyes *yes*, now I know who ye are! I thought ye had the look about you—Red Orm's son, are ye not?"

Michael was surprised as the name Red Orm stirred the memories within. Orm of Cornath, that had been the title, and Rifton had spoken of him as "my brother Orm, your father." The recollection came over him of a door swinging open and a young, muscular Rifton towering in the hallway. Behind him a house was burning while men with torches stood in the street and watched. In the background he heard the voices, "By the Saints, Red Orm and his family are dead." "Drag them out," another shouted, "and burn the house when you're done." Darkness descended over him, as the robes of the beloved priest covered him.

"The boy, the strange one, is he dead as well?" a voice shouted in the distance.

"Yes, " Rifton responded, "I shall bury him myself."

"That was your father, was it not?" the giant asked, interrupting Michael's silence.

"Yes," Michael said softly, "that was my father's name."

"I sailed with your father, I did," the giant stated proudly.

"Back '95 it was, my first voyage to the south. I owe him blood debt, I do—he saved my life 'neath the walls of Tir nan Loth. I never could return it, though, at least not to him."

He stepped closer, so that Michael felt he would choke from the smell. "Funny, you don't seem to take much after your father, but then *me* mother always said that Father had been a thief. And tell me now, do I look like a thief to thee? Tell me now." With that the giant broke into a thundering laugh.

"My name's Daniel Bjornson of North Prydain." He extended a gloved hand, which Michael hesitantly took. Daniel gave a playful squeeze that set Michael's bones to cracking, then released his grip and stepped back to gaze past Michael to the forecastle beyond.

Michael turned and was startled to see a man draped in a long black cape that blended into the gathering darkness. His right breast bore a glittering silver star, the only color to the ghostly figure that stood silhouetted by the Archlight. Wordlessly the apparition surveyed the crew. The men fell into silence as if awaiting his command. But as quietly as he appeared, he turned and disappeared into the forecastle hatchway.

"Halvin," Daniel murmured. And the others whispered his name.

Michael had stood behind Halvin when they left the harbor, but as soon as the walls were cleared the Lord Admiral of the Fleet disappeared into his cabin.

"I was with him at Gormath." Instantly Daniel had Michael's attention and several others gathered around to hear as well.

"Were you here on the *Thunderwind* then?" Michael ventured.

"Aye, that I was. We was having a rare, fine pillage, we was, working our way down the Ezrian coast. I was on the forward deck working the catapult," and his arm swept outward to point at the machine, "when we saw the *St. Manx* lose her runner and crash into the city wall. Lord, how Halvin raged at the sight! We put on more canvas and ran the barriers, we did, only inches from death as Halvin took us through the traps. But before we could reach the *St. Manx*, the Ezrians swarmed from the gate and pillaged the ship. As we closed, they set her afire and we could see prisoners being dragged off. It was madness, but we stormed the burning wreck beneath their very walls and searched her from stem to stern before the fire and the archers above drove us back. Halvin's brother we found dead, but of Halvin's two boys there was no sign.

"Halvin was in a blind rage and he ordered that the city be stormed at once. Madness it was, but we took the wall. That's where I got this, I did," and Daniel pointed to his misshapen nose. "'Twas a block of ice from above and it smashed me lovely face."

"What about the town?" asked a sailor standing behind Michael. "We don't want to hear about your pretty face." And with that the men chuckled.

Daniel shot him an evil glare and the man fell silent.

"Now if I wasn't being interrupted so much I could tell ye." He looked at them and, satisfied with their silence, continued.

"We took the town, we did, and there by the harbor gate we found them. Twenty Cornathians, and amongst them Halvin's oldest boy. A lad of but fifteen years.

"Saints above, they were all staked upon the Ice — have any of ye ever seen it now?" Daniel asked.

One or two of the men nodded grimly.

Daniel continued with his story. "Spread-eagled they were, hands and feet nailed to the ice, heads propped up so that they could clearly see what was to come. From a quarter-mile away the filthy Ezrians had lined up for their sport, and they took sail-mounted spears that rested on razor-sharp skates. Ah, it was ghastly, it was. By the torchlight we could see the horror frozen in dead eyes that had watched doom rushing down upon them."

Daniel fell silent again to let the image develop in the men's minds.

"He went mad, Halvin did," Daniel continued. "I was there to see it. Myself all covered in blood. He looked down at his boy and then, animallike, he screamed a terrible scream wrenched from the soul. Then he dashed away across the harbor. We went in after him, we took the city, we did, and our men died by the hundreds. With the coming of dawn Halvin still drove us on. At first light our Morians grew fearful of the Ezrian fleet, so they fell upon Halvin and bound him with rope. Placing him upon their shoulders, they fled from the city with him raving and screaming."

Daniel stopped again and gazed significantly at one of the men standing alongside Michael. The man shook his head but drew a flask from his tunic, swigged from it, then reluctantly gave it to Daniel. Daniel took a long thirsty pull.

"Ah, that's better now, it is.

"Well, it wasn't a moment too soon that they carried him out; those priests had smelt trouble, sure enough. We barely got back to our ships before the Ezrian fleet was sighted on the horizon. It was a hard run, it was, but in the end we got away.

"For days Halvin raved, the forecastle shaking to his oaths. Then suddenly he was silent. We had come to be so used to his shouts that the silence was every bit as frightening. For three days we heard him not, and then with the coming of the evening watch we saw him again on the deck. Since that day he's been a man without words, save those needed in his hunt to kill Ezrians. He's become a man without a heart; they killed more than his boy, they did. They killed his very soul."

The men around Michael nodded and grumbled over Daniel's words. Daniel walked over to the rail and spit over the side, then turned back to Michael and the other men. "'Tis getting rare cold, it is. Cold enough to freeze the spit to me lips. Let's go below before we freeze to this spot." And the men made their way to the main hatch.

"Come along, young scribe and reader, or come morning we'll find you here as stiff as a corpse."

Michael looked at Daniel and noted the disarming smile that Daniel gave him. He remembered Rifton's words about enemies, but as he looked at the stranger he could see that no danger awaited. He nodded with a smile and together they went below.

CHAPTER 3

HE STOOD ALONE UPON THE PROW OF HIS SHIP, THE ICE RACing past with blinding speed. Before the ship was a coiling, twisting wall of fire and smoke. He knew that death was coming to him at last. He closed his eyes, and even as he did so he could feel the ship drop away. The rattling of the blades was gradually replaced by the haunting sound of the wind whistling in the rigging. It wove a gentle, complex song that suddenly ended with a blinding flash of light.

Funny, he had no fear, and no pain. For what seemed like an eternity, he waited for the searing shock, the crushing blow of agony, but it never came. Hesitantly he opened his eyes. He was wrapped in a swirling gray mist, which turned and eddied in silence, then ever so slowly brightened and drifted away. His body lay in the broken wreckage below. It was horribly twisted into the impossible contortions that only the dead could hold. "I'm dead," he whispered. "By the Saints, I'm dead."

He knew that he was supposed to be afraid, yet he felt no fear, no anxiety, only an unusual sense of peace. The conflict, the struggle in which he'd been embroiled for the last forty years, was over and suddenly insignificant.

Wrapped in a strange, surreal quiet, he drifted up and away from his body. Within seconds, the form that had once been the center of his universe was only a twisted, bloody speck, then a point that disappeared without any regret on his part. How long he floated, he could not say. Time held no meaning and he felt as if his floating through darkness would consume all eternity. A hand touched him on the shoulder.

He screamed.

Turning, Gareth met the face of one that he had prayed to for over forty years. He was torn between horror and religious ecstasy. The face was just as he had imagined it—the dark, haunting eyes two wells of suffering; the clean-shaven head; the soft, enigmatic smile of a man who had transcended pain and fear.

"St. Mor," Gareth whispered.

St. Mor held Gareth's gaze and nodded slowly in acknowledgement. The mist behind Mor parted, and there, to Gareth's delight, was the Long Table of the Chosen, as wide as the largest ice runner's deck and carved from a single polished plank of wood that extended to a point far beyond the distance the eye could see. Blazing torches were spaced at even intervals, casting their light upon all who were gathered in the hall. The table was piled high with every type of game and drink imaginable, to meet the needs of the Everlasting Feast. The hall, however, was strangely silent; no sound of feasting or merrymaking was heard and Gareth realized that all were looking at him. All the Saints, all the Chosen, all who had found favor, were before him—to await the day of the Father's return. "Only the Chosen," thought Gareth. All others were condemned to the freezing darkness until Judgment Day.

"St. Mor," he whispered as tears clouded his eyes, "I am not worthy."

The hall was silent. The Chosen of two thousand years gazed upon him.

"You are not worthy," a voice whispered from the table.

Gareth looked up, panic edging into his mind. He turned to St. Mor with a beseeching gesture.

The Saint's eyes, the eyes of one who had died in fire,

started to pulse with a hidden flame, a flame of wrath.

St. Mor's voice boomed with a fury that brought Gareth to his knees. "You are not worthy. You have brought the evil one forth and suffered him to live."

The Saints of the Long Table responded in a monotone to the words of St. Mor. "He has brought forth the evil one."

"No, I didn't, I swear it," Gareth pleaded.

"You forgot the prophecies. You forgot, and now by your hand he lives."

"By your hand he lives, to bring death to the Holy Church and deny forever the return of the Father," the rest of the Saints intoned with angry voices.

Gareth looked to Mor then turned away from the loathing in the Saint's eyes. In desperation he faced those at the Long Table, but the fury in their eyes was the same.

"Oh Father above," he screamed, "forgive me."

"You have been found wanting," the Saints shouted, and the roar of their voices was like the crash of thunder above a stormy sea.

Above the chanting of the Saints, Gareth heard the voice of St. Mor: "You are doomed to darkness eternal, to the frozen realm of night, to eternal agony."

"And still that shall not be enough," the Saints responded. "Begone."

Even as he screamed, the room disappeared in a searing flash. "The cold, St. Mor, the cold."

He fell screaming into a black sea of ice that swallowed him, that sucked the warmth from him. And as he screamed, its piercing coldness tore into his lungs.

"Mor!"

The door was open, a terrified face looking in. Gareth sat sobbing upon the cot, trying to gain control of his fear. Several minutes passed before he was aware of the acolyte.

"Brother Gareth?" the acolyte whispered.

"Damn you, don't you know my orders!" Gareth shouted. "No matter what you hear, don't ever come in here again. Do you understand?"

"Yes, your Excellency. I only intruded since it is the hour

of dawn, and you asked that we fetch the deacon of St. Awstin to you at that time."

"Yes, yes. But next time enter here only if I call for you. Now let me prepare for morning prayers and then send this deacon to me."

The morning prayers were ended at last, and still he was shaking as he knelt before the image of St. Mor in the privacy of his room. Sleep was almost impossible now as the dream came more and more frequently.

He looked to the Holy Icon, and a wave of passion and fear filled him. "Oh St. Mor, have mercy on me. Show me the error of my ways so that I may be the servant of thy will. Point to me the evil one and wherever he is, I shall hunt him down and slay him for thee."

The icon looked down with blind eyes of fire.

Long he prayed in silence, until finally the knock sounded on the door. The deacon of St. Awstin had come.

"Just a moment," Gareth called softly. As he did so, the last vestiges of the nightmare slipped into the darkness—to await his return to sleep.

Gareth's vanity and meticulous mind were again in control as he scanned his quarters for any fault. The cabinets lining the starboard wall were secure. The massive barrel of the twenty-four-pound long gun was somewhat concealed by a simple table that rested on top of it. The table was suspended from four ropes that would lift the table to the ceiling when the ship was cleared for action. The sweat-soaked cot was still down, but with the pull of a rope it swung up against the wall and was secured in place.

Walking over to the small stove that was set into the portside wall, he opened its door and threw in two small logs. Only three men aboard the entire ship were allowed the luxury of a personal stove—the admiral, the sailing master, and he, the Essob Ulthane of Mor.

"You may enter," Gareth announced firmly as he walked behind the table and stood beside the Holy Icon.

The door swung open and the hooded form of a deacon of St. Awstin entered the room. The figure bowed to the icon of St. Mor then nodded to Gareth.

"Welcome, Michael of St. Awstin, welcome to a ship of Mor."

"Thank you," Michael replied coldly while throwing back his hood.

Gareth suppressed a gasp of shock. Michael bore the holy mark spoken of in prophecy. "The light of his eyes shall be as two. And they shall burn with the fire that can tear into the souls of men."

He looked into Michael's eyes and the fear swept over him. Michael stood quietly and returned his gaze.

No wonder the uncle hid him, Gareth thought. He examined Michael as if appraising a new gun, and all the time he could sense his own fear.

The boy's eyes held Gareth's until he could no longer bear to look at them. They were different colors—one the lightest blue, the other a cold steel-gray. They looked out at him as if from some incredible distance. The face was hard and lean, with the look of one who was already old from years of prayer and meditation. The shaved skull of a deacon accentuated the natural height of Michael's forehead so that he had an unworldly appearance to him. His light-blue robe hung loosely from his shoulders and Gareth could see the outline of a slender frame. A strange, undefinable sense of presence marked the lad. A presence that could not be linked to his eyes, his walk, or anything else that was physical. He experienced a deep sense of anxiety over this, yet the orders of Zimri could not be ignored.

Gareth turned his gaze aside and extended his hand.

"Greetings to you, Brother Michael. I have been looking forward to our meeting."

Michael smiled and took Gareth's hand in greeting. Gareth noticed that the deacon's hands were too large, the fingers incredibly long and thin, yet their grip was firm.

"Have a seat, my son, have a seat." Turning, Gareth beckoned to a narrow, straight-backed chair carved of ivory and bone, a chair taken twenty long years ago, in the sack of the first village Gareth had stormed.

Michael sat in the chair, which was facing the breech of the twenty-four-pound gun whose bulk occupied half the cabin.

Michael eyed the breech, which was carved and embellished with the finely wrought images of Saints. Across the top of the barrel was written the holy script necessary to prevent possession. He stood up and leaned over the barrel to read the holy words.

"Ah," Gareth said with a smile, "I must remember that I have in my company one who can read."

Michael looked back and smiled. "You can too, can you not?"

"Yes, of course, but only since I became Essob Ulthane. Before that it is forbidden in my order, as you know."

Michael merely nodded. Being of St. Awstin, he came from an order where all could read once they had taken holy vows. In the other orders only the highest officials were given the secret. Of course, all outside the Church were forbidden, and the Mord Rinn were quick to hear of any who tried.

"May I offer you some Aswingard?" Gareth asked warmly as he sat down in a chair next to Michael. He felt himself back under control and he fell into his usual masking of all emotion. "I think you'll find it to your liking."

Michael looked at him and hesitated.

"Michael, aboard ship our vows of abstinence are rescinded by order of our Holy Father. It's for our health, you know."

Michael nodded and Gareth, quickly reaching over to a cabinet, pulled out a decanter of icelike glass and two small, golden goblets. Uncorking the decanter, he poured a thick, ruby-colored liquid that filled the room with a warm, spicy scent.

"To a safe voyage," Gareth said, raising his glass.

Michael found the liquid surprisingly to his liking—especially after the icy cold of the morning's topside chart-reading.

"Tell me, Michael, do you indulge in the game of Flyswin?"

Michael's face lit up. "It would be a pleasure!" he exclaimed, unable to control his delight even before the priest of an enemy brotherhood.

Gareth looked at him and found that he too was relaxing a bit. He couldn't help but feel warmth toward the obvious joy that had surfaced on that hard, silent face.

"Excellent," Gareth replied, "a good game is hard to find

aboard ship, though I must warn you that I am a blue master."

"So much the better," Michael responded. "I have just taken the blue myself—only two months ago, in fact."

"You'll find the board in the desk along the far wall," Gareth said. And Michael rose to fetch the game. Of the eight levels of mastery in Flyswin, the blue was one step removed from the highest rank of silver. Gareth was pleased that at last his passion would be indulged—a good game with one of equal rank.

Michael returned with the ivory box and set it upon the table. As Gareth opened the box, Michael could not help but exclaim over the finely wrought pieces within. Michael, as the challenger to the board owner, took the white pieces and deployed his position upon the board.

To its devotees, Flyswin was far more than a game. It was also an art form, an addiction that, for many, was the sole source of entertainment in an otherwise harsh and demanding world.

The game was as old as the Ice itself—and a symbolic representation of what occurred upon it. The board was divided into 324 squares of alternating white and blue. Four great squares, two of blue and two of white, were placed at the four corners of the board. From his two corners each player would deploy his eighteen pieces—from pawn ship to the flyswin—while an inverted marker would be placed on each to represent the level of command aboard it. Each ship had limits as to the distance and direction of its move, and the command pieces would add or subtract from the power of the vessel. The game ended when both the senior command piece and the flyswin were taken. Great rituals had developed around the game, especially in the ordering of ranks. To step up a rank, the challenger had to defeat a player who was a step above him. The challenger then took his opponent's command piece as his own to use in future games, unless he was willing to ransom it back. There were only twelve silver and a hundred and forty-four blue in all of the Cornathian lands.

Michael drew his blue marker and placed it on the table. It was just a blue cylinder six inches high and two across, but it was a most prized possession.

The game opened with the usual sparring for position in the center board. Gareth deployed his pieces in the traditional two-arch defense in response to Michael's double-diamond attack formation. So involved in the game did they become that neither interrupted the other with idle chatter.

Michael was slowly driven into retreat, losing three pieces to Gareth's one in a neatly laid trap upon the middle board. Michael had held his flyswin in reserve so Gareth drove for it, smashing through Michael's defense in a savage attack, and took the center board. Michael's only reserves were three pawn ships on the right flank.

The final attack came and Gareth swept in upon Michael's flyswin with the necessary statement of flyswin's death. Gareth then unmasked his own commander, aboard his most powerful craft.

With a slowly spreading smile, Michael unmasked his own ship. "Master's death denied," he responded as he turned over the command ship to reveal that his lowest-rated commander rode his largest ship.

It was Michael's turn. "Flyswin and master's death," he announced as he revealed his senior command figure aboard a pawn ship. With the extra movement that assignment allowed, the pawn ship swept in and toppled Gareth's piece, ending the game.

Gareth looked up at Michael. The move had been so unorthodox as to border on foolishness.

"I can't use that one again," Michael said with a soft laugh. "I guess you'll be killing off all my pawn ships from now on."

Gareth laughed. "Well done, indeed! It's good to know that I can look forward to a game every day now. Michael, we might be of different orders, but at least we can find this in common."

Michael smiled his strange, disarming smile and looked into Gareth's eyes.

The fear returned, and Gareth quickly looked away again. "Tell me, Michael, is all according to your needs?"

"Yes. The cabin is small, but I'll make do."

"If there is anything you should want of Mor, feel free to come to me."

"I need nothing of Mor."

"Ah, yes—of course, Michael of Awstin."

Michael replaced the blue marker in his tunic pouch and, with a nod to Gareth, slowly stood.

"I have my duties to attend to. The log must be filled according to Halvin's command, and the charts must be read for today."

"Yes, of course. Shall we meet like this every morning, Michael? I would enjoy the game and your company."

Michael looked at Gareth and nodded, then turned toward the door. As he reached it he hesitated and faced Gareth again.

"Tell me, Gareth, has Zimri ordered you to kill me?"

Gareth was so taken aback that it took him several seconds to respond.

"What ever made you ask that?"

"You know who I am, the nephew of St. Awstin's archbishop. My death would be a blow to your order's archrival, would it not?" Gareth tried to look into the young man's eyes but found that he could not. He feigned interest in the Flyswin board and said softly, "I'll enjoy your company tomorrow morning at the same time."

"Yes, of course," Michael said. "Thank you again and sleep well tonight."

Gareth looked up. But Michael was already out the door.

He was alone again, and afraid. Zimri's orders had been clear. "As long as we keep the boy alive and aboard one of our ships, we hold a dagger over Rifton. The boy isn't worth much to us dead. Befriend him—who knows," Zimri said with a laugh, "with a little luck we could swing him over to our order. It could mean a lot to you, Gareth, or it could mean nothing at all." The tone of Zimri's voice had carried the message all too clearly.

Gareth poured himself another drink. The nightmare clung to him like a cold, damp cloth. There was only the one line from Prophecies so far, and his strange sense of anxiety when the boy had first entered the room. He had to get more information.

"Brother Mailcum," Gareth shouted.

The door swung open to reveal a portly subdeacon whose flowing robes only added to the huge expanse of his girth. "Yes, your Excellency?"

"Send for Seamus Bailson. You'll find him skulking around the galley, most likely."

"Aye."

"And my compliments to Lord Halvin. Inform him that I desire a conference with him this evening."

The fat monk bowed low and left the room.

How did the boy know about my dreams? Gareth thought. Damn him, how did he know? Is he the one the Saints warn me of? Damn it, why can't I sleep? He flung his goblet across the room. Damn him, why do I like him already?

The day passed under full canvas and a bright sky, while the ice shot past clear and black. After taking down Halvin's log for the day, Michael scrambled aloft to the small box atop the foremast. He took his charts and navigator's instruments with him to see if the ice had changed at all since the last charting. He tried to keep his mind on the task that he had set, yet concentration would not come; for long periods his gaze would sweep across the passing sea and register no detail.

The sun reached its low zenith in the southern sky and then quickly arched away into night as the ships came about and prepared their defenses. The call for prayer sounded. He watched from above as the men scrambled across the deck then fell silent as the procession came from the sterncastle. They seemed so small and pitiful two hundred feet below. His gaze swept upward to the faint Arch and then out across the Ice, which disappeared into darkness.

The wind moaned softly around him as he watched the service's end, and the men's quick scramble to the warmth below. The minutes passed and the last of the insectlike creatures disappeared as the darkness closed in.

Opening the bottom of his little windproof cubicle, he swung himself over to the ratlines and gradually made his way to the deck. The guards had been posted and with a gesture he indicated to one that he was going over the side. To do so without their knowledge was to invite an arrow in the throat upon return.

He lowered himself onto the ice and, half walking, half sliding, made his way out from the ship. The icy, dark splendor of the night calmed him. The aurora cracked and whipped in the northern sky, flaring with muted reds and greens. The ice was clear and windblown, its surface catching every streak of light and in muted mimicry repeating the wavery lines from the display that loomed overhead.

He closed his eyes and drifted on the point of nothingness. At last the sense of total loss came to him and all awareness of the world around him disappeared. The cold finally called him back and as he opened his eyes, he was aware from the position of the stars that at least an hour had passed in his contemplation of the light within. He silently thanked the monk who, long ago, had taught him the meditative arts.

He looked to the open sky and realized that for the first time in fifteen years he was free of the cloister's confines. For fifteen years he had lived in a hidden chamber, with only a handful of brothers and monks around him. Rarely any new faces, never any change, just the endless passage of days. His life had been a cycle of morning prayers before sunrise, hours of lessons in the reading of Holy Writ, noonday prayers, afternoon lessons in the charting of the sky and the other skills of St. Awstin, evening prayers, and then an hour or two of martial training from Niall before the last devotions. In the last three or four years, Rifton had spent more and more time with him late in the evening when no one else was around. But the great rituals, the processions through the town, the comings and goings of dignitaries and church councils, all this had been unknown to Michael. There was only the same endless routine, with a brother always nearby.

He had questioned Rifton often enough about his isolation and always received the same answer—the plague had almost killed him and another bout would be fatal. Therefore he must never venture from the hidden, inner monastery of St. Awstin. The chamber within the chamber must always be his, except for the occasional walk atop the highest parapet to watch the evening sky.

When Michael had started to chafe at the endless cycle that seemed worse than death, Rifton mentioned assassination.

"You are the last of my family, the last of my line. The knife hovers above you at every moment." Niall told Michael the same, and over the years had trained him to watch for the blow and always to be on guard.

There was only one problem. He knew they were lying. When he was seven he awoke one day to a terrifying sight. He could see a faint shimmering band of light around Brother Calum. He was so frightened by it that he went to Rifton and told him that Calum was possessed by demons and explained how he knew. With solemn oaths Rifton made Michael swear never to reveal that he could see "lights." But the lights would not go away. Michael was soon able to read and interpret the meaning of the aura and could tell when someone was happy or angry, calm or excited, and whether true or falsehood was told.

He knew that Rifton and the six other monks lived with some darkness, some fear. Then the other one came into his life. Calum disappeared one day and the others were silent as to his whereabouts. The next day a new brother came who was called Facinn. Facinn was assigned to Michael from midnight to dawn. One night Michael could not sleep and left his bed-chamber to seek out the brother for a talk.

Their talks were so revealing and disturbing that Michael went without sleep at night and caught but brief snatches during the day. Facinn spoke of a hidden book that he would reveal, and taught him the secret of meditation.

There came a night when Facinn asked Michael about the dark time of the plague, and of his father and mother. Long they talked that night, and at dawn Facinn looked him in the eye and said softly, "I believe that you are the one Chosen. Tonight I shall bring the book which speaks of you."

When Facinn opened the door to leave the room, Rifton was standing in the hallway with two armed monks behind him. Michael never saw Facinn again, nor would Rifton ever say a word about him except to explain that Facinn was a messenger from the evil one. Six months later, Michael was summoned to Rifton's office to be told that in a fortnight he would sail the Ice.

He looked across the Frozen Sea, his thoughts turning away

from the past. As he looked to the cold sky and felt the freezing ice beneath his feet, he knew that the world was a place of torment. All his life he had lived with fear—fear of the plague, murder, or eternal damnation, yet there, alone upon the wind-swept sea, he felt a sense of joyful liberation. All his life he had been hidden within the cloister, tormented by thoughts of eternal damnation. In the warmth of the caverns, before the chapel altars, he had burnt the incense and chanted when necessary, but it had never seemed real. There had always been the sense of emptiness, a fear that all the effort was nothing more than folly. He looked to the Arch to find comfort, but saw none.

He was swept with fear. The security and the rituals had been stripped away and he stood alone—the physical crutches that propped up his faith for so long were gone. He felt as if he were falling into a dark abyss. He tried to call on the Saints but the words would not come to his lips. Michael reached into his parka and grasped for his prayer beads, but they felt cold and dead. He ran across the ice until the ships were mere lines upon the darkened horizon. The spectre of fear stayed with him.

"Saints above," he shouted, "look down upon me and help me!" The wind answered him with an icy blast. "Send me a sign so that I can believe and save my soul!"

He tried to dwell on the Promise: the return of the Father, the melting of the seas, the return of the Garden, and the feast of joy. But here in the dead of winter's night, he knew that it would never return. He knew that for the heresy of nonbelief he would be condemned to eternal damnation.

Michael sat alone upon the ice while the aurora soared above him. He felt empty, like a vessel that had been drained and tossed away. The cold was slowly numbing him. He decided that it would be wise to return.

He slid across the ice, making his way back to the *Thunderwind*, which gradually grew before him. Reaching the ship, he looked up to the masts that soared to the height of a cathedral spire. The outriggers swept out gracefully from the hull and as he walked along the ship, he came to one of the rams. It hung from the side of the outrigger, its powerful form compelling

ICE PROPHET

Michael to draw closer and examine it. The hull of the ram was
four feet in diameter and supported by outriggers mounted with
razor-sharp blades. Its mast was collapsed and slung to the side
of the craft, ready to be stepped when the ram embarked on
its one and only ride. The oaken trunk was polished to cut
resistance to the wind. Michael walked the length of the ram
and came to the small cockpit at its stern. He swung himself
up and slid into the narrow confines of the box.

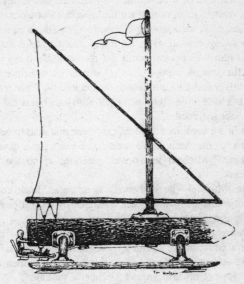

Ram

He sat quietly, looking over the cockpit to the massive form
of the *Thunderwind* that rose above him in the darkness. He
knew the ram's purpose, both for the fleet and its rider. It was
the seat of the Select. The ram was launched to seek the enemy
in battle, and then to crash into his ship. Since the Church did
not condone suicide, the pilot had a small lever that could be
pulled, cutting the cockpit free from the ram before it collided.
But few chose to escape. If the ram hit and destroyed its opponent after the pilot cut loose, then survival was acceptable;

if the ram missed, the pilot was an outcast both in this life and the next. To ride the Chair of the Chosen Ones meant that no matter what sins he had previously committed, at the moment of death the pilot immediately went to the Long Table of the Saints. It was a guarantee of salavation, even to a heretic who died as a nonbeliever in Holy Church.

A gust of wind shook Michael. Pulling himself free of the cockpit, he stepped onto the outrigger and again looked at the ram. The image of it held him even after he turned away and stepped over to a support beam that reached out from the hull of the ship. On all fours he climbed to the ship's railing and tried to swing himself over. He found that his hands and arms were so numb that they would not respond. He hung precariously for several seconds, until, suddenly, a helping hand reached over and pulled him onto the deck of the *Thunderwind*.

" 'Tis a bitter cold night, is it not?" said a soft musical voice. Michael stiffened.

"Ah, it's a night like this that can make one glad to be alive. A clear sky, the Arch above, and no one to trouble you."

"Facinn!" Michael whispered, reaching up to the man's wind mask.

"Aye, Michael," he said softly as he pulled back his mask to reveal a sharp, hawklike face wreathed by a short beard and a closely cropped head of brown hair.

"I thought you were dead."

"For a while there, so did I." Facinn laughed, looking Michael up and down. "Come, my friend, there is much to talk about." He put his arm around Michael's shoulder.

"How did you get away? I thought my uncle killed you."

"Michael, even the good brothers of St. Awstin can be bribed when necessary." Facinn's voice lowered. "I think it would be wise if my name from that place was not used again. Facinn in the tongue of my people meant the Far-Seeing. My real name is Seth, Seth the Far-Seeing, and it would be safer for us both if you used that."

"Yes, Fa-Seth," Michael said with a laugh.

"Good. Michael, you have much to learn about who and what you are. And we begin tonight."

CHAPTER 4

"MOVE HER CLOSER TO THE WIND. DAMN YOU." THE WILD-eyed captain roared. As the bowchaser exploded. he looked through the smoke to where the shot would fall.

"A pox on ye. Ioan. if you miss this time. You've had five good chances already."

"Keep her steady. Ishmael." the gunnery master shouted back. "and then I'll hit."

Ishmael roared with laughter and spit over the rail.

"A hit!" the lookout shouted. "A clean hit to the hull."

"Aye. pour it on to the black-souled bastards." Ishmael screamed. "Now feed it to them. Saints damn them. feed it to them!"

Two puffs of smoke eddied from the stern of their target. a single merchantman a half-mile away.

"To the left." Finson. the lieutenant. shouted.

Ishmael squinted with his one eye and watched as the two shots bounded past him. ricocheting off the ice a hundred yards astern and twenty to port.

"Hold her closer to the wind." Ishmael shouted to the helms-man.

They were directly astern of the fleeing ship and slowly gaining the weather gauge.

The bowchaser fired again.

"A clean hit to the deck," the lookout shouted.

Ishmael nodded with satisfaction as Ioan cheered and set back to his work.

"Two more!" came the call from the foretopman.

They heard the shells screaming in—the first one punched through the tightly rigged jib and fore staysail, the other plowed into the deck. A howling tornado of splinters and steel blew the forecastle railing apart and tore the length of the ship, tumbling over a half-dozen men. Screams of agony rent the air as blood-soaked men kicked and squirmed on the deck.

"Finson," Ishmael shouted above the roar of the bowchaser, "see to them. Help those who won't make it." Finson nodded and Ishmael didn't look back as some of the screams were suddenly extinguished. It was a rule as old as the Ice. In the end, it was better both for the dying and the living.

The volleys rolled across the ice as the pirate ship drew up before the wind of the merchantman. The deck suddenly rolled beneath Ishmael's feet as the first beam-mounted gun was brought to bear. The merchantman's broadsides answered in reply. The deck was swept by fire and smoke, and echoed with the screams of the wounded as the *Black Revenge* drew abeam its target and started to cut in.

"Aim for the deck and the guns," Ishmael ordered. "We want a prize, not a wreck."

Another shot tore through the forecastle and the deck lurched beneath Ishmael's feet.

"Ioan's hit," came a cry from below deck.

"Damn them," Ishmael cursed. A renegade priest was hard to find. "Damn them to hell," he screamed as the battle lust swept over him. "Finson, bring her over, we're boarding."

A cheer rose up from the deck of the *Black Revenge* as Finson put the wheel over and headed on a ramming course with the merchantman.

Another volley slammed out from the pirate ship, cracking the merchantman's mizzenmast and sending it crashing to the enemy's deck. The two ships were almost alongside each other. Catapults and ballistae fired their flaming shot and bolts, sweeping both decks with a deadly shower. The man next to Ishmael collapsed with a bolt in his stomach and vomited a crimson shower of blood. Ishmael reached down with a backhanded stroke and ended his friend's agony.

"Bring her alongside! Saints damn you, Finson, bring her along," Ishmael screamed.

The two boats were a dozen feet apart as they raced before the wind.

"Board!" Ishmael screamed. With a wave of his cutlass he leaped over the rail and ran down the outrigger's support beam. His crew was behind him, looking like fur-clad demons from hell as they swarmed over the side swinging cutlasses and heavy crossbows. From the enemy's foretop an occasional bolt flashed down, one taking a man in midleap and tumbling him to the ice below.

Finson edged the tiller over and the outriggers of the two ships slammed together. With practiced skill, Ishmael's men threw grappling hooks from outrigger to deck, so that within seconds a spiderweb of ropes firmly bound the two ships together. Ishmael leaped across to the enemy outrigger and found himself looking straight into a cannon muzzle. He ducked and the shot exploded over him, plowing into the deck of his frigate.

A thundering rage swept over him as he ran up the enemy's rigger support. A sword rose before him, there was a wild slash, a scream, and he was on the deck. A crossbow was raised, he dove to the deck and rolled as the bolt slammed into the railing behind him. He pulled out his dagger, and with a lunge he fell upon the archer, slashing his throat. He looked back as his crew swept over the deck behind him.

"Death to the Ezrians!" he screamed. "Death to the Ezrians. No prisoners."

Like a wave of death they swept across the merchantman. Several Horthian priests ran up from below with gun staffs in hand and quickly fell to the savage attack of the pirates, who laughed with glee as their hated enemy fell.

The fight swept below, and Ishmael stayed on the deck as

the remembrance of command slowly came back to him. He looked to his ship, where Finson was holding the place that he should now be occupying. Finson looked at him and raised his clenched fist in token of salute.

Ishmael quickly surveyed his ship. No fires. Good.

The sound of battle swept up again from below as the last of the Ezrian merchants was hunted down. He already regretted his call for no prisoners—one or two might have been useful—but that could no longer be helped. The fury of battle died away, and after ten minutes the men started to return to the deck with loot in their arms.

"What's she carrying?" Ishmael asked Jacob, who stood before him, his fur soaked from wrist to shoulder with Ezrian blood.

"Foodstuffs mainly—grain, dried fruit, the usual load of fungus and mushrooms, no gold or silver. Some casks of ale and wine, though," Jacob said with a smile.

"Good, good," Ishmael responded as he pulled off his wind mask to reveal an aging, weathered face. He rubbed the scar that cut across his brow and patch-covered right eye.

"Take a half-dozen men, Jacob, that should be enough to get her back to Bathan. Off-load enough to see our ship through, but leave the ale and wine aboard—it should fetch a fair price with Zardok's agent."

Jacob nodded. "That old pirate will outsteal even us, I wager."

Ishmael laughed. "Your uncle won't appreciate your accurate judgment. Now move, Jacob, we don't know if they had an escort to meet them."

Ishmael called to the lookout in the fore royal mast, "Any sign of the others?"

"Both our ships have run down their prey. One of the merchantmen is burning, though."

"God's blood! The smoke will be a signal for fifty miles. Come on, men!" Ishmael shouted. "Let's get back. Throw the dead over the side and let the Ezrian dogs find 'em. Jacob, cut away the mizzenmast. Save the canvas, we'll have tomorrow for repairs. Come on, let's move."

The men cheered and laughed as they swarmed back to the

Black Revenge. The loot was swung across and within fifteen minutes the frigate cut loose from the merchantman. Pressing on canvas, the *Black Revenge* swung about and ran back before the wind, her two heavy schooners and their captured prey followed in her wake. They doubled back along their tracks to confuse any pursuit that might come upon the evidence.

Ishmael stood beside the wheel. He was silent as the men busied themselves with repairs to the damage wrought by the Ezrians.

"Finson, what's the bill?" Ishmael asked grimly.

"Eleven dead, eight wounded. Repairs will take three or four days to complete. We were lucky: she was more heavily armed than you thought."

Ishmael was silent.

"We could have used some prisoners for information."

"Are you telling me how to run my ship?"

"Ishmael, I'm trying to talk to you as a friend."

"It's because of them that I'm out here."

"You forget, my friend, that we're all in exile. We all have family and friends back there."

Ishmael was silent.

"Ishmael, killing them won't help your daughter now. In fact, it could make it worse if the Ezrians find out who we are."

Ishmael slowly nodded.

Over a year earlier, the Ezrians had stormed Mathin while Ishmael and his crew were on a trading run. Their city had been untouched by the war till then, being considered an unimportant port. In the winter trade would come from across the Frozen Sea. In summer the ice would retreat and the Flowing Sea would bring ships from the Southlands that would trade food, ale, and wine for blackrock, fur, oil, and silver. But the permanent ice had pushed so far south in recent years that Mathin might have access to the Flowing Sea for only a few weeks out of the year.

It was there that the plague had hit hardest, killing two-thirds of the people in five years. The Church of Sol, a heretical branch of the Cornathian church, had collapsed under the strain and now the Ezrians and Cornathians were fighting for control of the trade lanes.

A number of free states had been declared and Ishmael, who at best had paid lip service to Sol, himself declared Mathin a free trade center—until the Ezrian fleet arrived.

He slammed his fist on the railing and looked at Finson.

"I know," Finson said, "I know. Our time will come."

"Ezrian, Cornathian—they're all the same. And I want them dead."

"There's not much we can do about it now, Ishmael. Besides, remember that your actions could hurt Janis."

Janis, Ishmael's daughter, was sixteen when the Ezrians came. The Ezrian commander had taken her as his wife and she had agreed to his demands in the hope of sparing her people.

"Finson, I would give my other eye just to free her from them."

"Our time will come, Ishmael, our time will come. But for God's sake, try to spare the prisoners. Our men are turning into bloodthirsty savages. This hatred will destroy them if you continue."

"I know," Ishmael said mournfully. He also knew what would happen the next time they sighted an Ezrian ship. He knew that his thoughts would be on his daughter's staying with her people and sacrificing her body for them. He knew he would think these things while he slashed his way across a bloody deck.

CHAPTER 5

THE CREW WAS ROUSED FROM SLEEP AS THE EASTERN SKY shifted from blackness to the deep indigo of dawn. The weary men were driven into the numbing cold, to prepare their ships for another day. Some went aloft to ready the sails, while others went over the side to retrieve the ice blocks and pull up the anchors. The men quickly hooked the blocks to the towlines, and the schooners dragged the barriers to the stern hatchways of the warships where they were stowed. It was easier to store the blocks than struggle each night with the cutting of new barriers. Too, they were excellent weapons when dropped against ships that pursued too closely.

Before the dawning sun had chased the last shadows of night, the fleet unfurled its stiffened sails. With a creaking, booming roar, the ice blades tore free of the sea's frozen grasp and the ships were underway. As the sun rose astern of the fleet, the morning light was reflected in the towering plumes of ice that were kicked up by the thundering passage of razor-sharp blades. Even the old veterans would pause to watch the graceful display of speed and light as the swirling columns of ice and snow held the golden light of dawn.

Michael was alone, the sailing master having left to plan the day's run after they completed the reading of the charts. In an hour Gareth would expect him, and he took advantage of the few moments that morning afforded to try and collect his weary thoughts. The joy of seeing Seth was overwhelming. Seth was the only one that he ever considered a friend. Michael had loved Brother Niall, but Niall was the hard master of defense, a person one loved and respected, but not someone to call a friend.

Michael and Seth had sat and talked about old memories and Seth's story of escape.

"I thought I was dead. The two brothers took me to a hidden chamber within the darkest folds of the mountain. There, I languished for days without food, having only the moisture from the walls to drink."

"So how did you escape?"

"Michael, shall we say that I knew one of the guards from before? He bided his time and one night the door opened to the sight of a corpse. The guard, if we can call him that, took a dead man from the town, and he substituted the body for me. I took the man's clothes and slipped away."

"But why did my uncle do this?" Michael asked in a shocked tone. "I've always thought of him as stern, yet somehow kind."

"Your uncle is a good man," Seth said. "I should know, I served in his order for five years—until I could finally get to you."

"Why?"

"Because I was waiting to see you. Let us say for now, that there are some who have studied the prophecies of the past. Michael, have you heard of *The Book of Prophecies*?"

Michael's thoughts were jumbled. He had heard a few veiled comments, but nothing more. He looked at Seth and was afraid. The man before him had the air of the fanatic.

"Michael, I've read the book. I read it long before I came to your order."

"But how? You're not a priest, so where did you learn to read?"

"Ah, Michael, but I *am* a priest, of Inys Gloi."

"So why did you come to me?"

"Because, Michael, there are some who believe that you have been preordained as the Chosen One. You are the one who shall sweep aside the old order and in its place return the favor of the Father and the retreat of the Ice. That is why your uncle hid you; he was afraid that you were the messenger sent to end the rule of the Church and bring forth the new time."

"But I'm not," Michael responded after several moments of silence. "Seth, you must be mistaken: I know who I am—I'm a priest of Awstin, not a messiah."

"Michael, whether you believe it or not, the signs say that you are. On the night of your birth a light hovered in the sky in the middle of the Arch, and it stayed in the sky for seven days and nights. You have the two signs of fire—you can reach into the nothing—and, Michael, I believe that you can also look into the hearts of men and see the fire of their light. These are but a few of the things that Inys Gloi has discovered about you in *The Book of Prophecies*. Michael, already there are hundreds to serve you, and my order has readied a place for you to live and to prepare."

"Where?"

Seth looked at him and smiled softly. "In due time my friend, in due time. We'll be riding this fleet till the spring. It will give you a chance to see the Ice, and to see what the good churches have done to it in the name of the Saints."

And so their conversation ended with the coming of the dawn.

A large sheet of double-bulged ice appeared on the horizon and Michael's thoughts were interrupted as he checked his charts. The obstacle wasn't noted, and with meticulous care he recorded its position. The fleet was still upon the permanent ice shelf, so the changes in the ice were few to note. However, the farther south they ran the more the ice would change until they finally reached the Broken Tracks.

The Southward Isles lay beyond the Broken Tracks in the region of temporary ice that disappeared in the brief moment of summer. The Broken Tracks were the between ground. There, as a result of the pressure of storm-driven waters laden with ice floes that crashed against the permanent cover to the Frozen Sea, the ice would take on fantastic forms, as large as mountains and as deep as any canyon seen on land. There, the levels of the two ice shelves changed as well, the permanent shelf resting higher than the one that melted each summer. Most of the area was too broken for iceboat travel, but some dozen passages did reach to the south. They would exist for years or even decades, until the pressure of the ice twisted them into impossible jumbles.

The Broken Tracks were difficult to sail, and there, more ships were lost in cracks and fissures than to enemy action.

The first watch of morning passed and Brother Elias came forward to take Michael's place. In Michael's opinion Elias was almost singular in his lack of conversation, and Michael felt he belonged more with the Braith de Narn and their silent prayer than to the friendly Brotherhood of St. Awstin.

Michael turned over his charts and went about his daily routine. Gareth awaited him with a game of Flyswin, and from there he would go to Seth. And gradually his existence was directed onto a path that he had never dreamed of before.

So the days passed in their endless succession, quiet hours of running across the wind as the fleet continued upon its mission of vengeance. Michael quickly fell into the cycle of life aboard ship and his confusion over his newfound freedom slowly gave way to an invigorating joy as his twenty-year-old's body took pleasure in the hard and taxing life. The conversations with Seth continued every night, and he found them disquieting. Whenever Seth began to speak of the prophecies, Michael rebelled and called the idea nonsense, so that after several days Seth learned to avoid the topic and instead spent his time educating Michael in the lore of the sea and the history of the churches.

Daniel would come forward during Michael's first watch and the conversation would inevitably bend toward war and battle, with Daniel boasting of his own exploits while giving advice on survival in combat. Michael never became accustomed to the stench of the rancid bear fat the giant used as protection against frostbite.

The fourteenth day of the passage dawned bright and clear, with a hint of warmth that most likely would bring the temperature up to twenty degrees of frost by midday. The fleet left its morning anchorage and swept out in open-search order. Michael soon drifted toward the edge of sleep as he sat alone in the navigator's box.

"Deck ho!" came a distant shout. "The *Snow Wind* is coming about."

Within seconds Michael was fully awake. as the crew stopped their routine and looked aloft.

"Deck ho!" the lookout shouted. "*Snow Wind* heaving to."

On the horizon's edge Michael could see the faint outline of sails swinging across the wind, then luffing as the ship came to a stop in the northwesterly breeze. The *Thunderwind* continued on her course and soon arched across the stern of the *Snow Wind*, coming parallel to her track—facing up into the wind.

"Lord Halvin," a voice hailed from the *Snow Wind*. "Tracks not two hundred yards ahead."

Halvin looked forward to see several fur-clad men racing back to the ships, using small, hand-held sails to pull them along. The men skated up to the starboard outrigger of the *Thunderwind*.

Halvin leaned over the rail. "What is it?"

One of the men, his goggles and mask removed, responded, "A dozen ships. Lord Halvin—ten merchantmen, I make it, and two frigates. Heavily loaded, I say. Bearing west by southwest."

"How old?"

"I'd say late yesterday afternoon. The tracks are all running close, so I'd reckon they were closing in for the night. If we're lucky, they might only be an hour or two ahead."

Halvin nodded and turned away. "Master reader, bring me your charts."

Michael stepped forward and laid the charts before Halvin.

"We are here," Michael said, pointing to a position a hundred leagues north of the Broken Tracks. "It appears that they're bearing toward the Bathanian Pass."

Halvin nodded. "Ezrian, no doubt; none of ours venture here."

Halvin turned to Elijah, the sailing master. "Order all ships to fall astern of our position. The *Thunderwind* will lead the chase. *Snow Wind* and *St. Almarth* to be on our port and starboard flanks."

The men cheered as the master turned and shouted his commands. The sails were banked over and the *Thunderwind* was soon pushed off from the wind's eye. Within seconds she was making a sweeping arc, turning to follow the merchant fleet's tracks. The chase was on.

In minutes the prediction of the *Snow Wind*'s tracking master was confirmed. The merchant fleet had indeed come about; the signs of its anchorage showed clearly on the ice. The Cornathians steered clear of the area because it was common for a captain to leave a couple of deadfalls to wreck a tracking ship.

"Clear the fleet for action," Halvin shouted as they rounded the anchorage point and the ice revealed tracks not more than an hour old. Within seconds the signal guns thundered and the fleet made ready for battle. Halvin smiled a twisted, wolflike grin of lust as he returned to his cabin.

Three thousand men now responded to Halvin's orders. Michael hurried to the charting table from where he was expected to advise on the lay of the ice and to log the key points of the action. He stepped to his place alongside the helmsman and watched as the ship prepared for action. The catapult crews swarmed across the deck and struggled with the canvas that shrouded their weapons. Directly before Michael rose two heavy ballistae capable of throwing ten-foot spears a quarter mile. These were assigned to Seth and Daniel in battle, and they drove their crews in frenzied preparation.

Crossbowmen ran past Michael, making their way aloft to fighting platforms set high in the mast, while from the deck, bundles of arrows were lifted on ropes. Part of the deck near Michael popped open, and Michael walked forward and looked down to see the twenty-four-pound bowchaser guns. The bulkheads in front of the guns were removed by straining crews and the guns were run out. Michael looked into the small room that he knew was Gareth's. The High Priest, looking up through the smoke port, gave Michael a curt nod and started back to his work. A man bumped into Michael, then hurried forward bearing two heavy buckets of sand, which he placed next to the ballistae. Another one brought a sealed bucket which smelled of oil.

The frenetic activity continued for another ten minutes until, finally, all the guns were rolled out on the deck below. Topside the catapults and ballistae stood ready, while placed strategically along the three-hundred-foot deck were bundles of shot, racks of rounded stones, buckets of sand, grappling hooks, boarding mats, nets, and the hundred other items that made up an iceboat going into battle.

So intent was he upon his examination of the scene, that Michael hardly noticed the hand on his shoulder. Turning, he beheld a man clad head to foot in bluish-black fur. Upon his head was a helmet of burnished steel that revealed only two small openings for the eyes. His chest was covered by a long coat of chain mail that dropped to midthigh. Over his shoulder was a light crossbow, while belted about his waist was a curved scimitar.

"Better get your armor on, Michael," the figure said. "Ezrians love to kill priests."

Michael recognized Seth's voice. He smiled, nodded, and went below, returning several minutes later with a helmet. A light coat of chain mail could be made out beneath his cloak.

"Do you have a weapon?"

"Priests of St. Awstin carry no weapons."

Seth laughed and, walking over to his ballistae, picked up a sword and shield. "Take them," he shouted. "After all of this, I would prefer to see you live."

Michael nodded and stepped back to his position next to the helmsman's box. Several minutes later the men started to fall silent, so that soon the only sound was that of the icy wind whistling in the rigging. Michael heard a strange, dissonant note. Looking up, he noticed that Seth had produced a lyre, which he strummed with an unusual, pulsating beat. Michael leaned back and, listening to the music, closed his eyes.

He relaxed to the soft rhythm, and the gentle emptiness of meditation flowed through him. His breathing came slower and slower, so that if any had noticed, they would have thought him in a state near death.

There was nothing, and then, suddenly, Michael stood before himself. He could see Seth sitting and watching his body, and he noticed that Daniel stood only a few feet behind. He drifted away from the confines of the *Thunderwind*, and in seconds, the *Thunderwind* was a small, insignificant spot crawling across the Frozen Sea, the rest of the fleet following in her wake. Not far ahead, he could see a dozen dart-shaped ships completely unaware of the doom closing in upon them. Michael felt a godlike power as he watched the insignificant struggle below.

The pursuit held his attention for a moment as he passed above them, and soon a thousand other ships were visible as he made his way across the sea of ice. Far to the north, he could see a burning frigate, while others raced in a death struggle as their crews looked to the Heavens for help. His vision swept past them to behold men living in the crumbling ruins of a forgotten age. He watched as the life of an entire race hung upon the edge of a two-thousand-year night. And he heard their cries of anguish and fear as they cowered amid rituals of darkness and death.

He looked heavenward and above him glowed the Arch, and a dark empty sea of a million stars. He looked out and found nothing—only darkness.

"Damn you!" he screamed. "Are you there?"

"Sail ho!" came a distant cry.

"Michael," a voice said softly, "are you all right?"

He slowly opened his eyes. The images were sharp before him, so sharp and intense that for a moment he had to shut his eyes to block the glare. He opened them more slowly and saw Seth kneeling before him, his face mask and helmet off, his sharp, hawklike face furrowed with concern.

"Michael, the ships have been sighted."

"I know," Michael said, loud enough for Seth and several others to hear. "There's a dozen of them—two frigates, two corsairs, and eight merchants."

Seth looked at him.

"It's all of them," came the shout from above. "I take it to be two frigates, two corsairs, the rest merchants."

Michael slowly stood up. The men looked at him and quickly turned away.

"You are the One," Seth said reverently.

The enemy fleet was visible from the deck of the *Thunderwind*, and the enemy merchantmen put on more canvas in their effort to escape. Halvin returned to the forecastle as the signal flags went up to the other ships. The light frigates and schooners on the windward side sprang ahead, while the *St. Regis* and the four armed merchantmen dropped off to the southwest to catch any ships that might try to run southward.

The two enemy frigates assumed the classic maneuver when surprised from astern by a superior force. They dropped all rams, in this case only eight, then one of them drifted astern of the fleet as a sacrifice while the other pressed on every inch of canvas. The sacrifice would try to delay the enemy while the other ship escaped to spread the warning. The merchantmen were on their own.

The minutes passed slowly as the range closed. The first frigate was keeping her distance as the *Snow Wind* and the *St. Almarth* were pressing forward to stop her.

It was Daniel who first noticed the act that sent up a howl of rage.

"Look!" he screamed. "The filthy buggers are dumping the cargo, pox on them, there goes the prize money."

The bales of goods were scattered across the ice, dumped by the merchantmen in a desperate bid for a few more minutes' time. Barrels of oil, bundles of fur, boxes of black rock, and finely worked metal goods lay across the ice as the *Thunderwind* shot past. If the battle ended quickly enough Halvin might send some schooners and merchantmen back to salvage the goods, but odds were that he wouldn't take the chance.

Michael stood next to Halvin and watched as several merchantmen broke to the south to try and run for the Broken Tracks, but the *St. Regis* shot ahead to cut them off. His attention was shifted back to the front at the cry from above: "Two shots coming from the frigate!"

Michael waited tensely for the impact, but after several seconds he remembered that it would be at least fifteen seconds at this range before the shots came in. The seconds dragged by and Michael tried to conceal his fear.

One of the men shouted and Michael looked to see a shower of ice kick up a hundred yards to starboard and a quarter mile ahead. No one could place the second shot. Looking back to the enemy fleet, he could see the attack of the *St. Almarth* and some of the corsairs as they swung past the enemy frigate and cut into the main body of the merchantmen.

"By thunder," Daniel shouted suddenly, "they've tumbled one of the buggers."

Michael walked forward to Seth's ballistae for a better view.

"Took the poor bastards' skates off, I reckon," Seth said coldly.

At this distance it was hard for Michael to tell, but as the shower of ice subsided he could see a small, dartlike shape tumbling over the ice, its masts whipping and snapping like broken straws. They rushed down upon the fallen foe as the *Thunderwind* turned slightly into the wind then straightened out again to avoid the wreckage.

They shot past. A great gouge had been slashed into the ice and it led like a beacon to the kindling that lay scattered for several hundred yards beyond. The hull rested in two separate parts, sails and rigging wrapped around them. Flames licked hungrily at what was left, and half a dozen survivors were staggering about the ice. As the *Thunderwind* whisked past the flaming hulk, Michael could hear the screams of the wounded trapped within. He watched as the burning tomb drifted astern.

"Ah, they're trying again, they are," Seth shouted as another plume of smoke shot from the frigate.

A quarter of a mile out, it hit the ice and both shots sprung off the ice and bounded upward again.

"A bit to the left, it be," said a short skinny man next to Daniel. And his forecast was true as the shot screamed past twenty yards to port while the other was a good deal farther out.

The deck rolled beneath Michael's feet and for an instant he was blinded with smoke as the *Thunderwind* responded to the enemy fire.

Once a minute the enemy frigate boomed its defiance, and every minute the heavier guns of the *Thunderwind* replied. The rest of the Cornathian fleet passed by on both flanks in pursuit of the fleeing ships and left the frigate to the *Thunderwind*'s guns.

Looking down through the smoke vent, Michael watched the action in Gareth's room.

"Set it another twenty yards to port," Gareth shouted, "and don't touch the elevation!"

On each side of the gun breech a chair was mounted for the gun layers. Before each gun layer was a crank that controlled the elevation or traverse of the gun. The portside man turned the traverse in response to Gareth's command while the powder boys rammed their charges home.

A shrieking roar passed overhead and Michael looked upward as a rigging line parted, the severed ends snapping with the impact from the shot.

Gareth's voice boomed out in the prayers of blessing—the secret ritual of Mor that prevented the gun's possession by a demon who could destroy it. Finally he shouted, "By St. Mor may this shot be laid true to the glory of the Everlasting Saints."

"Amen," the crew shouted in response as the linstock struck the touchhole. The deck swayed as everything disappeared into a swirling cloud of smoke.

The lookout shouted from above, "It's a hit to the deck."

Gareth's crew shouted with joy, their cheers drowned out by the firing of the other bowchaser.

"Now, set to it lads, and we'll send them all to hell!"

Yard by yard, the range closed as the *Thunderwind* approached the frigate. Most of the merchantmen, realizing that their fate was sealed, turned into the wind and struck their colors. Far ahead, the *Snow Wind* and *St. Almarth* continued their race with the fleeing enemy frigate.

The eight enemy rams came about and started to close with the *Thunderwind*. Gareth managed to get off one more volley then had to fall silent as two light schooners escorting the *Thunderwind* swung before her. The thirty-man schooners protected the capital ships, sacrificing themselves if the ram attack broke through.

The *Thunderwind* bore down before the wind and Halvin took personal command of the helm. The rams had only one chance for success; if they missed they faced a long stern chase and the heavy guns of the ship as they slowly regained attack position.

The *Thunderwind* swayed back and forth as Halvin pulled the wheel in an attempt to throw off their aim. With a thundering roar of "Helm a lee!" Halvin pushed the wheel over. The *Thunderwind* hiked up on its downwind runners in an incredibly tight turn to port that knocked Michael to the deck and slammed him against the railing.

Two hundred yards ahead, a schooner and two rams merged into an explosion of wood and steel as the schooner's captain gave himself to save his master's ship. The surviving rams swung about to chase the *Thunderwind* on a downwind attack. Without warning, Halvin put the wheel over again. The *Thunderwind* came down on all runners and a second later hiked up on her upwind runners as Halvin pushed the ship to its limit. Arrows swarmed down from above, while the guns below deck fired loads of grapeshot that caught one of the rams in an explosion of shattering ice. Another ram pressed in, trying to turn with the *Thunderwind*, but the target was swinging in too tight an arc. The boom arm of the *Thunderwind*'s starboard outrigger slammed straight into the ram's mast and snapped it. The ram catapulated underneath the outrigger and ran parallel to it as the mast and rigging collapsed onto the ram and tangled in its blades. Within seconds the ram shot clear of the *Thunderwind* and tumbled as the pilot lost control. The pilot tried to leap clear, then disappeared as he was crushed beneath the bulk of his death ship. The ram attack was over. The remaining schooner came about to run the four remaining rams down and to finish them off with light cannon and crossbows. The four surviving pilots were doomed.

The ram attack allowed the defending enemy frigate to gain half a mile, which had to be made up by a slow and painful chase. The *Snow Wind* and her escorts were hull down over the horizon, while the rest of the fleet was scattered as it chased down and captured what was left of the enemy.

The below-deck guns thundered again as both sides searched for the range. A puff of smoke burst from the target, and after several seconds Michael saw it hit the ice not a hundred yards ahead. It was coming straight at—

With a howling shriek the shell plowed into the bow of the *Thunderwind*. The port bow ballista collapsed as its support frame exploded from the impact of the ball. The torsion ropes spun madly, and the torsion arms rocketed across the deck like two deadly sickles. Shrieks of agony filled the air and a man with dazed eyes staggered up to Michael. A two-foot splinter as thick as Michael's arm was sticking out from the man's chest, his tunic becoming crimson as his torn aorta sprayed blood. Michael stood riveted, in fascinated horror, as Seth ran to the man's side.

"Don't touch me!" the dying man screamed. "Don't touch me."

With an unbelievable burst of strength, the man lurched over to the rail trailing a river of blood behind him. With an agonized scream of pain he shouted, "St. Karina, help me!" as he threw himself over the side of the ship.

The two cannons beneath the deck thundered in reply. The forecastle was a blood-soaked shambles. The exploding ballista had crushed the life from two men and almost a dozen others were injured. Seth looked at Michael, his face now masked by helmet and goggles.

"Are you all right, Michael?" he shouted above the wind and the roar of battle.

"I'm all right."

"Your arm, boy, your arm."

Michael looked down to his right arm and saw that a splinter had torn his jacket open from elbow to shoulder. He hadn't been touched, but already the freezing cold and wind were numbing him. He stood in a confused daze with the shriek of the dying man still in his ears. He had seen a man die for the first time, and he was afraid. He was afraid because he felt that he should be feeling all the civilized emotions of fear and anger but instead there was a different sensation—one that was far more terrifying. He was enjoying himself. He was caught in the swirl of battle and the joy of it washed over him with a savage call that he had never dreamed possible. He exulted as he became one with war.

And so the range closed downward and soon every shot found its mark. The light twelve-pounders of the frigate were no match for the heavier twenty-fours. Michael and the rest of the crew cheered wildly as the shots slammed home, sending up clouds of splinters and the broken bodies of Ezrian sailors and priests. One of the enemy shots plowed into the *Thunderwind* below Michael's feet. He could hear it crashing through the pine walls into the center of the ship, and he could hear the screams left in its wake. It was easy to imagine what the heavy balls from the *Thunderwind* were doing to the light hull of the enemy ship.

Before they had finished closing, the entire stern of the enemy was a broken shambles. Her guns were silent and sticking out of their ports at impossible angles, while from amidships puffs of dark, oily smoke were visible. The *Thunderwind* bore off to windward and as she did so she loosened a broadside at the enemy that brought down its mizzenmast. The frigate turned into the wind to try and cross Halvin's bow. Halvin pushed his ship over to port and cut astern of the frigate and slammed it with another broadside.

"No fire," Halvin shouted as the ballista and catapult men waited for the range and the oil-soaked bolts and shot were put aside.

"Ready," Seth shouted.

"Now!" Seth pulled at the ballista trigger and the bolt shot free with a booming crack. It whined into the frigate and plowed into a swarm of men standing on the enemy's forecastle.

"Well done, well done, I promise you a prize ship for that shot!" Halvin screamed, his hood now back and his eyes wild with battle lust.

while half a dozen flaming bolts from the enemy ship arched back in reply. The enemy ship weaved on drunkenly and all could see that Seth's shot had swept the helmsman's box and left the craft pilotless.

The two ships ran at ever-slowing speeds into the wind, with the *Thunderwind* a hundred yards to the port side. Several fire shots landed on the *Thunderwind*'s deck but were quickly smothered by buckets of sand.

Another volley tore from the *Thunderwind* and slammed into the enemy ship. The center of the frigate erupted into a towering explosion of fire as the magazine detonated with a bone-shaking roar, and the ship lifted clear off the ice. Halvin pulled hard over and all watched in grim fascination as the debris rose, hung in midair, and then rained down across several hundred yards of ice. An oily, black cloud rolled heavenward and Michael watched as the flames consumed two hundred men—the latest offerings to the return of God.

CHAPTER 6

THEY SAT IN SILENCE, UNTIL HALVIN FINALLY BROKE THE spell. "What's the price?"

Gareth looked down at the tabulation that his brothers gave him. "Fifty-three dead, another forty hurt—seven of those most likely will die. The damage to the *Thunderwind*, *Golden Night*, and *St. Almarth* can be repaired at sea. The schooner *Wind Hammer* was lost with all her crew, but it's the *Snow Wind* that we really have to worry about. Her master reports that she cracked her starboard outrigger frame for half its length. She can sail, but the slightest hike will collapse her. We need to hole up at least a week and replace the entire outrigger."

"Michael," Halvin suddenly shouted. The door swung open and Michael stepped into Halvin's cabin. "Bring your charts over here," Halvin commanded.

Michael fetched the charts and spread them on the table.

"Where were they heading?" Halvin asked his sailing master.

"The merchants claim that they were running to Mathin."

"Mathin? Never been there," Halvin muttered to himself.

"What about you?" Halvin asked, turning to his ship's master.

"Sire, it was a free port and the Ezrians took it last year according to our reports. It's not much—too far north and astride the last pass before the deadland. In fact, it's cut off more often than not by the ice."

"Bathan would be closer," Halvin said.

"Bathan's a freebooter's town, with extensive fortifications. We would have to storm it in order to get in," the sailing master responded.

"Then it's Mathin. We'll use the captured merchantmen to surprise the Ezrians." Halvin looked at Michael and with a nod dismissed him.

As Michael walked from the room he noticed that Gareth was staring at him.

"Tell me," Gareth said slowly, "what do you know of him?"

"Who?" Halvin responded absently.

"Michael, nephew of Rifton."

Halvin stiffened and tried to mask his feelings. "Why do you ask?"

"Just wondering. There seem to be some rumors going about among the men."

"How do you know this?" Halvin asked coldly. He needed the priests of Mor for his vengeance, yet he despised them and the bond that their leader held over him.

"It's just that I heard that you were once good friends with the boy's uncle," Gareth countered.

"Yes, but the boy was hidden from me. I never met him before this voyage."

"I see."

"Do you have orders from Zimri concerning him?" Halvin asked cautiously.

"Yes, to see that he returns safely in the spring." Halvin suddenly looked up at Gareth, searching his face for a clue.

"I think," Gareth continued, "that there is something more here, though. I was just wondering if you had heard anything."

"No, I haven't."

"Well then," Gareth said, "I believe that the time for the

services draws nigh. I must attend to my duty. We'll talk again, my Lord Admiral."

With a nod and then a wave of blessing, he left the room without acknowledgment of his passing from Halvin.

Halvin tried to form his plan to take Mathin and safely bring in the *Snow Wind*. Had it been any other ship, he would simply have sent it back to Cornath. But as the fastest ship in his fleet, she was too valuable. The plan slowly started to form, but the other thoughts, planted long ago, kept pushing at him.

"There's rumor that the Ezrians might have your boy," Zimri had finally stated. "We might be able to arrange something through one of the minor neutral brotherhoods."

He sat dumbly, wanting desperately to believe, yet afraid to. The image of his oldest boy was all too clear.

"I'll see what I can do for you, Lord Admiral."

"Thank you, Zimri. It is time to sail. I hope that when I return in the spring you'll have good news for me. I would owe you everything for this favor."

Zimri looked at him with his disarming smile.

"By the way," Zimri said offhandedly, "I've replaced your log keeper and chart reader for you. I think you know the boy—his name is Michael Ormson, he's the nephew of your old friend Rifton."

Halvin looked at him sharply.

"Interesting, isn't it? The old man never told me about him; I found it curious. I felt the cruise might do the boy some good, get him out of the cloister. So I asked the old man for him to be your St. Awstin priest. Did you know anything of him?"

Halvin looked at Zimri. "No, I thought he died in the plague."

"Curious, you two being such good friends and all. It would be a shame if he didn't come back now, but a personal sacrifice to our Holy Cause can sometimes bring unexpected rewards to others later on." Zimri smiled. "A good and profitable sail to you Lord Halvin," he said and left.

The conversation had tormented Halvin without letup. He remembered the boy before the plague, and how his birth had triggered the Inys Gloi rumors of a Promised One.

Yes, he remembered it all, and he remembered his boy as well—staked, a spear rammed through his body.

He buried his head and muffled the cry of anguish. A sacrifice to bring back the other, he thought.

"Let's us rejoice, for as it was said by St. Isaiah, 'They wait not, for already they shall feast at the Table of the Saints.' Amen."

"By the intercession of the Saints, may they find the everlasting warmth of the Long Table. And may they watch over us and guide us in our own hour of death. Amen."

The ships' companies stood before the great trench that had been cut into the ice and gave their silent farewells to friends who would never be met again in this life. The brothers turned from the grave, and in solemn procession formed into their separate orders to return to the ships. The cauldrons were brought forth, and amid bubbling towers of steam, the hot water was emptied into the trench where the weighted bodies of the dead rested. Within minutes the water formed a film of ice that etched a lacy network of lines across the grave. As the hour passed, the ice thickened and hardened, becoming one with the surrounding sea.

On occasion ice travelers would find such graves, some of which were a thousand years old, the cadaverous faces of the dead still visible and peering out from their frozen tombs. Such places were avoided by all and were called Marbth de lae—the Ice of the Dead.

The aurora was still tonight, the only light being the myriad of stars and the great, pale Arch. The crews were filing back to their ships, so that soon he found himself alone.

He stood alone, peering into the ice and the frozen stares of the dead. "What do you see?" he asked. "All the fears, all the prayers are past, and what do you now see? If only you could speak."

Silence.

As if from a dream, he could hear laughter echoing across the ice. Already they were forgetting. No, he thought, not forgetting—blocking out the sorrow, pushing it to the bottom of their nightmares.

He looked upward to the Ring of God. "Why do we torture ourselves? Why do we fight in Your Name?" The silent wind of night drifted past him. A wind that brushed against his shaven skull and touched his face with its deathlike kiss.

A muffled scream echoed from the *Thunderwind*. A scream of animal fear and pain torn from the soul, and Michael shook with the sound of it. Several priests of Ezra had made the mistake of being taken alive, and the three priests of Mord Rinn were visiting them. The muffled screams rose and fell, then slowly drifted away as the men clung to their belief in what they were sure was the nature of the universe.

Why? Michael thought. He looked into the faces in the ice, then looked heavenward.

A twelve-pound shot had crashed into Seth's cabin during the closing minutes of action. With an air of resignation to the fortunes of life, Seth spent half the night cleaning up the damage and repairing his hammock. It was quiet now and the other two in the room were asleep, the only sign of their presence the rumbling snore of the one and the bearish stench of the other. Seth relaxed in quiet thought and began the silent chanting that in one hour would bring the strength of a full night's sleep. But he found that meditation came hard as he pondered his task.

Michael's experience with spirit walking was totally unforeseen, and perhaps dangerous. One of the fools who had witnessed it was already spreading the word—and it was not yet time to start that. The other danger was the one that he and the Father had talked about so long ago.

"My son Seth," the Master of Inys Gloi had started, with his peculiar lisp, "we shall claim that Michael is the Prophet Preordained."

"Yes," Seth had replied. "Every sign is there—the ones spoken of in prophecy, and some other, unexpected ones as well."

"You mean the star signs."

"Yes, the star signs. Not only our own priests but some from other orders can cast those, such as the Master of St. Awstin. Consider that four years ago, on the night that he was born, the light held in the sky. The golden planet had entered the sign of Fir Calorth. We all knew that on that night the epic of over twenty centuries was at an end. That another twelfth of the twenth-four-thousand-year cycle was over and that the world had entered a new sign. Twice before in recorded times this has been the changing time, the time of the next prophet."

"Yes, I know that, Seth," the Father said patiently. "All the signs point now to him. But tell me, Seth, is he the creation of our dreams or is he more—is he truly the Wrath of God?"

They sat in silence and meditated upon the path that Seth was to take.

"Beware, Seth. You of all shall be closest to him if our plan succeeds. Through him we can break the power of the other brotherhoods, we can gain the secrets of the First Choosing and at last unite all the Ice under our rule of the One Church."

"But what if he wasn't really created by us and the prophecies that we invented." What if we are mere actors already set up to play a role for some other, higher plan? But Seth did not voice this to the Father.

What if . . . He now thought on that. The thousand brothers of Inys Gloi, all with hidden lives, slowly, through endless generations, had prepared for this moment. Prepared for the overthrow of the Churches and the return of their power.

Seth remembered the first meeting—the sheer presence of this young man; there was an aura, a sense of power about him that was compelling. What confused Seth was the total denial by Michael of any desire to be the Promised One. Seth had lived with the plan for twenty years and was bewildered. He expected the boy to embrace the idea of his destiny. But it was still better than the deeper fear that he had carried—that Michael would have already known that he was indeed the Chosen One.

Seth knew that the people would flock to Michael. The brothers of Inys Gloi had sensed the growing discontent for years, especially after the plague. Soon the people would flock to the new leader, the hidden priests of Inys Gloi pointing the way. The dream of the hidden brotherhood would at last be fulfilled as Inys Gloi seized the power of all three churches behind the banner of the Prophet.

He rolled over in his hammock and tried to organize his plans for the next day. The rumors of Halvin's plan had swept the deck and Michael had confided what little he knew. It was fortunate that Seth had been a master sailor before joining St. Awstin. He had Halvin's notice from yesterday and the ten other brothers aboard ship could help to make arrangements.

The bells of the middle night watch sounded overhead.

The words of the Father were with him as he drifted off to sleep: "Tell me, Seth, suppose he truly is the Prophet in the fullest sense of the word, ordained by a higher destiny than ourselves? Then what do we do?" The question remained unanswered.

At dawn the ships' companies assembled on the ice; while standing on the prow of the *Thunderwind*, Halvin addressed them for the first time.

"Men of our sacred brotherhood, I am well pleased. Already the hated church of the Ezrians reels from your blow, and we move another step closer to our final desire. Our moneychangers worked long into the night and it has been counted that to each of you shall come the prize of two shiden in silver."

The men looked at one another and smiled. Two shiden would bring them a night of drink or a few brief moments of pleasure in a house of the fallen.

"But we have just begun, my brothers, we have just begun. The ice shall be good for months to come, and in that time we shall make the Ezrians bleed a thousandfold more, so that you—all of you—shall return with your rags exchanged for cloaks of finest brocade. Your backs shall be bent double with the weight of the riches won."

The crews cheered at this and Halvin smiled. He knew that appeals to church would work with some, and revenge with others, but that silver and gold would reach into the hearts of all. To drown his hatred in blood he needed the men to drink deeply as well.

"Last night." Halvin continued, "we had a talk with several of our guests."

At this, some of the men roared with laughter; Michael heard a midnight echo of screams.

"They were making for Mathin, which stands two days' sail from us. They were making for Mathin and now, under the guise of their cloak, we shall go to Mathin in their stead."

The men stood quietly and looked at him.

"We shall sail to Mathin and take it!" Halvin shouted. "There the *Snow Wind* shall be repaired, so we may sweep from that island to raid the Southward Seas. From my hands shall flow streams of gold—for *my* prize money, *my* ten percent. I pledge now to you common men. With each drop of blood that you shed, another silver piece shall be yours. Now, what say ye men, are you with me?"

A burly sailor stepped forward, raised his fist into the air, and screamed, "To Mathin for Halvin!" In an instant all joined in with cries so loud that to some it seemed even in the city of Mathin there would be a warning of the fury to come.

The fleet was underway. The *Thunderwind* had been stripped of her crew to man the captured ships. As Halvin had promised, Seth received one of the craft—a small merchantman of sixty feet that he renamed the *Answered Prayer*. It carried one six-pound stern gun and three four-man crossbows.

As the master, Seth was able to choose the twenty-man crew. All were men whom he had known upon the Ice at one time or another, but he was startled when Halvin offhandedly offered Michael. Halvin stated that the raiding fleet needed a chartmaster and since the *Thunderwind* was the only ship with two aboard, he could spare the younger to Seth.

Seth's first instinct was to steal away for Inys Gloi, but he knew that if Halvin so willed, he could have a corsair run them down in two days. Even if he were to elude the corsair, there would remain two weeks of travel on the open ice, with only one six-pounder aboard to fight off the inevitable pirates and

Ezrian patrols. No, he would have to trust to luck. As the winter passed he would continue to court Halvin until a bigger prize ship was earned, then in the spring he would make his break.

Seth looked over to Michael, who sat upon the bowsprit with Daniel. Seth found that every time he looked at Michael he experienced a deep emotional bonding. Throughout his life Seth had wandered among thousands, but loneliness had been his only companion.

The memory of a father, his brothers, and a young laughing girl with long red hair swept through him, but all were gone— in the plague and the endless war. Yet when he looked to Michael he felt a stirring of love and friendship, sentiments that Seth had long since buried. I must not allow myself this risk, he thought. I cannot endure the pain again.

Michael sat in quiet fascination as the ice led them south-westward. He watched with acute interest the sudden and rad-ical changes in the texture and structure of the Frozen Sea. The ice shelf of the homelands had been solid and unbroken for almost two thousand years. The surface layer thawed of course, in the brief moment of summer, but froze solid again with the first heavy frost of Awst. The endless wind wore it down to a smooth polish that even the most ungainly of colliers and stone runners could pass.

But the surface of the Southern Sea held a different texture as they approached the edge of the Broken Tracks, and the blades chattered to the rougher surface. The helmsman kept a sharp watch in order to steer around the larger bumps as the ship bounced and swayed. From above the watchers called out the color and texture of the ice and kept a sharp lookout for fissures. As the ship crossed into the rougher seas, the crew left the warmth below deck to stand along the rail and watch the helmsman pick his course.

Most of the buckles were gentle affairs at first. An upturned edge of ice would rise up several feet, while double stackings lay scattered about as if two layers of metal had been hammered together. Occasionally a more spectacular form would appear—upended sections that pointed heavenward for ten or twenty feet. As the mornings passed, they approached the region of buckled mountains and the narrow channel that led to Mathin.

The ice mountains soon soared up around them. Their path led beneath the very brow of one such giant. The mountain soared upward to twice the height of the *Answered Prayer*'s mainmast, its huge form molded by some long-forgotten storm. For four leagues it stretched, dwarfing the *Answered Prayer*. The endless winds of winter had carved and twisted its form into a thousand shapes to catch and hold the eye. As they sailed beneath its icy brow the mountain blocked the wind from the *Answered Prayer*, so that they drifted noiselessly beneath the endless form.

Michael watched the mountain's passing in silent awe. The mysteries of the Ice reached into him and captured his soul, and he knew at that moment that the cloister would never hold him again. The mountain was like a thunder-laden cloud, its twisting folds trapped in ice to captivate and create images for the mind's imagination. As the fleet rounded one point, an ice giant stood before them, his frozen hand raised up as if to hurl a bolt of frigid death. Many, seeing this, mumbled prayers and made the sign of blessing, but even as they passed beneath the giant's cold fierce gaze, the folds and angles seemed to change, and the Ice became a battlement perched atop a strand of golden rock. The sun played across the mountain and each moment the light would bend and shift, so that the crystal hills took and held every color that could be imagined. A flaming red fire of wind-carved ice would change in an instant to a pale shade of chilling blue. Rivers of scarlet cascaded from dizzying heights, and would disappear immediately as the fleet moved on. Even as the men watched, the sun and the wind did their quiet work, chipping here and smoothing there, changing the images into new and ever-varied patterns. To Michael, the follies of man paled to insignificance before this timeless display.

Just when the men thought that the mountain could hold no more wonders, a jolt of fear washed through them. They heard voices. A soft singing of unearthly sounds echoed from the frozen hills, and a soft hush drifted upon the wind. The voices fell silent for a moment, only to rise again into a demonic scream that quickly dropped away to a whisper. Unnatural dissonant half-tones would blend in on minor keys as if some demented soul was playing a sardonic, mournful dirge upon a hidden organ, then in almost perfect harmony, the voices would start again upon their wordless chant. "Ilas de Marth," Daniel whispered—the voices of the damned.

Michael turned to look at him and then to the crew that stood on the deck.

"'Tis the cries and songs of all who are buried upon the Ice," a thin, gray-haired man said to Michael. As if by instinct, the man made the sign of the blessing. Michael looked from the old man to the rest of the crew. They were silent—even Seth, who was staring with fixed expression toward the cliffs that hung over them.

The mountain turned to the south, and as the sloop followed its line, they plunged into the shadow—the feeble warmth of the sun replaced by a cold and chilling darkness. Several of the men started to pray.

The men were frozen by some superstitious dread that, oddly, he could not feel. It was merely the wind, yet to the crew of the fleet it had become an insidious bringer of fear. It was a fear that in an instant drove them all back to the Church's teaching of doubt and pain.

Michael turned from them and walked over to the foremast backstays. Without a word, he scurried aloft to the small platform perched atop the towering mast. As he reached the top, the sun rose over the edge of the cliffs, flooding him with light so that all below was lost in darkness. The wind screamed through the mountain and the voices rose in their fury. He stood, and a long, rolling laugh burst from his lips.

The whole thing seemed so bizarre, so absurd, as he looked down at the fear-struck men. There they were, men capable of reason, living in a world of harshness, yet one of infinite beauty and challenge. They were alive, they built ships, and they challenged the Frozen Sea, yet they quaked at the whistle of the wind through the carved chasms. He looked up to the clear blue sky and remembered the endless nights of worship, the thousands of hours of prayer before a candlelit altar. In all those years, no matter how desperately he tried, he had never once felt he was praying to something—to something that really was *there*. Always he had been greeted by silence. Yet his fear, the fear bred of living with those who believed, had resulted in his never asking why.

"Have we been so reduced by our fears that we have to cower like animals?" he shouted to the cliffs, and his words echoed and rolled back to him.

"If you hear me, then show yourself—for I can no longer fear you." The wind howled above him and the sound of its fury shook through the cloistered halls of the mind that had held him prisoner to his fears.

The wind swept past him. Closing his eyes, he flowed with the rhythm of the Frozen Sea. He gulped down air so clean that he felt he was the first of all men to have taken it into his lungs. He held it for a moment and then let it escape to the realm of all the others. The cloisters, the wars, the threat of heresy, and the mad dreams of the secret brothers—all disappeared.

At last the mountain passed to the stern of the *Answered Prayer*, and the sails boomed outward to catch the unhindered wind. For an instant the *Answered Prayer* heeled over on its downwind runners; with practiced skill the helmsman let the ship dance along on slanting deck until the gust played out and the boat gently settled down again.

With increasing speed they shot past crevices and arching towers that reached to the sky, and Michael laughed with joy as the sun caught and held each passing form. Looking outward, he could see the fleet in long, open line arching back over the horizon. The narrows of the Mathinian pass slowly dropped astern—the broad three-mile-wide channel would run for the next eight miles. They were gradually coming down upon the Southern Ice.

He felt the cold cut through him as the wind picked up. He looked around once more at the shimmering mountains of ice, and with stiffened hands Michael Ormson swung himself off the platform and started down the ratlines.

They backed away from Michael as if he carried the plague. His fear abruptly returned when he looked into their eyes. He knew that the most dangerous thing of all was to be different, to call attention to yourself. The deck rumbled and shook as they passed over a rough spot, and his legs bent and swayed with the motion. Seth walked over to him. "Why did you do that?"

"I don't know, it was just something within me."

Seth suddenly turned and eyed the crew savagely.

"If one of ye pox-ridden bastards breathes but a word of this to the red robes you'll face my blade. And if I don't find you, believe me, others will."

The men looked away from him.

Daniel now spoke up from behind the crew. "Do you understand what our friend Seth speaks of?" he growled. With a lightning-swift motion he pulled back his cloak and whipped out his double-headed broadax with a gesture of contempt. "There are others who know the men aboard this ship, so mark my words. If one man goes to the red ones, all of ye will go in the end."

Michael looked at Seth as the crew broke up and went below deck, mumbling under their masks.

"Don't you realize that you can be killed for less than that?" Seth hissed at him.

"Don't you realize that it would kill me if I couldn't?" Michael replied. "Seth, I want none of your plans, none of your dreams. All I want is to live—alone, without fear, without cloisters, and with a freedom to think my own thoughts."

"But Michael, the red brothers will hunt you down. They would take you for what you've just said to me now."

"All I ask is to be free," Michael said softly, putting his hand on Seth's shoulder.

Daniel was standing behind Seth, his ax still drawn. Michael suddenly realized with a chill that the giant would kill at his slightest command. The power of it all was extraordinarily exciting, and the thought of that alone made him turn away.

"The two of you are my friends," Michael said, "but let me live my life outside of your dreams."

CHAPTER 7

THE NIGHT PASSED WITHOUT INCIDENT AS THE CREWS STOOD watch and considered the events to come with the next day. Michael could sense the electric tension of men preparing for war with the knowledge that before the day was half over many of them would be dead upon the Ice.

With the capture of the merchantmen Halvin learned the recognition signals of Mathin, and that the Ezrian garrison had no suspicion that a Cornathian battle fleet was cruising so far south. The defense of the city would be ill prepared at best. The captured merchantmen would precede the main fleet and sail into the harbor under the Ezrians' own recognition flag. Then their crews would swarm out and seize the main defense points before the garrison could be raised. The hard part would be the crews' holding their position until the main fleet could add its support.

Michael stood on the forecastle with Seth while Daniel held the wheel; the three were silent. Michael knew that the two men had no personal investment in the churches' war yet they were caught in it nevertheless. The thrill of the hunt was upon them, and Michael understood that in the hours to come they would immerse themselves in the madness with a fierce and violent joy, for it was the same with him.

As the pale sun cleared its first hour, the cry came down from above, "The three towers, dead ahead."

Seth turned to the signalman. "Break out the recognition flags."

Seth went below and returned bearing a bundle of merchant robes. "Put these on over your armor," he said, tossing them down on the deck.

The men laughed and wrestled over the garments.

"I brought weapons for you, Michael. They're in my cabin."

In the cramped cabin Michael found a gently curving scimitar that shone in the candlelight, and he felt a strange delight as he hefted the weapon and tested its balance. Alongside the sword he found a small, round shield of polished steel with a red dragon painted on the center. He smiled as the memory of his father's emblem came back to him. Next to the weapons rested a bloodstained purple robe, the owner dead less than forty-eight hours. He hesitated for a moment and finally realized that the sight of a light-blue robe aboard an Ezrian ship would ruin everything. He pulled off his outer robe and left it on the bed. Taking weapon and shield, he went topside.

"What about the priest's robe?" Seth inquired. "We really need one; otherwise, it might look suspicious."

"I'd prefer a merchant's robe instead," Michael replied evenly.

Seth merely nodded.

Michael gripped the hilt of the sword and felt a strange joy of anticipation. He looked back and saw that the main battle fleet was already far astern. The plan was in motion. The fleet would hold its position for three quarters of an hour and then would push forward with every yard of canvas pressed on. In the interval the merchant ships would gain the harbor entrance. All was going according to plan, Michael realized, but a thousand things could go wrong: the wind could shift or die; the Ezrians might already know—the list was endless. He pushed such thoughts away; he knew that if he dwelt too long on them fear might creep up and gain a hold on him.

"Now listen," Seth began slowly, "this will be your first real time in. Have you ever handled a sword in combat?"

"Only in practice with Niall."

Seth nodded his head and Daniel grumbled. "Michael," Seth continued, "I want you to stay to the rear, and keep alongside Daniel at all times."

Daniel gave Michael a toothy grin, his breath washing over Michael like the heat from an open oven.

"Aye, lad," he growled, "stay close to me now, we wouldn't want your blood to stain those nice furs you borrowed." With that Daniel broke into rolling laughter.

The merchantmen fell into line with a two-hundred-yard interval between vessels, the standard practice for friendly approach throughout all the Frozen Sea. The only exception was the corsair, which ran a couple hundred yards upwind and astern, and as they approached the trap and barrier line, would swing into line as well.

The ice channel was fairly narrow—with only a quarter mile of clearance between rough, twisting outcrops of ice. From the deck all could see the Three Sisters, the northernmost point of land in all the Southern Isles. It rose from the sea, a single sheer rock—a hundred feet across, and from it three spires rose heavenward for another thirty feet. Only three leagues beyond was the island of Mathin.

As they shot past the boulder, the one unsuspecting sentinel atop the highest spire waved from his guard box to the men below.

"We're sixth in line," Seth said to the crew. "Lord Joshua is in the corsair. The first four ships will clear the two towers that guard the harbor entrance and pass into the cove. Ship number five will clear the gate and then swing hard over and ram the inner side of the wall next to the port tower. We shall do the same to the starboard. Ships seven and eight will then cut their sails and drop anchor alongside our craft. They'll swarm over the deck and climb our rigging, which hopefully will be resting across the tower wall. The corsair will be held in reserve, to put its men where Joshua feels they're needed."

Seth stopped and looked at the men who had gathered around

him. "The main thing," he continued, "is for us to make sure that our mast snaps off and crashes against the tower, so our impact will be hard. Stand on deck and play your roles as long as possible, but when I give a shout, throw yourselves down and brace for the impact. Keep an eye aloft as well to make sure you aren't crushed by falling rigging. Are there any questions now?"

"But Master Seth," a high-pitched voice called from the back, "what if the mast doesn't hit the tower?"

"Then someone else will pray for us, you damned fool!" and the men laughed, to the discomfort of the questioner.

After the briefing, the men broke up into separate groups and lounged on the deck while the hills of Mathin came into view. It was a small island, not a dozen miles in length and that and half again in breadth. Her low hills were an unusual green, which all soon realized was a standing forest of pine and an occasional grove of hardwood.

At home, in some of the sheltered valleys heated by the hidden fires from within, one could find small stands of spruce and tamarack, but for the first time Michael was looking at a full stand of forest. He stood in silent amazement as the island drew closer. He heard a quiet cough from behind and turned to face two hooded forms—men typical of the Ice, bent from a life in the narrows between decks, their faces drawn and graying. The men pulled back their hoods and removed their helmets, standing silently until finally the taller of the two jabbed his companion sharply in the ribs.

The shorter cleared his throat with a rasping cough. "Havan here," he began, "wants your blessing before the battle."

"We know ye're the One promised in the Book," the taller one said with a nervous expression.

"Have you seen this book?" Michael asked.

"Of course not," the shorter one said, as if answering a stupid question. "Where would we have seen the Book? But we've heard tell of it since we was both younger than you, and that's a fact, it is."

Michael stood in embarrassed silence for several long minutes as the men before him waited for his reply. Finally he raised his hands in a vague gesture. "I wish you luck and protection in the battle to come. And may you return safely from the Ice."

"Amen," they mumbled, then pulled up their hoods and quickly walked away while Michael walked over to Seth.

"Did you see that?" Michael asked as Seth looked past him to judge the ice. Seth didn't answer while he turned the wheel in short gentle swings to avoid a series of cracks and bumps that stood in their path.

"Already it's starting for you, Michael."

The anger, the frustration finally exploded.

"What's started, damn it?" he shouted at Seth. "Ever since I've come aboard, you and that giant of yours"—he pointed at Daniel—"have been following me around mumbling about your prophecies and how I am the One." He looked coldly at both of them. "Well, I don't know a damn thing about it. I feel no different, I'm just Michael Ormson."

The deck shifted and rumbled as they crossed over a series of wind-carved ice ripples. The spray from the ship shot upward and eddied astern in a swirling cloud. Seth looked at Michael and could see the two dissimilar eyes beneath the wind goggles.

"Whether you choose to believe it or not really doesn't matter—they believe it, Michael," he said in a soft whisper. "And if enough of them believe it, then it will be true, whether or not you want it."

Seth turned on Michael with a sudden fury. "If enough of them believe you're the Prophet, then damn it, the Prophet you will be! You've been nothing but a cloistered brat whose biggest fear has been the darkness of the night, and you've mouthed your pious prayers and worried about your petty little problems. Look at *them*, Michael!" he commanded fiercely. "There are tens of thousands like them who want a dream to believe in, not a fear to run from. Who are you to take that dream away from them because of your own petty desires? Go ahead, Michael. Go back there right now and tell those two men that all the prophecies, all the dreams, all the longings are false—and then we shall see how you feel."

Seth put the wheel hard over to avoid a doubling in the ice, and the *Answered Prayer* rose up on her downwind blades and danced along the surface, cutting a graceful arc across the sea.

The Holy Books are full of examples of Saints coming down to tell men what they should do, Michael thought sadly. Why haven't they come to me? Why can't they send me a sign, so I might confidently go forward?

He tried to think, yet the fearful eyes of the two men stayed with him. They so desperately wanted to believe in some physical sign. Any physical sign.

"You've never walked the streets of Cornath, have you?" Seth asked.

Michael shook his head.

"Then you know nothing of life. When we take Mathin, walk the streets, sit in the taprooms and listen and watch. Watch the young couples that want nothing more than to be left alone. Watch the mother as she guards her child, praying that pestilence will not take him—only to have the child leave like his father to disappear in the churches' war. Then look at the old woman dying, wasting out her last years in some forgotten hovel, praying for death, yet fearing its coming. After that, Michael Ormson, return and ask me why people want to believe in some cause, some prophet. *Then* we shall discuss why they wish to believe in you."

"But why me?" Michael asked slowly.

"Because of the Coimhead de Adhar."

"The watchers of the stars?"

"As you know, they read the stars and know the twelve signs and the passing of the months. They watch the Arch as well to see who rises and falls in favor amongst the Saints. Through this they chart the paths of men.

"You see, Michael, not many know, but the twelve signs show us not only the division of the months and years, they also show us the passing of ages as well. With the coming of each second millennium there is the passing of an age, and at that time there comes the great change. We know this happened with the end time of before and we think that perhaps it had happened with the previous age as well."

Seth leaned forward and looked into Michael's eyes. "Michael, on the night you were born, the first moment of the new age began. The hidden brothers of Inys Gloi were in your city at that moment. As the first cry burst forth from your lips, the first breath of the new millennium came as well. On that night I was in your city and witnessed this to be true. That is why I now stand here next to you. That is why I, Seth Facinn, the Far-Seeing, believe."

"Tell me more of this moment," Michael asked softly.

But Seth fell silent, for the walls of Mathin were plainly in view.

The city of Mathin was the northernmost city of the Trade Isles. A place that was all but forgotten as the ice crept ever southward.

As Michael Ormson gazed upon its fir-clad shores, there was no hint, no sign, no Saint that whispered to him that here he would meet with his destiny. Here he would meet with a destiny that would link his name and that of this unknown city, and make them one.

He looked toward the city as the *Answered Prayer* bore down relentlessly upon its target. Dominating the view were the low-lying hills clad in thick, aged pine, enough trees to build a thousand ships, Michael mused. Even as the thought came to him, he found it curious that his mind would view the island in such a manner at that moment.

The hills behind the town swept down to the sea in two rocky strands that framed a natural harbor one half-mile across. As soon as the winter's freeze set in, the opening was sealed off with an ice wall that reached to five times the height of a man and was proof against most any attack. The entrance to the harbor was wide enough for only a single ship. Flanking the entrance, guard towers of ice rose to half again as high as the wall. Atop the towers were chains that could be dropped across the entryway, thereby preventing access to the inner cove. Even if an enemy should happen to gain the outer wall, there was still the citadel within. This was no seasonal wall but a thirty-foot-high tower of stone, its guns mounted to sweep the harbor in all directions if an attack should gain the outer wall.

With an alert garrison it could be a formidable barrier that could cost the lives of hundreds in its taking.

With measured commands, Seth ordered the sails to be reefed in so the *Answered Prayer* would match the slowing speed of the fleet. From the portside guard tower the green flag of Ezra was clearly visible, while from the starboard tower the recognition flags appeared—red over two blues, as the merchants said they would. From all the ships the reply came back—blue over two yellow—and the fleet sailed on.

The first ship gradually drew nigh the towers and all were quiet as the moment that would decide their fate closed in. The fleet sailed into the narrow approach channel. On both sides were traps and deadfalls concealed beneath a light layer of ice. If the Cornathians were to abandon the attack they would be forced to swing about into the trap zone, a maneuver that would destroy the fleet.

Tor Eldonson, a warrior of some fame in Cornath and a master sailor of years' experience, was in the lead. As he passed between the two towers he dipped his flags of blue and yellow twice, as the merchants had said, and the men atop the tower shouted in response. Not understanding their tongue, he feigned that the wind had carried the words away and conveyed by universal gestures that he intended to get uproariously drunk then planned to bed the nearest wench. The guards laughed and wished him luck, and so Tor passed into the harbor. Standing in front of him was one of the captured merchants, a dirk at his back; the merchant indicated the approach to the stone tower.

The second ship was manned by Tor's cousin, Grimbold of Halydim. With his helmet off he presented a frightful image, having lost an eye and part of his cheek in a half-forgotten battle more than twenty years before.

Once the first ship had passed, most of the guards atop the towers retreated to the relative warmth within the icy walls. One stayed, though, and he leaned over the tower to watch. Grimbold stood at the helm smiling his toothless grin and waving his hand to the guard while his other hand rested tightly on a merchant's shoulder. But as they passed under the shadow the tower Grimbold turned slightly to look up at the guard. With unexpected fury the merchant kicked out, catching his captor on the knee and bowling him over. The merchant screamed and ran to the railing, then leaped overboard to land sprawling on the ice below. A searing shock of pain struck him as his shoulder crumpled under the impact. He staggered to his feet, the world spinning madly as he made his way to the foot of the tower.

"It's a trap!" he screamed. "Cornathians, they're Cornathians!"

The guard on the tower looked down and almost started to laugh. It wasn't unusual for a cask to be opened when harbor was sighted. The merchant Saldin started to yell again, but a foot-long bolt tore out his throat. As he fell and the darkness set in, he saw his blood spilling out upon the ice.

"God's curse on you all," he groaned, and then he was dead.

The guard on the tower disappeared with a yell. Within seconds a great booming horn sounded, its call echoing across the harbor and into the town beyond.

"They're on to us!" Seth shouted. "Hoist the mainsail. Step lively there, you lazy scum."

Daniel turned from Michael and ran to the mainsmast halyards, the crew following. With shouts, and hard pulls, they ripped the covers away and sent the sail aloft. Seth raised up his gold-inlaid horn and with a mightly breath gave voice to it. Its high, clear call was picked up by the horns of the other ships' masters. The call stirred the blood of the men and set them to chanting their war songs as they smote their shields with ax and spear.

Trembling with excitement, Michael balanced himself as the ship shot forward with the booming of the sail overhead. Even as the *Answered Prayer* put on speed, several puffs of smoke issued from the starboard tower to be followed a second later by three from the port. A fountain of ice rose heavenward not a dozen feet from the portside outrigger, and with a demented scream the heavy shot thundered past.

"Three minutes I reckon it to be," Seth shouted. "We'll hold the mainsail till the last two hundred yards, then cut her away, Daniel."

The seconds passed in silence as the enemy reloaded. The cheers from the other iceboats rolled across the ice as they closed in upon their target. The corsair cut loose with its nine-pound bowchaser, and a shower of splintering ice exploded on the wall about ten yards north of the starboard tower. From the towers on land came a response to the corsair's single gun. Four shots thundered from each citadel and ranged out in a crisscross pattern. One of the shots holed a sail in the corsair, cutting her speed. Another shot whistled past the *Answered Prayer* and bounded harmlessly out to sea. It would come to rest over a league away, where eventually the winners of the battle would find it and take it back to be recast.

The third ship of the attack force was committed to running the gate, and she bore down relentlessly on it until a tongue of flame leapt from the towers and licked its sails and deck.

"Tarn de Marbth," Seth shouted, "the Fire of Death."

The men watched as it caught the ship abeam, her mast and sails exploding into flames that glared fiercely against the frozen, mirrorlike walls of the towers. The fire was the secret of the Church of Sol and known only by the members of its hidden brotherhoods.

"They must have captured a supply when they took the city," Seth shouted to Michael. "The harbor's closed. We'll take her from the outside."

Another volley burst from the two towers. This time the shots were better laid. The men of the *Answered Prayer* watched as their comrades' ship disintegrated under the thundering impact. All the shots had been aimed at her and all struck true at a range of less than four hundred yards. Some of the shots ripped the sails and swept the deck, but one, aimed by a priest with forty years of skill, caught the ship on its front rudder mounting.

The ship's blades dismounted and the bow of the vessel fell

on the ice, kicking up a plume of ice and snow. On smooth ice the ship would have survived, but a double buckle rose straight ahead, and the jagged block of ice was fatal to the crippled craft. With an agonizing shudder the hull slammed into the outcropping and the momentum of the craft lifted the vessel clear of the ice; the frozen block tore into her like a knife. In stunned silence Michael watched as antlike forms on her deck fell or jumped from the dying craft. From two hundred yards away he could clearly hear their cries.

Michael looked to Seth, and Seth was silent—staring straight ahead. He gently turned the wheel to steer past the wreckage, and without a sideward glance pushed into the attack.

"Less than a minute now," Seth shouted.

The range closed to three hundred then two hundred yards.

"Cut free the halyards."

Daniel gave a mighty swing to his battle-ax and the halyards snapped free as the massive blade sunk deep into the mast. The sails tumbled down.

"Remember what I said," Seth screamed as the canvas rained down around them.

"Brace yourselves, we're going into the trap area."

Seth put the wheel over and skidded out of the marked channel weaving past several obvious deadfalls. Even as he did so, the guns from the two towers thundered again, their rolling boom matched by the gunfire from the two citadels at the landside ends of the harbor wall. The starboard ice exploded as two of the shots ricocheted upward and crashed into the hull of the weaving attack vessel. A five-foot section of stern railing blew inward, cutting a bloody swath through the men huddled beneath its flimsy protection.

"Hang on," Seth screamed as a kaleidoscope of explosions and crushed wood swept the length of the ship.

"Fifty yards to the tower! Brace yourselves, we're going over."

The *Answered Prayer* turned violently to starboard and began a sideways skid that slammed her into the glistening ice tower. The momentum took the two masts clear of their mounts, and the stay lines snapped from the strain, whipping across the deck. One of the heavy lines caught a crew member across his helmet and crushed it. The man fell dead without a sound.

The outrigger telescoped in on itself, slammed its support beams into the *Answered Prayer*, and splintered out the other side. For several seconds all was quiet on the deck as the men recovered from the impact and rose groggily to their feet. A double-bladed ax suddenly rose heavenward and caught the rays of the morning sun.

"For Cornath!" Daniel screamed, and he waved his ax over his head. The reflection of the blade was like a mirror of the fire in his eyes. "For Cornath!" he screamed again, and with a bounding leap sprung upon the bent and twisted mast, the orders from Seth forgotten in the confusion of the assault. He had taken the berserker's way.

The two masts had snapped off as planned and their momentum had sent them crashing against the harbor wall. They had not come to rest on the towers but, instead, had skidded sideways and bridged the wall twenty feet from the overhanging tower of ice. Daniel's cry was picked up by the rest of the crew, and Michael drew his blade. He had seen death and stood helplessly by, but now at last he could strike back, he could smash the foe who had tormented him.

He jumped on the mast directly behind Daniel and started to claw his way upward through the tangled rigging lines. A block of ice tumbling down from above missed him by inches, then crashed into one of the men below, who collapsed with a horrible groan. Daniel in the lead, the crew climbed upward, screaming and shouting while the guns in the towers thundered at the attack ship trying to hit the other tower.

Michael was almost behind Daniel when the giant suddenly fell forward and stretched out flat on the rigging lines, his shield raised. Michael found himself staring into a bearded face not ten feet away. It was sighting down a crossbow.

Everything drifted into nightmarish slow motion, where the actors moved with leaden limbs. Michael watched the bow swing and aim at his face while he desperately tried to raise his shield. His vision locked onto the trigger and the finger that was flexing over it. With a feeling of deathly sickness,

Michael knew that he was losing the race. The trigger hand was moving, the face jerked backward—a shower of blood spattered the white tunic, and the bolt shot clean, whistling past Michael's ear.

Looking to the deck below, Michael saw Seth, crossbow still at his shoulder. Then, turning away, Michael loosed an incoherent scream, scrambling the rest of the way up the rigging and over the wall.

A form suddenly appeared, a bright flash of metal whistled past, he tried to swing but a weight fell on his back, pushing him aside. He fell to the corduroy floor which ran atop the wall, and several men trampled over him. Michael regained his footing as a hulking body waded past swinging a deadly two-handed ax. Then he fell in behind Daniel and they moved forward.

The battle turned into a swirling confusion of pushing, shoving men who screamed words of incoherent rage. They gained a foothold on the wall and Michael traded ineffective blows with several fur-clad men who yelled and cursed at him. Suddenly a man came running straight through the press with a pike aimed low. Michael jumped aside and the pike stabbed past. Michael braced himself and slashed out with his sword. It cleaved effortlessly into the man's stomach. For a second they stood, faces only inches apart, and behind the Ezrian's goggles Michael could see the eyes grow wide with astonishment. Michael watched the man collapse wordlessly as his sword slid from the wound that was emptying a torrent of blood. Michael stepped over the still kicking body with a cold and chilling sense of satisfaction. He had killed his first man. For the rest of his life the cold pleasure that he felt would haunt him. He had met death and triumphed over her messenger.

The Cornathians pushed toward the door of the tower, Daniel at the forefront swinging his great broadax and shouting a song of death as his enemies fell before his rage. The defense began to crumble beneath the pressure of the onslaught and the Ezrians retreated before the fury of the Cornathians.

Michael turned for a moment and looked out to sea as a merchantman skidded to a halt, her bow shot away by a volley.

Her crew was pouring over the side and running to join in the assault while the eighth ship turned to crash into the portside tower.

The defenders tried to hold the doorway into the tower, but Daniel soon crashed through with his bulk, leading the way into the citadel while a shower of ice and fire rained down from above. Men fell on all sides—crushed, holed, or aflame—but the Cornathians pushed on. Michael sprinted over bodies of his comrades and, holding his shield aloft, leaped through the blackened hole that would offer a semblance of protection.

He was blinded. From the glaring light of morning the world was suddenly plunged into darkness. As unseen blows rained down upon him, Michael swung wildly with his shield and sword. One caught him on the underside of his shield and lifted him clear of the floor, slamming him into the opposite wall. Struggling for time to regain his vision, Michael frantically twisted and turned across the floor. He could hear an ax smashing into the corduroy surface and the grunts of his assailant as he pulled the blade free to attack again. Blindly Michael slashed out with his scimitar, striking repeatedly. But still the attacker pressed him. A shadow loomed over him, he rolled inward. As the blow came Michael slashed upward, his sword slicing first into the attacker's ax then his groin. A howl cut the air, and Michael's sword was almost torn from his grasp as the attacker fell away. Michael rolled over into the corner of the room and tore off his goggles.

As his vision adjusted to the light it revealed a room filled with men. The tower walls had been cut from ice over four feet thick, so the sunlight that filtered through on all sides gave a translucent glow to the room. The floors and ceiling were of wood and there was a small stove with a chimney, which Michael huddled behind as he got his bearings. In the center of the room were two cannons that the fur-clad men now fought around, with the smoke from the guns adding to the confusion and lending a surreal appearance to the battle. Cornathian reinforcements were pouring through the door and the few sur-

viving Ezrians were driven into the far corner where they fled
up a staircase to the platform above.

Michael watched as Daniel stormed up the stairs, howling
like a madman. In an instant Michael was on his feet and
bounding across the room to rejoin the fray. He raced up the
stairs and re-emerged into the blinding light above. Again there
was a swarming confusion as men grappled and killed to the
sickening sound of bodies being crushed by clubs and axes or
falling away or crawling underfoot to be hacked at by their
maddened opponents. Suddenly it was over except for the cries
of the wounded and the dying.

Panting for breath, Michael looked about at the carnage.
From a corner a thin, wounded man in green robes stood up,
a look of surprise upon his anguished face. He jumped atop
the wall.

"Al marth non Ulimak," he screamed, and tried to leap from
the battlement. But instead, he smashed heavily against the
wall, hanging upside down, while Michael clung desperately
to his feet.

"Let him go," Daniel shouted, even as he helped Michael
to pull the struggling man back up. The man screamed and
kicked in rage as Daniel hoisted him back. Finally, Daniel hit
the fellow across the back of the head with the butt of his ax
and he collapsed into unconsciousness.

Seth walked over and looked at him.

"A priest of Sol." He bent over and pulled the man's gloves
off. Michael was sickened: the nails were missing, the hands
scarred and puffy from healing burns. "Most likely tortured
him and he broke. That explains the Fire of Death—he showed
them how."

Seth looked back up at Michael.

"It would have been more merciful to let him die, he's
betrayed his religion."

"If he betrayed it once, he can again," Michael said coldly.
"Bind him up and make sure our own priests don't find him."

The men leaned against the wall panting for breath, while
some searched the fallen for loot. Seth's quick count revealed

that he still had eighteen under his command, eight from his own crew and ten from Cynric's merchantman, which had crashed a hundred yards out on the ice. The men were looking over to the other tower, where the sounds of battle still raged, and shouted their encouragement. They watched as the last of the Ezrians were driven to the wall and their bodies hurled over the side. The corsair's crew held the foot of the towers; her nine-pounder was brought into play to keep a channel open for the fleet to pass through. From across the harbor all could hear the sound of battle as the assault on the citadel continued.

"There's hell to pay," came a shout from behind as Cynric beckoned to the men and pointed along the harbor wall to the landward tower. As if in answer, puffs of smoke jetted from the tower and the yells of the men were drowned out as two shells screamed in, burrowing into the wall beneath them with a rumble that knocked them off their feet.

Michael and the others ran up to Cynric's side and looked to the far tower. Advancing along the wall was a swarming knot of men, their swords and axes gleaming in the sun, their battle cries sounding clearly in the morning air as they shouted oaths of death and defeat for the Cornathians. In the middle of the group was a long, dark object—they were bringing up a battering ram. As well, dozens of men were approaching across the harbor on skates and one-man sails, while several iceboats were making sail to challenge the corsair's hold on the entrance.

Seth watched as the attack developed.

"Cynric, keep your men up here. Try and maintain fire from above." With a wave of his crossbow Seth shouted, "My men follow me," then he ran for the stairs.

Michael pushed after him. As he made the stairs he noticed a bloodied corpse hanging over the one cannon on the platform. It was Havan, the man who had asked for his blessing before the battle. He ran down the stairs to the dimly lit room below.

The doorway was still open. The original defenders had been caught by surprise, and in their eagerness to come to blows, they had swarmed out of the tower to meet the attackers. In the press of battle the move had been fatal.

Some of the men fell upon the bodies by the door and dragged them clear, while Seth braced himself behind the massive oaken door and slammed it shut. It was mounted on iron hinges, which in turn were bolted to great oaken beams that ran from the base of the tower to the very top. Encased in four feet of ice, the beam was a solid foundation against attack.

The men piled up the bodies of the fallen against the door, along with blocks of ice and any other object they could find. They would have rolled the cannon over, but there wasn't enough time to cut them free of their moorings. Even as the last body was piled up against the barrier, the screams and shouts of the attackers came from the outside as they met the arrows and blocks which showered down from above.

Seth climbed up over the barrier of flesh and ice and, bracing himself up against the door, he pulled open the peephole. Shoving his crossbow up against the opening, he fired through it. A scream gave answer to his shot. Michael could hear the shouts of Cynric's men as they rained death upon the attackers.

The door buckled and cracked as the battering ram struck. Fissures ran up and down the ice wall and arm-length splinters flecked from the door's surface as the ram hit again and again.

The fury of battle rose to thunder as the shouting Cornathians braced against the door. The hinges started to work free and the attackers cheered as they felt the barrier yielding. Even with Daniel's great back against the door, the barrier could not be held. It broke from its hinges and crashed in on the Cornathians. The soft, translucent glow of the fortress was pierced by a blinding shaft of light that silhouetted the shouting, cursing mob pouring in. Seth fired again, his bolt passing through the first man in the doorway. Dropping his bow, he drew his scimitar to meet the rush.

Man after man, they jumped in with the fury of despair, and each fell to the blows of the defenders until it seemed as if the doorway would be clogged to the ceiling with the dead and dying. Finally a giant of a man crashed through the pile of corpses, and his shouts were like the voice of death. Daniel swung wildly with a savage blow, but the giant, with catlike ease, slipped his shield beneath Daniel's ax and slammed him up against the wall, knocking him unconscious.

Seth, with scimitar drawn, jumped in front of the giant as the Cornathians backed away from him, and the Ezrian shouts rose to a higher pitch as they rallied behind their captain. Seth swung low to catch his opponent's legs, but the giant's ax descended with a savage blow and shattered Seth's blade. Using a backhanded sweep, he brought his weapon up, hooking Seth above the wrist. The hand that drew the bow, that worked the harp, and had piloted the ship was gone in a blinding moment of pain and a gout of blood.

Seth crumbled, and the giant, laughing with joy, jumped on top of him, his ax swung high to cut the life of his foe. The laughter froze on his lips to be replaced with a howl of astonishment and pain. From the shadows Michael's blade slashed through knotted muscle and cut through solid bone. The head tumbled backward, while the body crashed down on Seth, a shower of scalding blood spilling out across the tower floor.

With a madman's fury Michael cut his way through the press. Casting aside his shield, he grasped the head of his foe and pushed through to the door. Holding the head aloft, he screamed savagely as he stabbed and slashed. The lifeless eyes of their leader looked out at the Ezrians — and they fell back before his gaze.

Michael was the instrument of war now. The backs of his enemies so enraged Michael that he drove after them, hurling the head of their captain at their retreating forms. They ran along the length of the wall as the sound of gunfire swelled in the distance. Suddenly a shadow came down from above and crashed into him. His thoughts fled away and he fell into darkness.

CHAPTER 8

He awoke to darkness and the throb of pain. He knew a moment of panic because there was no sensation other than an all-consuming fire of aching darkness.

"Am I dead?"

A nausea swept over him, and he fought down the urge to scream. He sat up.

"Seth, Seth."

A gentle hand was upon his shoulder, bracing him.

"Seth!" he screamed louder.

"Sleep, Michael, go to sleep," a voice said softly, and the hands gently pushed him back down upon the bed.

"Sleep, Michael, Seth is alive in the next room."

"But his hand . . ."

"Sleep," the voice whispered.

His vision began to clear and he could make out a shadow leaning over him in the darkness.

"Where am I?" he whispered.

"In the house of my father, in the city of Mathin."

He asked no more questions, as darkness came back to him.

* * *

Even as he lay in darkness he walked. There was a high floating chamber that hovered above sunlit seas, and he passed it as if his spirit was at one with the wind. Upon that wind he crept down hidden alleyways, then drifted off to the highest peaks of unseen mountains in far-distant lands. A strange power coursed through his body.

He had a vision of heaven that swirled and drifted around him with its sharp colors and dark, pulsing light. It was green— no ice, no cold, an ocean of green mixed with the wildest profusion of colors and shade. It was a garden of sounds and smells that overwhelmed him with a haunting nostalgia. It reached into his essence and called to him.

He soared with the wind as the day swept through time, so that the green was tinged with red in the glow of late-afternoon light. He looked heavenward again as the world drifted into darkness. He froze in terror—the Arch was gone, and in its place was the light of another sun.

Dawn filtered through the double-pane window and gently stirred him to life. As he opened his eyes the sunlight on the chair alongside his bed brought out every detail. For a few moments he watched dust motes dance in the light, then he moved his gaze to the chair of embossed leather. Its arms and back were highlighted by a swirling design of silver thread. The latch on the door clicked, and he looked upward as a cool draft swept into the room from the hallway beyond.

She stood before him, tall and slender, in a simple high-waisted dress of darkest burgundy. Long black hair tumbled down her back and was braided with a silver cord. Her lips were red and sensuous, matched by the high full cheeks common among women of noble birth. Michael found her dark-green eyes compelling and strangely impossible to read.

Michael nervously realized that for the first time in fifteen years he was alone with a woman. He was afraid of her and of the desire that she provoked. Without realizing what he was doing, he looked deeper—the colors swarmed about her and congealed into the patterns that showed him a terrible sense of loneliness and confusion, but above all else were the patterns of longing and hatred.

"I'm used to being stared at," she said coldly, "but not in the manner that you seem to practice."

Michael blushed and turned his head away. "You see," he said haltingly, "I haven't been this close to a woman since I was five and went into the monastery."

He started to sit up and the world began to spin. "My head!" He groaned and he brought his hands to his bandaged skull.

She started forward, a look of concern replacing her scowl of reproof. She sat on the edge of his bed. "Lay back down, it will be a while before you're up and about."

"Who are you?" he whispered as he lay back.

She gave him a faint smile.

"I am Janis Tornson. My father, Ishmael Tornson, was the Primary of this town... until the Ezrians came."

"The Ezrians," Michael said, and the memories flooded back. The confusing memories of battle came over him as if they belonged to a different age.

"Your fleet took the city by storm two days ago."

"I can't remember," Michael said weakly.

"I can see why," Janice said softly as she touched his brow. "I understand that they found you in front of the landside tower. You've been asleep since then."

"What happened?"

"Your fleet arrived late, but they finally took the rest of the garrison. Your men say that you saved the ice tower from being retaken, and your High Priest was here to see you."

"How is Seth?"

"He will live," she said softly. "He is weak, of course, but already he asks for you."

She rose and walked to a small table by the door. A crystal decanter rested upon it. Removing the stopper, she poured a small measure into a golden cup then added a handful of herbs from a pouch that sat beside it. She turned and with a mysterious smile brought the cup to Michael.

"Drink," she said firmly, her expression betraying a seductive charm.

Michael looked into her eyes. He had promised himself to Holy Church, yet he was swept by a desire that was inexorably linked with guilt.

The scent of the cup was warm with spice. Moreover, her scent came to him—and it was warm with life. The coldness was gone, the damp mustiness of empty altars could never call to him as she did now.

With trembling hands he took the cup and drained it. In seconds he could feel its drowsy warmth. "Why am I here?" he asked as the spices gently took him.

"Because of the 'Ceuth Arren.'"

He knew the words yet his mind could not bring the meaning clear.

"Do you remember the captain you faced upon the wall?" she said coldly.

Already she was drifting away. "Yes," he replied numbly.

"The Ceuth Arren, is the first right. The man you killed was the captain of the garrison. Michael, you killed my husband."

"Yes, I remember," he said softly as he drifted away.

"You killed him, and by tradition and law you can now claim me."

"Such a damn good player, too," he mumbled. "Not often one finds a blue."

"What's that you say?" a voice asked from behind.

Turning, Gareth looked again at the man. It was sad the rumors about Halvin were true. During the executions after the fall of the town Gareth watched him—and the mad light that shone in his eyes. Gareth killed because it was the law of Holy Church for heretics, but he realized that Halvin killed Ezrians for the pure sadistic joy of it.

"What was that you said?" Halvin repeated.

"Nothing important, Admiral. I'm just considering our next topic of conversation."

Gareth was tired after another sleepless night, and the meeting with Halvin that he wished was over. They had gone over the reports all morning—the number wounded, at least, was

not serious, but repairs on the *Snow Wind* would take at least a week according to the most optimistic of the master carpenter's estimates.

For form's sake Gareth argued against tolerating the Church of Sol, but in his heart he knew Halvin was right. Allowing the church to survive would bring support from the townspeople. Halvin didn't have enough men to garrison the town, so it was best to leave the islanders hating Ezrians and loving the Cornathians. The missionaries and the Mord Rinn would have more than enough to do after the Cornathian Church consolidated its hold on the area.

"I'm concerned about our new hero," Gareth began cautiously, and he watched Halvin closely. He was tempted to ask if Zimri had given orders to Halvin as well. Zimri was a master at seeking his goal through a dozen different sources without any of the individuals knowing the plans of the other.

"Well, what of him?" Halvin asked coldly.

"His name is linked to this Tornson woman, daughter of their ruler in exile."

"Yes, yes, I know," Halvin said. "First Rights and all of that."

"I have other concerns, as well," Gareth continued.

"Such as?"

How could he explain it? How could he explain the nightmare? It had come again—the falling, the death, and the terrifying rejection. Yes, it had come again last night; his screams echoing through the ship. Now the brothers whispered as he passed. His agent Seamus had sailed on Cynric's ship and reported how some of the men were saying that Michael was the Deliverer, the one mentioned in the Books of Prophecy. How could he tell of his fear to a mad admiral who most likely would do anything to protect the nephew of his friend?

"I'm just concerned, that's all, that he'll be safe in the city."

"Yes, it is dangerous in that town, but his presence will be good for us. The people like him and we should leave him free to roam. It can only help us."

Gareth was silent. The orders of Zimri were clear. Let nothing be blamed on the brotherhood. Yet a larger fear, a fear even larger than Zimri's wrath, was hanging over him.

Halvin looked at the priest and wondered what his orders were, but decided that it was dangerous to ask. "Leave him in the city," Halvin said, "and if there is no more business, then leave me as well."

"Yes, your Excellency." With a bow, Gareth left the room.

Halvin turned to the icon of St. Regis that hung upon his wall and to the two portraits hanging enshrined below. The one was gone, the other a maddening possibility of life, and he remembered Zimri's words. He knew how dangerous a free port could be, especially after a taking. He would not raise a hand directly against the family of his old friend, but he could not step the other way—to protect as Rifton had asked. He looked again at the portraits and buried his head in his arms.

Michael awoke to a clear morning of blue skies and puffy, fast-moving clouds that cast fleeting shadows across the wind. As he sat up, he experienced a slight discomfort, but it was nothing compared to the blinding pain of the day before.

He swung his feet from the bed and with unsteady legs made his way across the room. He passed before a tall mirror and was shocked at his nakedness. He could not remember the last time he had stood in such a manner; it seemed there had always been the scratch of rough wool in the cold, cloistered halls. And a bath was a luxury indulged in only once a year. He realized that he had been bathed. A memory came of soft hands and a faint, haunting smile, and he shook with fear.

He went to a small chest in the far corner of the room and opened it. His gaze fell upon a long cape of ermine. Beneath it were trousers of the finest wool, dyed a faint blue, alongside a shirt and doublet of soft, rich velvet. To his surprise, they fit as if they had been tailored for him, and he put them on to cover his nakedness. As he finished dressing he sensed that he was being watched. Turning, he faced a massive form that filled the doorway and realized that it was Daniel.

"Well, Michael, so you're up and about again at last."

Michael nodded and sat on the trunk lid.

"Where are we and what is this place, Daniel?"

The giant smiled at him and from under his cloak pulled out a large skin of wine. From across the room, Michael could smell the cinnamon richness of the drink. "Draw up to the stove"—Daniel made a beckoning gesture—"and we'll talk." He walked over to the small black stove in the opposite corner of the room and, picking up a chair, pulled himself up alongside the black box. From an ornate brass bucket he pulled a couple of logs and opened the door to throw them in. Michael was about to protest the extravagant waste of wood when Daniel raised his hand to stop him.

"Ah, I know, Michael, but they've no wood-laws here. It takes a bit of getting used to, it does, but 'tis wonderful nice. In fact, you can even leave the door of yer stove open if you wish." With a wild flourish of his hand Daniel pulled the stove door back.

Again Michael wanted to protest, but as he watched the flames his objections died on his lips. In his entire life he had never seen wood used in such a wanton manner, and he found it exciting. The caverns of the monastery had been passably warm from the hidden fires within, but there had still been a chill in the air and an open fire was a rare thing indeed.

Daniel took a long pull off the sack of wine and handed it over to Michael. "Well now, I guess you're brimming with questions, and I might as well start at the beginning if you don't mind."

A bit puzzled by the giant's tone, Michael looked at Daniel. Suddenly he realized that Daniel had employed the slight change of inflection used with one's superior. Gone was the playful tone that an older brother might use with a younger. The roughness was still there, to be sure, but it was covered now with respect.

"What happened is rather hard to say. The last I remembered was that devil of a man coming through the door. To think, I, Daniel Bjornson, defeated."

He shook his head and took another long pull on the sack. "Never before have I been bested. He threw me as if I was a broken doll. Ah, the fates laughed at me that day, they did.

But when I came to..." and his eyes flashed as he looked at Michael beside him.

"Aye, when I came to, there you were, howling like a madman, and, that giant's head in your hands, I followed you. As you cleared the door a couple of Ezrians tried to take you, but they fell back when they saw your prize. You started to laugh—a strange, chilling laugh—and all were silent as you looked to the sky like there was a sign up there, and many turned and looked with you. I think we half expected a Saint to appear. 'Twas then that you charged them, hurling the head of their captain—and they broke and ran before you, Michael."

"It was then that Shem shouted, 'He is the Chosen One.' Some of the men shouted it also, and our few survivors were away and after you. You drove the Ezrians back until we reached the landward tower. They couldn't open the doorway of the battlement and were forced to turn and face us. I came up alongside you as a shower of ice blocks rained down from above. You were struck a glancing blow and crumpled like one dead."

"What happened to the Ezrians?" Michael asked, not sure that he really wanted to know.

"When our men saw that you were stricken, they were filled with a deadly fury and fell upon the Ezrians and slayed them all."

Michael was silent.

"Michael, you should never have rushed forward like that. I thought for a moment that you had been killed."

Michael looked at Daniel and could read the fear in Daniel's eyes.

"I picked you up and carried you back to the tower. The enemy had lost his fight and we were not attacked again before the *Thunderwind* arrived about a half-hour later." He hesitated. "It took them a long time coming."

"And Seth?"

"Seth will live. It wasn't until the end of the battle, when I was carrying you back to the tower, that I realized Seth was missing. Rushing to where I last saw him, I found that Cynric had dragged him from beneath the giant's carcass and burned the wound shut with a heated sword. Ah, the stench was terrible, and Seth was awake through it all, but when I came in bearing your body his first question was of you."

Michael's eyes filled with tears.

"He's in the next room, he is." Daniel said softly. "Would ye care to see him?"

Michael rose and followed Daniel from the room. As they turned into the corridor, Michael noticed the richness of his surroundings. Finely woven tapestries depicted scenes from the Ice, and above them was the smoky darkness of intricately carved wood ceilings that arched the corridor.

As they entered Seth's room, Michael tried to conceal his shock at his friend's appearance. The lean, ascetic face was skull-like, with a translucence which suggested that at any moment Seth might disappear into the world of spirits, without leaving a trace of his existence.

A smile crossed Seth's face as Michael entered the room. "Some of them think I'll die," he said with a mocking laugh. "But not yet, Michael. Ah, not yet." He beckoned to Michael to sit by his bedside.

"I saw you out there," he whispered, "and I saw the others follow you. Already the word spreads—I know that, too. At this moment, in every tavern and aboard every ship, it's being told and retold, and the older tales are remembered as well."

He grew silent for a moment, then looked up to Michael again. "Tell me, Michael, have you found the way in your own heart?"

Michael looked at Seth and smiled at the question.

"Well, what do you say to our quarters, Michael?" Seth asked, sensing Michael's answer.

Daniel grunted his approval from the far corner, raised his depleted wine sack to the two of them, and drained the rest of the contents.

"Help me sit up," Seth said. With a groan he started to raise himself into a sitting position, and Michael leaned over to help him. "And throw some more wood on the fire while you're at it."

Michael crossed to the stove and threw in a couple of logs,

taking a perverse delight in wasting wood so wantonly. Returning to Seth's side, he sat down and asked, "Where are we, Seth?"

Seth nodded slowly, and there was the trace of a smile on his face. "In preparation for things to come, I've traveled far, Michael, and so have many others of my order. The city of Mathin is well off the traveled paths, but it is known to those who wish to hide from something. Granted, it is supposedly a city of Sol, but really it is nothing more than a free port—a city for people to disappear to. It's the northern- and westernmost of the Trade Isles and, as such, has little if any value, since its open-harbor season is short."

Seth paused for a moment, as if there was a memory to smile over.

"Ah, Michael, I've been here before, years ago, and sailed with some of the men here. I'm known and trusted, for I've always brought advice and truth to the ruling family of this isle. Daniel, bring over another damn sack, will ye?"

Daniel looked vacantly at Seth for a moment, then his eyes lit up with a recollection. Reaching under his tunic, he pulled out another sack and handed it to Seth. Taking it clumsily in his left hand, Seth raised the sack to his lips. Pain briefly clouded his expression but he waved off any help as he drained a good measure.

"Ah, that's better now, even if there be a vow."

"When we received orders for Mathin," Seth continued, "I thought of Ishmael, whom I haven't seen in seven years. Little did I expect the part *you* would play, Michael. You complicated things terribly when you killed his son-in-law, even if he was an Ezrian bastard."

"I see that you've already found out then," Michael said. Seth and Daniel broke out into ribald laughter.

"Yes, Michael, by the Ceuth Arren you've complicated things in your life, haven't you? You being a vowed deacon and all."

Daniel chuckled at this, but Michael's angry stare silenced him.

"More than that, though," Seth continued, "the men who

saw what you did spread the word of it, and now the entire town looks upon you as some sort of deliverer from the oppressive Ulstin. As a result, you and those injured with you were brought here upon the request of Ishmael's advisor. Halvin had to agree since he wants to keep the people on our side after we've gone."

"Who was this Ulstin?" Michael asked, trying to conceal any real interest.

"He was the captain of the garrison and the ruler of the town appointed by the Ezrians. He took a liking to Ishmael's daughter and forced her to marry him. Had she resisted, he probably would have killed her, and quite a few townspeople as well. Besides, she most likely figured that she could soften his rule a bit."

Michael did not respond.

"She did what she had to do, it was her duty."

Michael nodded, and as he recalled the fight he found a satisfaction in knowing whom he had struck down.

"I'm weary now, Michael, and I feel sleep coming on again."

Seth eased down, his right arm resting on a soft cushion. Despite the covering of bandages, Michael could see that the limb was swollen to nearly twice its normal size.

Seth followed his gaze and said softly, "Now don't worry, it will take more than this to finish me. Besides, I'm called the Far-seeing," he said with a smile, "and I know there's a lot more for me to do before the end."

Michael tried to smile.

"Oh, yes," he whispered, "remember the priest of Sol? He's hidden in the basement, like you wanted, but I don't see why. He's madder than St. Lalime."

Seth fell silent and gently drifted away.

Michael sat by Seth and watched. He heard Daniel leave, but he didn't turn or say anything. The sunlight traced its daily path across the polished floor, but Michael looked straight ahead and did not see. The only sound was the soft, shallow breathing of his friend. The thoughts flooded over him and he sat quietly, as if waiting for some voice to speak.

* * *

It was late afternoon as he walked through the corridors and out the front door into the busy streets of Mathin. Except for the Cornathians, there were no signs of life in the house. Even the girl was nowhere to be found. The guard in the corridor, a crewman from the *Thunderwind*, told him that all the men had free leave for four days unless the horn of attack sounded. The men expected at least a week to pass, though, before the *Snow Wind* was fully repaired and aligned for sail.

A light snow was falling as he opened the door. Gusts of wind sent the flakes swirling along the narrow alleyway. He was used to the caverns of Cornath where half of the town was carved into the mountain and people lived below ground for months on end. He stood in silence, not sure which way to turn. After fifteen years he was free of his prison, and his feelings were elation and fear. He turned to the left and started to make his way down the hill toward the harbor. The alleyways were wider than Cornath's, so that two horse-drawn carts could pass abreast. The filth was not quite as bad, but was still enough to shock someone who had not spent time in an iceport.

Michael was fascinated with the towering log houses that rose to three and sometimes four stories. Each floor jutted out a foot or two farther than the one below, so that only a thin shaft of light penetrated from above. With the constant upheaval of thaw and freeze the buildings had tilted and buckled so that a cross-lacing of supports was necessary to keep the houses from falling into their neighbors across the lane. Though more than a few homes in Cornath were still vacant from the Great Death, their fire-gutted windows staring like eyes from a skull, Mathin, where the Death had struck hardest, showed little sign of decay.

He made his way down the alley past crowds of boisterous men walking up from the harbor and women leaning from the upper windows who beckoned to them with shrill calls and lewd suggestions. The shouting, the riot of color, the sense of abandon and celebration intoxicated him with a heady sense of joy.

From every building hung a sign announcing what was to be had within. The sign of the Silver Runner had a cask above it. Looking in the window, he saw Cornathian ice runners with mugs of steaming mulled wine.

As he turned a corner, a sign hung down before him and the image upon it caught his eye. It was a sailing ship, a strange, ungainly thing, of squat shape and high, ponderous sides. It was not of the Ice. It was sailing upon a blue flowing sea. He looked at it for several minutes then walked to the double-pane window of the tavern and looked in. The few who were within were of a foreign look. Their garb had a looser fit to it and the colors were brighter. They were dark-haired and swarthy, dressed for the outside, even though they were in the warmth of the tavern. An overwhelming compulsion seized him and he walked in.

He stood in the doorway for several seconds as his eyes adjusted to the darkness. He noticed that the noise level dropped to a whisper and he regretted having left the safety of Ishmael's home as he sat in the far corner of the room behind a rough-hewn table. When he sat down, he pulled the hood back from his head and the room became silent as death—they stared at his shaved skull.

The patrons gazed malevolently at him, and with a rash defiance Michael looked up and fixed them with his gaze. For a moment he felt as if real danger awaited there and he let his hand drift to the hilt of his dirk. But one by one the gazes fell away and a low buzzing gradually filled the room. Michael suddenly realized that they knew of him, and were afraid.

The tavern master unhurriedly walked over, his grease-stained woolens and long leather apron smelling of the thousand tankards of spilled ale mopped up through the years. His burly form and massive, hairy arms loomed before Michael and he knew without a doubt that there was a tavernkeeper who could maintain order.

"What will it be, master?" the keeper asked with a rumbling voice, as he bowed slightly in acknowledgment.

For a moment Michael was confused. Never in his life had he ordered any type of spirits. He had tasted the ceremonial wine of the Church, but he doubted that they would have such. Memory of Gareth returned to him.

"Do you have Aswingard?"

A smile flickered across the keeper's face and a stifled laugh came from the other side of the tavern. The keeper turned and the laughter fell into silence.

"Young lord," he said as politely as possible, "we carry no Aswingard here. Try some Colinmarth from beyond the Flowing Sea—it is the drink for men such as yourself."

The wine appeared in a finely made flask, and Michael sat back to savor his first experience of freedom. Seth's words came to him as he watched the comings and goings of the people in the tavern. So intent was he that when a hand came to rest upon his shoulder, he almost jumped from the chair.

"Young Michael, you should be more on your guard in a place such as this. Instead of a hand on the shoulder, you could receive a blade in the back."

Michael turned and looked into the eyes of a short, portly man of sixty-odd years standing next to him. His clothing had a faint glimmer, as if they somehow spun from the essence of the sun to catch and hold the blues and reds of the evening sky. The man's face bore a thin wisp of a graying beard, full, ruddy cheeks, and dark, coallike eyes that sparkled with sly amusement.

"Hey Ulimar," he shouted, "bring another flask of Colinmarth for my friend and one for myself—and no cheating now, the full measure without the water. Remember, I sell you the stuff so I know what the quality is! Make that a full round of it for the rest of my friends here, as well." And with a slight wave of acknowledgment to the other patrons he sat next to Michael.

"So, this is the young hero that has set so many tongues to wagging!"

The man fixed Michael with his gaze, which Michael returned. After several seconds the man's smile died away and he grew serious.

"Yes, I see now, you do have the look about you. You do have the look, Michael, but it will still take some proving on your part before I'll believe such tales. My name is Zardok of Mathin, and I've not made my fortune by believing every wild tale that comes across the Ice or drifts up from the Flowing Sea."

Ulimar brought the two flasks of wine, and Zardok grabbed one from the keeper and drained off half the measure with a long, noisy pull.

"Ah, that's better now," he said, smacking his lips. "Now, as I was saying, I don't believe every half-baked rumor until it be proven before my own eyes."

Michael could feel a swell of anger. "I never asked you or anyone else to believe. I don't even believe it myself. Anyhow, who are you to come along like this?"

Zardok threw his head back and laughed. "Good, very good. So you don't believe everything that Seth says. Well, I find that amusing, I do. Here's Seth's prophet, not even believing his own story. Well now, what shall we make of this?"

He leaned back and took another long pull on the flask. "I'm glad I noticed you leaving the home. I find it better, I do, to meet a man without all the fanfare and nonsense. It pulls the mask off one, so to speak."

Zardok looked to the tavernkeeper. "Ulimar, another one for myself." He looked back to Michael with a smile. "As I was saying, I'm Zardok of Mathin, head of the guild of free merchants of both the Ice and the Flowing Sea. I am also distant kinsman to Ishmael Tornson, and one of the Inner Council. As his chief advisor and closest friend, I want to know who you are and what your plans are?"

Michael stiffened at the tone of authority in Zardok's voice, and looked at him suspiciously.

Zardok reached into his tunic and, leaning over the table, withdrew a gold medallion. Stamped on the face of the medallion was a single tree of spruce; above it, in plain script, was the word Mathin. "'Tis the city's seal, it is. And for a year I've kept it hidden from the Ezrian dogs. If I intended harm to you, you would already be dead."

Michael was silent. The memory of the girl came back to him—the memory and the longing. He sat in silence and was torn by the horrible conflict. For fifteen years he had been trained to suppress all desire, to think only of his immortal soul. The body of a woman was the path to damnation. The conflict, the desire, was tearing at his heart, yet the monastery and its life was still there. "I'm pledged to take the Holy Vows," Michael said without a trace of emotion. "I therefore will renounce my right to Ceuth Arren, and with that, any part of the city as well. I give her freedom to do as she pleases."

Zardok sat in silence for a moment then drained off the rest of his flask. "Know this," he suddenly began. "I am a friend to Ishmael, but to his daughter I feel as if she was my own child—like the one that I lost so long ago. I wanted to kill that Ezrian pig for taking her, but you denied me my wish. I love her, Michael, and for your deed I thank you, and will be indebted to you forever. But hurt her, Michael, like the last one did, and you shall answer to me." Zardok leaned back from the table and nodded slightly. Michael saw several men get up and leave the tavern.

"Most perceptive, Michael," Zardok chuckled. "In fact, I think I might even like you."

"If you didn't," Michael said with a trace of a smile, "I'd be leaving now through the back door with those friends of yours."

Zardok gave him a sly smile. "It was easy enough to divert Daniel with a sack of wine and a young wench. A couple of payoffs here and there, I felt that sooner or later you would come out alone."

Beckoning to Michael, Zardok stood and threw a gold coin to Ulimar, who made a ceremony of biting it, drawing a round of snickers from the other customers.

As they walked out into the street, Zardok continued, "Michael, if you wish to venture into higher places, you must first realize how the world really is: first, you must realize that there are several different groups that might want you dead for a variety of reasons, yet like a naive child you wander about alone. No excuse for that."

Michael noticed that the three men who had left the tavern were following them at a discreet distance yet close enough to be at their side at the slightest sign of trouble. Michael could not help but feel that he was still being judged and that if he made the slightest mistake he would disappear into a dark alley and meet with a bloody end.

"Ah, Michael," Zardok continued with a gentle, almost fatherly tone, "there is something about you that I like. It's certainly not your shrewdness—but that will come in time. I think you don't believe one-tenth of what people say about you, yet somewhere deep inside there's a part of you that finds the while thing intriguing nevertheless. Am I not right?"

Michael felt exposed, as if his thoughts were being stripped away by the little merchant who for the moment held the power of life and death.

"How do you know this?"

"If I couldn't read men, Michael, I wouldn't be rich. All men crave power—some ruthlessly, others slyly. You, my friend, are frightened by it, especially when this prophet talk starts. You do know that you have a strangeness about you—a fire in your eyes that can enervate people, the way you did the customers in the tavern, and myself for that matter. That alone is enough to set the simpler folk talking."

"And what then?"

"Some fear power, others rush to it blindly. I think you see Seth and the others and what they can do with you, and that type of power frightens you. I like you for that, Michael, but I also think that if once you decide to seize that power, you will be a scourge terrible to behold. You could wash us all in blood with the dream of the people to end the darkness."

"The End of the Darkness? Don't tell me that you really believe that, Zardok?" Michael was shocked by his own cynicism, his open statement of disbelief in Holy Writ.

Zardok laughed. "No, Michael, no. Seth's tales hold nothing for me. I believe in no church other than whichever is in power. The darkness I speak of is far different than that."

He paused for a moment, and then in an offhanded manner said, "Tell me, Michael, have you ever read any of the Old Books?"

Michael looked at Zardok as if he was some kind of fool.

"Only the Cynth Raith, the Brothers of the First Truth may

read such things. Anyone else who does so is as good as dead. Why do you even mention it?"

"Just curious, that's all."

They turned a corner and walked into the square that led to the city harbor. Michael realized that Zardok was appearing with him in public as a show, so that people could see that the head of their guild was accepting, at least for the moment, the new stranger. Michael turned and, looking at the man and those around him, felt like laughing. Zardok, 'head of the Merchants Guild'? Head of the pirates was more like it.

So Michael walked the streets of Mathin, as Seth had asked, and no sight was lost to him. The cavelike alleyways echoed with the shouts of peddlers and the calls of the merchants as they sold their wares to the thousands from Cornath who had come with money in their pockets. Halvin had been strict with his order — no pillaging except for the barracks of the Ezrians — all had gone well except for an occasional fight and one or two murders, so the city was happy.

Exotic smells came out of one of the alleyways and Zardok guided Michael in that direction, where they passed food stalls that sold wares from beyond the Flowing Seas. Strange fruits in rainbowlike colors greeted the eye, great slabs of smoked or frozen meats hung overhead while men cried out in strange tongues and beckoned to all to try their treasures. From homes and stores came the smell of herbs and spices that would grace the table of a king or be offered on some distant smoking altar to the chanting of hooded priests. Thinly veiled women braved the cold to stand provocatively in the doorways, displaying the wares that they had to offer; and the ice runners of Cornath shouted lustily to them and were lured within.

"You still have the look of the priest about you," Zardok said seriously. "You mentioned your vows before — Tell me, have you ever had a woman?" and with that he beckoned to a young girl with flaming red hair who stood in the doorway of a pleasure house. She noticed Zardok's gesture and smiled seductively to Michael, her transparent black veil revealing a supple young body that left nothing to the imagination.

Michael stood for a moment in astonishment and the fear

in his heart wrestled with a hidden desire. The image of the girl faded into a tall, lithe figure with flowing black hair and green, sparkling eyes. He turned quickly and made his way past the door and down the street with Zardok laughing alongside.

"Ah Michael. I was once like you," he said, "but not for long." And he chuckled softly with his hidden memories.

Michael made no response. His thoughts returned to the strange voice in the night, and he knew that the doors to the monastery were slowly closing forever.

They walked to the edge of the city, where the ice met the rocky, frozen shore. Michael could see the bustle of activity surrounding the fleet as the *Snow Wind* was covered with a swarm of carpenters, sailmakers, iron fitters, and blade masters who in the closing light of day were seeing to the repairs. Great cranes on long-bed sleds had been pushed alongside the ship and had raised the *Snow Wind* off the ice and set her up on chocks. All along the starboard outrigger the men sweated and worked to remove the hundred-and-fifty-foot-long outrigger.

The *Thunderwind* dwarfed the other ships in the harbor. Michael could see the finishing touches being applied to the repairs from the last two battles. As well, the darkened patches from dozens of older hits were visible alongside the newer patches of pine, oakum, and tar, which made the between decks airtight and smooth-surfaced for the fastest run possible. His gaze swept past the *Thunderwind* to the harbor walls over a half-mile away. They seemed so distant, so small. It was hard to comprehend the pivotal role that the ice towers had played in his life.

His gaze returned to the *Thunderwind* and he noticed that Gareth and Halvin were on deck. Halvin was looking straight at him, and he felt a wave of darkness settle over his thoughts.

Strange, Michael thought. Rifton told me that he would be an ally, a friend, yet somehow I feel I can't trust him.

He turned away. Walking along the harbor's edge with Zardok pointing out the sights of the city, Michael finally came to the ships that had so often captured his imagination. The first sight of them was a deep disappointment. He had expected a craft of sleek and beautiful design, like the ice runners. Instead, they had a curious, rounded shape, like great barrels, with their beam almost a third of their length. The light forms were not here, and compared even to the slowest merchantmen of Ice these ships looked for all the world to be wallowing, ungainly tubs. Nevertheless, they could venture where no ice-ship would ever go—unless someday the ice did cover the entire world, as some Saints had foretold.

The ships were set up on blocks for the winter. In the spring, when the ice broke, they would be lowered into the water and packed with the trade goods of winter. They would disappear over the horizon and venture out into the Flowing Seas.

A crippled old sailor, bent with age, sat in a shack alongside the greatest of the craft and for a few coppers he told Michael about sailing the Flowing Sea.

He spoke of the dreadful sickness that seized men and left them weak and gasping as the water rolled the ship beneath them, and how they would sail south by east until they came at last to the Islands of Trade. Here was the farthest that north-men were allowed to venture, and here the Southlanders would come in great galleys with five hundred slaves chained to oars that moved to the beat of drums that were hidden within.

The old sailor's face wrinkled with disgust as he described the fetid stench that trailed astern the galleys, and how on occasion he had seen the slaves, some as dark as the night. The old man swore it to be true, then said that some of the slaves were ice runners who had dared to venture into forbidden lands and now would row the Flowing Seas forever. Michael asked him what lay beyond the Trade Isles, but the old man fell silent and would say no more.

So Michael walked the streets again, and heard and saw things that he had never dreamed of. True, the war had touched these people, but they were not yet caught up in the blinding fury that swept the north. The people around him seemed to survive somehow, to live off the prey that fell to them. It was a pirate island, to be sure, devotion to the Church of Sol a faint flicker, at best. Twice in the last year the war had reached them, and Michael knew that it would come ever more often. The people of Mathin had been in the background for too long. Their city would ally, learn to defend itself against the power of the two churches, or perish.

Of this and many other things Michael and Zardok talked, until finally their path led them to the doorway of Tornson's home. Zardok beckoned to one of the men who had shadowed them, and the man disappeared only to return a few minutes later with a small bundle. In the light of the torch that flickered alongside the door, Michael opened it and found several strange, red fruits that seemed to be molded of wax.

"Michael, when I was your age, I made my first voyage away to the Trade Isles in a craft not twenty feet in length. That was forty years ago, and I've earned a fortune since, yet I would give it all back again to be able to see the world in all its freshness for just one moment. I see that freshness in your eyes today."

He turned and started to walk away, then stopped. "Share that fruit with my old friend Seth, but tell Janis that if she wants any, she'll have to come and visit an old man and get them herself." He smiled a strange, wistful smile.

"Good night Michael, I've enjoyed our walk. Through your eyes I remember the wonder of a young man about to embark upon the journey of life. Come visit me when you wish to talk. But for heaven's sake, don't walk alone."

He disappeared into the shadows of night, and the three men drifted away after him.

"Damn my eyes," Seth said weakly, "so you met Zardok already?"

Michael took the apples and offered one to him.

"I should have figured on this," Seth said in a more serious tone. "Where the hell was Daniel?"

They sat for several minutes and Michael told Seth about his meeting with Zardok. Seth's gaze suddenly lifted from Michael and his eyes widened slightly. Michael turned.

"Good evening, Michael Ormson. I am pleased to see that you are up and about." Janis stood before him in a lavender dress, silhouetted by a flowing white fur cape. The timing seemed rather obvious to Michael.

"Tell me, Janis Tornson," Michael ventured, "has Zardok stamped his seal upon me?"

A slight quiver betrayed her quiet expression but she otherwise ignored his comment. "Seth, I hope that all meets with your satisfaction."

Seth nodded his head and eyed her coldly. He could see the threat she represented to his plans.

She smiled at him as if she could read his thoughts. "If you will excuse Michael, I wish to talk with him for a while."

"Enjoy the fruit, Seth, we'll talk again later."

She led Michael into the corridor and he noticed a look of concern on her face. They walked down the hall and he closely studied her slim body, and the gentle, feline grace of her stride. He thought he could see the hardness of a woman who had married for the sake of her family, and who was considering doing it again. He respected her, and as he looked at her his heart quickened.

They turned into a large empty chamber where five logs blazed cheerily in an open fireplace. Michael walked over to it and stood in wonder, watching the logs crackle and pop in the blazing heat. The fire was the only light in the room and it cast a pleasant glow to the walls, which were hung with tapestries depicting the history of a family that had been on the Ice of the Southward Isles since the days of colonization a thousand years before.

"Michael," she began without any hesitation, "I want to ask you of our plans."

"What do you mean?" Michael replied.

"Our island has been a free port since the Great Plague. We've managed to have our indiscretions overlooked and so Mathin has survived."

Michael smiled at her diplomacy. What you really mean, he thought, is that your lucrative trade in freebooting has been threatened. "Really?" Michael said with a smile.

"With the coming of the Ezrians, our trade was closed down. My father was upon the Ice, otherwise he would have been put to the sword. I was held hostage for my people and forced to marry." Her shoulders straightened. "It was more rape than marriage," she said with a deadly whisper. "You robbed me of my one desire, Michael Ormson, that I never had the chance to use the blade on him."

She turned and Michael could see the tears streak her face, the drops of moisture reflecting the soft firelight.

He stepped closer to her, but she seemed to freeze. "So now you want to know if I desire the same," Michael asked.

She remembered how they told her of Ulstin's death while the people in the street cheered. For an hour she lived in a dazed joy—until she remembered the law as the men carried a cloaked form into her father's house. From the moment that she saw him she felt a closeness that she had never known before. She bandaged his wounds and nursed him through his delirium, and all the time his young, strong body and the powerful, penetrating look to his eyes made her tremble.

It was all so ridiculous, so undignified of a Tornson. She had known Michael for less than four days and yet she felt an overwhelming desire for him. She wished that she could drive him from her presence, but in her heart she knew that she would still desire him, long after he was gone.

She tried to hold back the words even as she lashed out with them: "Did you ever think what my desires might be? All my life I've been a pawn to this damnable island. Not once have I been able to do as I wanted. Tell me, priest, do you want me—do you want my body?" She made a sweeping gesture as if she were going to rip open her dress for him to examine her.

"That's all I've been—nothing more than a piece of meat to be dealt out to someone else's desire." She tried to control her tears and, failing, turned away.

Michael stood before her. The torrent of emotions made her even more attractive to him.

"Janis."

She still stood with her back to him.

"No, I could never do that to you. You've been hurt too much. I never would want you under those conditions. Marry whom you please, but do it of your own free will. I release you of any obligation."

She turned back to face him. "Is this what you truly desire."

"Yes."

She lowered her eyes. She reached out to touch him but he stood as one frozen. She sensed rejection from him, a rebuff, as if the ghost of the Ezrian would stand beside her forever.

"Good, then it is settled. You may have the free use of my home—and your friends as well—until your fleet leaves, and you shall always be welcome in my house."

"Must you be so formal, Janis?"

She looked into his eyes again and could see the fear in him as well, the fear that just barely masked the desire.

Her thoughts were still confused. Without another word she stepped past him and walked silently from the room.

As she opened the door Michael thought he could see another form in the hall.

Michael turned back and faced the fire. Three weeks ago he had been alone, in a monastery, and now a woman that he desired beyond all imagining had offered herself and he had turned her away. He shook his head and threw another log on the fire.

"So you turned her down after all?"

"Come in, Zardok, I half suspected that you were listening."

"Ah, my boy, you do me a disservice. As I told you before, that girl is like my own daughter—like the one I lost in the plague so long ago. Your turning her down was a sign of good breeding, as a priest of your brotherhood would be expected to do. But, my boy, I think you care for her far more than you would let on, and she for you. It's a shame for all of us that something can't be worked out."

"What do you mean?"

"Michael, I'm going to speak now as a realist. I told Janis this before she came to see you. She knew my words to be true, but she rebelled, and I really can't blame her. We've been a free port for many years, but with the war increasing in its scope, we need protection, for our one, small city cannot stand alone. If you would marry Janis you could be our contact to the Cornathian Church. After all, your uncle is an archbishop of the church and, if I'm not mistaken, will be the next Holy Father."

"Why do you keep thrusting your plans on me?" Michael shouted. "Seth, with his prophet. You, with this damn town. Why can't I just make a decision for Michael Ormson and be left well enough alone?"

"Because, Michael, if you wish to survive you must align with somebody. Stay with us, give her some time, and I think she would see you for what you really are. We can have protection then, and we can protect you from the designs of Mor, as well. Besides, Michael, if I'm not mistaken, I believe that you are already in love with her, in spite of your brotherhood."

Michael looked away and they sat in silence. The fire flickered and flared, then slowly dropped away. The smoldering embers held a thousand different pictures—an end to Seth's prophecy dream, the ability to live quietly in this back corner of the Ice, with the green-eyed girl next to him.

Yet there was the darker image, the image he was still slave to. The fifteen years of prayer and fear. The fifteen years could not be pushed away by a gentle touch and a flashing look of desire. The hold of the Church was still too strong. He desired sin, and with that desire came guilt. The cycle pressed in upon him and he longed for an escape.

He could not accept. He could not accept, even when he wrestled with the fear of his own heresy and the threat of eternal damnation.

"I'm sorry, Zardok, but I cannot accept, even if I wanted to."

The days passed without incident. At the first light of every dawn, Halvin would dispatch a half-dozen schooners and corsairs and a frigate as support to sweep out in all directions for sign of the Ezrians. And each evening they returned without report of contact.

The repair of the *Snow Wind* continued as the shot holes were sealed and the shaping of the new outrigger and forward support beam continued with three crews working ceaselessly.

Teams of carpenters fashioned the support beam to the measurements of the master shipwright, while joiners and iron-wrights worked arduously at knocking out the support pins and bolts that fastened the crossbeam and the outrigger to the ship. Two men were crushed to death before Michael's eyes, and a third lost his right leg when the support beam slipped from its chain and crashed down on the men working below. Work stopped for only a moment as the bodies were dragged clear. Then on the still bloody ice, a new team took over and the work pushed on.

Michael's only duty was to report aboard ship during the morning watch to note the progress of repair in the ship's log. For the rest of the day he was free to wander. He noticed a companion or two always seemed to follow, but when he mentioned that to Seth and Zardok they feigned ignorance.

Seth was a source of worry as his stump refused to heal and started to discharge a foul-smelling liquid that sickened any who drew near. Finally a Braith de Dochas was called. He came with two acolytes before him, one ringing a bell and the other carrying a censer that gave off a pungent smoke. It took four men to hold Seth down while the Healer cut open the stump to allow the river of pus to flow out. The priest placed a long thin knife in the stove and waited till it glowed white-hot. He then laid the knife into the wound and cut out the decaying flesh. The screams of Seth could be heard throughout the house and even in the street below, but the following morning he awoke clear-eyed and the fever was gone.

When not by Seth's bedside, Michael found himself drawn to Zardok and the welcome conversation to be found in his simple chambers. The talks would rarely touch upon Mathin or Zardok's business. Of course, Michael realized that Zardok, as an "agent," helped to unload stolen booty from privateers.

"Ah, young Michael," Zardok started one afternoon, while uncorking a sack of mead, "the Southward Islands are a curiously hellish place. In some ways I hear that they be like the Garden of Promise, yet in others they are more like a nightmare."

"But what are they really like?"

"Have ye ever seen St. Judean's Bane?"

"I've seen it on the maps, it's twenty-five leagues west of the Mathinian Pass, almost within the realm of the Dead Lands."

Michael, of course, knew the legend of how St. Judean had been cast out of favor from the Long Table and had fallen to Earth. Occasionally, farsighted men from Mathin claimed to see the smoke of the Bane when the wind came from the north.

"Well, I've seen it," Zardok stated, "and much else, besides. At the bane there is a rent in the ice, a dozen leagues long and two or three wide. It's a land of flaming skies and water that will never hold ice. Michael, 'tis said that the lands beyond the Southward Trade Isles are like the bane. There are small kingdoms, but most of the land will not support life. What's curious is that the people there believe quite the opposite of what we believe. They follow a false prophet who claims that God, upon the murder of the Son, threw down his Son's body in fire and smoke and that the lands will burn until the entire world is consumed. That day will be the moment of salvation. It's curious, Michael, that we take the worlds that we live in, even though they are opposites, and blame it all on the Divine Will of the Angry Creator."

Early on the morning of the eighth day, Michael felt a need to escape the city and seek the solitude of the hills. Borrowing a pair of skis from Zardok, he walked down the city streets and, as he turned a corner, broke into a run, weaving through alleyways that he had scouted the day before. After several minutes he was satisfied that he had shaken his self-appointed guards. Leaving the city through the west gate, he put on the skis and set out for the hills beyond. It took him a while to master the balance and stride, but he soon found his pace.

As he poled his way through the deep powder of the pine forest, he let his mind become absorbed by the steady rhythm of the stride. The old towering trees had been planted hundreds of years before to supply fresh timbers for fleets then undreamed. Their girth could barely be spanned by two men. The stately rows had the symmetry of columns in a cathedral.

In the forest the noise and bustle of the city drifted away

until, finally, there was nothing but the silence of the snow-covered forest, occasionally disturbed by the sigh of the wind and the shifting whispers of the snow. Shafts of sunlight beamed down through infrequent gaps in the dark-green canopy a hundred feet above. He was skiing through a dreamworld where shimmering crystals of light drifted down like buoyant diamonds.

He was not completely alone, though—he crossed the path of a hare running ahead of a fox, and the deeper markings of deer as they browsed the snow cover for nourishment.

Up through the hills he cut his track, stopping occasionally to observe the snow as it drifted down in a sudden squall, or the strange, razor-sharp edges of a mound that towered to half again his own height. The frost of his breath froze to his face mask but he did not notice the cold as he merged into the sterile, icy world. There was a wild, stark beauty to it. A beauty that he had never found anywhere else. At that moment he would have been satisfied if the Garden never returned. The snowdrifts caught and held the essence of the wind, their graceful lines curving around the trees and boulders. At times he felt a sense of guilt when he broke through a drift that had coiled and shifted into something that was almost alive. But even before the drift was out of sight the wind was repairing the damage and covering his tracks, as if to demonstrate how puny he really was in the face of winter's strength.

The trees gradually thinned out as the slope steepened and the lush soil gave way to bare, windblown rock. Passing through a line of scraggly trees that clung tenaciously to the stony edge, Michael came upon a wide, sloping monolith that rose above the forest like a pagan altar. Removing his skis, he scurried up the sloping pinnacle to where it flattened, revealing an enormous platform carved in the shape of a giant's chair. Michael sat down in the chair, which was positioned to give him a sweeping view in all directions.

Wherever he looked the Frozen Sea was before him—the Broken Tracks to the north, the smooth, open ice to the south. He stood in the glory of the view and let its joy encompass him.

The hard breathing from the long climb gradually gave way to a slower, steady pattern as he sat on the flat pinnacle with the grove of trees rising toward him. A particular group of towering pines drew his attention, and leaving the giant's chair, he made his way down the thirty- or forty-yard path that appeared to have been created to guide one's feet to a place of quiet solitude.

The trees towered above him. They were set in a little dell that formed a natural depression. A dozen pines rose up and over the dell to form a canopy that diffused and softened the light. Pulling off his cloak, he lay down and slowly let his mind wander.

He thought of Mathin and wished that he had never seen it and all the temptations that it had created for him. Had he never left the cloister, he would then have been in noontime prayers. Why was it that fate was seeking him out, thrusting itself into his life and limiting his freedom of action? He wondered if his thoughts, if his very life were really his at all. He could sense the storm that was gathering around him. He could almost see the lines of history coming together and forcing themselves into his life.

His breathing slowed and his thoughts drifted up to the clouds, yet the image of Janis would not leave him. Her image became more and more real. The shadows gently turned as the sun slipped toward the west, and his thoughts held on her. A twig suddenly snapped behind him.

He jumped up and turned. She stood before him.

Her skis were still on, and her long white cape dragged across the top of the snow. A light gust of wind swirled through the forest, sweeping the snow from the boughs above, so that the grove was bathed in crystals. She stepped out of her skis, her face aglow with the climb up the hill and with the deeper fire that burned within.

"Michael, in your thoughts you called for me and I heard you," she said softly. "Really, Michael, you don't understand the strength that you have. But you should be a little less explicit." She smiled a mischievous little smile that made Michael blush.

She walked up to him, putting her arms around him, and he raised his head to look into her eyes. "I've watched you, Michael Ormson, and I've come to love you. But I will never submit to you."

"I know," he whispered.

"You called for me just now in your thoughts, didn't you?"

"Yes."

"You called for me, and you dreamed that we made love and you cast aside forever your vows to be a priest."

He could not respond to the truth, even as he wondered at the power that could summon her there.

"Your desire is my desire," she whispered as she drew off her cape and laid it alongside Michael's. She sat down and, taking his hand, brought him down alongside her. Her hands gently brushed his face and her eyes searched into him. "Michael, I am yours now because I want to be. Someday many may call you a prophet, but Michael, you are more than that to me."

He looked into her eyes and saw the love and devotion that were kindling in her. Memory of the vows, the promise to the brotherhood disappeared. Her arms coiled around him, and in her warmth the dreams of the priest died as he had always known they would.

A gunshot rolled in the distance, a muffled thunder that penetrated into the quiet of the grove. He stirred. Another shot followed, and he was fully awake. A swirl of fine powder blew off his cloak when he stood.

A wave of realization struck him with the enormity of what had happened. Turning, he looked down, saw her looking up at him, wrapped in the other half of the white cape, her eyes wide with wonder.

"Michael," she whispered.

The memory flooded over him—the first light kiss, the strengthening embrace, and the gentle yielding as he unbuttoned his tunic to a swirling, blinding fever of desire. He had fallen. He looked at her in her nakedness and he could understand why, and the desire started to overtake him again. But she had destroyed his world. She had destroyed his one road back to security; the vows of the Church were gone forever. She had unlocked the door.

"I must leave," he said gruffly as he pulled his cape off the ground.

"Michael, don't leave yet."

"Janis, I have to go."

"Michael, I love you."

"Oh really! Was it Zardok who told you to say that?"

"Michael!"

He was afraid and he lashed out at her. "We could make a good alliance, couldn't we?"

She stood up, naked in the frigid air, and slapped him with a crashing blow across the face.

He stood silent.

"God damn you, Michael. Priest, I did this because I wanted to, because I thought that I loved you. Forgive me, oh Prophet, for having taken your virginity and priesthood from you, and shown you instead what it's like to live."

He lowered his gaze.

"Look at me, Michael."

He turned away from her.

"Are you afraid to look at me?" she asked coldly. "Afraid of human desire? Michael, I love you for what you are, not for Zardok, nor prophecies, or anything else."

He began to walk away, and she sank down on the robes that still held the warmth that only moments before had been shared in quiet intimacy.

"Go, priest," she said sadly, "lock yourself up. You could have had so much that would have been different, if only you would dare."

She watched him as he walked from the grove and disappeared over the pinnacle to his skis. She was tempted to get up and run to him and ask him to stay.

No, she thought. If it's ever to work he will have to come to me. He will have to come, damn him. And she pulled her cape tightly around herself.

CHAPTER 9

FOLLOWING HIS TRAIL BACK THROUGH THE FOREST, MICHAEL skied down the slope to the gates of the city. Even before he reached the walls, he could hear the bells and horns as their strident calls sounded the alarm. Michael skied to the west gate and Daniel came out of the shadows to greet him.

"I heard you were in the forest, so I thought I'd wait for ye here," he mumbled.

Michael looked at him and searched for the truth, but found that there was no knowledge of what had occurred.

"What's happening?" Michael asked breathlessly as he pulled his bindings loose and stepped off the skis.

"From what I can piece together, it appears that our patrol schooners had a brush with the enemy. One of our schooners overhauled a small Ezrian patrol craft with a crew of six aboard. They were persuaded to talk."

Daniel became excited and he waved his arms in an agitated manner as they walked through the gate and into the city.

"There's a fleet, Michael, and no mistake. 'Tis a big one — half a dozen merchants and again as many frigates."

"We should be able to handle that," Michael said.

"But there's more. They've got three big ones, they do. Three ice cruisers as big as the *Thunderwind*, if not bigger."

Michael fell silent.

"Ah, but you ain't heard all yet," Daniel continued. "They know about us. They knew when we left Cornath, and this here fleet's been searching after us. They thought we had run one of the more easterly passes, but they know we're here now. It seems that the Ezrians know far more than we thought."

"Interesting, isn't it?" Michael said thoughtfully.

"We lost a frigate too, Michael, the *St. Ioan*. That's the bad part of it. Our schooner that brought the patrol craft came about to try and pick up the *St. Ioan*. On the way she sighted the other two patrol schooners on her flank and signaled them in. They ran for several hours, until they came across the tracks of the *St. Ioan*, not a half-hour old. They followed her for several leagues, until they saw the smoke and signs of a pursuit by half a dozen frigates and merchantmen. The *Ioan* is gone, Michael."

Michael was silent as they pushed their way through the increasing crowd of men who were making their way to the harbor.

"The schooners ran for it. We've been found for sure, Michael, there's no mistake, especially if any survived the *St. Ioan*. There'll be hell to pay, and soon enough."

They came to the harbor and all was confusion, until a deep, thundering horn sounded from the forecastle of the *Thunderwind*. It sounded three times, and by the final blast all stood in silence. Halvin appeared on the forecastle, ringed by priests of Mor who held sparkling torches that cast an eerie green light on the upturned faces of the Cornathian crews.

"Men of Cornath," he started, "the false believers have been sighted not thirty leagues from here. The *St. Ioan* has been lost."

A rumble of noise and shouts drifted through the crowd, and from the deck of the *St. Regis* there was a loud shout and the crashing of swords against shields. Two of the three sisters had been lost. *St. Regis* was alone.

"Men of Cornath!" Halvin shouted, cutting through the cries

of lamentation. "I am Halvin—the death dealer. Halvin—the vengeance bringer. And though they be ten times our number, we shall still triumph over them!"

He paused for a moment as if expecting a cheer, but he was greeted instead with silence. His face turned red, and with a mighty voice he shouted, "We sail within the hour." Then Halvin turned and disappeared below deck.

Michael looked over to the *Snow Wind*, where a swarm of men worked the cranes at a frenzied pace to lower the injured ship onto the ice. She would sail with the rest of the fleet because the outrigger was in place, but the final carving and the important adjustment to the blades would have to wait for another port. Another day would have seen the job done correctly, and Michael pondered how this might affect the survival of the fleet when speed could mean all the difference.

"Come on, Daniel," Michael shouted as he joined the milling crowd of men who started to make their way up the streets of Mathin. The pushing and jostling mob thinned as each man went to his quarters for his gear or to bid a quick farewell to the friends and lovers he had found in his short stay.

The merchants were deeply disturbed at the departure of such willing customers. Within a day the Ezrians would be back, and the memories of that occupation did not rest well with them.

Michael reached the Tornson house and saw a familiar shadow standing in the doorway across the street. "Daniel, could you get my things together for me?" Michael said quickly, as he went across the street to Zardok.

"Well, my friend," Zardok said sadly, "I hope that we shall meet again, for I have to come to value you far more than you could possibly know."

Michael looked at him coldly. "Do you know what happened this afternoon?"

Zardok looked at Michael and held his gaze. "I think I might," he said hesitantly. "I saw her return from the grove, and from her expression, I felt it wise not to approach her."

"Did you have anything to do with this?" Michael asked fiercely.

"A week ago, I would have, for you were nothing to me. But not now. Michael, why are you two hurting each other? Her with that damnable pride, and you with your foolish vows and fear of the world."

Michael looked past Zardok.

"She loves you, and I think, my son, that you love her as well but are too afraid to admit it because it would wreck your nice little world and force you to stay here and be a part of hers. Michael, if she destroyed the cloistered monastery forever, I promise you that I had nothing to do with it. It was of her own choosing."

Michael nodded. "Farewell, Zardok."

"Farewell, Michael."

Michael turned into Tornson's house.

Much to his surprise, Michael found Seth on his feet and feebly trying to dress himself. He had yet to learn how to function with but one arm, and he grimaced with pain as he pulled on his tunic. Ignoring Seth's weak protests, Michael clothed him then ordered him to lie down as he packed up his gear.

Daniel entered the room with Michael's gear and closed the door behind him.

"Michael, it's all been arranged," Daniel whispered.

Michael looked at Seth.

"What does he mean?" Michael asked suspiciously.

"Michael, there's no longer any purpose in staying with the fleet," Seth said. "With the dozens of things to attend to in the next hour, it will be simple enough for us to hide here until the fleet has gone. Once the battle has drifted away to the north, we can start your work in earnest."

"What do you mean by my 'work'?"

"Michael, you are the Prophet, and will be the founder of the new religion. That is why you have been sent here. The people of Mathin will follow you—at least Zardok has assured me of this. From this woman Janis, I know we could get a ship to help you go to Inys Gloi, where your training will start."

Michael stood and glared at Seth. He could see the ravages that the wound had worked on Seth's body. In spite of the weakness. Seth's face was aglow with a fanaticism that reminded Michael of the icons of the Saints—their eyes alight with religious fervor.

The vision came of what Seth's road would lead to—a holy war, unlike any that had ever passed before, and upon the faces of a hundred thousand would be that strange, fanatical light. And they would call his name, and the sound of their cries would be like the rolling of thunder in the hills.

He could see it! And upon seeing it he wanted to reach out and claim it. But with that desire came the other faces—the faces of the dead, of the thousands of maimed, and over it all hovered the spectre of defeat, and the death of one more important than any other.

"Michael, come with me," Seth whispered.

Michael looked at him for a moment. When they had first met, Michael was the student and Seth Facinn, the Far-seeing, was the leader. It was changed forever. Michael turned and walked to the door.

"Michael," Seth shouted. "Michael, where are you going?"

The memory of a woman called out to him. "Michael," she whispered.

"Where are you going?" Seth shouted again.

"I would hope to a death of my own choosing," he said, and then he was gone.

He made his way into the street, where he found himself surrounded by half a dozen priests of Mor. Immediately Daniel thundered through the doorway, his hand on the head of his ax. One of the priests quickly blurted out that Gareth had sent them as a guard of honor to escort Michael back to the ship. Michael nodded with a soft smile and realized that the last thing Gareth needed was to tell Zimri that Michael had slipped out of his hands.

"One of your friends is inside, is he not?" the head priest asked softly.

Michael realized that it was senseless to lie at this point, because the priest already knew the answer to his own question.

"Yes, you'll find him on the third floor."

"Good, we have our orders concerning him."

"And what might that be?" Daniel asked gruffly.

"Lord Halvin has decided that those who are too seriously wounded to withstand the rigors of the campaign are to be sent home with the captured merchantmen."

"Isn't that rather dangerous?" Michael inquired.

"The captured corsair will accompany them. They should have a safe passage. Besides, it's better than leaving them here to the tender mercies of the Ezrians."

Daniel gave a low, throaty growl. With a corsair in escort they stood an even chance at best. A couple of armed merchantmen could sweep them up without any trouble. Halvin didn't want the slower ships around for the fight, knowing that the ships and wounded would be a hindrance in the battle to come.

"I should go up and help him," Michael said.

"I'm sorry, but there is no time for that. We sail in half an hour. Brother Seamus here will see to your friend."

Michael looked at Daniel and nodded. He knew that with a word he could command the berserker to fight, but that would solve nothing.

"Come, Daniel, we've said our good-byes to Seth. We must be off."

They walked the narrow streets with their escort and reached the harbor ice, where a steady stream of men climbed the ships' boarding ladders. Daniel and Michael slipped under the outrigger and Death Rams to the portside forecastle ladder, and went aloft to the ship's deck. Stowing his gear below, Michael returned deckside to watch the casting off. The last of the men trickled in from the city with armed squads of Morian priests dragging those malcontents who had tried to stay. Only a few attempted desertion because all knew that by the morrow's night Mathin would be an Ezrian town and they could expect no better treatment than the Cornathians were about to deal the lines of Ezrian prisoners standing by the flagship's portside outrigger. The captives were soon drawn up in a circle, their arms tied behind them. Halvin came on deck and looked out at them. The scene was lit by the flickering glimmer of wind-swept torches.

Halvin began to speak, and a short, dark man next to him translated the words. "I shall make this offer but once. We shall not force you to renounce your faith at this time, you have five minutes to decide. You can sail with us or stay here."

With this he nodded to three brothers of the Mord Rinn who stood next to him, and the implication was clear. Halvin busied himself with other matters as the minutes passed then, turning, he faced the prisoners.

"Decide now," he shouted.

About half of the prisoners stepped forward and made their way to the side of the *Thunderwind*, their voices clamoring for mercy. A dozen brothers of Mor stepped from the shadows and led them away to be distributed to the various ships. They would fill the places made empty by the casualties of the last two battles. Halvin looked to the others who stood quietly, their heads held high in defiance. He nodded to the three brothers of the Mord Rinn and, turning, made his way below.

One of the brothers stepped forward into the torchlight. His face was concealed by the burgundy mask and cowl, and his high, quavering voice echoed across the ice. "He who is not of the True Faith of the Saints is of Satan, and as Satan's servant, he shall therefore be destroyed."

With these words ringing in their ears, the guards, who were brothers of Mor, drew their scimitars and fell upon the Ezrians. In their fear some of the Ezrians fell to their knees and cried aloud, recanting their decision, but their words went unheeded as blood streamed forth upon the ice.

Michael stood upon the side railing and forced himself to watch the slaughter. The scent of blood aroused the guards to a savage passion, so that many of them prolonged the agony of their prisoners.

One of the prisoners broke clear of the circle of death, and in his panic ran straight at the *Thunderwind* with several priests at his heels. He managed to crawl under the outrigger and ran along the side of the ship while the crew above watched. Some stood in silence, but many started to jeer and laugh at him.

The terrified prisoner ran along the outrigger until he fell sprawling on the ice. He realized at last the futility of resistance, and rather than trying to flee, the Ezrian rose up onto his knees and waited. It was then that he looked at Michael.

His eyes bore into Michael—they were the eyes of a fifteen-year-old who didn't understand why his life was to end like this.

His terror reached out to Michael as the guards fell upon him and gleefully hacked away. The Ezrian's body trembled with red, searing pain as the Morians held him down and cut off his arms. Laughing, they threw his arms aside and propped the kicking body up as a priest came from behind and with a vicious sweep of his scimitar beheaded the screaming boy. A pulsing shower of blood washed against the side of the *Thunderwind* as the body tumbled over onto the snow, kicked spasmodically, and then was still. Michael watched as the blood slowly soaked into the snow and changed it from white to a pink slush that rested like a hole of darkness in the pale torchlight.

A hot rage swept over Michael as the jeers continued, and he turned to watch as the Cornathians cheered at the entertainment that the Morians offered them. Even Halvin had returned to the deck and looked down upon the carnage with a wild light in his eyes. The words suddenly poured forth, and the voice spoke from a hidden, inner soul that at last was starting to awake.

"And we call ourselves the servants of the Saints," he shouted. "We call ourselves the servants of God, and yet we have sunk to this!"

He pointed an accusing finger to the crumpled body below. As if in answer, the last pitiful cries of the dying whispered in the background.

"Is this the Will? Is this truly the desire of the Saints? That we tear at each other like maddened beasts! Can we not even lend dignity to the death of that boy down there? If we must soak ourselves in blood, let's at least give a sense of dignity to it, and not mock them like raging madmen."

Michael pointed at the fat, sluggish brute who had jeered

loudest. "When you die. my friend. I hope that boy below is there to meet you. Somehow I don't think he'll laugh at your last moment. Then let us see what you say, you filth disguised as a man."

"He was an Ezrian dog and deserved death." the fat man snarled.

"If he's damned. then so are you!" Michael shouted in rage. "You're all damned for the joy that you take in his agony. Get out of my sight, and take your twisted pleasure into some dark corner where it belongs."

The men around Michael were silent. The tone of his voice held a compelling ring of command that riveted all and forced them to stand in silence. It reached the guards below, who stopped their grisly work and looked to the torchlit deck. The men on the deck backed away from the man Michael confronted, as if he carried a curse.

"You heard my words." Michael shouted. "Begone! Such as you are not fit to stand among men."

Michael held the man with his gaze, and the man turned with a nervous cry and fled below deck.

Michael stood for a moment and surveyed the men. None dared return his gaze. The three brothers of Mord Rinn were silent. What had been said could be viewed as heresy. But they had the sense not to state it, for all could see that a number of men stood behind Michael and what he had just said. Daniel's hand lay on the hilt of his ax. For a long moment there was silence, then without another word. Michael went forward to stand alone in the navigator's box. He didn't notice the small group of men who took positions behind him. ready to challenge any who dared to defy him.

As he passed the helmsman's booth his gaze fell upon Gareth and Halvin. They looked at one another for a moment, and in silence he passed on. He would know soon enough the results of his actions.

The harbor gate loomed up out of the darkness, the only forewarning of its approach the two small fires that marked the safe channel that had to be passed in single file. Far ahead of the fleet the light schooners spread out to feel their way across the ice and look for signs of danger. That night their task was even more difficult, for the night was overcast and there was no star or Arch to steer by.

As the fleet cleared the harbor, Michael stood upon the prow and, looking back along the deck of the *Thunderwind*, watched Mathin's lights disappear into the gathering darkness. His thoughts strayed far—over all that he had found and lost in the last week. Try as he might, it was impossible to forget that only a few hours ago he had held Janis in his arms.

He looked into the darkness and prayed for an answer. He knew that if only a sign would appear he would grasp it, believe in it, and return to Holy Church.

There was nothing.

CHAPTER 10

THE LANTERN BOBBED AND WEAVED AS THEY HIT A PATCH
of rough ice. All of them were tense. Running an ice cruiser
at night was an exacting and dangerous business so far south.

Gareth watched as the lantern swayed back and forth, casting
its shadows on the other four men in the room. How could he
ever tell them? How could he ever explain the dreadful nightmare that had swept through him again last night. The Table
had been there as before, the rejection certain, and then had
come the moment of shock, the moment of revelation that he
had half suspected but now knew as truth.

As he fell from the Heavens, that long terrible fall into
darkness, the Saints had parted the mist. He plummeted to
Earth, a rejected soul bound for damnation, yet they had let
him see. Eyes wide with terror, he watched, and there upon
the Ice was Michael Ormson. Michael was the cause of his
damnation.

"Brother Gareth, are you with us?" came the sinister voice
concealed behind the burgundy robes.

He looked up.

"Yes, yes, of course I am with you."

"You've known him better than anyone else aboard this ship, at least from the brotherhoods. Tell me your opinion on this."

Gareth was torn with fear—fear of the dream that drove him to the edge of insanity, and the fear of Zimri if his orders concerning Michael were not carried out.

He sat in silence for a moment. What was Halvin's design in this? Everyone knew that Halvin was a close friend to the boy's uncle. Gareth maneuvered for an opening.

"I am a simple warrior priest, and not a searcher for the Holy Truth in others. I must therefore refer the question back to you and the brothers of Mord Rinn."

The three monks sat in the darkness, their hooded forms barely visible.

"St. Regis, chapter seventeen, verse one: 'And the infidel shall die by the sword of Truth,'" the tallest of the three whispered.

"What our good brother Druce has said means that this deacon of St. Awstin, this Michael Ormson, had defied the Holy Word of St. Regis in denying the task of destroying the infidels."

Gareth looked to Halvin, expecting some defense for Michael. He knew that the grounds for a heresy accusal were slim. If any spirited defense was offered, the case would be a hard one, since they were dealing with no ordinary man, but with an archbiship's nephew. But all knew they were dealing with a man who was starting to think differently—and it was the job of the Mord Rinn to stop such infections before they could spread.

"He is a brother of St. Awstin and, as such, deserves the opportunity to prove his innocence," said the leader of the Mord Rinn.

"We therefore have the choice of trial by Inquisition or trial by Ordeal," the third priest said. He had remained silent until then.

The leader of the three spoke again in his soft, hissing voice. "A trial by Inquisition at such a time would be inopportune. He has a following already and such events take time. A ship is not a place for such dealings. Therefore I recommend serving the Good Church and redeeming his soul at the same time. Which, of course, is the goal of our brotherhood."

"You mean the ram," Gareth said coldly.

"Yes, brother."

Gareth did not resist. "This then is your decision, a decision by the brothers of Mord Rinn?"

The three brothers were silent.

"It is not our decision," the leader said, "since this is no Inquisition. It is the Will of the Saints to decide; the responsibility of no order. Since the rams are weapons aboard a Morian ship, it must be you who make the offer."

"That I must disagree with," Gareth replied.

"Then of course we would have to go with the Inquisition, because you refuse our good brother Ormson the opportunity to prove his innocence," Druce said sarcastically.

Gareth knew what the Inquisition could bring. Several days of questionings was demanded, then three times on the rack if there was any doubt or if the prisoner refused to recant. All could then be laid on Mor's doorstep. The ram would be quicker, easier, and the soul of the alleged heretic would be saved, as well. And most important, the nightmares would end at last.

"If the good brothers of Mord Rinn insist, then so it shall be. I will offer him the choice of the ram."

"We only requested, good Gareth."

Gareth was silent for a moment.

"So shall I report it to Zimri upon my return, that the Council of Inquisition met and decided upon this course for the salvation of his soul."

The brazier was brought forth, the three cups of incense were burned, and all arose.

"What about those other two? The ones whom we have heard are followers of his?" the leader of Mord Rinn asked.

"The one is crippled and has been sent home. I doubt he'll survive passage. The other is on ship."

"I'm concerned about his soul, as well," the priest said. Then the three of them left.

Halvin and Gareth were alone. Each was silent, each glad

that at last the confrontation was over. The nightmares would end, the dream would come closer. They sat in silence as the ship sailed through the night.

As expected, the messenger had come, and before the last chant of morning prayers had ended, Michael made his way to Gareth's cabin. Without a word Gareth beckoned to the board, and Michael sat in silence across from the priest and they played their usual game. Gareth's defense was weak and Michael pressed the advantage.

"Brother Gareth, your game is off this morning."

Gareth looked up but did not reply.

Michael picked up a ram piece from the board and examined it closely. "I've been chosen," Michael said as he gazed unblinkingly across the board into Gareth's eyes.

"Yes."

"Because you've come to fear me."

Gareth was silent.

"I never wanted anything more than to be left alone. Why did all of you have to drag me into your struggles?"

Gareth looked away from Michael. "Michael, I am only a pawn, like you."

"Sacrifice the pawn to capture the bishop, is that it?"

"The Mord Rinn decree that you shall have the choice of trial by Inquisition or trial by Ordeal—with the ram as your means."

The ram... The memory came of the first night alone on the Ice. If anything, the ram would atone for his sins. He smiled at the thought. If he truly wanted to return to the Church, this could be his way. No matter what sins he had committed, the ram would wash them away with his blood and give him release as well.

"You're of the Church, and your blood is that of the Church, so the ram is offered. Die upon it, Michael, for the sake of us all."

"Ride the ram, and do not return," Michael whispered.

"Yes."

There was silence as both considered the path before them.

"Daniel is to go with you. as well." Gareth said evenly.

"Why? He's only a friend."

"A friend and an apostle—and we need no apostles after you are gone."

Michael nodded. He knew that to argue Daniel's innocence was meaningless.

"You can inform Daniel. if you wish. See the master of the Death Rams and he shall give you your robes and instruction. From now on you are bound by Holy Tradition. You may eat and drink your fill, but to no man other than a fellow initiate or a Morian priest may you speak. If you successfully ram a ship and survive. then the Ordeal has ended and you are judged innocent by the Saints. If you survive and fail to ram. you shall be left upon the ice to die. To violate any of the traditions shall result in your death and the disgrace of your family." Gareth placed a special emphasis on the last statement.

"Farewell, Michael Ormson, and may we meet again at the Long Table and rejoice in the Everlasting Feast." Gareth pulled up his cowl to cover his face.

Gareth began the ceremonial blessing. "Rejoice. my son. for soon you shall feast at the Table of the Saints. Rejoice. my son. for the sorrows of the world shall pass away from thee since you are the Select. the Holy One of Divine Mission. Rejoice. my son. as you embrace sweet death. the Release from the Cold. the Release from the Ice Forever."

Gareth looked at the door as it closed in front of him. and then to the table. The white ram piece was crushed: alongside it was the marker of the Blue Master.

That evening the nightmare did not return.

The long day passed, and with the sounding of the second horn of the morning watch most of the hands were on deck to look to the sacred platform on the sterncastle. The two had come out of the chapel door and they wore the sacred marks of their fate—the black cowl and cape with the blood-red trim. The mark of Ruither de Marbth—the Runners of Death. All knew them, though the cowls covered their faces. giving them a deathly visage. They joined the others who were so marked.

and stood in silence and waited. The crew was silent, and many made the sign of blessing, for some took Michael's presence among the Select to be a sign.

For Michael there was a strange fascination with the fact that he had been removed at last. The wild dreams of Seth were insignificant, a crazy errand lost forever in a distant, dreamlike world that no longer existed. The long afternoon passed, and Michael sat with Death.

As the day continued the wind dropped, so that by sunset it was nothing more than a faint breeze that pushed the ships at less than three leagues per hour. Passing under the great ice mountain that had enthralled the crew the week before, Halvin ordered the dumping of the ice blocks. The smallest of the armed merchantmen came about into the wind.

"Ah, they are Ruither de Marbth as well," one of the men next to Michael whispered.

Halvin stood upon the forecastle and watched as the ship turned into the wind, her men cheering him as the *Thunderwind* drifted past. Those with any foresight knew what awaited them before dawn, yet they cheered Halvin nevertheless. Michael marveled at their cries.

As soon as the merchantman came to a halt the men started to swarm over her side. Before darkness fell they would have a barricade of blocks and trenches set up across the channel. With any luck this tactic would net two, maybe even three ships in return if the Ezrians pursued at night. It would delay the pursuit by an hour or two, as well. The rest of the fleet pushed on, leaving a small part of itself as sacrifice.

The prayers came late that night, and the priests grumbled and said that it boded ill. Halvin had pushed his men until, finally, not even the sharpest of sight could see the difference between the black and white thread, the traditional sign that the first watch of night should commence. Halvin felt lucky, believing that he had eluded pursuit. The order was given to halt the sail. It was still another two hours, though, before he felt satisfied with the defense and ordered the crews to stand fast for Holy Service.

During the night Michael watched above deck while all

around him men slept, exhausted after the day and a half of running. With the first coming of dawn he stood up and faced the light in the southeast. He watched its crimson flame then turned his gaze southward. No other eyes looked where his now did, and he alone saw the brief rise of light, and the darkness that closed down again. He looked back to the flame that chased away the last light of the Sacred Arch, and the red sky spoke of sails and flame to sweep across the Ice in the day to come. The trap had been sprung.

CHAPTER 11

As the fourth hour of day passed, the ice broadened and soon the Broken Tracks fell astern of the fleet. It was good clean ice that ran beneath the fleet, and the men laughed and cheered as more canvas was inched unto the yards and the ships danced across the Frozen Sea. The tension of the last two days melted away, so that even the ram pilots started to smile to themselves.

The wind blew fair and strong out of the south. The crews settled back into the daily routine, with most of the men going below to sleep between watches.

Michael and Daniel found themselves alone upon the sterncastle as the plumes of snow and ice kicked up by the *Thunderwind* swirled and billowed behind them.

Daniel turned to Michael and watched him closely.

"Aye, Michael, you seem unhappy at our luck. Why, we've cheated them off, we have. That Halvin is still a rare good one."

Michael was silent.

"What is it, Michael?" Daniel asked as he lowered his voice in an anxious tone.

"We haven't escaped," Michael said softly.

"What do you mean?"

"It's over with. Prepare yourself."

Michael was silent again and would not answer any of Daniel's questions.

Eastward they ran on a beam reach. The day progressed with the sky clear and the wind full and hard. The sails were taut with the pressure, and as the sun climbed heavenward the men on deckside duty sat behind the barriers and enjoyed the warmth of the Southern Ice.

Michael felt detached as he watched the men mingling on deck. It's fascinating, Michael thought, how we dream our dreams of immortality and deny death. How good it is that we usually know not the hour of our passing—and what torture it is when we do know. How the unknowing waste and laugh their way through their existence as those men below are doing now. They will be dead before nightfall, yet they skylark and laugh while I am tortured. He looked across the ice, the torment filling him.

He could feel the trap closing in and the lives of all around him ticking away their final brief moments. A burst of laughter from the foredeck drifted back with the wind. He was terrified to the point where he could barely conceal his shaking. He wished the agony was over with, and he cursed his second sight, which had given him the brief glimpse of what this day would bring.

From an eternity away the cry came down from above.

"Deck ho . . . Deck ho, the *St. Almarth*, she's coming about."

Michael was torn from his thoughts as a shock passed through the crew. The men stood up and raced to the rail, looking to the southeast, where they knew the frigate was running, just visible on the horizon.

The tiny, toylike sails were lined up at a right angle to the *Thunderwind*, and turned as the ship completed her jibe and made for the flagship of the fleet.

The maneuver of the *St. Almarth* was warning enough; even before the command was given some of the men went below to put on their armor. Long moments of silence passed as the

Thunderwind's crew waited in anticipation. All eyes were upon Halvin as he went forward and stood by the helmsman's box. A series of signal flags could be seen from the *St. Almarth*'s mizzentop, but even before the signal flags were readable the three lookouts from above gave voice.

"Deck ho! Sails on the horizon. Nor'east to southeast. Six . . . eight . . . at least a dozen!"

Halvin, throwing aside any pretext of dignity, ran to the foretop stays, and with an agility amazing for a man of his years and injuries, he scurried aloft. There was a chance that the ships were merely a fleet belonging to Sol, but the behavior of the *St. Almarth* spoke against this.

Halvin gained the foretop and hung on the ratlines outside the lookout's cabin, braving the wind to catch a better view. His hood was pulled back and his shoulder-length hair streamed behind him in the morning breeze. His voice boomed down from above.

"Deck ho! Come about there. Come about west by northwest. Signal all ships to prepare for battle." His voice rose up with a fury as he cried, "All hands prepare for battle."

Halvin swung himself off the foretop and, grabbing hold of a line, lowered himself. Reaching the deck, he ran back to his post alongside the helmsman's box. Far astern, Michael stood with the Select and watched as the opening act of the battle was laid out before him like a vast, magnificent play.

Even before Halvin had hit the deck the helmsman started to put the wheel over. Plumes of spray shot up from the upwind runners as the pressure increased on the blades. The craft reared and canted upward, so that Michael had to grab the railing to keep his balance. From the hatchways the crew poured forth as the great horns sounded below, rousing the men to their duty. Men swarmed to the rigging, some going aloft to prepare the fighting tops, others to trim the sails for the new heading. Boarding nets were brought up and the catapults were prepared for action. After a quarter mile of turning, the ship faced the eye of the wind and her massive bulk slammed down on all the runners. She hesitated for a second, then swung past the eye—with an explosive roar her sails bellied outward and raised the ship upward on the opposite tack. The sail crews swarmed across the deck, trimming the canvas and adjusting the booms to the chants and curses of their captains.

Across the ice, the enemy sails were already visible on the horizon, their blue and gray colors a certain sign that they were ships of the Ezrian church's fleet. Nearly a dozen were already in view, and the lookouts kept calling out the sightings of even more sails as the enemy pressed to the attack.

From port to starboard all could see the rest of the fleet as it turned. The *St. Almarth* was astern and to port, but slowly gaining. The rest of the fleet was spread out in a vast circle surrounding the *Thunderwind*. The four light schooners and small escort ships taken in Mathin started to drop astern to act as a screen. Halvin was already regretting his decision to send the captured merchantmen and corsair homeward with the booty and the wounded. They would have been valuable as decoys to throw astern.

Immediate concerns taken care of, the fleet settled down to the long race. The Cornathians had managed to avoid the trap, but Halvin had been second-guessed, and this had a disquieting effect on the crew.

Michael had seen the charts and could visualize the race that was being run. The Ezrians had run to the next pass in the Ice and cut in front of his route. Coming about, the Cornathian fleet had a clear run on the Ice for the next hundred and fifty miles. If they kept that heading they would squeeze past the southern end of St. Judean's Bane—the smoking hell that Zardok had spoken of with a reverent fear. Once clear of the bane, they could swing northward between the bane and the Forbidden Lands, then streak onward to safety. If the Cornathians tried to run due north, the Ezrians would have the wind abeam, while the fleet ran on the slower heading of wind astern—the enemy would quickly catch up. The race with the bane as barrier was the only way to shake the enemy. It was going to be a long one, and the crew settled down after the initial excitement. The knowledgeable ones on the between decks explained the strategy to their friends and confidence was slowly restored. Michael drew his robes around himself and waited.

During the first hour of the chase the Ezrian admiral sent his fastest frigates and corsairs on a more northerly tack in order to gain a downwind position, thus cutting off any escape in that direction. Halvin ordered the *Snow Wind* to move in and screen the northern approach in anticipation of attack from that direction, but the assault never came. The enemy refused to close or launch its rams, and the Cornathians grew uneasy and started to question the strategy. Halvin paced on the deck like a cornered bear, and his anxiety was visible to all as he tried to guess the next move of the superior enemy force.

"Deck ho!" a shout echoed down from above. "Deck ho. Sails . . . six, eight of them bearing dead ahead, running straight toward us."

Halvin ran across the deck and again scrambled aloft. No sooner had he gained the foretop when his voice thundered across the deck.

"Frigates and a cruiser, damn their pox-eaten souls."

Halvin clenched the ropes with a fierceness that whitened his knuckles. "Fire and hell, I curse thee," he screamed hysterically. "Away all rams, away all rams. Signal the fleet to run northwest."

His commands drifted into incoherent screams as he lowered himself back to the deck.

The trap had been sprung at last. The enemy had split their superior fleet and sent almost two-thirds of it down to the next channel in the Ice, where it cut in front of the Cornathians. Turning about, the Cornathians had run back down to where the other third of the Ezrian fleet awaited them.

From out of the shadows of the sacristy the brothers of Mor marched, one of them carrying two leather-bound hammers and another a round brass drum as large as a full-grown man. Cluigin de Marbth, it was called, the Ring of Death, and its sounding was the call to the Ruither de Marbth. Behind them came three more brothers carrying Adharchin de Beannach, the Horn of Blessing. Harwinth, the mightiest of all the brothers in the fleet, gave wind to it, and its low, booming tone shook

all on ship and set up a chilling vibration that set men's teeth
on edge. The drum started its steady, rolling beat that would
continue through the rest of the battle, as the rams went to their
doom. Together their song was the call to Death.

The Chosen Ones ran to their assigned rams. Michael turned
and looked to Daniel. Defying all tradition, he walked to Daniel's side and threw his arms around him.

"This is where it ends at last, Daniel. My blessing upon
you."

Daniel pulled him back and looked at him gravely. "You
are the Chosen. You will survive." And then, in a voice that
was barely a whisper, he said, "To the Broken Tracks."

The horn sounded again and a brother came up to Michael
and touched him on the shoulder. Michael turned to face him.
It was Gareth. Michael started to speak, but the cold look in
Gareth's eyes and the hand outstretched in a sign of silence
stilled Michael's comment. Together, they walked across the
deck to the starboard stern railing. They looked into each other's
eyes for a moment, and Michael could see that he was looking
into the eyes of madness.

"This is the fulfillment of your dream, Gareth," Michael
whispered as he lowered himself over the outrigger boom.
Gareth looked at him with terrified eyes then fled back to the
bow of the ship.

Several crew members were ahead of Michael, preparing to
raise the single mast. Michael made his way out to them and
threw his additional weight onto the lines. The mast broke free
of its icy frame and rose up to be stepped into its socket. The
Thunderwind hit a patch of rough ice and turned into the wind
to avoid the worst of the outcropping. The outrigger rocked
and groaned with the strain as the ship rose up and hiked on
its downwind runner. Michael had never seen the ship heel
from this vantage point, and he stood in awe as the giant bulk
of the three-hundred-foot ship hovered above him.

Michael heard a stifled scream as one of the men farther
forward lost his footing and slipped off the outrigger to the ice
below. Rolling with the blow, he tumbled out and away from
the ship with a scream of anguish. The man regained his footing

while holding his broken shoulder. No one turned, no schooner would sweep him up. He was the first casualty of the battle.

Michael turned back to his ram and watched as the crew slammed the steel bolts into the socket that would brace the mast in place and secure the stays to the forward outriggers. The men grabbed the halyard, and with a mighty pull the sail broke free and was quickly run aloft. One of the men shouted to Michael that all was ready and Michael jumped aboard the swinging oak trunk. He scurried astern to the pilot's compartment and squeezed inside.

He noted that the boom cleared his head by less than a foot as he stretched himself up to look over the top of the ram. He kicked the rudder blades and they gave smoothly on their greased pivots. Grabbing the sail sheet, he checked to make sure that the rope ran full and easy on its block and tackles.

The sails were secure and the outriggers were locked into place, and all down the starboard side of the *Thunderwind* the rams were ready for launching. He felt alone and frightened. His heart pounded with such force that he thought it would kill him. To divert himself, he adjusted his parka and goggles and pulled his ceremonial black robes tighter, making sure that no flesh was exposed to possible frostbite. Looking to the deck, he saw that many of the men had stopped their tasks to watch the launch. He swept them with his gaze and some nodded. His eyes settled upon the forecastle as he awaited the rising of the starboard black flag, the signal to launch. He could hear the booming of the drum and the low, steady moan of the horn. Michael raised his left arm to signal that he was ready and a priest on deck acknowledged him with a wave of a small black pennant.

The *Thunderwind* started to keel over again, and ran directly into the eye of the wind. Michael gripped the sheet with both hands, his feet firmly braced on the tiller board. A flag casing shot up on the starboard signal line and broke free to reveal the dreaded signal — the black flag with a silver hand embossed upon it.

The three assistants sprang into action and with a hearty cheer seized the lowering lines as the *Thunderwind* continued

her turn. Michael felt the ram drop, then, with a high, grating
whine, the skates touched the ice. Mounted on the side of the
ram was a round, blue knob that Michael reached out for and
yanked with all his might. The knob jerked back, releasing the
three pins that cut the ram from the lowering lines. Michael
kicked the tiller hard over, with a dizzying swing the ram arched
off and away from the *Thunderwind*. Within seconds he was
free and astern of the great ship.

The wind bellied out the sail as Michael put the tiller over
and back in gentle pulls to get the feel of the craft. Still drifting
into the eye of the wind, he eased the tiller over and the ram
drifted into a starboard tack. With a snapping roar the wind
raked the sail out and Michael could feel the raw pull of speed
as the ram started to skate across the Frozen Sea.

A dull, rumbling vibration ran through him then quickly
smoothed out as the ram accelerated across the frozen, howling
wind. The other rams were clear as well, and strung out in a
long, diagonal path as the *Thunderwind* turned away from the
wind and swung back onto her regular course. The launching
had taken just over a minute, but in that minute the enemy
ships had loomed ever larger ahead. From astern, a small Cornathian schooner shot past, maneuvering to protect the *Thunderwind* from Ezrian rams. After several minutes of running,
Michael slowly overtook the *Thunderwind*. Along with a half-
dozen other rams they formed into a loose attack formation.

The fleet was running north by northwest, while the Ezrians
were forming up into three distinct groups—three points of a
triangle with the Cornathians in the center. Running due north
of the Cornathians and on a westerly heading were a half-dozen
frigates, several corsairs, and a light cruiser. Directly ahead
lay the Ezrian group that had followed them and run the barriers
that Halvin had set. They numbered five frigates, a cruiser,
and several merchantmen and schooners. Directly astern of the
Cornathians was the main van of the enemy—two cruisers and
a host of armed merchantmen.

If Halvin turned north to fight the frigates, he would be at
a slower sailing angle and the enemy astern would close in.
He couldn't turn into the eye of the wind, and even if he could,

he would pin himself against the Broken Tracks. If he engaged the fleet ahead, his fleet formation would fall apart in the action and the enemy would pick them off. His only hope was to try and cut between the frigates to the north and the intervening fleet to the west.

As the pursuit dragged on, a point of smoke grew on the horizon—St. Judean's Bane. Halvin was running between two jaws that with every passing moment were slowly squeezing in, and when they closed, the enemy strength from astern would rush in for the kill.

The echo of thunder rolled across the wind as the *Snow Wind* and an Ezrian frigate traded shots at extreme range. As the volume of noise increased, Michael and the rest of the ram pilots sped toward the opening encounter.

The enemy frigates from the west and north started to swing in and Michael watched the *Snow Wind* exchange volleys with two ships of equal strength. Occasionally an errant shot bounded back from the battle and skipped through the ram group, disappearing southward across the ice.

The armed merchantman *Mawr Thona* charged into short range of an enemy frigate, and a boiling cloud of smoke gushed out from her side, while from her deck a rain of burning shot slammed forth to be joined by the whistle of crossbow and ballista bolts. The enemy's foremast snapped at the foretop into a tangled confusion of wreckage, but the enemy frigate still had a fight in her, for the pilot slammed his vessel up against the *Mawr Thona*. The Ezrians let go with a blazing sheet of bolts and cannon fire that swept the *Thona*'s deck and turned it into a bloody hell of deadly splinters and flaming sails. The two ships locked together as grappling lines snaked out and boarding crews swarmed down the outriggers and fought on the booms, while their comrades in the riggings continued to rain forth their deadly hail.

An enemy merchantman tried to pass the *Mawr Thona* on her windward side, but as she pulled abeam, the two engaged ships swung wildly out of control and slammed into the bow of the new attacker, shearing its bowsprit and crushing the starboard outrigger. The attacking ship broke away, spinning out of control while the two other ships, hopelessly tangled, drifted into the eye of the wind and slowly came to a stop.

Within minutes Michael overtook the crippled ships and passed them to windward. The ice was aswarm with men who poured from their craft to fall upon their foes. Michael saw several Ezrians hold a prisoner down while a Horthian priest hacked his chest open to remove the beating heart. Several arrows and a ballista shot arched outward, but none found their mark as the rams whisked past the bloodied ice. The crippled merchantman tried to swing back into the fight by pursuing the rams, but her crushed outrigger and missing jibs soon left her far astern, her pilot steering wide to avoid the *Thunderwind* and its escort.

Michael knew that the Cornathian merchantmen and frigates were in a wedge formation to the front, trading shots with the enemy while the slower ships kept pace with the *Thunderwind*, which rode a half-mile astern. For the moment, at least, the Cornathian rams were between the two halves. But from the north a new situation was developing—the Ezrian rams were coming into view.

An ice battle can develop with deadly swiftness, but it can also rage for hours across thousands of square miles of ice. The first brush left the crippled ships astern, and for the next ten leagues the two sides traded shots at long range. The two Ezrian wings could not get in front of the fleet since the Cornathians were sailing at the best possible angle to the wind. The only action possible then was to run the same heading.

As the minutes passed, the direction of the heading became more and more ominous as the sky from the west to north was slowly obscured by a black, boiling cloud. The fleets approached St. Judean's Bane, the place where the Saint had fallen a hundred years ago, leaving a boiling rent in the earth. Halvin had wanted to pass south of this place, but the enemy was driving them straight into it.

Morning had long since passed, and the afternoon waned as the Ezrians dogged the flanks but refused to close. The sun drifted behind the darkness that rose up to meet the fleet with the beckoning of death. Halvin grimly hung to his course, hoping that the enemy would break off first and he could then ride the edge of the bane to freedom. The entire sky from horizon to horizon became a boiling mass of darkness and the men on the foretops could clearly see the flaming island of St. Judean. As they drew closer, the sea started to turn foul with rotten ice and ash-covered floes.

Both the Ezrians and the Cornathians broke away at almost the exact same instant and ran north by northeast. One of the enemy schooners hesitated, and the ship hooked into a patch of rotten ice, flipping over on its side, crushing its crew.

Looking back to the *Thunderwind*, Michael could see the signal pennants flying.

"Run northeast, engage, and break out."

Even as he watched, the *Thunderwind* came hard over with towers of icy spray kicking up from her stern as she made a valiant attempt to run across the bows of the pursuing cruisers, and from there head out onto the open ice.

Michael kicked his tiller over to follow in the wake of the *Thunderwind*. A voice began to whisper to him, "Live, Michael, live. There's so much yet to be done. Don't waste it here."

He hesitated as he watched the horror of the battle unfolding beneath the shadow of the Bane. The oily darkness that reached to heaven was matched by rolling clouds of cannon smoke and the pyres of flaming ships. A slow, steady roar rumbled across the Ice—it sounded like the ending of the world.

His hand rested on the release knob as he struggled with his thoughts. It's madness, he thought. Madness, yet he could feel a strange fascination as he watched the battle rage around him. He was in a ram of the Select and it was all over. If he died and the Church was True, then tonight, despite his doubts, he would be at the Long Table. He was afraid of death, but he was more afraid of living. His hand drew away from the release knob.

The ice around Michael exploded with a howling roar of iron and spray. An enemy frigate had swung in behind him and at less than a hundred yards had let fly with a volley. Three of the eight rams running with Michael crumpled and rolled over, throwing the pilots out and crushing them in the wreckage. Two rams swerved, crossed Michael's bow, and charged in to attack, shouting for the Saints to witness their deaths.

The pilots guided their steel-tipped weapons straight at the enemy frigate. Another volley thundered as the rams dodged and weaved their way through the splintering ice. As Michael and the rest of the pilots drifted away from the encounter, they watched the frigate pour a rain of arrows and shot, which slammed into the ice around the attacking rams. One of the sleds detached and pulled over to port while the ram continued on its course. As the pilot released, the frigate rose up on its starboard outriggers and shifted to port. A beautiful column of spray shot up under the pressure of the blades and reflected against the towering darkness beyond.

The ram passed astern of the frigate and continued on its way. The second ram lined up for the attack, but out of the frigate's spray a small schooner cut in front of the ram while its archers pinned the pilot to his seat with a deadly hail of arrows. The ram continued toward the Bane and disappeared from view.

In a parting act of vengeance, the frigate aimed straight at the ram pilot who was still skidding across the ice. In a graceful display of speed and movement, the frigate weaved from side to side, like a snake running down its prey. The ram pilot desperately tried to evade, but the steel blades of the frigate caught him at last with a crushing blow that cut the Cornathian in half while his sled disintegrated beneath him. The frigate pushed on.

Searing volleys thundered and rolled, while ahead the enemy rams moved in on the Cornathian flagship. Halvin pulled the tiller over and swung out on the same heading as the rams. The two schooners escorting him came hard about and crossed behind the *Thunderwind* to rake the rams with arrows and small ballista shot. Halvin ran southeast for a half-mile, straight at the main force of the enemy fleet, then he pushed the tiller over to turn into the eye of the wind. This maneuver pointed him straight at Michael's group. From the *Thunderwind*'s side a volley of grapeshot was fired into the enemy rams. Michael desperately weaved to avoid the enemy rams and the fire from the Cornathian ship.

From astern of Michael the *Snow Wind* of Cornath came up to lend her aid. Half of the enemy rams decided to break away from the cruiser to try their luck on the smaller craft. The *Snow Wind*, seeing the danger, swung hard over as the pilots released at two hundred yards. Believing that all the Ezrians had released, the *Snow Wind*'s captain brought his ship around in an arc to come up on a course behind the *Thunderwind*.

It was a fatal mistake. One pilot had kicked his sled free but he still rode behind the trunk of the ram. He had become Feywarth, the Doom Seeker, and he knew his work. He pushed his tiller over and tightened the main sheet.

Had she been the old *Snow Wind* escape might have been possible, but the blades were not aligned and as she rose on the damaged outrigger the ship bucked and pulled. They collided as the ram pilot stood atop the log and laughed as he rode to his doom. The horrified Cornathians screamed in rage as the ram sliced through the portside outrigger and slashed into the bottom of the ship, ripping out the keel and smashing the foremast socket. Skidding across the ice at sixty miles an hour, the ship broke apart, her mast snapped, the sails and rigging collapsed. Tons of wreckage slammed onto the disintegrating deck, pinning and crushing the crews. Terrified men screamed out their lives as they fell from the fighting tops to the rock-hard ice below. With a terrible grinding roar the *Snow Wind* went over on its side, its heavy guns smashing through the sides of the ship, crushing the gun crews trapped below. The ship burst as the magazine exploded—the wreckage of the *Snow Wind* rose heavenward and rained down across a quarter mile of ice.

Any semblance of fleet action soon disappeared as every ship fought for survival. The armed merchantmen were hunted down, while the lone surviving frigate was engaged several leagues to the north in a vain attempt to break free of several Ezrian ships. The main action centered on the *Thunderwind* as she twisted and turned upon the ice like a stag fighting off the encircling wolves. Two of the enemy cruisers closed with the

Thunderwind, and every minute a third of a ton of iron was hurled from the *Thunderwind*'s guns, to be answered by twice that weight in return. Whole sections of deck and hull were shot away. Sails collapsed with tons of rigging, which rained down to crush the deck crew below. Bloodied bodies, many still living, were tossed from the deck to keep the ship cleared, and Michael raced past their twisted, squirming forms as he pushed onward into hell.

From out of the smoke and fire, at a distance of only half a mile, Michael saw one of the enemy cruisers swing about to make another pass on the *Thunderwind*. Michael braced himself and set a course that would converge on his foe. The seconds passed and the ship drew nigh. He looked over his shoulder for a moment and thought that he saw Daniel swinging in to join him in the assault. He could imagine the frantic crew aboard the cruiser as the rams pressed the assault. A shot screamed by, holing Michael's sail, and another tore a furrow of ice to starboard.

Daniel! Michael watched in horror as Daniel's ram swung wildly off course, one of its starboard outriggers sheared off by a shot. The ram hung on the edge of tumbling and disappeared into the smoke. Daniel was gone, and Michael grimly pushed on. Another enemy ram pilot, seeing the peril to the flagship, swung directly in front of Michael to take the blow. Michael hesitated, hoping to bluff him off. Finally, with a hard kick, Michael pulled the ram out and away from the attack. The enemy pilot skidded up and bumped against Michael's outrigger. They eased off from each other, not ten feet separating the rival pilots. Michael looked over to the Ezrian, who like himself was dressed in black. The pilot looked back and gave Michael a playful wave. Then pulling hard over, he came about to go in against the *Thunderwind*. Michael smiled and waved back as the enemy was quickly lost in the confusion of battle.

The ice was littered in all directions with the sections of decking, smashed guns, scorched sails, lengths of rigging, torn bodies, and burning wreckage, around which men fought and grappled. From the center of the battle came hundreds of round shot that rolled for leagues in every direction. The ice was carpeted with bodies, most of them twisted in the impossible forms that only the dead could hold. Some were rolling or twisting in agony, while others staggered in shock, blindly making their way to nowhere.

Schooners darted across the ice to give aid or ruthlessly track down the fleeing. Michael passed some of the schooners' handiwork—men cut in half by razor-sharp blades or bodies that had been pinned with arrows. From a distance he could see a Cornathian schooner that had roped some Ezrians and was dragging their broken bodies across the ice. No quarter was given that day.

The enemy was keeping control of the situation. With each desperate turn the *Thunderwind* found enemy ships across every line of retreat, and the pressure inexorably pushed the *Thunderwind* closer and closer to the Bane.

The Cornathian rams had all been expended, except for Michael's and one other. From the enemy command cruiser a series of large and brightly colored pennants broke out. Out of the southwest the rest of the Ezrian fleet, which had stood in reserve, swung from their holding position and moved in for the final attack. It was the last blow to end a long and bloody day. It was obvious to Michael the course that he had to take.

Adjusting his tiller, he started a series of rapid tacks that after several minutes brought him a half a league south of his original position. Bracing the ram over, he started a straight run on a southwesterly heading. The other pilot took up the lead, and since his sail was not holed, he was soon several hundred yards ahead and upwind.

The two forces converged, closing at over eighty miles an hour, and as the wind gusted and shifted a point to the east, the speed suddenly leaped up to over a hundred miles an hour. Neither side diverted from its course. The enemy schooners arched out to either side then swung in on a converging course to shower Michael and his companion with bolts and shot. The heavy ballista on one of the schooners fired with a deadly efficiency and with vision-blurring impact her bolt slammed into Michael's ram directly in front of the pilot's box. Lighter arrows whistled past, holing the sail and striking like quills into the ram and pilot's box. He could hear the jeers and curses of the Ezrians as the schooners roared past and came about in an attempt to track him down and finish off the last Cornathian rams.

One of the armed merchantmen streaked ahead of the Ezrian cruiser and her guns came into play as shot and arrows roared past Michael. The other two merchantmen of the reserve force came to the attack as well, and let fly with all of their guns as they swung outward to loosen their broadsides. Their act sealed the fate of their command ship.

The smoke of forty guns rolled and eddied across the ice and the first ram shot through it and disappeared from Michael's view. Directly ahead, Michael could see the sails of the giant ice cruiser bearing down from a range of less than half a mile. Seeing the first ram, the cruiser turned to port; the first ram whisked past as its pilot released, and the cruiser came back onto its original heading. The smoke rushed up on Michael, and he sailed into it and ran blind. The cruiser had reacted to the first ram, and in the swirling confusion of smoke, the captain thought the second ram had been destroyed. The range was less than a quarter mile and they were heading straight at each other.

Michael burst out of the smoke, and directly before him was the enemy cruiser, with the black sky of St. Judean's Bane boiling up behind. The giant ship rose up out of a swirling, flaming madness of night that reached out to engulf him.

The world froze to a maddening slowness as the giant loomed closer and closer. He smiled; the dreams of Seth were all over with; the cloister and the memories of Rifton tugged at him as he pushed on. The range was down to two hundred yards as the cruiser started to react to his attack. He knew he would hit and he stayed with his ram. Salvation was assured.

It was over, Mathin was gone... *Janis*—the memory screamed at him. Before he even understood his action, he pulled his feet up and hit the release knob. The sky beyond flared up as St. Judean's Bane burned and roared in the darkening afternoon, silhouetting the cruiser that desperately tried to veer away from him.

As he released the lever the sled fell backward and slammed onto the ice, almost flipping on impact. Shifting his weight, he leaned with savage desperation to keep the ram upright. The world was a roaring confusion of madness as the ram shot away. The ship loomed higher and higher, so that it engulfed the entire world.

"My God, I'll hit!" he screamed, and closed his eyes as the giant blade of the outrigger bore down upon him. There was a roaring explosion of wood, ice, and steel. The blade lifted above him as if to crush out his life, then it was past. Looking over his shoulder in dumb amazement, he watched as the giant reared off the ice—its masts rocking, the stays snapping and flailing. He heard the screams of half a thousand men locked in terror as the climax of death came to them.

He had released too soon, and his ram had not hit the body of the ship but sheared into the ship's port outrigger instead, taking off the portside steering blade, which was bearing the pressure of the turn. The ship weaved erratically as one of the schooners came out of the smoke in search of Michael. The Ezrian cruiser, weaving out of control, cut in front of the schooner's path and the small ship impacted into its master's side, completing the damage that Michael had started. The bow of the cruiser lifted off the ice as the schooner crumbled underneath.

The front of the cruiser smashed back onto the ice, its outriggers collapsing under the impact. Then ever so slowly, the ship collapsed in upon itself as it reacted to the rules of wind, friction, and ice. The front end of the ship dragged its split bow across the ice, sending up a hundred-foot shower of spray, which rained back down to the flaming deck. The ship skidded away to its death.

He was alive. Alive, and a mile away from the final death agony of the Ezrian cruiser. There was no exhilaration, no rejoicing, just a blind numbness as he witnessed the drama that should have ended in his death. He knew that he should have died back there in the pyre of flames.

For several minutes he sat, oblivious to all else. He arose at last and stepped from his motionless sled. From horizon to horizon it was a nightmare of death. Flaming shot and twisted clumps of wreckage dotted the landscape. Directly behind him and half a league away was the edge of the Ice, and above it rose an endless column of smoke and flame that lent its gloom and foreboding to the final moments of battle.

Three thousand men were dead or dying, another three thousand were refugees looking for help or fleeing from the doom that sought them out. Michael Ormson stood alone, detached, watching them in their madness.

On the horizon the *Thunderwind* was fighting on, as Halvin turned again and again. It finally disappeared beyond a pall of smoke.

It was Gareth who saw the doom come at last. His cabin was a shambles, his crew dead or dying, the walls a holed and splintered wreckage; the Holy Icon was just a shattered memory. His dark-blue robe was singed and scorched and covered with darkening stains of blood, from the bodies that he had pulled clear of the gun that stood quiet in the smoking ruin. Out of the smoke Gareth finally saw what Halvin could not see. A blast at fifty paces had swept the forecastle with a swarm of splinters and Halvin's face had been torn apart, his vision destroyed. He stood alone, a towering image of madness, blood pouring in a great river from his scorched and twisted face as he swore and raged at the enemy.

Gareth watched as a crippled schooner appeared suddenly out of the smoke then crossed the bow of the *Thunderwind*. The *Thunderwind* bore down upon the crippled craft, and Gareth heard the screams of her doomed crew as death reached out to them. The *Thunderwind* plowed into the craft, smashing it into a torrent of splinters and rag.

Gareth could feel the difference as the broken hull of the ship passed underneath and drifted astern. Climbing past his gun, he swung himself over the smashed bulkhead and pushed aside the wreckage that had showered down from the collision. Bracing himself on the splintered siding, he swung himself over to the catwalk that lined the front of the ship then grabbed hold of the edge, leaned over, and looked down.

The steering blades had been locked and bent; the impact of the schooner had jammed the support plate up against the frame of the ship and destroyed the tiller. The *Thunderwind* had no control other than to attempt to balance and steer by sail alone.

Gareth stood up and listened to the shouts of the crew above. Leaning out, he looked at the torn sails and tangled madness that had once been the pride of the Cornathian fleet. Walking along the catwalk, he swung himself up onto the bowsprit and made his way out to the forward edge of the spar. He drifted into his death chant as he gained a vantage point amid the wreckage, to watch the final act of the drama.

At last the dream will end, he thought as his chant went on. At last he could sit in peace at the Long Table, a martyr of battle. The *Thunderwind* was pointed straight at the Bane, which grew larger as the *Thunderwind* relentlessly bore down on its course. It appeared to be a living, coiling thing that reached upward and outward to draw all living things into its folds.

. . . until the Ice shall give up her dead, he thought. He laughed softly as he saw the smoldering sea that in another moment would be his grave. The *Thunderwind* started to turn slowly as her crew desperately worked the sails. It was useless—he didn't even bother to go back to help. Even the Ezrians could see what was coming and had eased off, standing astern to watch the Bane finish its work.

He felt a strange calm descend over him at the coming of the end. The burning wreck of a ship shot past, and Gareth watched with detached interest, his gaze drawn back to the approaching doom.

The dream, St. Mor, the dream!

He screamed.

Ripping off his goggles, he pulled his hood back. A scream of anguish welled up from the depths of his soul: "St. Mor, forgive me!" His fear became a raging blindness as the tiny figure grew and took form.

"You removed him from death and gave him life, and in so doing you destroyed us."

The prophecies and the dream were true. Michael Ormson stood upon the ice and watched as the *Thunderwind* raced to its doom.

Gareth wrestled with madness as the fear of a thousand sleepless nights took hold of him and came to pass before his terrified gaze. With an anguished scream he cast himself from the bow and was crushed on the ice below.

Michael Ormson was alone upon the ice when out of the smoke of battle came the *Thunderwind*, the last ship of the Cornathian fleet, its torn hull and sails plainly showing the fight that she had made in a last bid for survival. He could see blind Halvin atop the forecastle, still shouting oaths of defiance as death rushed up to swallow him.

The robe, the dark-blue robe—it was Gareth. Michael's gaze reached out and he could feel the madness that raged in Gareth's tormented soul. Gareth looked at him then, and the visage of one was believed that he was doomed to the eternal torment of hell seared itself into Michael's soul. The ship approached Michael, and Gareth seemed to fill the sky.

"You sent me to death, and you gave me life instead," Michael whispered.

Gareth screamed.

It was a scream of primal fear. The priest reached heavenward and cast himself off the bow, as if he could fly up and away from his madness. He fell, and his scream would echo through Michael's soul and take a thousand forms in the years to come as if one nightmare was ending and another was just beginning.

"St. Mor, forgive me!" he screamed, then crashed with a sickening blow into the ice and disappeared beneath the grinding blades of the ship.

The *Thunderwind* was past him. A ship of death on her final voyage. The towering flames of the western sky flared in greeting as the ship rocked from side to side as it passed onto the rough ice. For a second it seemed to rise up, as if imitating the gesture of the dead priest, and then the ice parted and the ship disappeared from mortal view.

The moment had passed. Michael Ormson walked over to the blue robe. Looking upon this last link with his now dead world, Michael bent over and closed the corpse's eyes. Standing up, he swept the darkening seas with his gaze. He started to walk south. South to the Broken Tracks. Southward to Janis and Mathin.

He was alone upon a frozen sea, his nearest companions the stiff, frozen dead who lay thirty miles to the north. In making his way past the wrecks he came across a frozen corpse wearing a pair of skates. Taking them, Michael made his way southward, keeping low and skating on the edge of the Bane to avoid detection by the schooners that scoured the ice for both friend and foe. The only sounds that came to him were the soft, dirgelike whisper of the wind and the steady clicking of his blades. The unreachable Arch hovered above him, and served as his guide on this, the first night into the new world.

As he watched the Arch fade with the morning light he sensed the power that was to come. He knew that he was the desire of others, the dream of millions, and in that strength he could move the world. As he moved ever southward he believed that perhaps he could change it, after all, to end the madness and the death worship, and destroy the shadowy fears.

He remembered his old links to the church, and with a contemptuous gesture he ripped aside the black robe of the ram runner and skated on in the heavy parka that he had worn beneath.

He felt as if he had been purged of everything and left an empty vessel to be filled with a new dream, a new world. And there, beneath the starry Arch-encompassed sky, the dream started to take form. To find birth in an empty vessel that would become the Prophet.

B O O K II

Frigate

CHAPTER 12

THE ICE WAS EMPTY, THE SEA BARREN AND STILL. THE LAST
cutter had made its way into port two weeks earlier, plumes
of water in its wake. Now was the brief moment of life, the
two-month passage of warmth that would see the emptying of
the tunneled cloisters to the joy of the late-evening sky. But
the Haf Haulen, the long day of feasting and merriment, had
already passed. The star readers were already marking the progress of the sun on its voyage back beyond the far side of the
Arch—a portent of yet another winter to come.

Rifton walked alone, his tired gaze examining the muddied
beach and the iceboats that rested on their frames, awaiting the
coming of fall. In the distance he heard the laboring of a thousand
men as the fleet continued to grow in the late-evening light of
summer. It was the sound of a new merchant fleet growing. A
fleet to replace the one consumed by the war, which, for the moment at least, had ceased.

For the first time in a generation the fleets could sail in
peace, except for the occasional freebooter, and the ships of
Mor would not put to sea. For two generations he had waited

169

for this moment, yet he felt a great emptiness—a sense of detachment from it all. He continued to walk, making his way past the muddy refuse.

The sense of being alone was a pleasure, even if it was artificial. He looked over his shoulder and they were behind him. "Always following, always watching, damn them," he whispered. They stood at a discreet distance yet were present nevertheless—Niall and two burly brothers who wore the light-blue robes of St. Awstin. They stopped as he stopped, and moved again when he moved. They were the Braith de Iladden, the Brothers of the Knife—the trained bodyguards of the high officials of St. Awstin. They had become such an ingrained part of his existence that he barely noticed them anymore. One had died already, taking the blade intended for him. He had never been able to figure out where it had come from, but he had his suspicions. He could remember when such things were unnecessary. Since the plague, though, all had changed, and the world had become more serious, more deadly. Or was he simply getting old?

Rifton looked across the ice as the sun's flaming red disk slipped behind a bank of clouds, lighting them with a soft, fiery glow that bathed the hills behind the city. A gentle breeze wafted in from the sea, carrying the bracing scent of salt and the brief touch of summer's warmth. It was a scent that could carry him across forty years and a hundred launchings—the proud ships putting out to sea, he a young man aboard his first ice runner, with a friend long dead. A chill crept though him; he drew his white cloak across his chest and walked on.

I'm growing old, he thought sadly. Why must I continue this struggle? Why could it not be as it once was, without the cares, without the fears?

He fondly remembered the idealism, the unshaking belief. The Ceuth Cearth, the First Choice, came to him again. He pushed it away. He would not wrestle with that now. There were far more immediate questions of concern.

The riders had come in not more than an hour earlier, bearing word that Zimri was almost at the watchers' tower and expected in Cornath before the night was an hour old. The spies had warned him of the unfolding plan, and he was torn with a desire to know.

In the last year he had sent three ships to learn the truth, and none had returned. Not one word had come from the south. No evidence concerning the so-called prophet. The first warning had been no more than an offhanded comment about a new madman in the south. There had been dozens before and undoubtedly more would come. Yet for some reason this first small warning had been enough to create a gnawing sense of uneasiness. What was Zimri's game concerning this? Rifton felt a twinge from that deep, innate sense of warning that had helped him to survive forty years of church politics and maneuvers. Something deadly wrong was in the wind. It was only a faint scent, a barely detectable breath of air, but it could roar into a storm that would sweep all before it.

"Michael, where are you?" he whispered to the wind.

There had been the sense of presence on two occasions. He awoke in the middle of the night knowing that Michael was near, that somehow he was alive. But the few survivors who filtered back swore that his ship was lost with all hands. It had been three years since St. Judean's Bane. At the end of the first winter came a rumor of a new leader on a freebooters' island in some Saint-forsaken corner of the Southward Isles. The rumors were even stronger after the second winter, and Rifton finally sent the ships to find the truth.

The nagging questions kept returning. Is Michael this Prophet, this Holy One? The question held endless peril. What would it mean for him in his quest for the Holy See? What about Zimri? But most of all, what about Michael—if the Prophet truly was Michael? Was he the Chosen One? And if so, what would it mean to all that the Church had worked for? The thoughts were numbing. He could not reach an answer, and the horn for vespers broke into his thoughts. He quickly turned and made his way back to the cloister, the Braith de Iladden moving silently ahead to clear the way.

* * *

"Yes, Brother Niall. Do show him in."

"Certainly, your Excellency," Brother Niall replied softly. His large frame stiffened with distaste at the mention of Zimri's name. Niall was getting old, his bushy jet-black eyebrows were starting to show streaks of gray, but his body still held a tremendous presence. His angular, craggy face bore the scars of a hundred fights upon the Ice. He was head of all the brothers of the Knife, responsible for guarding the key people of St. Awstin, and he had done his job well. For fifteen years, he alone had been responsible for Michael. It was a task that had come near to breaking him, especially when Michael disappeared. Rifton could see the masked pain—the love of a man for a boy who had become a son, to one who could never father a son of his own. Niall had begged for permission to sail with him, and, later, when the news had finally come of the long-overdue fleet, to search for him. The years had been hard on Niall, especially when the quiet rumors started to circulate. Niall was torn between his love of Michael and his commitment to the Holy Church and the man he had served for twenty years. Niall turned away and started back down the corridor to the entrance of the abbey.

"Brother Isaac," Rifton called.

The door swung open to reveal his secretary, a lean, pale monk with disarming features that concealed a razor-sharp mind. "Yes, Holy One."

"Isaac, fetch up a bottle of Yawinder. And see that it is heated."

"Yawinder, your Excellency?"

"Yes, damn it all," Rifton shouted crossly.

"But there are only two bottles left. It will be six months before we can resupply."

"I know, I know, but it must be done."

Isaac turned to leave.

"And be sure to be in the necessary place."

Two bottles left, Rifton thought, and I have to waste one on that bastard. He grumbled in disgust and rose from behind his desk, his rounded bulk slowing him down and causing him to breathe heavily with the effort. He felt a slight tremor in his chest; he waited, and it passed. He barely noticed them now, but he knew that they were just another sign. Don't think about that now, damn it. Purge your thoughts. He took a deep breath and tried to clear his mind. He had to watch for every movement, every statement, every detail.

A gentle knock sounded on the door.

"Enter," Rifton said as he crossed the room. The small, round door swung open to reveal the ceremonial robes of an Archbishop of Mor, the dark-blue cassock trimmed in gold. Zimri's flowing black cape appeared to swaddle its owner in the darkness of night.

The doorway was like all other doors in the monastery, designed for the conservation of heat while serving as a symbolic representation of the sacred sign. Its low, arching frame cut a half-circle with a rise only four feet in height. The guest bent low to pass through, and as he stood up he had the presence of a strong, agile god of night, with a compelling aura of dignity and command.

Rifton stood before him, arms folded, and hands concealed beneath his robes, with no sign of welcome to extend. Zimri rose to his full six and a half feet and with deliberate slowness cast back his hood.

Rifton was accustomed to wounds, Saints know. He had seen enough of them on the Ice, yet every time he met Zimri and cast his eyes on the twisted face, he felt a sadness, for the right side of Zimri's face revealed the reason for his torment—a twisted scar that ran from temple to jaw. It had the sickly pink appearance of a burn that had reached to the bone. From the way he favored his left side it was obvious that every movement was painful. Rifton knew that the scar was the legacy of a bursting cannon mold, and that Zimri had hovered for weeks at the doorway to death until the healing crafts of the Braith de Dochas brought him back. They had spared him to attack life with the fury of despair. In the twenty-one years that had passed since, Zimri had risen to the Archbishopric of Mor, to the Council of Fourteen, and now the position of Secretary to the Holy See. And every passing day more came to believe that the Final Seat was to be his as well.

The adversaries stood silent, their mutual hatred concealed by the practiced manner of high office. In spite of conflict, there is a sense of respect that a leader can feel toward an enemy who he knows is as good as himself.

Zimri broke the silence at last. "Your Excellency, the Holy Father sends you his greetings and prays that you and your brotherhood are well."

"And I pray that all is well with our Holy Father," Rifton replied softly, while waving Zimri to a chair next to his desk.

"As usual with him, Brother Rifton," Zimri replied evenly. "And I as usual keep close watch on him."

Over a year ago the hands of the Saints had passed over the Holy Father. Since that time he had been unable to speak or move from the bed that served as a coffin for the living. And Zimri acted as regent, as befitted the office of the Secretary to the Holy See. For this reason Zimri guarded the life of the Holy See as jealously as his own. While the Holy See lived, Zimri held the power. If the Holy See were to die soon, chances were that the Council would vote Rifton the new head of the Church. Rifton knew that it would be to his advantage to send one of his Brothers of the Knife to do the job; with enough money and the proper bribes it might work. The temptation was there. But it was hard to consider such for the man who had been one of his closest friends. He knew Ioan would welcome the release, but Rifton would not take the scepter of power that way. Rifton looked at Zimri and decided to open the attack.

"Tell me, Zimri, to what do I owe this visit? Is your brotherhood looking for another crusade, now that the last one has ended in a truce?"

Zimri hadn't the time to pass a half-hour in gentle maneuvering. "I've come about your vote in the Council," Zimri replied, his smoldering eyes trying to penetrate into Rifton's thoughts.

"Vote on which issue? There are so many, you know."

"Damn it, Rifton, I've come to ask you if you would reconsider your stand. Don't you realize that we're giving up when ninety percent of the battle has already been won? By the Sacred Arch, we could win this war once and for all if only we would press the dagger home!"

Rifton shook his head sadly. "You refer to Sol, of course."

"Yes, I refer to Sol. The Ezrians have been checked for the moment and now is the time to fall upon those heretics who left our brotherhood. It is time that we brought all of them back into the fold."

"Zimri, must it always be with blood? Their church is dying anyhow. In another generation they will be gone forever, just like the half-dozen other schisms that have gone before them. They have split away and we the parent have always survived, and always will survive. It has forever been the same: they have their brief moment of glory and then they're gone. Why can't you simply wait for the process to lead to its natural end?"

Rifton was confused. A fool would know his position on this matter, why had Zimri journeyed fifty land leagues to argue this with him? Zimri parried Rifton's response. "The path of heresy is death by the sword of the righteous. And we of Mor are the sword of the Good and Holy Church. This is Holy Writ," Zimri said with an icy tone. "Tell me, Brother Rifton, do you doubt Holy Writ?"

Rifton eased back in his chair and smiled at the onslaught. He loved Zimri when he drifted into one of his self-righteous moods. Rifton knew that someday the man might destroy him. Nevertheless he found Zimri's zeal amusing.

"Of course not, my friend, of course we all believe in Holy Writ," Rifton said with a sarcastic tone. "'And the Return of the Garden shall be watered with the blood of heretics'—fourth pennod of Malcum. But, my good man, must you be so serious about it?"

"In this case, we should be," Zimri said maliciously.

"And what does that mean?" Rifton said, sensing that the issue was coming.

"This new prophet."

Both men fell silent. Mastering any sign of emotion, Rifton sat quietly, the only movement the slight tapping of his hand on the desk.

There was a knock at the door.

"Excuse me," Rifton said. He got up and crossed the room, taking advantage of the time to marshal his thoughts. He opened the door to find Isaac holding a tray upon which was a flask and two golden goblets encrusted with rubies.

"The Yawinder, your Excellency."

There was a subtle gesture of Rifton's hand and the doorway closed behind him as Rifton returned to the desk with the tray in his hand. "Would you care for some?" he asked, offering a goblet to Zimri.

Zimri smiled and reached across the tray to take the other cup. Rifton poured the heated wine, which instantly flooded the room with its full, heady scent. He felt in control again.

"A year doesn't pass without some madman declaring himself to be the Promised One. Why should we take any particular note of this one?"

Zimri looked straight into Rifton's eyes. "There's something about this one, Rifton, something that makes me uneasy. From what I've heard, this one is actually starting to get a following. It could be dangerous, if we allow it to continue."

"How?" Rifton responded, feigning boredom.

"At best the situation is unstable in the Southward Isles. We control a quarter of them and Ezra another quarter, as the treaty we signed arranged. But Sol has not the strength to maintain what is technically theirs. Already dozens of islands have broken away to become free states, at best, or pirate havens, at worst. Yet something far more dangerous than this anarchy might arise. This leader could gather in the pieces if he plays his game correctly."

"So why are you telling me this?"

"We must stop him and crush the free states before they unite as a new, fourth power. If we don't, the Garden could be even further from our grasp."

Rifton couldn't help but chuckle. "The Garden. Come, come, my dear Zimri," he said in a rich, condescending voice, while draining his cup. "Do you still believe that you can bring that about?"

There was an angry flare in Zimri's eyes. Ah, I've touched something, Rifton thought.

"We must acknowledge the Garden at all times, Rifton, even when we are alone like this. It's demanded by the First Choice, or must I remind you of that."

They were silent again for a moment.

"Tell me, Rifton," Zimri resumed softly, while looking Rifton in the eye, "what do you know of this so-called prophet?"

Rifton held his gaze while reaching over to pour another cup for Zimri. "Nothing."

"I see." He was silent again.

He suddenly changed his tone and leaned back, but the aura of tension remained in the room. "Then I must assume that you stand firm in your votes concerning both Sol and this new prophet."

"Zimri, can't you see beyond your wars?" Rifton replied, going over to the attack. "We're at the edge of exhaustion. We barely broke even with the Ezrians—it was only our good luck that cost them their fleet at Ord Eilean. We got our revenge and what do we have to show for it? A handful of islands in the south—at such a bloody cost, Zimri, such a damnable bloody cost." The memory of Michael, Halvin, Padraig, and a hundred others came back to him, frozen ghosts from the past.

"We've lost a hundred thousand in this, the latest round. Every family's lost somebody, and still you want to move on. I tell you, Zimri, you can't push the people any further, even though it might help some in their power and bring more profit to others."

Zimri stiffened; the connection between the House of Gwen and the brotherhood was well known. To that house came much of the profit for the laying out and rigging of ships. As well, Zimri was the illegitimate son of Comarth of Gwen.

The ploy worked.

"I refuse to be insulted any longer—I came to talk," Zimri shouted.

Rifton rose, and walking around the desk, he put his hand on Zimri's shoulder. He tried to look him in the eyes, but Zimri turned away.

Something of Michael was in him—a compelling, almost

magnetic personality that one wanted to like. Rifton remembered all the pain that the man had caused him in his ruthless drive for power, yet still he could find a part of him that was appealing. If anything, it was the raw determination and drive. How often had he wished that they could be allies? Nothing could have stopped them. Together, they could have found a way to deal with the ultimate paradox and to plot the course that would lead the Church against the growing power of Inys Gloi. He wanted to confide in the younger man; he wanted to reach out, to trust him . . . But he knew that would be impossible.

"Now my friend, no harm was intended by my words," Rifton said in a smooth, even tone. Zimri finally looked at him, and both knew the lie in Rifton's statement.

"The Council meets at the first of the new moon, which is only three weeks hence. Zimri, stay here with me for that time and we can go together to the meeting. It would please me and give honor to our order." And I can keep my eye on you, as well, Rifton thought.

"I thank you, Rifton, for your generous offer, but I merely stopped here as a side trip. In fact, I plan to leave within the hour. I am charged with the transfer of papers to the Ezrian Embassy, which awaits me in Conwy." Zimri rose from his chair.

"The Saints' blessing upon you, and may they preserve your health for your forthcoming journey," Rifton said with a vague gesture of blessing.

Zimri gave a cold, tight-lipped smile. "May the Saints be with you, Rifton."

Zimri bowed and walked to the door with Rifton following. As he was bending low to exit he stopped, and whispered softly, "Suppose this prophet really is the One?"

Rifton hesitated for a second. "Do you believe that?"

"Of course not, but it is an interesting thought, isn't it?"

"It's pure foolishness. If he was the One we would know."

"How?" Zimri asked, his voice still a whisper.

"By the signs, of course."

"But many claim that the signs have already come to pass."

Rifton was silent, afraid of what might come next.

"But then, if it was true," Zimri suddenly said loudly, "we would be destroyed." He broke out into laughter, and his voice echoed through the corridors. "Good-bye, Rifton," he said with a flourish, and ducking low he disappeared down the hall.

"Brother Isaac," Rifton shouted.

Isaac stepped from the shadows.

"Have him followed. I wish to know which road he travels. And have Niall come to me."

"Yes, your Excellency."

Isaac disappeared and Rifton returned to his study. Zimri was on to something, that was obvious. But what? The pretense about the vote was a farce; Zimri and all the other archbishops knew his stand on this issue. Zimri was on to something. There was a knock at the door.

"Enter."

Niall stepped in and walked to the chair that Rifton offered him. Niall was only his bodyguard and Isaac would someday be the new archbishop, but some things were best not discussed with young men eager for power.

"Did you hear?"

"Yes." And Niall's glance flickered toward the icon on the north wall, which concealed a small booth entered from the next room.

"What do you think?"

Niall sat back in his chair. "I'm not sure. The question of the vote was obvious. He and everybody else knows what your stand will be. But of this new leader, I don't know what he thinks."

Rifton was silent. He would like to believe that Zimri was casting in the dark or throwing out a confusing trail for Rifton to misread. "Could he know of our interest in this new leader and the three ships we dispatched to check on him?"

"Anything is possible. There is always room for a traitor, even in the heart of our monastery."

"Yes." Rifton fell silent. He had never even learned who sent Facinn. For a while Rifton had trusted him almost as much as he trusted Niall. More disturbing, after Facinn escaped, his accomplices were never found.

"Yes, you're quite right, Niall. But I think if he did know he wouldn't have come here with the knowledge, he would challenge instead at the Council. I think he was just casting."

Niall was silent.

Rifton's thoughts came to the question that had tormented him now for so long. He reached over and poured another cup of wine.

What if it is Michael? Worse, what if he truly is the One?

It was the hour before morning prayers, and twilight colored the eastern sky as Zimri turned in his saddle and looked down at Peter.

"Nevertheless, my dear Peter, despite his age and gentle ways, I still fear him."

"But why, your Excellency? He really doesn't have all that much time left to him, if our reports are true. It seems that he started to slip three years ago."

"His nephew," Zimri said softly, then lapsed into quiet. Zimri looked at the early-morning light and then to the cloaked and hooded form riding next to him. Behind were the shadows of his bodyguards, who kept a respectful distance and mumbled their morning prayers.

They rode in silence for several minutes as the eastern sky lit up before them. They finally reached the pass, and the long coastal plain fell away behind them. In the far distance the faint glimmering of lights marked the walls of Cornath, while ahead was the solitary beacon of St. Parthius.

In the brightening light of dawn Zimri looked again at Peter, who had the refined, angular face of good breeding, the breeding necessary for a secretary to the Cardinal of Mor. His heritage was unknown; a good half of the brotherhood was illegitimate. The Brotherhood of Mor was the traditional home of such children, and it was the source of their strength. From that came the unswerving loyalty to the substitute parent. It also brought the money necessary to keep certain origins quiet.

The lucky ones, like Zimri, were acknowledged by their family, and the influence helped. But as for Peter, nothing was known.

"As you were saying, your Excellency," Peter said, picking up the line of conversation. "You said that you fear Rifton. If this is true, then what are your intentions?"

Zimri smiled. "I trust you, Peter, but not that much."

Zimri lapsed into silence for another half-league. They crested the coastal ridge line, and as they did so they drew nigh the beacon tower, where the guards were dousing the flame as the sun appeared on the horizon beyond. From the tower the great horn suddenly signaled the start of day. The monks on watch faced south and began to chant.

"To the return of the Father..."

The monks in Zimri's column stopped and dismounted. Kneeling, they joined in the prayer.

"Oh Father, who has turned away, hear us now as we cry to thee..."

The prayer ended and all touched their foreheads to the ground and rose. Zimri and his secretary walked off the road and stood on the spongy grass of the moor.

"Peter, I've heard of some sailing master skulking about the port of Conwy. He's a follower of this prophet. I want him located and arrested."

Peter nodded.

"Find some reason, but don't have him tortured. And for Heaven's sake, don't let the Mord Rinn get him. Make it a smuggling or theft charge. And keep him quiet, we might need him later."

"It shall be done."

"Next, I think we've confused our good brother Rifton. He'll think we're not going to Conwy, but of course that's precisely where we'll go." Zimri laughed. "He'll never guess that we're working on Xavier. I hope that wench you found for our good cardinal is all that you claim," Zimri said with distaste.

"But of course, your Excellency. I've seen to her myself."

"I assumed that you would." How he disliked all of this. To bribe men with power was understandable, but wealth or lust held no meaning to him. and he looked with scorn on any who succumbed to either.

"I also want my personal guard increased. I fear Rifton might misread my intentions and resort to something that he normally wouldn't consider...especially after the conference."

Peter smiled.

"I take it from your foolish grin that all has been arranged."

"But of course, your Excellency. Arranged to your every specification."

"If it should fail, it will mean your head."

"I know," Peter said, "and it won't."

"Such confidence!" And turning from Peter, Zimri looked back to enjoy the view of the valley and sea bathed in the first light of early morning. The roadside watchtower echoed to the chants of morning service. It was a tower of the Before Time and, as such, was a sacred spot of pilgrimage—its white stone and rusted metal, a place of holy devotion.

He looked away from the tower and out to the open sea.

"I wonder who this prophet is? The others are the known factors in the game, but will he cooperate as well?"

He walked to his horse and mounted. Clods of mud were tossed up as he kicked the stallion into a gallop, which left the rest of the monks scrambling after him. Together, they weaved their way into the snowcapped hills, into the rising light of day, and the question still haunted him:

"I wonder who and what we are dealing with?"

CHAPTER 13

HE STOOD IN FOG-CLOAKED SILENCE. HE WAS ALONE ON THE hill, looking out over the sea, and his thoughts were on a strange, gathering darkness. He had sensed it often of late, a dim foreboding, a feeling that destiny was at last returning to hunt him and draw him out.

The blanket of gray softened to a shimmering, translucent light as he walked down to the Grove. He sat in silence, pondering. His time alone was short; when the morning fog lifted they would come to seek him out. It was hard on Janis to awake each morning to an empty bed, but the compulsion to find a brief moment alone was overwhelming.

The memory of the battle returned again, and Gareth's haunted eyes still stared at him. He had evaded capture but it was a near thing at best. He found the wreck of a Cornathian schooner in the pass, and from it he salvaged supplies and a one-man skate sail. He traveled by night and hid in the ice mountains by day, his only companion the insane howling of the wind. He stayed for a month, until he knew that Mathin was safe. He arrived to find the city in celebration. The day before, Ishmael Tornson had arrived and driven out the tiny garrison that the Ezrians had placed there. Michael was the first survivor of St. Judean's to reach Mathin.

For the first year Mathin's independence had been a near thing. The Ezrians were busy exploiting the gains won at St. Judean's Bane, but twice they turned their wrath on Mathin. Michael held the tower that he had once taken and lasted out a siege of four weeks that left it a pile of icy rubble. The action enhanced his growing mystique, and in a city with such a transient population, Michael quickly found himself to be one of the inner circle.

He went to Janis on the night of his return. It was a night of stormy, scornful tirades, but in the end she joyfully led him to her bedchamber. The priest stopped shaving his head the next morning, and that night they were married.

The city had flourished, her population almost doubling over three years. Sol collapsed and could no longer offer protection, so men pulled up and searched out the city-states and pirate havens that would. The word spread across the Ice that Mathin was a place where a man could live without question of religion or guild.

Michael had not sailed again, but helped Zardok and sat in the taverns and talked of his dreams—talked of his desire for an end to the wars—and as he talked people listened. With the coming of the third winter it had started. The self-appointed baptist returned.

Seth returned to the harbor with the first ice, and for two weeks they had argued, Seth trying to pull Michael back to Inys Gloi. For two weeks Seth stayed, and then as mysteriously as he had come, he was gone. Soon thereafter the people had started to come. Only one or two at first, but soon it was a constant procession seeking him out. Some came just to see and then they were gone. Others though, the disturbing ones, came and stared at him as if they were gazing at a statue or idol. He tried to drive them away but they stayed, and the word spread across the Ice that a teacher, the "Promised One," had come to Mathin. The people of Ishmael started to turn away from their warrior leader and look instead to the strange, com-

pelling figure who could hold all with the sound of his voice
or the fire in his gaze.

There was a stirring behind him and Michael was pulled
from his thoughts. He looked around. A shaggy, bearlike crea-
ture stood at the edge of the Grove. "Yes, Daniel," he said
wearily.

"The people are coming."

"Yes, I know."

It would be a short while yet before the fog burned away,
and he tried to savor the last few minutes. What a shock Daniel
had been! He had thought him dead and frozen on the distant
Ice. But Daniel had survived. Daniel had thought Michael's
ram was destroyed by a schooner. He had searched for Michael
after the battle and then headed south, where a band of freebooters picked him up. He rode with them for two winters,
until a new member joined. With the new member came a night
on the bowsprit standing watch.

"I was to Mathin this fall, and there I talked with a man. . . ."

The bear had come back. Michael knew that Daniel in-
formed Seth and Inys Gloi about actions in Mathin, but he did
not argue the point. Daniel became the bodyguard.

Michael closed his eyes and meditated for several minutes,
then, knowing that they were approaching, he opened his eyes
to greet them.

The usual faces were there, the dour innkeeper Ormath,
Rafe behind him, young happy Rafe, the man who spoke of
peace yet chafed for a good fight. The priest of Sol was there
as well, the one who had begged for death but now served
Michael instead. His sad, empty eyes were the sign of a man
who could no longer believe, yet still wished for faith. Scattered
behind them were fifty others who had come to talk with him.

What have I started? he asked himself as he looked at the
crowd.

Michael stood and looked out at them, and their dress told
of a dozen different cities and guilds. No new Cornathians, he
thought with relief. Half a dozen times there had been Cornathians, but none seemed to link him to their home. His secret
was still safe, and with it his uncle. But he knew that a day

would come...Michael sighed softly with the thought, then with a graceful sweep of his brown robe, he sat down on the pine-needle floor of the grove. There was silence. The first comment or question was sometimes long in coming.

Finally a gaunt man stood up, an ice runner from back north by the cut of his clothes and the pale milkiness of his exposed arms. His eyes were deep gray. He began in an even, self-assured manner. "Tell me, Michael, how you ever expect to survive? I served Ezra upon the Ice for three years, I did. I gave to them heart and soul, and I saw their power at St. Judean's Bane."

Daniel looked to Michael, but Michael ignored him.

"I saw the power of their fleets. Tell me, where are yours? You have precious few guns, with only a couple of renegade priests to serve them. Why, therefore, should your religion be worthy of my respect. Answer me this, Michael—how upon this sea do you expect to survive?"

There was a bit of angry stirring, but Michael's gaze swept out over the crowd and the ominous words were stilled.

"First of all," Michael started softly, "I am not preaching a religion, though I do find it interesting that you equate religion with ships and guns. To me, a religion implies a faith in one creed or belief. Let's take an example for this. How many different types of craft did you sail during your three years on the Ice?"

"Half a dozen at least: a couple of frigates, the rest armed merchantmen."

"What cut were they?"

"Barkentines, an old foretop schooner, the rest sloops."

"Well, my friend, the Ice is the same, is it not? Yet we as men have designed any number of craft to sail—with men ready to argue violently over which one is the best—and all of them, though they sail differently, reach the same goal."

"This, my friend, is my view of religion. To say that one is right and all others are wrong is a denial of logic, for it shuts out the thoughts and beliefs of so many others concerning the questions of man. To say one is right above all others is to deny logic."

"Look into your hearts, all of you, and you will see that this is true. In this Grove are Ezrians, Cornathians, Sols, free-staters, and even some from beyond the Flowing Seas. All of you are different, yet all are the same. The reason that we will survive is because guns cannot kill the thoughts that are born here. We are not a religion, we are a way of life."

Michael hesitated for a second. "No, let me change that. We are not a way of life, we are a way of living."

An old man sitting in front of Michael spoke up: "Master—"

But Michael interrupted him with a tone that carried reproach. "Please, I am no master. I've never claimed to be nor have I ever intended it."

Daniel and others who knew him could read a hint of despair in his voice.

"Excuse me then, Michael. In my life I've had four sons, each of whom has gone to the shadows before me—three at the hands of the Ezrians"—with this he shot a look of scorn at the Ezrian— "and one by the followers of the false prophet of Wornth." He was silent for a moment then drifted on in a low, singsong voice, "I am dying. There are no sons after me. Where are they, Michael? And where am I to go, as well?"

The Grove was silent. Michael sat for several long moments and then got up and walked over to the old man, who was softly crying.

"I'm so afraid, Michael. I just can't believe, no matter how I try. Night after night I pray for a sign—any sign—to believe in, for I fear the freezing of all who die unbelieving, but nothing comes to me—only the night. And it haunts me, Michael."

"I don't know," Michael said softly. "I just don't know."

Those who had not heard Michael before stirred with disappointment, for his words were not what they had come to hear.

"That is what I've been trying to say to all of you. I just don't know the answer, and my voice is raised up in challenge to any who claim that they do. I raise my voice even higher, though, across the entire Frozen Sea to those who claim that they not only know the answer but that theirs alone, their belief or sacred book is the right way and all others must follow them for salvation.

"Look out to the sea," he shouted, and his arm swept out, his brown robe swirling out around him.

"How many thousands have died out there arguing this point? How many and for what? A promise, a hope, a whispering dream that flees with the light of dawn? We scream our arguments when we doubt them the most."

Michael took the old man's hand. "To promise you anything would be the start of yet another cycle of belief. It was such words that took your sons before their time. Do you wish such a thing to happen for those whom you leave behind?"

The old man shook his head sadly. "But what of me?" he whispered.

"You are alive. That is the miracle. We deny our living in our fear of dying. Live, old man, and take glory in each moment, that is the true miracle."

Michael paused for a moment, then with a slow, even tone he continued, "If you wish me to speak of the beyond, I will only say this. We are part of some cycle that is beyond our ability ever to express in thought or word. We are cloaked in some mystery far deeper than we shall ever understand. On occasion the curtain is parted for a moment, and we glimpse light from beyond, but as quickly the curtain is drawn shut again. We shall part that curtain soon enough, and then there shall be time enough to deal with it. This is a mystery far beyond our ability to comprehend. If it cannot be expressed, then to speak of it will only confuse. I believe then that the more I am silent on this, the more I will be heard."

They sat in silence, for the thoughts that he had provoked were so alien that the impact was almost numbing. In an age of religion he taught that religion was not the answer. Several people stood up and fled from him, unable to bear the burden of Michael's offering. Others, though, drew closer and he could see in their eyes the light of thought, as if the first of so many veils had been pulled back. His words were simple, and each man thought, I could have said that. He puts into words what I've thought myself.

In the distance a horn sounded and its voice flowed with the breeze, so that all turned and looked to sea. Another ship was returning to harbor. Michael rose and walked to the knoll above the pines, and they followed him. A single ship was clearing the outer reefs, its high prow gently pushing aside the ice floes that were not worth maneuvering past. Her sails swelled proudly in the morning breeze and the sound of distant cheering fluttered up from the sea as her men rejoiced after an absence of two long years.

He turned back to the group. "My friends, let us live within our senses and stop worrying of what is beyond. In that we can create our Garden again, and with that I will be content. It is a revolution of thought, and that is what I've been trying to say. To learn to have new thoughts, to think beyond what has been told, to make things yet undreamed of, so that one day perhaps we might be able to reach up and touch the essence of the Arch itself, and in so doing, touch the essence within."

"Blasphemy! Blasphemy to dare dream of touching the image that our Father set as a sign of His anger."

The group turned and looked to the edge of the clearing, where a man in tattered robes pointed an accusing finger. His hair was matted, his face gaunt and ascetic, his defiant look born of the total assurance that he knew the answer.

Daniel silently drifted through the crowd with a deadly, practiced ease. He came up behind the shouting man then looked to Michael. But a subtle hand gesture caused Daniel to step back a pace.

"You cry blasphemy and I have heard you, so now listen to me. You come here without doubts or questions to trouble your mind. You know then that you are right."

"What I speak is Holy Writ, and its words cannot be doubted."

"Yes, I see," Michael said softly, sensing that many were getting the argument that they had hoped to hear. "In blasphemy there is blasphemy, I could say in response. In your act of denying me and attacking my beliefs, you deny the ability of free men to think and act for themselves. If there is a Creator he gave me a mind that can think, and your argument is asking me not to think, not to question, but instead to obey blindly and follow. I believe that is far more of a crime than speaking of the dreams in my heart. I have not denounced you, nor your belief—so why must you so vigorously attack mine?"

"But you are wrong. You deny what the Saints decree."

"Let us say that I am wrong, and everything you believe is right. If that is so, then in the end you will have the supreme satisfaction of seeing me punished for all eternity while you and those with you are saved. So why are you in such a hurry? Aren't you willing to trade a few decades for all eternity? Can't you see that this is the source of our suffering? Why can't a man believe as he wishes while his beliefs hurt no one else?"

"But your words are poison, and mislead others into the darkness, and in so doing deny all of us the Garden!"

"That is the road of madness that has crippled us for a thousand years," Michael said coldly. "There is not a man here who has not seen men killed or killed men himself because of our struggle over belief. For a thousand years we have done this. We have been so busy killing each other over this question that we have wasted an eternity. Think of the effort, think of the time, think of all the energy that could have been spent creating together, rather than destroying. Liberate your minds, turn them to new thoughts, and cast aside the darkness. *That* will bring the return of the Garden."

"Your words are the words of the Dark Seducer. You've been sent to lead men into damnation."

"My friend," Michael said sadly, "hasn't there been enough suffering already? Haven't enough men died? Live in peace then, for I shall not say that your beliefs are wrong. Believe in your Saints and be happy with them, but give me the right to think differently, and let all upon the Ice think freely, as well." Michael extended his hand and walked to the tattered man.

The man looked at him and started to recoil, then he leaned back, looked to the sky, and screamed; "Saints above, bear witness to me!"

He threw aside his cloak and drew a dagger that glinted wickedly in the morning sun. He flung himself on Michael screaming, "Death to the Heretic!" and the dagger arced downward.

Michael jumped while swinging out his cloak in an attempt to throw off the assassin's concentration, but the aim was true and the blade bit through cloth and slashed into Michael's upturned arm. The assassin ripped his poniard free and, recovering with ease, swung the double-edged blade upward in a vicious cut toward Michael's stomach. Michael tried to jump back and, in so doing, knocked down a young Mathinian boy who in turn tripped Michael, and he crashed to the ground.

The slash for the stomach met with thin air, but now his prey was at his feet desperately trying to regain his footing. With a shout of triumph the assassin threw himself on his foe, his blade outstretched for the kill.

There was a blinding shock from behind, a stunning explosion of light. It was Death, reaching out with icy hands to seize him. Yet even as his thoughts fled into the night, he felt his blade sink home with deadly ease. "By the Saints, I've killed the Heretic! . . . Saint . . ."

Daniel stood over the assassin and, screaming with rage, swung his ax and severed the dead man's head. Great gouts of blood splashed all who stood nearby.

The crowd pushed back and forth screaming in terror and rage, so that the voices were heard even to the gates of the city below. "The Master is dead! Michael, Michael . . ."

And yet he lived. His thoughts returned to him with the roaring of the crowd and the realization that he was soaked in blood. He pushed a body aside and sat up. Daniel was towering over him, and at Daniel's feet were the bloodied remains of the assassin. Alongside Michael lay another body, a poniard buried in its chest. It was the old man Michael had talked to only moments before.

"You are alive, my son," he whispered. "That is good, then it is worth it after all."

"Why? Why did you jump in front of me?"

"Because I heard you, Master, and now . . ." He coughed spasmodically, and a torrent of bloody foam bubbled between his lips. A great sigh escaped him. His eyes glazed over and he was still.

"Tell me what you see, old man," Michael whispered softly, as he reached out to cradle the body. He sat in stunned silence while chaos reigned around him.

"Michael," came a voice, as if from a great distance.

"Michael!" A bloodied hand touched his shoulder. Michael turned with a start and gazed up at the bloody ax that was in the other's hand.

"Michael, we must go back. You're wounded."

He gripped his useless arm and tried to struggle to his feet. A wave of nausea washed over him and he sat back down.

"Why, Daniel?" he said softly. "Why this?"

Before Michael could speak again a half-dozen hands lifted him and carried him from the Grove, which for the first time was stained with blood.

Through the spinning darkness Michael looked back to see the curled corpse of an old man who had given his life so that he might live. With a numb horror he could clearly see that the old man was the first of thousands.

"How is he, Andrew?" Janis asked nervously.

The group stood up and eyed the healer with apprehension.

"He'll live, no fear of that. I bled him. Not much, mind you—just a capful—and the blood flowed quick, a good sign, showing there was no poison."

The tension that had held them began to ease. Janis looked at the renegade priest-healer with gratitude.

Andrew continued in a satisfied professional tone, "It just tore through the muscle, it did. A wicked-looking slash, but it touched not the bone. But, even so, my skill would have been sufficient to save him. No fear, my lady, he is in capable hands. I shall now prepare—"

"Fine, Andrew, fine. You have served him well. Now if you would please leave us, there is much we must see to."

"Of course, my friends, of course." Bowing low, Andrew started his exit. "I've prepared some rare and costly herbs with

which to bathe him, and I shall return in the evening to do so.
Most costly are they, but nothing is too good for him."

"I understand, Andrew, and I shall see that you are compensated."

Andrew bowed low, hiding his smile as he left.

Janis turned wearily and sat down before the crackling fire.
Even in the summer Michael loved to sit before a fire, and
watching it brought her some comfort.

"I'm sorry, Lady Janis, it was my fault. I should have seen
it coming."

"Daniel, you served him well. He should have known better,
and this is the price he must pay."

"He can't pay it again."

Janis turned to face Zardok. "No, he can't—we would all
lose too much. You, Father, the power he brings to us; you,
Zardok, the trade; me, a husband; and you, Daniel, the cause
that more and more of the people believe in."

"But we still haven't answered the question," Ishmael said.
"Was the assassin sent by the Church?"

"I doubt it," Zardok said evenly. "From what Daniel said,
Michael was a perfect target," and he looked at Daniel with
reproach. Janis might forgive Daniel, but Zardok realized it
was time for professionals to look after Michael. "Michael was
an open target. An assassin, especially a Black Brother, would
have made short work of him. Secondly, the blade was not
poisoned, an assassin's almost always is. If the Church had
tried this, Michael would be dead or he would be begging us
to kill him."

"Then it was the isolated act of a religious madman," Ishmael said.

"Not isolated," Daniel replied. "What Michael is saying
will bring more of them in the future."

"Damn it!" Ishmael shouted. "Damn all of your plotting
brothers"—he raised an accusing finger at Daniel—"where is
your brother Seth now that this has happened at my own back
door?" Ishmael walked to the fireplace and tossed another log
on the flame. Why this? he thought to himself. We finally get

rid of Sol only to be saddled with another religion, and its leader is married to my only daughter.

He turned and looked around the small circle lit by the crackling logs of pine. "What happened today was the act of a madman, but more shall follow." He was silent for a moment. "I know the three of you are starting to believe this new religion he teaches."

"It is not a religion. It is merely a way of living without fear."

"Damn it, girl, call it what you will, but to most it is a religion."

Janis looked at him defiantly.

"Those people out there," and Ishmael waved his arm toward the window, "they believe that he is the Chosen One, or whatever it is that Seth's brothers have cooked up."

"He *is* the Chosen One," Daniel said reverently. "The one preordained to lead us to the Garden."

"Now don't start that again, damn it," Janis said, looking at Daniel. Then, turning to Ishmael, she started, "Father, can't you see—"

"Janis," Zardok interrupted her forcefully, "you can believe what you want about Michael, and so can Daniel, but the fact is that the reaction of ignorance to truth is never very pretty. Today is only the start. They will come for him individually at first, and then in groups, and then by nations, until either he is dead or they are dead, for truth and ignorance by their nature will always war to destroy each other. In coming for him they will come for us, as well."

Ishmael turned to look at Zardok. "I can see that, and they will come then to Mathin since we harbor him."

"Yes, and Mathin," Daniel said softly. "Why do you think he is here? Since he wouldn't come to Inys Gloi, this is the most out-of-the-way place we could find for him."

"Damn you," Ishmael said, "and damn the day I pledged sanctuary to your brotherhood."

"It is done," Zardok said. "You cannot change that now."

"Then Michael must be stopped," Ishmael said. "He is a

good warrior and a good leader. He could help Mathin hold onto her freedom, but what he is doing could kill us all."

"No." Janis looked defiantly at her father. "You talk as if he were ours to command. He isn't. He walks by another dream and we can't stop that."

"But much of it *is* a dream, Janis."

"It is preordained, Zardok," Daniel replied grimly. "He shall bring the Garden back, it is no dream."

"I meant that his inspiration is a dream, Daniel. He dreams that by reason alone men will listen to his words. Perhaps someday, but not yet. His new world will come. I believe that, but it will come with fire and sword."

"Then we do agree," Daniel said. "The Prophet will return, but with the sword, as we all knew he would, and we must prepare."

"But what of Michael?" Janis asked.

"He will not stop," Ishmael said softly, "and I know that I cannot stop him. But in his hands rests the fate of us all." Without another word, Ishmael stalked from the room.

Zardok watched him go. The power that stood behind Michael had turned the heart of Ishmael away. Perhaps Michael was the Bringer of the New Age, but Ishmael Tornson would stay forever in the last—with his dead wife and children.

Zardok looked back to Daniel and Janis. "Then it has come to what we all knew would come."

They were silent.

"The alternative," Zardok continued, "is to go into that room and plunge a dagger in his heart."

Daniel started to rise out of his chair. "How dare you," he shouted.

"Daniel, if I desired that boy's death I could have arranged it long ago. Now sit calmly."

Daniel looked darkly at Zardok and returned to his chair.

"You failed today, Daniel," Zardok said, going to the attack. "Without the sacrifice of that old man, Michael would be dead."

"Is there a guard with him now?" Janis asked.

"Yes, Ormath stays with him."

"Good, Daniel, but I want more from now on," Zardok

replied. "I know some people we must hire. Daniel, we must never let our guard down. The next time, a Dark Brother could be waiting for him."

"I shall do what is necessary," Daniel said grimly. He looked to Janis and she nodded to him. He stood. Her dusky features radiated a genuine concern for him, and he bent his knee to her. He couldn't help but feel a moment of sexual longing, for she was lovely. With a shock he realized that she was Michael's chosen, and it purged him of desire. He bent his head lower and quickly kissed her hand; blustering about the need to check the guards, he rose and stormed from the room.

"He's in love with you," Zardok said.

"It's harmless, and besides, his devotion to Michael will always rule first."

"Let us hope so."

The room was silent, yet Michael was burning into their thoughts.

"Why can't he be left alone?" Janis asked, as if to the fire.

"We must prepare. The whirlwind is coming far sooner than I ever expected. It will cost much, but there is nothing else anyhow."

Zardok turned to pat Janis's knee. She looked over to her father's oldest friend and she slowly smiled. Reaching into his pocket, he enacted the ritual for the thousandth time. With a chuckle, she accepted his bribe of chocolate as she had when still in her mother's arms.

"Let us hope that there can be peace for a while longer."

The taverns were crowded late that night as the people heard about what had happened. Those who were in the Grove would stand for many free drinks in the nights to come as they told and retold the story of the attack on the Master, for some were most free with their money—the Brotherhood of Mor paid its spies well. And so the days and weeks of that brief summer of peace passed quietly away, and the arm healed. Where once there had been a handful, now there were hundreds, and the words that he spoke were told and retold — and in the retelling, reached the deepest longings and deepest fears. The word drifted and spread like smoke from a flame not yet seen.

CHAPTER 14

He TURNED HIS ATTENTION AWAY FROM THE ROOM AND blocked out the ceaseless drone of their voices. He opened the small, ruby-colored window and looked out to the twisting streets and sordid hovels below. The brothers of the Clach Guilta, the stonemasons' guild, were laboring on the north wall, swinging another granite block into place, and he listened to their shouts, and appeals to the Saints, as they inched a ten-ton block into place. Zimri remembered watching them work on the same wall when he had first come to the city almost thirty years before.

From the windows of the Eaglais du Buioth, the Cathedral of the Holy Writ, he could see the sacred city of Dulyn, the capital of the Cornathian Federation and the center to which the fourteen brotherhoods bowed. Within the walls of the cathedral lived the Holy See.

He looked out the window and watched as a sacred procession of the Morian brotherhood flowed from an alleyway and snaked across the great square before the cathedral. The shouting relic merchants and chanting pilgrims fell silent as the basses in the procession picked up the chilling minor-keyed chant, "To the Garden of Mor." And Zimri silently joined the tenors that gave voice to the response.

All in the square fell to their knees, hands raised in the Sign of Blessing as the head of the procession passed before them.

At the front of the column, six brothers carried the Great Icon, the blessed and sacred image of St. Mor. It was believed that the Saint's hands had touched it before he died. Only the Archbishop of Mor could touch it now; the six brothers who carried it wrapped their hands in black capes that trailed to the ground. Behind the Icon six more brothers followed, swinging censers which gave off rolling green clouds of sulfurous smoke that swirled and eddied about the column. The smoke all but obscured the ten brothers who carried the symbol of the Church. Their staffs rose fifteen feet into the air, and atop each staff was a silver hand that pointed heavenward; above the hand was a silver arch.

The chanting swelled and echoed across the great square. At the opposite end of the square loomed the Eaglais de Mor— the Cathedral of Mor—center for the entire brotherhood. The great doors of the cathedral swung open, and the priests from within came out in full ceremony to greet the procession.

The centerpiece of the Morian procession entered the square. Fifty Morian deacons marched to the chant as they pulled five separate ropes that led back to a large, wheeled cart. Monks stood at each corner of the cart, holding the symbol of the Church, while at the front of the cart rode two archdeacons— one who gave wind to a great horn and one who beat upon a large round drum that marked the cadence of the chant. Resting on the middle of the cart was a cannon, still warm from the foundry at the edge of the city. It would be set before the altar in high ceremony, to wait until winter, when it would be sledded to the coast.

The procession continued across the square, and from the alleyway came the end of the holy ritual—the brothers who had sinned and who now carried the Mark. Their blue robes were replaced by purple, which hung in tattered shreds from their backs. Each monk or deacon carried a whip, and as they marched behind the column in trancelike numbness, they

whipped themselves with the thorn-tipped leather. At the sight
of them the people bowed even lower and covered their faces,
for it was a sin to look upon those who were being punished.
All was silent except for the steady, haunting beat and the
dirgelike chant, which disappeared into the open corridor of
the Morian cathedral. The last of the Brothers of Punishment
marched into its darkness as the doors swung shut behind them.
The hundreds of people who had gathered in the square rose
and the hum of their conversations shattered the momentary
silence. Zimri smiled as he watched the pilgrims flock to the
Morian cathedral to watch the ceremony within, while the relic
hawkers were right on their heels selling Saints' bones, sacred
soil, and miniature icons that hung from long poles and danced
in the afternoon sun.

He stared at the cathedral for a moment, then looked across
the city toward the Foundry of Mor. Its walls were of the Before
Time, made of stone that the ancients were able to mold into
the strangest of shapes. Beyond the foundry he could see the
green fields and small trees that exploded with color in this
brief moment of life. Over all hung a light haze, the heat of
St. Duly, that kept the ground warm even in the darkest days
of winter and gave life to the earth.

As he looked across the fields he could remember his first
task as an acolyte—month-long expeditions in search of metal
scraps. He could remember many a frightening night upon the
moors, which all knew were populated by vengeful spirits.
Covered with moss or hidden in glades, the buried treasures
would be found amid the tumbled ruins.

A shower of sparks shot heavenward in the late-afternoon
sky as the sign of another casting appeared. He rubbed the torn
and scarred side of his face. He still remembered the pain,
even when everything else was forgotten.

"Zimri, what is your opinion on this?"

He turned away from the nightmare.

"It appears that the learned Zimri finds our conversation too
tedious for his attention."

Zimri smiled a secret smile as he turned to face Rifton's
challenge. "I shall be with you, Brother Rifton," Zimri said,

feigning weariness, "when I feel that our conversation is finally leading to some common good. For eight days we have sat about this table and argued with no end in sight."

The other archbishops were silent as Rifton leaned back in his chair and nodded in an exaggerated manner.

"In two weeks the first frost shall be upon us, and still we argue," Zimri continued. "Let us decide one way or the other— but let us decide so that we can plan our actions and prepare."

"What he really means," Rifton said, "is that we can prepare for the war that he wants. Brothers, we have decided that now is not the time to attack Sol, for to do so would endanger our fragile peace with the Ezrians, and there are the other reasons which are implicit in the First Choice." Rifton looked significantly at Zimri. "If that is the case, then why must we argue his other point? For in my mind they are one and the same."

Zimri threw up his hands in a gesture of desperation and looked up to the ceiling as if appealing for divine aid.

The ceiling let in a strange, translucent glow from the four rounded bubbles that the Morians had salvaged from a ruined temple. Since they let in the winter cold, they were an extravagance in a society obsessed with heat, but for the meeting room of the archbishops this was something that could be accepted.

The room was simple enough, with a plain, long table of oak running its length. Around the table were fifteen straight-backed chairs, thirteen of which were occupied by the various archbishops of the accepted sects of the Cornathian Church. The seven archbishops of the original orders were gathered at the north end of the table, while the seven of the newer orders were ranked by date of acceptance at the south end of the table. There had been ten original orders to the church, but two had disappeared from the wars and the plague, and the other, Inys Gloi, had resigned shortly after the founding of the Church. The seven new orders had risen from the minor sects. An order was recognized when it had a thousand brothers in its monasteries. There was one exception—the Archbishopric of Cynth Raith, which had only fifty priests. Upon the death of one of the brothers a new one was selected from St. Awstin. They were the keepers of the First Choice, and their power was sacred.

Fourteen of the chairs were filled as Zimri walked over and sat to the left of a higher vacant throne. The Holy See was dying, thereby locking the Council into a helpless debate. Traditionally a simple majority was needed on all votes. The Holy See carried the weight of six votes and made the decision a two-thirds vote as required by ancient law. Without him the Council had to decide each issue either for or against on a two-thirds basis.

"Our brother Zimri is being most difficult," Rifton said, easing up from his chair to the right of the vacant throne. "He's not getting his way and so now he wishes to ignore us. Can you ignore reality, Brother Zimri?"

Rifton turned to face the archbishops. "As our Blessed Father in the next room slowly slips away from us, so does the age that we were born into. Let us end this cycle. The price has become too high. A hundred thousand have died, and are we to start another adventure that will kill a hundred thousand more? True, there must be war, as stated in the First Choice, but must we press for it so soon? For once let us turn aside and wait, for this generation has suffered enough."

Archbishop Balor rose to speak. His deep, melodious voice had a richness more befitting an orator than a brother present for public prayer but once a year. "Zimri, your brotherhood found its power in war. Without war there is no longer a need for the thousands who serve you, and for yourself as well, as far as the people are concerned."

Zimri looked up at the round, wrinkled face of Balor. "Ah, my dear Balor, without my guns where would the power of Good Church be?"

"It saddens me," Nairn of Mord Rinn whispered, "that we so easily forget what Mor has done for us all."

"Brothers, there is far more here than a simple debate for peace or war. We are standing at a dangerous moment," Balor replied as he swept the Council with his penetrating gaze.

"Mor has forged our guns, fought our wars, and has kept the balance as is proper by Holy Decree. But I remind you, brothers, never has one of their order *been* the Holy See. We are not debating the issue of some minor heretic's surviving another year—no, my brothers, we are debating Zimri as the Holy See."

The room was silent as Balor stopped and walked from his chair to rest his hand on the throne.

"Mor is an order unto itself, and if it ever gains the last power then what shall become of the directive handed down to us across the aeons of time? I tell you that a vote for war against this heretic, who has yet to raise a hand against us, is a vote for even more power to Zimri. True, the Missionaries shall find more converts, and Mord Rinn the heretics, and the guilds shall make more ships, but, my brothers, what shall become of the original purpose of our sacred trust?"

Zimri stood and faced the archbishops, ignoring Balor, who stood between him and the throne. He began slowly, so that the brothers had to lean forward to catch his words.

"Rifton and Balor confuse the issue. We are not debating the Holy See. Our Blessed Father is making a slow recovery, and with the blessing of the saints, he should still see long years of service to Good and Holy Church."

Several of the archbishops smiled at him in a gentle, almost mocking way.

"True, if the wars continue they will bring power to my order. I would be a fool to argue against that. But if the wars continue they will bring power to *all* our orders, as well. We have an opportunity here that can't be missed. We have given the Ezrians a bloody repulse and have shattered their home fleet. The Ice is open to us. The Ice is open—but already it is starting to form the future threat. You have voted to leave Sol alone, and since you have voted I shall not argue that issue. But the city-states and the heretic's city are another matter. As Sol melts away, the Free States shall grow, and with them the power of this heretic. We must act now! This new leader can only grow in the vacuum that we are creating for him—until there will come a day to reckon with, for Ezra and Sol are bound by certain laws that *all* have agreed to, but the heretic has not."

"This is ridiculous," Rifton replied. "Every year there is

another new prophet or new teacher, and every year they disappear. What is so different about this one?"

Zimri looked closely at Rifton while he spoke. He sensed something, a vague uneasiness that couldn't be defined.

"This new one comes at a time of recovery from the dark plague. He is filling the space that we should be filling."

"Filling the space with bodies, you mean," Rifton countered. "We haven't even seen this prophet, and from what little we've heard he appears to be harmless."

"He still speaks heresy," Nairn replied.

"He just asks to be left alone," Rifton countered.

"Zimri is right," Nairn said, his burgundy robes billowing out to either side as he stood to speak.

"Remember what Zimri has said here today, for there may be a day when it returns to haunt us all. The three churches are bound by the same laws. But this one—the prophet's— could be different. He is bound by no law, and like all heresy, should be hunted down and destroyed before it can take root. For if it shall ever take root, then in tearing it out we may destroy ourselves."

His words chilled the archbishops. His order instilled a certain level of fear in even the highest officials of the Church, for all knew the power of his trained assassins.

Zimri now decided to cast a shot.

"Rifton, I really can't understand why you are so adamantly against this issue. At times I think that you are almost protecting this heretic."

Rifton knew it to be a comment without weight, but still he hesitated. He could hear his heart pounding, and he spoke quickly in an attempt to make light of the comment.

"Why are you so intent on sending an army to kill one man? We always have the alternative." Rifton nodded to Nairn.

"The death of a single man cannot wipe out a heresy, it merely creates martyrs," Zimri replied. "This requires the might of the Holy Church."

Rifton continued the attack: "My good brother, it seems as if you fear that this teacher could be more than we believe. Do you fear that he might be the One?"

"I don't, but it sounds as if you are toying with heresy."

"Could prophecy be heresy?" Rifton responded evenly.

The issue was provoking that which should be left unsaid, and all knew it. All feared Inys Gloi and its army of hidden agents. Any one of the archbishops could be a secret holder of their cassock, and as such could cause an "accidental" death. A two-thousand-year tradition prevented any challenge to the Casters of the Stars.

Zimri realized that the issue was deadlocking again, and he walked over to the ruby-glassed window, which had grown dark with the onset of early evening. Looking out for a moment, he shuddered and pulled up his cowl so that only the shadow of his face was visible in the dimly lit room.

A hollow boom echoed through the room as the massive oaken door behind Rifton was struck three times by a wooden staff. Zimri turned with a worried look and walked to the door; all eyes were upon him as he opened it to reveal his secretary, Peter.

"Your Excellency," he began while bowing low, "forgive me the intrusion but it's the Holy Father."

"What's wrong?"

"He's taken ill again and is in pain."

Zimri turned to face the other archbishops. "My brothers, I must leave to see to our Blessed Father. Anyhow, it's late and we are all a bit weary. There are many things that I feel should wait until tomorrow's light. Do we agree at least on this?"

The archbishops nodded.

"Good, then, my brothers. If you will excuse me I must see to our Father." He turned to Peter. "Please see to it that their secretaries escort our brothers back to their quarters." Turning back to the archbishops, he bowed, "My brothers, until to-morrow."

The door opened to his response and Peter entered Zimri's chamber, which was directly across the corridor from the apartment of the Holy See.

"I trust that all is in order," Zimri said.

"Everything has been prepared."

"Have you found that disciple?"

"He's been taken care of."

"Who is the brother?"

"Bartholomew. We've known for some time that he's been giving information to Archbishop Landson."

Zimri was silent and looked closely at Peter.

"I hope you've made the right choice."

"Oh I have, your Excellency."

"Good. Awaken me before it is to begin."

Peter turned and left the room. He smiled. Bartholomew should have known better—a thousand gold pieces had disappeared with the "lost ship." You can cheat me a little, Bartholomew, he thought, but never try and make a fool of me.

Rifton awoke to someone's pounding on his door. For several seconds he was confused by the noise and the unfamiliar setting. Finally the door was flung open to reveal Isaac with the dim light of the hallway behind him. "Hurry, Rifton, get up. Saints be praised, you're safe!" There was a note of panic in his voice.

"What is it?" Rifton demanded as he swung himself out of bed.

"It's the Holy Father."

Without another word Rifton grabbed for his cloak, and throwing it over his shoulders, he ran out into the corridor.

The cathedral was in an uproar. As Rifton stormed through the doorway he was nearly bowled over by a column of priests of the Select, and their curved scimitars glinted evilly in the flickering torchlight.

Rifton started to run after them. His fear caused an unexpected well of energy to spring forth, and for a man of his years he showed an amazing speed. Rifton turned a corner and bumped into a confused knot of priests and guards all trying simultaneously to force their way through a low and narrow doorway that led into the apartments of the Holy See. Upon entrance into the apartments they conversed in whispers.

With Niall behind him, Isaac caught up to Rifton and whispered, "I was going to the chapel of St. Adrain when I heard the clash of arms from the inner chamber. I started to run toward the commotion when I heard the cry. 'Assassin.' I didn't stay to see what happened but ran to get you instead."

They pushed forward and finally turned the last corner and stood before the bedchamber of the Holy See. As if on cue, the doors swung open, and there in the doorway stood Zimri. A trickle of blood dripped from his hand onto the pearly whiteness of the marble floor.

He was obviously shaken, but he made an effort at an appearance of calm. At his feet lay two forms surrounded by ugly pools of blood. A third man lay in the corner, his tunic covered with blood. The smell of death and fear pervaded the hallway, and gradually the crowd fell silent.

Zimri stared thoughtfully at them, and then ever so slowly, with measured words, he started. "The Holy Father is safe. Fortunately I was with him in his chamber and was able to stop the madman. This, my brothers, is the price of our weakness. The assassin fell upon the two guards at the door, shouting that he was the messenger of the new prophet. He slew Brother Yarvin and grievously injured Brother Farnath, who managed to wound the madman fatally."

Zimri paused, and walked to where Brother Farnath was lying in the corner, a dazed look on his face as the blood welled through an ugly wound in his shoulder. Zimri leaned over and made the sign of blessing, then, kneeling, he hugged the wounded priest. "Perpetual blessing on you, brother. I shall pray to the Saints for your speedy recovery."

Several priests hurried to Farnath, and taking him up gently, they led him away.

With a gesture of disdain Zimri waved his bloodied hand. "Farnath's blade was true, and he mortally wounded the madman, who nevertheless, still came on. If he had been without hurt I could not have stopped him."

"This is the reward of weakness!" Zimri shouted unexpectedly, then he turned to point at Rifton. "We talk of peace, and madmen come in the night to slay our Holy Father."

By now the hallway was packed with priests and several of the archbishops stood at the back of the hall.

"The Holy Father is safe for now, but what of the next time? Answer me that."

The crowd parted and Peter stepped forward with a brother of the Select at his side. The brother shot nervous glances at the crowd. Upon seeing Zimri, he froze.

Zimri eyed him coldly, and the savage ferocity of his mood could be felt throughout the crowd.

"Your name, brother."

"Bartholomew, your Excellency."

"Are you not captain of the watch for tonight?"

"Yes, your Excellency, I am."

"Then how came this to happen?"

Bartholomew looked at Zimri, and then to Peter.

"Brother," Zimri started softly, "you are of my order. Therefore I am to judge. Speak honestly and the Saints will be just, for so it is written."

Bartholomew threw himself onto his knees. "Forgive me, your Excellency. I was asleep and did not secure the eastern gate. Forgive me. But who would have dreamed of this?"

The room fell silent, so silent that all could hear the quick and nervous breathing of the archbishop before them.

"Brother, your sword."

Bartholomew drew his scimitar, kissed it reverently, and handed it to the archbishop, who towered above him.

"Brother, I absolve you of your sins by the power that the Saints have vested in me."

Bartholomew looked to his side and saw Peter's eyes. He had thought it strange that Peter had offered him the thousand gold lomans for this trick to 'embarrass Rifton.' A madman would be let into the cathedral and killed. The attempt would be blamed on Rifton and Bartholomew would receive the thousand lomans and a transfer to a private merchantman, where he could get his fill of things not available to the Select, who lived the most austere of lives.

Beheading was once the punishment of those who failed in the duties of the Select, but over the years the practice had devolved to a ritual in which the offender would be absolved of sin, his neck merely tapped with the flat of the blade. Yet as he looked at Peter, who smiled savagely at him, he suddenly realized. In panic he started to stand up. "Wait," he screamed hysterically.

With all the force he could muster, Zimri smashed down with the blade. Zimri's skill was still with him, for even as Bartholomew rose, the blade cut upward in a gentle arc. The fine blade sliced through Bartholomew's neck, cutting him off in midscream. The head tumbled forward and a fountain of blood showered those who stood nearby. The body collapsed on the floor and kicked for several seconds, then it was still.

"Brothers," Zimri stated, "when it comes to the protection of our Blessed Father and our Holy Church, *that* is the reward for negligence."

No one dared to move or break the deadly silence.

Rifton stood to the side and his heart raced as the full impact of what had happened washed over him. He had a good vantage point to the drama, so good in fact, that he looked in horror at the spattering of blood that had showered his cloak. Isaac was standing next to him, ashen.

There is more to it, Rifton thought. There's damn well more!

Zimri interrupted his thoughts. "Brothers, let us return to our chambers to pray. Brother Moab, see to the removal of the bodies and give Bartholomew the full ceremony of interment. He died absolved and shall rest forever at the Long Table. Poor Bartholomew could not serve in this world, but forgiven, perhaps he shall serve in the next."

Zimri walked back through the doors into the Holy Father's bedchamber.

"Your Excellency, I would like to see our Blessed Father," Rifton announced. "I fear for him and will not sleep until my eyes have told me that all is well with him."

Zimri smiled. "Of course, my brother, of course. You must excuse my tirade out there," he said as he led Rifton into the chamber. "I was overwrought. I hope you did not take offense."

Rifton approached the canopied bed draped with white hangings. It gave the illusion of a cloud floating in a sea of blackness.

while overhead, the solid-gold arch that spanned the ceiling glinted faintly in the shimmering candlelight.

It was always a shock to see him like this. The Holy See— Good Ioan. He was awake, staring vacantly toward the ceiling. Rifton moved forward and bowed reverently as he approached the side of the bed.

Zimri, in respect, drew back.

"Ah, my old friend, how fare you tonight?" Rifton whispered as he brushed aside his tears at seeing his friend so, crippled and trapped in a dying body.

"Sleep my friend. I'll be close by." Rifton stood and in the shadows wiped his eyes. He started toward the doorway while Zimri stood by the edge of the bed and watched. As Rifton reached the door he turned and in a casual, almost offhanded way, pointed at Zimri's wounded hand.

"Really, Zimri, I think you got more than you bargained for this time."

Zimri gave a grudging smile to the most formidable and perceptive of his enemies. He bowed respectfully to Rifton as he left.

As soon as Rifton's back was turned, a cold shiver washed through Zimri. I'd better get this scratch bandaged, he thought, and give Peter a good going-over. There is more than meets the eye with his choice. And lost in thought, he left the room and closed the door.

The Holy See was alone as the candle gutted away, its dying sparks reflected in tears that spoke of unspeakable pain and simple longing.

CHAPTER 15

"ST. ULIMAR, SAVE ME," THE VOICE DOWN THE CORRIDOR shrieked for the thousandth time. The hysterical chant had droned on for days—just one maddening note in the deafening cacophony of screams that he desperately tried to ignore.

Suddenly there was silence, and he turned from his thoughts. Rolling over in the fetid darkness, he looked through the crack in the door that admitted the one thin shaft of flickering light. Yes, they are coming again, he thought.

The sound of boots echoed down the dank, foul-smelling corridor. They came to his cell and stopped for a moment, then, with a low command, the group pushed on to the next cell.

Seth of Inys Gloi knew the ritual that was to be played, and with a sickened heart he tried to block out the drama that was unfolding just a dozen feet away.

"Simon Gutherson," a voice suddenly intoned in the corridor, while in the background Seth could hear the strains of the "Am Sythric for the Fallen" start their eerie half-tone keening.

"And the light shall shun him as he falls to eternal doom."

"Simon Gutherson of Dubla," the voice repeated.

"Simon Gutherson of Dubla, relapsed heretic," it said for the third time. "You have been found wanting and shall face the punishment of Good and Holy Church, for your sins and the return of the Garden of Light. You shall be taken from this place to the House of Death where ye shall be stripped, quartered, and burned, on this, the twenty-second year, first month, and fifteenth day of the Holy Guidance of our merciful Father, Ioan III."

Seth listened to the muffled sobs as the chained prisoner was led forth from his cell. Perhaps this one will go quietly, Seth prayed. But the thought had no sooner passed than he was proved wrong.

"Oh Saints, please no! He owed me money, he did. Oh Saints, he lied, please listen to me!" The sound of scuffling broke out in the hallway and there was a jarring thud of wood against bone. The screaming stopped, to be replaced by a low, sobbing moan. The moaning retreated down the hall and was washed over by the chanting of the Inquisition brothers. Seth could hear the rusted door groan shut and for a moment there was silence. The screaming started again: "St. Ulimar, save me...."

He found it interesting that in total blackness the ability to smell and hear became so acute. The smell he tried to block out. It was a horrifying stench of excrement, dampness, and rot. The various sounds started to filter in again—the steady drip of water in his cell, the sobbing of the prisoners, and the soft scurrying of rats in the walls and corridor. Above him he could hear the steady drone of wheeled traffic, so it must still be day, he thought. The sound from the next room, though, was disturbing. Simon was gone on the one side, but Brian should still be alive in the next cell. He could hear the rats in there, and with a chill Seth knew that they were enjoying another feast. There would be little enough of Brian to bury if they ever finally got around to it.

He had been there for at least a month, as far as he could reckon. Who had betrayed him? The thoughts flooded back. He had been in Cornath all through the spring, spreading word of Michael and winning converts. He and fifty other brothers from Inys Gloi had been doing their jobs well. One or two had been picked up, but Seth always felt that he, as the shrewdest, would never be caught. His cover as a displaced Mathinian merchant had been convincing enough, and outwardly he swore allegiance to Cornath. Who had betrayed him?

They had come in the night, as they always did, and had seized him and four other brothers of Inys. In spite of his training, he was terrified. There would be the question asked three times: Are you a heretic? The burden of proof would be on him to show that he was not. If he failed to convince them, three times he would be burned, racked, immersed, and hung. They all talked before the end.

He heard the corridor hatch open again, and all fell silent as sandaled feet stormed down the hallway. They stopped in front of his cell. Seth could feel the thundering of his heart as the door slammed open. He pulled back and looked into the blinding light that silhouetted a hooded form.

"Seth of Mathin," he heard a voice say. "You will come with us."

"My friend, when I heard about this terrible mistake I came here as quickly as possible to see to your release and to offer you my apologies."

"I see," Seth said cautiously as he sipped the glass of mulled wine that had been set before him.

"The real thief of the sacred chalice was only found this morning, and when he confessed it came to my Master Zimri's attention that five innocent men had been imprisoned for this same act. He sent me, as his secretary, to make amends personally. He would have come himself but he has been busy with preparations for the war."

"War?" Seth asked, feigning a bored lack of interest.

"Yes, there is to be war."

"Oh, the Ezrians again," Seth said, trying to find out more. "It's a good move to go for them now. They can never have enough punishment, I say, after what they did to me." And he waved his right arm before Peter.

Peter looked at the stump and softly responded, "According to our information, you lost that to an Ezrian off Valdinmar a couple of years back."

"Ah, that I did. I've fought your enemies well, I have," Seth said. "But there is another one in my mind now; he who drove me from my homeland."

"Oh, I see," Peter said. "You mean this new heretic."

"Yes, him," Seth said, and stopping, he looked Peter in the eye.

Peter smiled inwardly.

"My master first of all bid me to give you this as a token of our regret for all that we have done," and so saying, Peter reached into his robe and brought out seventy-five gold pieces. "Divide it up among yourself and your friends."

"This is most generous."

A fifty-fifty split between you and me, Peter thought. Not a bad day's profit.

"I understand," Peter continued, "your ship carries four good ballistae, and you've fought her often."

"Aye, that I have. She's a rare good craft, can outrun most anything upon the Ice."

"Considering where we are bound, we could use you as a pilot and scout, we could," Peter said in a conspiratorial manner. "The fleet sails to punish the one who sent an assassin against our Holy Father."

"What would be the pay?" Seth asked.

"Half of whatever loot you take is yours, plus one-half of a percent of the total pillage of the fleet, as long as you are in sight of an action."

"That is generous—for a craft my size, it's usually half of that."

"My master wills it so, in payment of your grievance."

"Where is the fleet to marshal?"

"At Cornath, in seven weeks' time. We sail on the Night of Supplication."

"I shall consider it."

"Good," Peter said, and rising and walking around to Seth,

he put his hands on Seth's shoulders. "We could use you, since you say that you were expelled by this so-called prophet."

"Oh," Seth said evenly.

"It should not be told, and I hope I am correct in thinking you can keep this quiet, because Heaven knows it will mean our heads if word gets out. . . ."

"You have my word," Seth said, while looking into Peter's eyes.

"We sail to stamp out this new heresy. We go to avenge you against your enemy. The Council has decided to take Mathin."

Seth kept the eye contact and his expression didn't waver. "I thank you for your confidence. We will meet again upon the Ice." And so saying, he turned and walked from the room.

"I have done as you commanded," Peter reported.

"Good, the Council has decided and we have defeated Rifton. Let us hope that Seth does his part as well."

"It's a terrible risk you're taking," Peter said.

"This prophet can be used."

"Zimri, this is a dangerous game that you're playing."

"Look, it's already been done, and if there is one thing you must learn it is to not worry once the decisions have been made. The Council has given us what we wanted—half the home fleet to go to Mathin."

"So why play this move with Seth?"

"It's easy, Peter. You must learn to see these things. This prophet has no fleet to speak of, we know that. If four cruisers, eight frigates, and a host of transports and merchantmen descended on him, the city would fall in hours. Remember, we did it with a quarter that strength three years ago." He hesitated for a second and looked out the window.

"And?" Peter prompted.

"Oh yes," Zimri responded. "You see, I don't want the city to be taken."

"So that is why you had Seth arranged like this?"

"Ah Peter, you are learning," Zimri said sarcastically. "I've seen the maps of Mathin. Given eight weeks' warning, they could turn it into an impregnable fortress. They hold till spring, we retreat, and the following year the brotherhood is needed again. This keeps our presence in the South, gives us a war without too much cost, and keeps the brotherhood in strength for the real conflict to come."

"And that is?"

Zimri looked at Peter, and with an uncomfortable feeling Peter knew that he had been dismissed.

Peter rose and started to walk to the door.

"Oh, by the way Peter . . ."

Peter had felt it coming for some time. "Yes," he said grimly.

"Ah, my dear Peter, you are learning the game after all, but the next step you must learn is never to show that you already know."

"Then I must assume that I am to take Holy Power of the fleet."

"But of course, Peter—I need someone there to make sure that all goes according to plan. I'm arranging for Lord Conneachson to command; you should be able to control him easily enough.

"Now, you have much to see to, but we shall talk again."

Without another word Peter was gone, leaving Zimri alone with his thoughts.

It would be good to get Peter away for a while, Zimri thought. He's capable enough to see the job through, but if it goes wrong I can sacrifice him easily enough.

Zimri pulled his blue cloak tighter about himself. The step to the Holy See was drawing closer, but he needed something to destroy Rifton first. He knew that Rifton and his followers would never join together for his final dream. He was confirmed to the Ceuth Cearth and his dream was to see it confirmed forever. In order to do that Rifton and Balor would have to go, and their orders destroyed. But there was an even bigger obstacle to overcome. He would have to destroy Inys Gloi. Mathin would be a minor training ground to keep his fleets ready and the rationale for his power intact.

He thought of Mathin and he had that feeling again—that

sense of chill. He walked to the window and looked out. The first snow of winter was falling; its icy fingers rattled the pane with a foretaste of the cold to come. "Damn, I wish that spy would return," he mumbled out loud.

The storm that was swirling down the narrow alleyways of Dulyn covered the coast of Cornath with the first sign of winter. Deep within the mountain of St. Awstin, winter's approach was barely noticed, for Balor of Cynth Raith had come in the middle of the night as if storm-driven himself, to discuss the impending crisis.

"Are you sure then that it was him?" Balor asked as he settled into the chair across from Rifton's desk.

"We're positive of it. It was Niall who saw him."

"What were you able to find out, then?"

"He claims to have been a Mathinian merchant. Zimri had him arrested on a charge of theft. He was seen on the streets of Conwy just five days ago."

"Does this Seth know that we're aware of him?"

"I don't think so."

"So what is your conclusion?" Balor asked. "And it better be a good one to drag me twenty leagues through this storm."

"Michael is alive."

Balor was silent for a moment as he took the Vinlander that Rifton offered him. Rifton had aged visibly since the conference and his hand shook as he poured a cup for himself.

"Then our fears were correct after all," Balor said coldly. "Do you think Zimri knows?"

"No, I don't think so."

"Why?"

"Because Seth was arrested before the conference. If Zimri had known he would have finished me off right there."

"True—so what do you think his plan is?"

"He wants Michael to know of the attack. He knew the link between Seth and the Heretic without knowing who they really were. To hire Facinn's ship for the campaign can only result in one thing."

"I see. The campaign will be tipped off to the Heretic, they'll have time to prepare, and Zimri will have a nice long war on his hands to keep Mor occupied."

"There is nothing else that I could think of. Zimri is orthodox with the First Choice, therefore he knows the agreement between us and Ezra cannot be broken for at least a generation in order to give us both time to recover. This is the agreement of the Council and he is bound to it. Therefore he needs this new enemy."

"But he doesn't yet know who it is," Balor interrupted.

Rifton was silent.

"I now understand the reason why you have sent for me," Balor said.

Rifton turned away to conceal his emotions. "Damn Inys Gloi forever," he finally choked out.

"I wish that we could," Balor said as he came around the table and put his hand on Rifton's shoulder. "But they are too strong. And if we ever were to try a move against them, their Brothers of the Knife would find us. Such has always been the fate of leaders who interfere too much with them. I don't think that Zimri sees the danger, nor would Michael, but we must do something about both."

Rifton nodded his head.

"Zimri can't see how this could affect the First Choice."

Balor was troubled as he lapsed into quiet contemplation. The plan slowly started to form, as Rifton knew it would.

"Someone in Mor must be made aware of the risk that Zimri takes," Balor said, "but it must be done in such a way that we would not be betrayed."

"I know, and that is what I hoped for," Rifton said.

Balor hesitated, and then looking Rifton straight in the eyes, he said coldly, "Eighteen years ago I came to you and told you that for the good of the Church Michael must be destroyed, that Inys Gloi had traced the signs of birth to him. Michael was no longer one of us from that moment on, even if he was of your blood. I know that he is the last of your family, but he is too big a threat, not only to you but to our entire Church. Rifton, Michael must die."

"I know," Rifton whispered.

"I therefore shall release the Black Brother to him, and he will sail tonight."

Rifton looked at Balor. "I knew that, and that was the reason I sent for you. But as his kinsman, I must claim the right first to warn him and to offer him exile beyond the Flowing Sea."

"So it shall be," Balor said. "But I fear that already it is too late for him."

"Olin, set the course west by southwest."

"Aye, Seth, west by southwest, it is."

The ice schooner, answering to the wheel, heeled over and ran a close reach to the wind. The deck rode on a steady slant as they pinched as close to the wind as they dared.

"We're running free and clear," Seth shouted from atop the foremast. What a day to be alive, he thought.

The Ice stretched to the horizon, clear and unbroken. The sun held like a small, dimming lamp on the western horizon, while the wind blew hard and strong from due west. It was a day to make an ice runner's heart swell with joy—the first good sail of winter, the tracks clear before him, and the virgin ice to plow across.

He pulled aside his goggles and looked out to the late-afternoon sun. In another hour it would be dark, but he felt that he could risk it. They had lost a week because of the storm and every moment was the difference between success and failure. Grabbing hold of the flying jib, he slid a hundred feet to the bowsprit, and with the agility of a cat he ran down the bowsprit to the forecastle deck.

"Ah, Olin, what say ye now?"

"It will be good to see the fight start at last, will it not, Master Seth?"

"Aye, that it will be."

Together, they stood upon the deck, two brothers of Inys Gloi, their mission ready after years of preparation—the fight for mastery of the Church was beginning at last. But for the moment they were enthralled by the freedom of the Ice and a stiff breeze to run close to. The wind picked up and the deck heeled over. Olin gently put the tiller over and dropped off a point from the wind; the deck eased back to its original cant. From astern Seth could hear the shouts of the other brothers and he knew that they too were rejoicing over having finally broken free of the storm which had stalled them.

Seth prayed that the ice was good and that he could find a track quickly. This was the earliest he had ever sailed, and he had no idea which tracks through the Broken Ice were open. Tonight he would meet with the Master. There, the final plans and orders would be revealed, and, he hoped, a report on the Ice, as well.

"Tonight we harbor at Inys Gloi!" Seth shouted to the crew, and they cheered in response.

CHAPTER 16

"SO MUCH IS YET TO BE DONE," MICHAEL SAID ANGRILY, "SO why do you always return to the same subject?"

"But Michael," Zardok replied wearily, "you must face reality. Your conversations in the Grove are drawing notice. There must have been two hundred with you this morning. As the ships come out of the north this year, *thousands* will hear you. Some will say that you are crazy, others will listen and be moved, but many will say that you are either the Prophet or a heretic. Both conclusions are dangerous."

"So what in hell do you want me to do? Deny that which I feel I must say?"

"No, but you must consider the war that will come as a result."

"It might be years before it comes."

"But it will come nevertheless."

"Zardok, what about the Dead Lands, and the sailing to the Southward Seas? And the library to be built? There are so many other things to call our resources and energies."

"Don't speak about the Dead Lands again—in my mind that subject is closed."

"But Zardok, it only stands a day's run to the west."

"The churches are right on that one. It is said that the plague that afflicted us came from those lands."

Michael fell silent at this. Just the mention of the plague was distressing to Zardok.

From the half-completed watchtower out on the harbor wall a horn sounded.

It sounded but once—a single ship approaching.

"Ah," Zardok suddenly brightened up, "the first ship of the year. Let's see what news it brings." And together, they followed the swelling crowd that made its way out to the harbor.

The ship, a small six-man cutter, made a graceful arc through the gate and stopped in mid-harbor. A single skater leaped from her side and made his way to the quay. His strong, steady stride carried a note of urgency to it, and Michael felt a wave of apprehension.

Without even waiting for the messenger, Michael lowered himself from the dock and started to make his way out to him. Daniel and Ormath pushed their way out of the crowd and, jumping off the dock, ran up alongside him.

The skater drew up to them.

"I seek the teacher commonly called the Heretic," said the man who was bent over, panting for breath.

"You have found him," Michael replied.

The skater looked keenly at him for a moment.

"Right. You are to go alone to the cutter."

"Now wait a moment," Daniel growled.

"And who asked me to do this?" Michael said.

The skater held up a golden seal for Michael to look at.

The moment he had dreaded had at last arrived.

Michael turned to Daniel. "I'm going, I know who they are."

"But I don't, and you're not going alone, Michael—it could be a trap."

The messenger looked at Daniel. "My orders are simple—he is to go alone. I will stay here as hostage."

Daniel looked at the messenger and snarled. "And what the hell good are you, compared to the Chosen One?"

Daniel turned to Ormath. "Get the men. We're going out to see about this."

"Hold," the messenger said fiercely. "I've received my orders and so have those aboard this craft. If more than one person approaches within bowshot range there is four hundred-weight of powder aboard her and a match will be put to it."

"The devil, you say!" Daniel shouted.

"It is true, we have our orders. If anyone but the Heretic approaches, the ship and all aboard her will be destroyed."

Michael looked closely at the messenger and fixed him with his gaze, then turning, he started to walk toward the ship. "He speaks the truth," Michael said. "I shall go alone."

"But Michael—"

Michael spun toward Daniel. "Silence," he shouted, then turning again, he walked to the ship.

"I donna' like this at all," Ormath mumbled. "I smell trouble a comin'."

Michael swung his leg over the railing and landed on the deck. A fur-clad ice runner stood in the hatchway and didn't move or speak as Michael came over to him.

For several long moments they stood, looking at each other. "It is you then," the ice runner whispered.

"Niall?"

"So, now I see," Niall said. "I thought Rifton mad at first. How did he know?"

"Rifton," Michael asked. "How is he?"

"He is well, but that is all I am allowed to say," and suddenly Niall's voice grew cold. "Michael Ormson, the Heretic," he said in a speechlike manner, "his Holiness Rifton of Cornath, Archbishop of Awstin, Protector of the Faithful, has charged me, Niall of Cornath, to bring you this message. His orders are that you are to read it and then to hand it back to me."

So saying, Niall brought forth a simple letter that bore no seal or mark.

"Niall, what is going on?" Michael asked.

Niall stood silent, holding the package before him. Michael finally took it, and opening the letter, he started to read.

It was in Rifton's usual cramped scrawl, and just the sight of it made Michael's heart beat faster.

"Michael, my boy," it began, and Michael stopped for a moment to wipe the tears from his eyes.

> *Michael, my boy, in my heart I knew that you had not perished, as all had said, and there finally came a day when I knew that my fears were true—the heretic was you. I speak to you now, Michael, from beyond the veil of Holy Church, for you have already been listed in our hearts as one who has never existed.*

Michael stopped reading and looked at Niall. Niall turned his back to Michael.

> *Niall alone could I trust with this mission, even though I knew it would break his heart since you were like a son to him as well. Michael, you are already the adversary, but you are also the last of my blood, and even Holy Church cannot deny me that.*
>
> *Zimri does not yet know who you are, but he suspects. He has convinced the Council that you are a danger, even as you read this letter his fleet is preparing to overwhelm you. Michael, you shall be completely destroyed, as all the power of Holy Church will bear upon you, and tens of thousands will die.*
>
> *Michael my boy, accept exile while there is still time. Flee to the Flowing Sea—and let not this war take place. Only Zimri can win from it. You think you act as your own, but you are merely the pawn of Inys Gloi and of Zimri for control of the Church.*
>
> *I have always loved you, Michael, and will pray for you, though I know that I shall never see you again, in*

*either this world or the next. Take heed of my warning,
for there is so little time.*

  Your Uncle and Protector

Michael held the letter for several minutes, rereading it again
and again—as if additional words would suddenly appear to
reassure him that everything would be all right. So Rifton knew,
and Zimri was not far behind. Once Zimri found out, that would
be all for Rifton, and perhaps for the Brotherhood of St. Awstin
as well. He turned again and looked at Niall. No wonder there's
hate in his eyes, Michael thought.

Without another word he walked over to Niall and handed
the letter back to him. Niall produced a small brazier from a
recess behind the hatchway. He took a flask from beneath his
cloak, poured oil upon the letter, then dropped it in the brazier.
Niall added another liquid from a tightly sealed flask and the
paper smoldered then burst into flame. In a minute the evidence
was gone, as the paper turned to ashes, which Niall ceremo-
niously ground into dust and cast to the four corners of the Ice.

"I would like to send him a message," Michael said.

"Already the door has been shut, already the light extinguished," Niall started to intone the rite of excommunication
from the brotherhood.

Michael turned and made his way to the railings.

"You must decide, Michael Ormson," Niall suddenly said.
"Do you sail with us, or do you stay here at Mathin?"

He could see the pain in Niall's eyes.

"Where would you take me?" Michael asked.

"Off of the Ice forever. You would be exiled to the Flowing
Sea."

"The alternative?"

"Already the Black Brother awaits you."

"I know."

Niall stood rigid and silent.

Michael walked up to him and embraced his unyielding
form. Turning, he walked back to the edge of the ship.

"Already the door has been shut, already the light extinguished . . ." Niall began again.

"Farewell, Niall."

Niall stopped the chant for a moment. "To say who we were, or where we came from, could only hurt an old man whom we both love," Niall said with a look of anguish.

"Yes, I know, and shall say nothing."

"You have been told and warned then, my task has ended." Niall looked at Michael, then his eyes drifted. His voice came thickly. "Michael Ormson, it would have been better if you had died upon the Ice." And Niall resumed his chant.

A half-hour later Michael stood alone upon the frozen harbor and looked to where the ship had disappeared over the horizon. Suddenly a brief flash lit the evening sky, and several minutes later a faint rolling sound came from the east.

Even if it had not been ordered, Niall would not risk loose tongues among the brothers on board. Michael knew also that it was a message from Niall. It was the thunder of the approaching storm.

And no one detected the single figure who slipped in from the Frozen Sea that night.

"Damn it, Zardok, I must leave!"

"You can't run away from it, Michael. You can't run away."

It had been a night of torment and debate. Fortunately the rest had stayed clear. Ishmael had said nothing. Janis had pledged to support Michael no matter what his decision. And Daniel had wanted him to go to Inys Gloi.

But Zardok had remained adamant. "Sooner or later they would track you down anyhow. At least here you have support, hundreds in this city who would fight for you."

"Fight for me as their Messiah, their Prophet."

"It doesn't matter what they call you, as long as they fight for you."

"To hell with you, Zardok, I don't want their blood."

"But it's in your hands anyhow."

So it had gone on through the night.

At dawn he left them and made his way up to the Grove. The demons of fear were upon him, and he wrestled throughout the morning with them. One side of him believed that he was merely an individual who thought differently and that, as such, he was simply tapping into the feelings of others. The other side, the side that he feared, spoke loudly, but he shouted it down. Slowly the decision was formed. He could not lead the people into a senseless war that merely made him a pawn dancing to Zimri's music.

No, he would ask Zardok for a ship. He would leave them all, and sail to the west, to the Dead Lands whence no one returned. Maybe then he would find peace.

The thought of leaving settled over him, and in it he found comfort. The sound of a horn in the distance barely disturbed him and he quietly slept, his mind resolved to leave behind the religious madness forever.

He awoke with a start; someone was nearby. He realized with surprise that several inches of snow had fallen upon him and that it was still falling through the trees, muffling all in its silky silence. But he was sure he sensed someone's approach.

Without moving he quietly thought of Daniel, and for the first time in a long while wished he was there.

"No, Michael Ormson, you don't need Daniel to protect you from me."

"Seth!" Michael shouted joyfully.

From out of the trees stepped the old friend whom he had driven away in a rage the year before. Michael ran up to Seth and threw his arms around him, thumping him wildly on the back.

"Ah, Seth my friend, it is so good to have you with me."

Seth looked into his eyes and smiled.

"Why are you here? When did you arrive?"

"Didn't you hear my ship's horn?"

"No, I didn't realize, I guess I was lost in thought. So, you've just arrived, then."

"Not a half-hour ago. I would speak to no one until I found you."

"You don't know?"

"Know what?" Seth asked.

"Zimri is coming for me."

"But how did you find out?"

Michael put his hand on Seth's shoulder and, together, they walked through the grove while he explained most of what had happened. But he took care to keep Niall's identity a secret and spoke merely of friends in Cornath.

"Interesting," Seth said softly, "so interesting."

Then Seth briefly spoke of his experience with Peter.

Damn it, Michael thought. Damn it all, it's starting to fit. "Are you sure it was Peter who did this?"

"Yes, he made it a point to say that he was the voice of Zimri."

"He knows," Michael shouted. "The bastard knows."

"What are you talking about?" Seth asked. "Just what is going on?"

"Rifton knows, and so does Zimri. Zimri set you up, my friend."

"How?" Seth asked in surprise.

"Look, Seth. Zimri knew your connection to me, and he wanted you to come back here to let me know that he was coming. He figured I would prepare, hold out for a siege, and then give him an excuse to come again next year, and the year after that. To keep Mor in training, to keep Mor in power—until the Holy Father is dead.

"Damn it, Seth, I can't run. He'll level this city anyhow. Even if I flee, Mathin will defend itself and Zimri will have his war. Damn it, we're all his pawns."

"By spring his agents will know exactly who I am, and Rifton will be politically destroyed from having been protector of a heretic—and a relative at that! So Rifton is beyond saving as well . . . Damn it!" Michael screamed, flinging his arms upward. "Damn you all, can't this pass from me?"

"It cannot," Seth said in his low, rolling voice. "It was ordained before you were ever born."

"Do you believe I am the Chosen One?"

"Yes."

"But tens of thousands will die."

"They will die anyhow, Michael, but you can give them a dream to live with even as they lay down their lives."

"Why?"

"So the cycle can be broken at last. The churches are ready to die, Michael, and you can give them the final blow. Michael, think of the power I offer you. Look to the city, and you can hear the shouts of the people who go to hear what my crew is saying. They already know, Michael. And already they wait for you to lead them."

"Can't you see? Can't you see what you are doing to me, Seth?"

"I am making you what you are meant to be—a leader for the ending of this age."

"Damn you and Inys Gloi, who made up all this trash of prophecy."

"Even if we made it up," Seth said coldly, "it is you, Michael, who fit the bill of what was said, and therefore you must serve. What can you fear in that? You can have your dream in the end, you know—an end to the cycle of war."

"What do I fear?" Michael shouted. "What do I fear? Damn you, Seth—I fear that one day I will crave this worship, this power, that I will one day believe I am the Messenger of God and that men shall and must die for me."

"If that need be, Michael, so let it be. Inys Gloi will stand by you."

"What if I should just walk away from you and your damn secret. What then?"

"You won't, Michael, you cannot escape what must be. War is coming, like it or not. You know that if you leave, this city will fall and all will be put to the sword. If you stay, though, it will live by your leadership."

"But I'm not sure."

Seth started to laugh, and he walked up to Michael and put his hand on Michael's shoulder. "Michael Ormson, you are only a man. And as such, you will always wrestle with doubt. Some future history will put assurance into your mind, the voice of God at your ear, the clear sight of genius into your every word. That is the way it has always been. You will always be in doubt. But the people Michael—ah, the people will not, for the people have always needed something to believe in. You can give them a choice. You can give them their Church with its fear of torment and darkness, or you can give them you."

"The Garden is a metaphor—Inys Gloi has known that. Our astrologies have merely seen that the cycle of two thousand years has ended, and as it has happened before, with each ending has come a new age with a new leader to set its stage."

"That is you, Michael Ormson. Whether you like it or not, that is you. In your heart you know this to be true."

And Michael looked inward and finally acknowledged that which he had fled from all of his life. And the taking of it shook him to the core of his existence. Whether he truly was the One or not, he would never know, but he could not escape that which the world around him wanted to believe.

"I shall lead them," he said. "I know I will lose myself in the process, but I shall lead them."

"People of Mathin," Michael began, "we have heard the words of Seth the Far-seeing and of your own Ishmael, and I feel that I who have started so much of this should speak as well." Michael looked out over the sea of faces before him. The entire city must be here, he thought.

"Seth has told you of Zimri and the Cornathian Church's plans. Within a two-month span we can expect their fleet to be outside this very harbor. Ishmael has called upon you to fight, and you have responded that you would. And now I shall ask you why.

"Remember always that it is I, more than anyone else, who Zimri wants. I am the one he desires. As such, it is I who brought this down upon you. Therefore, if you wish me to leave I will."

Michael stood in silence for a moment; the only sound was the gentle whisper of the afternoon breeze.

"Ishmael has called you to fight for your homes, and we will. But I now call upon you for more. Let this be the start of the end of all that the churches have stood for—the fear of ourselves. Let us end our thoughts of death! Let us turn our thoughts to what we can do today to make this world a garden again, by our own hands. Let us decide that now is the time to end the two-thousand-year night."

Michael turned and walked away from the dock.

"Michael!" a voice echoed from the background, and in a moment the crowd started to chant his name in a deep voice that carried far out upon the Ice, so that it seemed to reach to the very foundation of the world.

Seth looked back to Michael, and then he turned to Daniel. "I think," he whispered, "that I am beginning to fear what we have started here."

And Daniel was silent.

CHAPTER 17

"By the Saints, Michael, it's all well and good to make your wonderful speeches, but what the hell is going to happen to my city now? Don't your realize what's coming?"

"You forget, Ishmael," he said softly, "I rode a ram at Judean's Bane. I know what it's about."

Ishmael gave him an exasperated look. "Look, Michael, your dream is all well and good, but see what it has called down on us. In another five years we could have been ready for it, but not now. There aren't fifteen thousand people on this entire island. At best we can muster three thousand experienced men. We've only forty-five guns with some renegade priests to serve them. Michael, look at the numbers! Cruisers— we have one small one to their four. Frigates—two to their eight. Merchantmen—we can't even guess how many will come against our half-dozen. If we venture out onto the Ice we'll be slaughtered."

"But we must go on the Ice," Michael replied.

"I see," Ishmael said sarcastically. "I guess you believe these priest stories, as well," he suddenly shouted. Turning, he looked at Seth. "We've been friends for fifteen years and I've always trusted your word. And in payment you give me a man who believes the trash that you preach."

"Damn it, Ishmael, what do you propose instead?" Michael answered angrily.

"It's simple. We have six weeks to prepare. In that time we could work a miracle of defense—a triple ice wall across the harbor, false traps, entanglements—and zones of crossfire could be laid. With a little luck we could hold till spring."

"And then?" Michael asked rhetorically.

Ishmael looked at him coldly.

"Prepare for the next year."

"That's precisely what they want, can't you see that?"

"So what else do you propose? Suicide?"

"Damn it," Michael said softly. Ishmael was right and he knew it. If he went out on the Ice to meet them they would be overwhelmed. Damn Zimri, he'd laid the cards.

Michael looked to the others and they were all lost in silence.

Seth began softly, "If we survive this winter, you can hope for twice as many followers next year."

"I can hope," Michael said, "but Zimri will still be there!

"Sooner or later it must be him or me. In the end one of us must destroy the other."

He walked across the harbor; already the work had begun. Beyond the gates crews of laborers were busy carving the ice into blocks that were dragged to the wall where they would be placed around wooden pilings and cemented with buckets of water. In some areas the walls were already ten feet high and climbing. Twenty yards in front of the walls more wooden piles were being sunk at an angle to impale any ship that attempted to ram. It was a good suggestion on Daniel's part, especially after their success with the city years before.

For several moments he stood watching the work, then, putting on a pair of skates, he pushed off from the harbor's gate and made his way out to sea. He knew they were following, and looking over his shoulder, he saw a half-dozen men fanning out behind while on either flank ran two four-man cutters. The guard was like an article of clothing that he wore but was hardly aware of anymore. Of late, they had come to call themselves the Companions. There were twenty of them—led by Daniel.

For over an hour he skated in long, steady strides, until only the hills above the city were visible. Finding a small, double lapping of ice, he sat down behind it to protect himself from the wind.

He sat and waited. He could see his guards forming a circle several hundred yards out, and they too settled down to wait. The hours passed without hope or thought. Day reached its zenith and drifted into afternoon, and from there into darkness, and still he sat alone.

He relished it. Alone, to be alone. The Arch came out above him, and as the hours passed it wheeled its way across the frozen sky. The thoughts were purged away, one by one. The confusion, the noise, the emotion. The dawn came in its passage—and still he sat alone. And the day passed its plotted course, until suddenly the Arch was above him again and the purging was complete. He felt the doubt replaced by knowledge. The course was clear before him.

He would face Zimri, but he must face him on the ground of his own choosing and not Zimri's. Zimri had chosen the town, therefore he must choose the Ice. The breathing came slower, until many would have thought that he had frozen to death. The concentration gave way to nothingness, and self disappeared.

There was an old man, tossing in nightmare-ridden madness, and he came to him and spoke to him softly. "Yes, I live," he said, and the old man wept and looked away.

He stood to watch the rising of the sun in the east. A storm, which was sweeping the Cornathian coast, was only a faint whisper of wind and high clouds fleeing to the north.

The images had come together at last, and he knew what needed to be done. He had seen the answer on the way out—and skated by it. Only now, after the time alone, had the realization arrived.

Daniel looked up with apprehension when he saw Michael coming. Damn, it's been cold out here the last two nights, he thought. Why can't he think like other men, in front of a warm fire with a tankard of ale? From out of the dawning light he was coming, and as he drew closer Daniel could hear his laughter.

Without stopping Michael swept past him. "Back to the city!" he shouted. "It's time we begin."

Mathin now knew no night. As the sun set in the southwestern sky, great fires would be lit in the harbor. Fires that ringed the shipyards and the harbor's entrance beyond, so that night was banished. Never would there be a moment of quiet or rest, as men worked in shifts of eight hours on, four hours off. Michael could be found most anywhere—one minute heaving on a block, the next lending his back to a saw. Yet most often he could be found in the woods during the day; for it was there that the most painful task was performed. Most of the great trees of Mathin were falling to the ax. The Grove, of course, would be untouched, but all the trees beyond that one spot were put to the ax.

His plan had come as a shock when he had sat down with the council and told them of it. As in most things, the simplest answer, the answer that remains hidden for a thousand years, is usually so childlike that all feel stupid for not having seen it before.

"We are faced with this," he started. "If we defend, we stop Zimri, as Zimri has planned. And by so doing we give him what he wants. Granted, we survive, but that will not end the threat. Therefore, let us take what *we* desire—and attack!"

"What?" Ishmael shouted as he rose up, sending his chair clattering to the floor.

"Michael, we've been over this before. Attack with what? Our fists and a couple of prayers from you?"

"With our fleet."

"What damn fleet? One broadside from the Cornathian ships of the line and we'll be splintered wrecks. The *Black Revenge* has twenty guns, she'll be facing ten times her mettle."

Michael looked at Ishmael and then said softly: "The *Revenge* will sail, but her guns shall remain on the Ice."

"On the Ice?"

"Yes, we'll strip our ships of their guns to build a barrier line. Our ships will run without cannon."

"God's tooth. Michael . . ." Ishmael looked at him darkly.

"Hear him out, Father."

Michael looked at them and there was silence. "For now at least, the day of the ice cruiser is dead."

They looked at him with varying degrees of disbelief. To an old ice runner like Ishmael, and even to Seth, it sounded like heresy. He might as well have told them that an ice ship could fly, or that he held a charm against shot and bolt.

"What is an ice cruiser? It's nothing more than a large platform to mount and fight the guns of the churches. The merchants, and even the small city-states, can make or sail the merchantmen, and even the frigates, but it's the cruiser—the giants—that only a church can afford to build and to lose. For it is the church's guns that fight her, the church's masters who make and sail her. It has the power to smash a frigate in a single blow or reduce a wall to rubble. And for the three churches, it is the symbol of their power. I say, not only can we win a battle against them, but we can shatter the entire order of things upon the Ice. We of Mathin have the power to smash the entire fleet in a day!"

They were silent.

"In battle we can shatter them, and in peace as well. The Church needs the cruisers, for they are a visible sign of her power, but that power can be broken. The chance is out there to seize a weapon the Church has feared for too long—our imaginations.

"Look at how we fight upon the Ice. We sail into action, the battle swarms and breaks down, and in the end the side with the most metal usually wins as it hammers its foes into rubble. It is a battle without discipline."

"So what do you propose?" Seth asked, his curiosity aroused.

"We destroy them with a disciplined fleet, a fleet made of rams."

Daniel stirred and looked at him.

"But the ride of the ram is death," Ishmael said. "Do you propose that my people kill themselves?"

"No, of course not. Daniel and I both rode the rams and lived. The ram is a dangerous weapon, to be sure, and ponderous to carry. Its effect is limited at best, to an occasional hit. It is more a part of ritual than battle.

"Let's look at the problem. We cannot build enough cruisers in time to meet them. We don't have the resources, even if we did have the time. But we have hundreds of trees that can be converted into rams!"

"But, Michael," Zardok interrupted, "you can't possibly ask hundreds of our men to ride to their certain death. There's honor to be found in fighting and dying aboard ship, but a ram's death has always been for the condemned who wish to be redeemed."

"As I was skating out I stopped a moment to watch Rafe lead some Mathinian men in crossbow practice. It was simple enough. He set a target and trained them to fire in volley, so that, as he said, 'You can be sure that one arrow will always find the mark. When only one shoots, the target can use his shield better to ward off the blow.'

"It took that simple lesson, and during the night it came to me. Our ram attacks have always been like the firing of a single shot. The enemy can twist and weave, or smash the blow. But what if we trained our men to act and think as one? Disciplined them to fight as a team, rather than to run wildly off to their individual deaths and glories?"

"It would be hard," Ishmael said.

"We will build a fleet of rams. They will actually be like small, two-hulled schooners, each with a crew of, say, five men. They will maneuver in groups of five and attack in lines of five. Attached to the back of each attack vessel will be a small lifeboat with a light sail.

"As the battle draws close, all but one of the ram's crew will board their small lifecraft, which will cast off while still out of range. The steersman will stay with the craft and pilot it in. If it seems as if the ram will collide with its target, the steersman can cut off on a small sled and be picked up by his comrades. If he misses, the crew can rejoin him, and under the command of their squadron leader they can come about and try again.

"Our fleet of merchantmen will be assigned the task of coming alongside the life rafts and picking up crews, while the light schooners and cutters will provide escort and rescue to any the merchants can't reach."

Michael stopped for a minute to gauge the reaction.

"But, Michael, the enemy's frigates will be able to smash down an attacking ram."

"Yes, we will lose many, but by the sheer number of attacks many will get through. It's discipline that will count. We'll attack in trained teams spread across miles of Ice. In fact, most of the rams will not even be aimed at the opponent during the attack, they will simply follow the course set by their commander. The enemy will turn to evade one ram and will swing in front of another. No matter which way he turns, there will be death. In such a way, the battle cruisers and the frigates will find themselves trapped in a stinging web of death, their guns powerless. Gone will be the battle cruisers, gone the frigates, and thus will we break the power of the churches."

While he talked Michael produced two charts. One had a number of diagrams indicating how the squadrons of five could maneuver, while the other was of the Ice from Mathin to a hundred leagues beyond the Broken Tracks.

"You realize what you're asking," Ishmael said.

"We either win it all with this or none will return," Michael replied.

Ishmael then looked to the chart. "Where do you plan to fight this action?"

Michael pointed north of the Broken Tracks. "Here, where they would never expect it."

Ishmael said softly, "You gamble it all, because if you fail there will be no retreat."

"I know that."

"Are you afraid?"

Michael sat silently for a moment. "No," he said flatly.

Ishmael turned away from him. "Ormson is right, it is our only opening. But you will be afraid, my boy. Oh yes, you will be very afraid before it is done." And so saying, he walked quietly from the room.

Seth leaned on the table across from Michael and looked at him closely. He had cut through to the core of power and had unveiled it. With this new weapon, rams mated to iron discipline, they could sweep the entire Frozen Sea. He looked to Michael and sensed the power that wss to be unleashed. He experienced fear, and with it a touch of doubt as to what he had helped create.

So the days passed in endless hours of work, and the forest of Mathin drew back ever farther from the city walls as many a fine, old pine or oak was sacrificed.

Tons of metal were needed for the fittings and blades. Many an iron kettle or pot was sacrificed to the insatiable appetite of the forge. From the church towers the bells were lowered, so that a strange calm filled the morning air. The bellows roared and the work went on, but no more would the bells ring, even if in these years it was just a tradition to announce the coming of the dawn.

The hardest shortage to fill was that of the canvas for the thousands of yards of sail. The warehouses were stripped bare. The riggings and sails of the summer ships disappeared overnight. Soon dresses, tapestries, and hangings were pressed into service, so that some of the craft looked as if they were to sail beneath the quilting of a demented woman.

While the working and rigging continued, the men trained to a school of warfare unknown in the history of the Ice. There were no rival brotherhoods, no peasants, no nobles, no faction, each out for its own part of the loot. Michael demanded that all booty be divided equally. He wanted no race for prizes, but disciplining the men to that was hard. Michael's presence and that of the brothers of Inys Gloi was enough to strike superstitious fear into many of the sailors, so that they would follow his word. For others, and there were many, it was the iron hardness of Ishmael and, on occasion, the lash of Finson, the sailing master, that turned the trick.

From dawn until dusk they drilled, first individually to learn the feel of a ram, and then, as the assembly of the ships progressed, in squadrons of five, so that the men learned to steer as a team. They learned the line abreast, the echelon, the wedge, the column, and how on a given command of flag to change formation and direction, until finally the chants, the flags, and the thunder of blades seemed to fill their sleeping hours as well.

Each day more rams came from the dockyards, until the sections of five were soon maneuvering in squadrons of twenty-five, and in fleets of a hundred. Every man knew his number and place, and Michael stood upon the battlement of the three sisters and was pleased. There were other things that were new as well, many things that had never been thought of before, and the men spoke of Michael with reverent fear.

And so the fleet grew as the days turned shorter and shorter, until finally, one night, the fires were not lit on the harbor's shores. It was the night of rest. On the morrow they would sail at last.

CHAPTER 18

He was alone upon the tower that rose two hundred feet above the Ice. The smooth, sheer walls were carved from the rock that formed Inys Gloi. The Grand Master stood alone while the others looked and observed from the lower battlements. He had waited since dusk, and in the light of the false dawn the fleet was observed at last.

He looked to the heavens and the signs were correct, as correct as the charts of a thousand years ago had said they would be. They showed the final sign of the ending of the age, the two-thousand-year passage that was but a twelfth of the Great Age. Yes, the signs were correct.

He watched the fleet pass. The sails showed dimly in the light of the Arch while, overhead, three Saints fell. He watched until dawn swept aside the images of night, and then he retired to the highest and most secret of all the chambers of Inys Gloi.

He was the Grand Master, the sixty-third in the line. The tradition of each passed down by word to the next to succeed. Five hundred were his servants on the island, another thousand concealed upon the Ice as merchants, priests, peasants, and princes. All three churches were known to him, their inner councils not often concealed. He was the master of the first brotherhood, father to all the others. His was the brotherhood that existed even before the Church rose from the ashes of night and declared the Prime Choosing.

None had ever dared to raise a hand against him, since his brothers were masters of the garrote, the knife, and the deadly leaf. All bishops, all princes knew the fate that awaited the attacker.

For a thousand years Inys Gloi had been content to manipulate, but that time was passing. The power of an individual with the brotherhood was meaningless, the power of five hundred years, a passing moment. What Inys Gloi desired was an empire that would last for an Age. By using Michael correctly, that power could be ensured. All three churches would be overthrown and Inys Gloi would move in to take the pieces. The key was control of Michael. He had not followed all of their plans, as had been hoped for. However, the lines of the future could be read and would show that his actions had fit their plan all along. There were areas of concern, the girl for one, but they could be taken care of in time. Yes, Inys Gloi would come to control him, giving him weapons not dreamed of in two thousand years, and when he died their power would sweep the Ice. The Age of the Prophet had come at last.

Long he thought of Seth Dublarth el Facinn and Daniel Neive Lomarth, and with a chill he realized that winter was coming again. He closed his eyes and let the force of the silence sweep over him.

"Was that Inys Gloi?"

"Yes, your Excellency."

"An interesting order—at the completion of the campaign I would be curious to stop and ask them to read my stars."

"Your Excellency, they are a strange sect indeed. 'Tis strange the Holy Fathers have not questioned their dabblings in sorcery and such."

"Why do you find the decision of the Holy See to be strange, Brother Iolairson?" Peter turned and looked at his ship's archdeacon.

Iolairson was wrapped in the usual garb of a Morian ice runner, blue tunic and dark-blue leggings bound with fur. His face was entirely wrapped and his eyes were concealed by goggles, so that Peter could not see the flicker of emotion on the brother's face as he realized the danger of this conversation.

"I repeat only what others have said, your Excellency. Many have rumored that Inys is linked to this prophet."

Peter looked at him for a moment and decided to bury the subject. With a curt nod of his head he turned from Iolairson and walked away.

A voice cut in from behind.

"I think we'll be shortening sail, your Excellency. The storm is freshening. Damn the wind anyhow, 'tis strange to see a southwesterly blowing this late in the year."

Yes, it is strange, Peter thought, another thing that Zimri might not have planned for.

"If you'll excuse me, Excellency, I must see to the ship."

Peter turned to face the captain. "Yes, of course, Ceadac."

Ceadac bowed slightly and went astern. As if to give credance to the captain's words, the wind suddenly increased in its fury. The *St. Talmartin* of Cornath rose off her upwind runners, and Peter had to grasp for the windscreen to keep from tumbling across the deck. The wind shrieked through the riggings and the rumble of the skates rose in pitch as the great ice cruiser ran as close to the wind as she could.

I don't like this at all, Peter thought. Already we're a week late, and still another four days to the Broken Tracks. I should have told Zimri to go to the freezing ice.

Peter leaned up against the windbreak and was diverted as he watched the men going aloft to shorten sail. He never ceased to be amazed at the bravery of men who could hang aloft on icy lines a hundred and fifty feet up while the ship heeled over at speeds of eighty miles an hour. He tried to imagine himself with them, but his mind rebelled, and turning, he went below to his cabin.

Peter's cabin displayed none of the elegance in fashion with others of his high rank in the Church. The icon was in its proper corner, but it was of simple wood and had none of the silver or golden embellishments then so popular. His bunk was set into the far corner of the room and was folded during the day.

The usual symbol of war—a large, thirty-two-pound stern-chaser—evenly divided the room with its bulk. On the port and starboard walls and framing the entranceway to the cabin were the few luxuries Peter allowed himself—finely woven tapestries from Barnin showing the life of St. Peter the Wanderer. The tapestries not only improved the heat of the room but also gave it some color, with finely hued blues and greens that showed St. Peter on his journeys during the last days of the Garden. Peter's favorite was a rather fanciful rendition of the Saint after he had risen into the skies to survey the cities of sin below.

It was the far wall that Peter favored the most. Two sliding panels could be rolled back to reveal the luxury of windows. A craftsman of infinite skill had centered four large double panes of glass into the two panels and had edged them with stained glass befitting a cathedral.

Now that the storm was upon them the view was limited, but on a clear day he found endless pleasure in watching the sunrise, which reflected the four great plumes of spray thrown up by the passing of the ship. The stained glass edging the windows enhanced the effect with a rainbow of colors.

Peter gazed out the windows for a moment and watched the storm swirling past. The ship shuddered as another blast of wind rocked the boat and set it up on its downwind outriggers. The ship hung in the air for a moment, and then with a rolling boom, settled back down to run on its westward tack.

It was not until late that afternoon that the wind backed around and the storm abated in its fury. A layer of windblown snow covered the Ice, something quite rare for that time of year, and it slowed the progress of the fleet. The ships made their way southwestward with a freshening breeze from the north-northwest. The great billows of snow that the fleet kicked up created the effect of a giant tumbling cloud that stretched off to the southeast like a coiling plume of sparkling diamonds.

Peter tried to rest, but that was impossible as he wrestled with the questions that had been raised in the hour before sailing.

"Michael, it's time."

He awoke gently, the touch at his shoulder bringing him to the first level of consciousness.

He opened his eyes but the room was still dark, except for the glow of the hearth. The room held a brisk chill to it, which made awakening all the more uncomfortable; the thought of leaving his warm bed was just unpleasant at the moment.

Janis stroked his arms and then softly enveloped him in an embrace that he returned with an awakening ardor, and so she brought him to face the day.

The first light of dawn was streaking the morning sky, a welcome sight for the start of the campaign.

"Janis, it's time for me to go."

"Just another minute, Michael." She held him tightly, and he realized that she was trying, unsuccessfully, to hide her tears.

"Janis, don't. I'll be back in a week and then it will all be over."

She shook her head without answering.

"What's wrong, then?"

"I'm losing you, Michael. You'll never come back to me now."

He laughed softly and held her tightly. "You're being foolish, love. I'll be back."

"Michael, can't you see it's over, the way we were, the way we lived. That fanatic of yours has come back."

"But Janis, he saved my life."

"Saved it to destroy it, filling you with these wild dreams. So now you go away to fight. I know you have to do it, my love, but he won't let you stop. Already the people call you the Promised One, they won't let you come home to me."

"But Janis..." And his words failed him. She was right. Gently he turned away and rose. The shock of the cold air brought him fully awake.

"Oh Michael!" she suddenly cried. and pulling aside the covers and furs. she jumped out of the bed and hugged him.

"I'm sorry. Michael." she sobbed as she buried her head on his shoulder.

Her long black hair shone in the early morning light. and the tears from Michael's eyes rolled gently down her shoulder.

"Michael. I'm carrying a baby." she whispered.

"A baby?"

"Yes." she laughed. "a baby."

He held her back and looked at her closely.

"Oh don't be foolish." she laughed. "you can't see yet."

A baby! The shock of it washed through him and filled him with a warmth that blotted out all other thoughts. There was a growing clamor from the courtyard. yet for the moment she held sway. so that the sound drifted away as she eagerly led him back to the bed.

He walked down the corridor and out into the main hallway. where his men waited. The Companions. now fifty strong. stood ready. and Daniel beamed with pride when Michael noticed the uniforms that they wore—white sealskin furs for parkas. fine chain-mail tunics that went to the knees. Atop their heads were finely wrought. pointed steel helmets capped in fur. Their goggles were pulled up to reveal eager faces that were creased with smiles at the sight of their leader. Daniel had finally convinced Michael that the simple brown robe of a former monk would not serve a leader of war. and Michael accepted a tunic of chain mail. a sable cape. and a helmet. Upon the face of his shield was the symbol of the Grove—a circle of spruce.

With his guards. Michael went out into the foyer of the palace. there to meet with Ishmael. Seth. Zardok. Finson. Olin. and the other household retainers. The shouting in the square grew to a fever pitch as the door swung open. The leaders of Mathin went forth to lead their people to war.

For two hours he stood upon the forecastle deck of the schooner *Fire Wind*. with Seth on his one side and Daniel and the Companions on the other. He watched the fleet go to sea while along the double line of ice walls the crowds cheered. The ice walls were simply a pretense for the city; her able-bodied men were sailing, and only the old, the infirm, and the very young stayed behind. They could put up a stout resistance for a week or even a month, but if the enemy ever reached so far the defenders would know that the men of Mathin would never return. He could see her upon the high tower, cold and stern, the leader of her people while her father was away. Every time he looked to her she felt his calling, and turning, she smiled to him.

From out of the harbor came the old cruiser of Mathin, the *Black Revenge*. At her helm stood Ishmael, and the cheers rolled like thunder as he ran her down the channel and out onto the open ice. The two frigates of the fleet followed in the *Revenge*'s wake, and they passed on out, with every inch of canvas set.

Then came the fleet of Michael. At the sight of their sails one would have thought the fleet fitted out for some strange religious rite, for their patchwork sails showed every color of the rainbow. Mathin would be a cold and dreary place that winter, as every scrap of clothing, drapery, tapestry, and abandoned sail had been pressed into service. In the van came four crude rafts, a hundred feet long and half as wide, with several thousand square feet of sail upon them. Their decks were piled high with hidden cargo. Their making and what they carried had been kept a secret. The crowd pointed to them and debated long on what these strange craft would mean in the battle ahead.

The ponderous craft negotiated the harbor entrance, then slowly pulled out to sea. For several minutes there was silence, then from beyond the harbor walls Michael could hear the sounding of horns and the raising of a cheer as the first rams cleared the harbor gate.

First came the green fleet, of a hundred rams. Their command vessel was in the fore with old Finson at the foremast. As he passed Michael's vessel he raised his hand in salute. Behind him came four sections of twenty-five—a hundred battle rams—and each of the four units moved as one as they swept across the Ice.

Each ship was a catamaran made of two logs almost forty feet in length and four feet in diameter. Mounted beneath each log, three sets of runners sparkled and shone in the morning light. A flat wooden frame was built between the two logs, and upon that was a small shanty that rose up not more than four feet, to keep the wind resistance down. To the rear of the ship were two lifeboats. One was a small dinghy that could carry the catamaran's crew of five and was stocked with provisions and a small gaff-rigged sail. Alongside the skiff was a small sled that was not unlike the sled carried by the rams of old.

The pilot and four crewmembers of each ram stood upon the platforms of their craft and raised clenched fists into the air as they passed Michael. They were grim and silent. They were men prepared to die, and Michael experienced a strange thrill with the realization.

In sections of five they passed, with their small command and rescue craft out front. After the green fleet of Finson came the red of Olin of Inys Gloi. There was a sailing master who truly believed that Michael was the Prophet. He rode forth with a religious fervor in his eye. Michael and Ishmael had chosen him because Olin had been like most of Inys Gloi, a brother of two cloths. He had sailed with Ishmael for fifteen years, and was known by most of the city. His fleet passed behind him and his crews were not silent. One of the men started it, and it was quickly picked up by the others in the fleet. It was a simple, primitive chant. "Mich—ael, Mich—ael," and it pulsed and rolled with power, and the crowds upon the wall picked it up, and the chant echoed across the sea.

Behind the red fleet came the twenty-five rams of the gold; this was the section commanded by Daniel. They maneuvered up and stopped behind Michael's craft while the chanting swelled.

Next came the six armed merchantmen of Zardok, which carried upon their sails the emblem of the golden circle and the three trees. Zardok was before the mast in his armor of old, and Michael waved as the old man led his fleet to open Ice.

Finally came the assorted crafts—schooners, catboats, and light merchantmen—which were the messengers, auxiliary rescue ships, and eyes of the fleet. They darted and swept across the Ice as they swung out and took up positions on the flanks. The harbor was finally empty. The *Fire Wind* stood before the harbor gates, and Michael watched the sails of the fleet move northward.

He looked at the windswept battlements and the huddled figures on it. Each of them was giving a loved one to the forthcoming battle. His gaze swept out over the ice traps and pitfalls, the double walls, and the high tower beyond. If any ships attempted to strike, the island would become a bristling, deadly fortress.

The enormity of the gamble started to strike home. Almost three thousand men had just sailed from the harbor, cheering his name. How many would return? All because of me, he thought. He looked to the walls and realized that he should say something to them. Turning, he gazed back out to the Sea. It had been three years since he had been upon the Ice. He was going out again, and with the realization there came a fierce joy. He was going out again to sweep the Frozen Sea.

He waved to the tower and the crowds on the walls and docks saw the gesture and started to cheer again. The cheering rose to a deafening roar.

"Mich—ael! Mich—ael! Mich—ael! . . ."

CHAPTER 19

Dawn. In the first light of morning a light breeze had sprung up from the northwest with a promise of a clear, wind-swept day. They knew that the time had come at last. The days of drill and practice had ended, for in the middle of the night one of the scout ships had come in, her horn and drums sounding the alarm.

Michael did not need to tell the men of his fleet. Within minutes all were awake and preparing. He walked the Ice, alone except for Daniel and Olin, and as he walked he listened and watched, and knew that all that could be done had been done.

The horizon grew lighter and no horn summoned them to prayer, no one uttered strident commands to form up, and yet they gathered together, replacing the old rituals with a new one. They came in ones and twos, and then by the dozens, until finally the entire fleet was gathered around him.

There was no cheering, no chanting, just an overwhelming silence. He looked at their faces, the faces of men who had been on the Ice for twice his age, and the faces of boys who were sailing to their first battle. He looked at them and knew the power that he held. These were his men, the men who had drifted to Mathin because of him and what he was saying. They were a handful who now went forth to challenge the power of the mightiest brotherhood on the Ice. In their silence he could sense the strength, the determination to at last stand and rebel against the churches and their ritual of war.

He began softly as if he were speaking more to himself than to those around him.

"And so it has come at last," he began. "All we asked for was the right to be left alone, to sail the seas, and to live and think as free men. I don't know; maybe this world is made of pain, made to bring forth endless fear and sorrow. But at least let us question this. As we stand here, not a hundred miles away a great fleet is preparing. They have families, they speak the same languages that we speak, they have the same fears and the same joys as we. And yet they have come in the thousands to take from us the right to speak and to live as we wish.

"Look around you, my friends, and remember that they are only men like ourselves. Let us remember this moment, for I know that we shall start something here which can never be stopped. We shall throw them back! Yet let us then show them compassion as well, for to do otherwise would make us like the thing that we now dread.

"We shall fight today and we shall fight well. For as long as one of us lives, as long as one of us is willing to stand up and say no, we will have succeeded. We have discovered at last that we are men, who can think. To many, a people who can think is a mortal danger. A people who question and will not follow blindly is a people who must be destroyed. Therefore, let us remember what we fight for. I shall not now offer you blind promises of what shall happen to our fallen, for to do so would be a lie and a defiance of all that we have stood for. That mystery will be met by many today, yet let us meet it like men. Let us go forth like free men of Mathin! Remember that we fight not only for ourselves, but for all people upon the Ice who yearn to be free."

"We fight for you, Michael Ormson, the Promised One!"

and the cheering of his name swelled and roared across the Ice.

He tried to stop them but they would not listen. For some minutes he looked away from them, until finally the cheering died.

He looked out at them. How many will be alive at day's end? he wondered. He looked to them and felt as if he could read the aura of death that was descending over them all. Many of the boys before him would be frozen in their graves before the sun rose again.

He looked over to Daniel and smiled at him, and Daniel, as if sensing his memories, smiled back. Daniel projected a strange, pulsing aura, and Michael noticed it around the other men, as well. He looked to Daniel and a stranger who stood behind him, watched for a second, and then turned away. He walked back to the *Fire Wind* and mounted its outrigger.

"We sail with the rising sun!" he shouted, and the cheers rolled across the Ice as the men broke away and stormed back to their craft and positions. Mathin was ready.

The last conference had been held the night before, and the fleet commanders led their men into position. As if by one hand, the sails of the red fleet of Olin were run up the masts. They formed into columns against the backdrop of the rising sun, and made their way southward to their command position. Finson and his hundred were running close hauled to the wind, their sails pulled tight and the double-hull rams hiking and dancing in the steadily mounting breeze.

Ormath and his gunners were out of their ice huts and standing in the line of death that Ormath had designed. For Ormath this was a moment long dreamed of. He had been a master of fortifications, having learned under the old Dalmin Brotherhood of Sol, before the Ezrians first came.

Michael could just barely distinguish their white-clad figures on the ice when from behind came a loud, rumbling noise. Ishmael's fleet was sailing. Upon the forecastle stood his father-in-law; his face was grim as he rode the *Black Revenge* into a battle, and his memories rode with him. The memories of when

Sol still stood as a power, before the plague, and when Ishmael Tornson was sailing master of Mathin and commander of the small cruiser *Somarthen*, now the *Black Revenge*. Her timbers were going to powder and her gun decks were stripped bare. She was going forth not to fight, but as bait. He did not look to Michael, for his eyes were elsewhere, and the Ice cried to him with the voices of those long dead. He stood in silence, for already he could hear Hell calling his name.

The *Black Revenge* heeled over as she ran abeam the wind to the northeast, toward the last reported position of the enemy, her two frigates and three schooners spread out on her flanks. Michael watched them disappear over the horizon. He knew Zardok waited with the reserve of armed merchantmen and heavy schooners. He looked across the deck of his command ship and a chill came over him again. He stiffened for a moment, and decided to wait for what was to come. So the hours passed as the sun cleared the horizon and climbed in its short turn across the southern sky.

"Sail ho! One point off the larboard bow."

Even from his cabin he heard the cry. Within seconds it was picked up and echoed back through the fleet, the signal pennants dipping and rising to the ships far astern.

Peter threw down his pen and ran from his cabin, not even bothering to don parka and goggles. Topside, the cold was numbing, and he knew that he was risking frostbite, but his uneasiness was almost overwhelming.

"A report from the *St. Regina*, your Excellency," the deck officer shouted over the wind. "She's running before the fleet and reports a sail."

Peter strained his eyes to look forward.

"Send someone for my gear," he shouted. The *Regina* was clearly visible on the horizon and she appeared to be approaching them.

"What means this?" Peter shouted. The deck officer stepped closer to him, while two men helped Peter on with his heavy parka and goggles.

"She's run into something bigger, I'd say, and she's coming about."

He didn't like that at all. The Broken Tracks were on their lee thirty leagues below the horizon, and the navigator indicated that the main pass to Mathin was five hours ahead. All had counseled to take this route. Of course, one of the frigate captains laughed, "They aren't expecting us anyhow." In spite of his own judgment he had agreed with the admiral's decision to follow the route; the next passage was already a hundred and fifty miles astern, and was far more hazardous.

"It could be a couple of privateers," the deck officer said casually. "If so, we'll just sweep them in."

Peter was worried. If they're coming out, he thought, then they must be confident of success.

A cry came down from the fore royal lookout. "Deck ho! I see them—two, three, no, it looks like four sails dead ahead, running abeam. Can you see them?"

Peter strained his eyes forward, and was suddenly aware that Lord Conneachson was standing next to him. "Could be Mathin," Lord Conneachson said softly. "They are supposed to have three frigates and a cruiser, but why would they be out here, unless they somehow knew?"

Peter turned to look at Conneachson. "How could that be?" Peter said innocently.

"Oh, the usual thing, spies and such. I heard speak of a craft that slipped out almost two months before we sailed. In fact, it was the very night we ordered all traffic closed. Sailed from Cornath, it did. Only a cutter, though, the chances are it was harmless."

"Why didn't you tell me?" Peter inquired.

"Didn't think much of it at the time."

At least our own wasn't noticed, Peter thought, but this other cutter now...

"Ah, there they are," Conneachson said. "I see a fore-top-sail." Peter looked to where the admiral was pointing at a small splotch of dirty white on the horizon.

"They must see us by now," Conneachson said. "Ah, the *St. Regina* is coming along."

Peter watched as the *St. Regina*, a light frigate of twelve guns, cut across their bow, and as she did so a beautiful plume of spray shot up to the windward side of the flagship. She pulled up to hailing distance.

"Your Excellencies," came the voice of her captain. "We could see their sail: they're of Mathin, and come on in battle deployment."

Conneachson was silent. "Very good, resume station," he shouted.

Turning, he looked at Peter, then walked away.

"Clear for action!" he shouted to the men behind him. "Put all canvas on. Signal the fleet for standard pursuit. Perhaps we can run them down before they make the Tracks."

"Launch the rams," Peter said quietly.

"What? That's pure waste, it's a stern chase, it is—what good are our rams in that?"

"Launch the rams."

"But your Excellency, I've fought for years—"

"Lord Conneachson, must I remind you that this is a brotherhood ship, and I am secretary of that brotherhood? You've received your order."

Conneachson looked at the priest. A damned blue-robe, giving him orders, he was tempted . . . But the man's mystical ability to have enemies turn up dead came to him.

"Clear for action," he shouted, "order all rams away!"

"Clear for action," the cry went up. And the ship swarmed with life. Hatchways were thrown open and great columns of smoke shot heavenward as the boilers were doused below decks. The crews of the catapults and onagers came running on deck, and they were laden with racks of shot and great bundles of quarrels.

The rams were made ready and their pilots came running across the deck then swung out across the outriggers while the archdeacon of the ship climbed up to the forecastle to give them benediction. On twenty other fighting ships and the dozens of smaller craft the preparations were basically the same, as ten thousand men prepared for battle. The frigates swung out on the flanks while the armed merchantmen, ketches, brigs, and schooners formed a protective ring around the cruisers and transports.

The ship's archdeacon came to Peter's side and watched as the dozen rams of the cruiser swung out and away at almost the same time the other three cruisers launched theirs. Suddenly a ram on the starboard side lost control in a gust and swung wildly out of line, the pilot screaming in terror as his ram flipped over and collided with two others coming up astern. Within seconds they exploded in a swirling mass of splinters and jagged ice.

"You're feeling differently toward it, aren't you?" the archdeacon asked.

"What's that you say?"

"Just that you feel a deeper danger to this."

Peter looked over at the young man. "I don't understand what you mean, brother."

"We're facing more than we think, your Excellency. A good many men have felt it. You should stand on the deck of an iceship in the clothes of a common man and you'd see what I mean."

Before Peter had time to react a cry came down from above.

"They're turning about, they're running, the filthy buggers."

A ragged cheer came up from the deck.

"After them," Conneachson shouted, "press on the canvas."

Conneachson turned and Peter could see the broad smile partially concealed by his hood.

"They must have thought twice after seeing our full size."

Peter watched the stern chase as the ice rocketed past.

A faint cloud blew off the deck of the lead frigate, and a half-minute later a faint rumbling boom sounded across the ice. The *St. Allman* had opened with her guns. The chase was on.

At one-minute intervals the echo of the guns rolled back to them. The sound became almost constant as three more frigates slowly pressed to range. But the frigates were not able to close, in fact it appeared the enemy ships were slowly outdistancing them.

After nearly an hour of running, Conneachson started to comment on it. "She must be stripped down, else I can't explain the speed—either that or there is some devilish spell of the Heretic upon her."

"Lord Conneachson. I don't like the feel of this at all, there's something afoot here. Send a couple of frigates upwind—over the horizon if need be—I think there's more here than the enemy's taking fright and running. That cruiser is stripped of all guns and gear; she never intended to fight."

"Yes, your Excellency," and for once there was no hesitation in Conneachson's voice.

"Make that three frigates, and send a cruiser with them."

Within minutes the four ships and a couple of light schooners veered off as close as possible to the wind. With the close reach they slacked off in speed, so that they gradually fell astern as they made their way northward.

"If there's anything up there our ships should be on their flank . . . Conneachson, order all transports to swing downwind for a league and send the rest of the fleet upwind a league. We'll go in echelon—our light craft above, the three cruisers in the middle, and the transports downwind."

Conneachson nodded and, turning, shouted his commands.

Peter watched as they were carried out. He was no fighting brother but his years of survival in the climb upward had taught him much. A trap lay ahead, and he wasn't going in blind. This prophet had come out to fight, and he therefore must be coming out with a plan he thought would let him win.

Peter hung upon his hesitation for several moments and wrestled with his fear. Damn him, he thought, he's not here, he doesn't see. I'm not to win, but by the Saints, I'll be damned if I lose.

"In fact, to hell with Zimri completely," he suddenly whispered. "We must end this heretic now!"

"Conneachson!" Peter suddenly shouted. "Call off the chase."

"Call off the chase? What's wrong with thee, man? The men's blood is up. We'll catch them yet, we will. How the hell can I call off the chase?"

"By God's blood. I'll show you how, and I'll see you in hell afterwards." Peter shouted.

Conneachson swung on Peter with a vicious snarl. "Go

ahead you pox-eaten son of a whore. You and your damned brotherhood have been ordering me for too long. There's been something wrong with this campaign from the start. And now you turn coward on us. I care not if you be the secretary of the Father himself, I'll take no more orders from you."

Peter turned to his archdeacon. "Tell all of our deacons—"

A cry came down from above, "A star. It's a star, rising dead ahead!"

Peter shot a savage look at Conneachson, then with a dash he ran to the foremast ratlines. With an agility that surprised him, he made his way aloft and scrambled to the fighting foretop. Dead ahead, he could see a shining light that sank back to the horizon. "What in the name of the Saints?"

Another light rose, this time from the enemy cruiser. "Damn them!" Peter shouted. "They defy Holy Writ." He stood in wonder and watched as the rocket shone in the morning sky and then flared out. They had taken Holy Powder and burned it in the air.

Suddenly, in an arc from north to south, half a hundred rockets of green, gold, and red rose heavenward. Peter watched in numbed silence.

He swung himself off of the foretop and slid down the rigging, shouting to the deck. "Conneachson, order all ships about. Order all ships about!" There was a thundering echo from forward, and looking out, Peter realized that Balor was right after all.

"I hear guns, Michael!"

Michael turned to the boy standing alongside him. Andrew looked up at him eagerly, with that expression of joyful anticipation that seemed to be characteristic of Zardok and his innumerable nephews and nieces.

"Are you sure, Andrew?"

"I'm positive, it's coming from the northeast, it is."

"They'll be here soon enough," Michael said. "Tell me, Andrew, where is your station?"

Andrew turned bright red beneath his mask, and mumbling

some excuse about searching for a bundle of quarrels, he made his way back to his post astern.

Michael looked down from the forecastle deck to the large room below him. Upon a table fifteen feet on a side was a model of the Ice for thirty miles. There were dozens of wooden models of the ships expected in the enemy fleet and of their own fleet as well, coded by color to the various commands. It reminded Michael of Flyswin, in fact it had been inspired by the game, as a means of grasping at a glance the lay of the battle. On a low platform over Michael's head stood fifteen boys of Andrew's age who had been trained to observe the action and to tell the model movers the positions of the ships. It was another one of Zardok's ideas and Michael had understood the control it could give him.

"Deck ho! There's gunfire to the northeast. I think I see something, as well."

Michael looked upward and then back to the officers and Companions standing off to one side.

"Prepare to make sail," and his command was picked up and echoed across the ice to the twenty-five rams of the golden fleet, and to the merchantmen three leagues astern.

"Deck ho! Firing increasing, I can see them now."

"Any moment now, any moment," Michael thought, and he could feel his stomach knot up.

"Saints preserve—" he caught himself. The traditions were hard to break.

"Our fleet is dead on," said the lookout, "they're on the mark."

Michael looked out and could not see them.

"There're the enemy ships—three, I think."

Where are the rest of the frigates? he thought. They should have brought up all their frigates in pursuit. He felt a wave of hesitation. Why— Are they on to us? A grain of doubt was planted, anhd he looked over to Seth. Seth stood in stoic silence.

Where were the rest of the frigates?

"Another minute at most," the lookout shouted.

Does the commander know it's a trap? Michael thought.

"Michael, look out!"

Before he had even the time to think, Michael threw himself on the ground as a figure lunged past him. He rolled off to one side and, turning, saw his attacker.

The attacker rose to his feet and a dagger glinted in his hand. He faked to the left and did a slash to the right that laid open Michael's parka but didn't hit flesh.

Michael desperately weaved as the attacker came back for a third strike. Suddenly, from over his shoulder Michael heard a crossbow fire, and a bolt exploded past him to slam into the attacker's chest.

The blow lifted the man off his feet and threw him up against the foremast. With a dazed expression he slumped to the ground. Seth was already on top of him, his dagger raised for the kill.

"No!" Michael screamed.

Michael pushed his way up to the attacker and held Seth off.

"The bastard almost—"

"I don't care. He'll be dead in a minute anyhow."

"Who are you?" Michael asked.

The man looked at him. "A Black Brother," he whispered.

"From whom?" and Michael could hear the whispers around him at the mention of the legendary order of assassins.

"Your uncle."

Michael grabbed hold of the man and shook him. "You're lying."

"No," the man gasped, "it's true. I came with the messengers. I was told to strike only if you failed to heed your uncle's warning. They dropped me off just before the end . . . Your guards are good—twice I . . . I thought I had you, but they were too close. I slipped aboard this morning, and except for one arm there—" He started to cough spasmodically. A pink foam gushed out from his mouth and ran down his chest.

"But why?" Michael shouted.

The assassin looked at him. "I have failed, but there'll be others . . ." He seemed about to succumb, then smiled gently and rallied for a moment. "Michael, Rifton said . . ." He coughed, and Michael leaned over. With lightning speed the assassin drew a small dagger from his tunic and slashed upward. A Companion elbowed Michael aside, and on the back stroke the Black Brother slashed his own throat; in seconds he was dead.

Even as the guard look dumbly down at his forearm, it swelled visibly.

Seth ran to the guard, who looked at him beseechingly.

"It's only a scratch," he groaned.

Seth looked at the guard and at the finger-length cut on the guard's hand, then shook his head.

"Michael!" the guard screamed. "Save me!"

But Michael was sitting on the ground in numbed shock.

Seth shouted for one of the Companions to take the guard astern, while several other men picked up the body of the assassin and threw him over the side.

"My uncle," Michael said numbly. "Why, Seth? Why him?"

"Because he's afraid of what you are, and what you might do."

Michael looked up to see the crew staring at him, awaiting their orders.

He wavered for several seconds then stood up and walked to the forecastle. In the background he heard the screams of the poisoned guard who would take several hours to die. The screams were suddenly cut short, and Michael turned to see several of the Companions holding their lost friend. They were covered in blood. Because they had loved him, they helped him to cross to the other side.

From above came a cry, "Michael, Ormath has fired!"

Michael turned to Seth. The seconds ticked by, and the voice in his mind tormented him and memories tore at his heart.

"Damn you," Michael whispered.

The roar of the guns rose to a thundering crescendo.

He knew that they had to wait, and he was proud of the discipline shown by his men. That is what he had feared the most, that they would shoot before all was ready. Ishmael's fleet had made its way through the barrier without any problems and was only half a mile away. The three frigates in pursuit would be the only catches. He had taken a good week to build the line and camouflage it—and all that for three frigates. He had hoped that one of the cruisers would have been in the van.

The entrapment was almost a league in width. In front were a series of pits dug into the Ice and designed to rip the blades off of the enemy's ships. Next came the personnel ditches to break up any attack. And last came the six star forts at quarter mile intervals, each with five guns. It was a barrier that Ormath had hoped could smash a good part of the fleet as it leaped ahead for the chase.

They were closer now, closer, a quarter mile, another couple of seconds.

There! A cheer went up from the line. The first frigate hit the ditch. The ice covering the ditch broke away to reveal a pit six feet deep and thirty feet across. The front blades of the frigate slammed into the wall of the ditch, tearing out the bottom of the craft. Her masts snapped like twigs from the shock, and the ship exploded into a shower of splinters.

The other two frigates reacted almost immediately.

"Send up the signal flare!" Ormath shouted. And the single rocket rose up to signal the start of the action.

The next frigate heeled over sharply in a desperate swing to avoid the traps. She hung on the point of coming about, then her leading-edge skate slipped into a deadfall and the ice gave way. The frigate flipped over and her crew was lost.

The third one turned and weaved, her captain reading the Ice and the tracks of the fleet that had run before him. He knew that the path of the Mathinian fleet followed the safe channels. He shot onward. Ormath watched, muttering a curse and a compliment to the enemy captain.

"Open fire!" he shouted.

The guns roared, and in seconds the other guns volleyed forth in a shattering crescendo of noise. The men laid their shots with a passion, sponging their pieces and running them forward, as renegade priests directed the battery. Smoke choked the hidden battery, and Ormath jumped on the wall of the fortress to get a better view.

"Load, damn you, load!" he screamed as the frigate bore down. Her bowchasers fired, and the Ice exploded around him.

The first gun fired, and then the others, in a ragged volley.

"A hit," Ormath screamed, "a hit!" The frigate's lee out-rigger buckled, and the ship careened across the ice. Ormath stood in mute fascination as the frigate spun ninety degrees, sending up a showering spray of ice and wood. The image filled his mind as the craft swept closer, hit the sloping walls of the camouflaged fortress, and then, towering above him, finally rolled over onto her side. The image of the shattered frigate filled his universe, and finally blackened it forever.

The sails snapped out like the reports of a dozen cannons while rockets on the decks of the ships arched up and away. The booming echoed and rolled, and yet it was drowned out by the cheers of the men as their ships leaped before the wind. Within seconds they were away, the rumble of the blades and the shrieking of the wind added to the noise of the men, and the sense of unleashed power that had waited coiled for so long filled them.

To the north and hull down over the horizon, Michael could see the fleet of Finson slowly bearing down as they jibbed across the wind.

To the southeast rode the fleet of Olin running close-hauled, the other end of the sweeping arc that gradually closed in on the enemy fleet.

Seth stood at the helm of the *Fire Wind* and kept the heavy schooner at the fore of the attack. Overhead, Michael could hear the calls of the battle observers, which were quickly answered by the boys who moved the markers.

From the southern wing four rockets rose heavenward—green, red, blue, green.

Michael turned and looked to the deck officer carrying the code book.

"Olin signaling, Michael. The enemy is coming about, running back northeast."

"A quick response," Daniel shouted. "Almost too quick!"

Michael was silent.

The minutes ticked by, as Michael's fleet shot past Ormath's barrier line. There was scattered fighting as the survivors of the frigates tried to rally around their wrecks. Michael saw that the central fort had been smashed by one of the ships.

Rockets arched across the sky. "Signal from Finson. Enemy cruiser and three frigates appearing on northern flank."

Michael watched as the information was plotted on the board below. Seth looked at him.

"We want the main fleet," Michael whispered.

Seth nodded. The rockets went up.

"Press home on main fleet."

The enemy fleet was clearly visible—three separate columns running about two leagues ahead. The forces of Mathin crossed over the tracks where the enemy ships had come about. The sound of gunfire echoed down from the north. They're hitting us, Michael thought.

Michael could see the trap closing as Finson's fleet strove to cut in front of the enemy ships. It would be a near thing; the fleet had not hit the barrier firmly enough.

A thundering roar opened up from in front, and the Ice was obscured by smoke. "The enemy fleet's opened up," came the shout from above.

"Signal from Finson. Red, white, red."

Michael already knew. "Pressing attack on enemy."

More signals came in.

"Enemy fleet bearing off to the lee."

A cheer went up.

They were giving way before Finson and running straight into Olin.

"Finson is going in," was the shout from above. A second later: "Enemy fleet coming about."

All was confusion now as the enemy fleet turned with the wind in a desperate attempt to throw off the ram attack. But the rams ran through the screen of light ships and pressed into the center of the van.

"A hit!" came a shout from above. "A hit!"

"A frigate definitely down!" The smoke blew clear to show Finson's fleet passing astern of the enemy with at least ten sections intact. Already the order was starting to break up. Half a dozen rams continued purposefully on their way, their crews pursuing them aboard small rafts. Schooners wove in and out, and one of the enemy merchantmen fell astern to do battle.

"Signal general attack."

The four rockets went up—red, green, gold, white.

Seth started to swing the *Fire Wind* out of line by gently pulling the tiller into the wind. The rams of the golden fleet shot past with Daniel in the lead. Their target was bearing down head on, less than a league away. The entire enemy fleet was coming in.

Michael looked to the north and saw a far closer threat bearing down. The cruiser and three frigates that had cut to the north were above the action. They aimed themselves at the most substantial target they could find, the merchantmen that were Michael's reserve, and his command vessel was between the two.

The gold fleet under Daniel's command sailed for their target, but the enemy fleet held its fire until the range closed to half a mile, then the first volley burst forth. Michael could see the shots winging in as they bounded across the ice. Still a bit too far for such small targets, he thought. The rams pressed in front of him as Seth eased off and away. To the east Michael could see Olin's fleet slam into the enemy, while to the north, half of Finson's sections followed suit.

The four enemy ships closed. A volley was fired, and a shot hummed across the *Fire Wind*'s bow, while aloft the forestay sail was holed.

The ram-attack teams started to spread out. Most of the crews tumbled into their rafts while the commanders stayed at the tillers. Another volley. One of the rams on the larboard side of the attack force rolled over into a gyrating tumble, and the crew was tossed into the air.

The nearest enemy frigate swung away and tacked into the wind in a tight skidding turn. The rams ignored her and drove on to their main target. A lifeboat cut away, and then another, and another. Even as they cut away, the cruiser let fly with another volley. Another ram collapsed.

Within seconds they were passing. At the last second the two starboard teams broke off as the cruiser started to jib evasively across the wind. The teams turned away and headed into the main battle. As the cruiser turned back before the wind, one of the larboard attack team cut in a tight turn, and Michael watched in stunned silence as the men drove their ram home. There was no time to release in the violently maneuvering battle—the crew knew that, and went to their deaths piloting the ram. And Michael stood in silence as he heard them call his name.

The cruiser heeled over, half her rigging collapsing from the shock of impact. She skidded across the ice toward the *Fire Wind* and Michael watched in quiet fascination. He didn't even notice the frigate that shot out from behind the cruiser. The frigate weaved past the wreck and slammed across the bow of the *Fire Wind*. A howling roar tore the air as the frigate's volley exploded at a range of fifty yards. A shower of arrows and catapult quarrels rained down upon them. A Companion standing next to Michael was picked up and thrown across the deck by a ballista bolt that impaled him to the foremast. The six-foot bolt quivered in the man's chest and he kicked and screamed in anguish. Seth ran up to the guard and slashed his throat to end his agony. The frigate passed the command ship and went down a hundred yards astern after two rams split the ship open for her entire length, spilling the horrified crew onto the bloodied ice.

The *Fire Wind* flew clear of the action, and the two surviving frigates were astern, with a team of five rams trying to circle in for an attack. Daniel's command vessel sent up a series of golden flares to rally his group, but the five pressed on and drifted from the main battle. Daniel had less than a dozen rams left, and with a wave to Michael, he swung his vessel over and pressed into the main battle, which was swarming across the ice less than a league away.

So it wore on. Within minutes of the destruction of the first ice cruiser Finson's fleet smashed another with two hits to the bow, while in the rear of the action a transport went up with a hideous explosion when one of Olin's rams penetrated to its powder magazine. The explosion lifted the vessel fifty feet into the air and scattered bodies and wreckage across a quarter mile of ice.

Command started to break down on both sides. The enemy fleet turned, and turned again, to throw off the attack. Twice the *Fire Wind* was racked by shot as Michael moved with the battle to lead and rally his men, and the screams of the wounded and dying filled the ship. The battle board had been smashed by a twenty-four-pound shot, and the bloodied bodies of the boys who had worked it were covered by a red-soaked piece of canvas.

The thunder of battle dropped off for a couple of minutes and the wind blew a few holes in the smoke, so that Michael could see that the enemy was running again to the northeast.

A stern chase was ordered, and for over an hour the two fleets sailed northward, giving Michael's commanders time to sort out their rams. Olin still held to the south and Finson had the foresight to keep the wind gauge; ever so gradually they pressed ahead of their opponents.

The enemy admiral ordered his schooners, corsairs, and light frigates to sweep outward to harass the rams, but Zardock's merchantmen and the other schooners kept them at bay.

Michael's ship kept to the rear and center, so that both wings would be in view. And with every minute the wreckage of conflict drifted past—bodies, flaming ships, sails, rigging, and shot were just part of the flotsam of battle scattered across forty miles of sea.

"They're coming about again!" the signaler shouted.

Michael looked aloft, to find that Andrew was missing.

"Where's Andrew?" Michael asked.

"The last volley," Seth noted softly.

Michael turned away. "Order an anvil attack."

Rockets rose.

The enemy fleet turned hard over and bore down on the *Fire Wind*. Half their strength had been maintained, and looking quickly, Michael realized that half of his was gone. The enemy was bearing down from only a league away. Daniel and his ten rams were in the front. Michael realized that they would have to break the enemy on this attack. If the enemy was not turned or held up, the two sides of his own force that had tried to cut across the enemy to the northeast would be astern as the Cornathians ran to the southwest. The two sides would be the hammers, but Daniel and Michael's command ship would have to be the anvil.

"We go straight in!" Michael shouted with a passionate scream.

The men, seized with battle lust, cheered his command and pounded their shields with swords and ax handles and chanted the death songs of their ancestors.

I wonder who he is? Michael thought as he looked across the narrowing gap. Even as he pondered, the bowchasers of the Cornathians opened up and swept the ice before him.

The fury of the first attack had come with blinding speed. At first he was so taken by the sheer audacity of the rockets that he had little time to notice the host of sails bearing down in a deadly arc. The crew had been near to panic for several minutes, but then a curious calm settled over them as they realized that the ships were just small cutters, with the most bizarre coloring of sail. Some of the men started to laugh and shouted to be turned about and led to the attack.

Their tone soon changed. The Mathinians had come on with deadly purpose, maneuvering in groups of five and twenty-five. Conneachson took command of the fleet, as was proper in battle, and Peter stood upon the bowsprit to watch the action, which unfolded with stunning speed. The cutters came on, and the crew no longer laughed as they realized that the small ships had one purpose only—ramming. The hundred rams of the northern attack group slammed into the fleet of Cornath with deadly effect, and Peter stood horrified as a cruiser crumpled under the simultaneous impact of three double-hulled rams.

The losses were severe—two cruisers, half a dozen frigates, and a transport within the first hour. The Heretic had shattered the conventional way. Equally shattering was the fury of the attack. Peter could see crews unflinchingly pilot their rams home as shouts of defiance left their lips. They weren't afraid to die. They were just as religiously fanatical as any Cornathian pilot.

With a cold fascination he watched the battle unfold as the wreckage swept past. The ice was littered with the dead and dying, and still the groups of five swept in, smashing and tearing at the edges of the fleet. He could see that they were starting to reform and Peter knew that the morale of the enemy was just too strong. They would shatter themselves as long as in so doing they could bring the Church down.

After this, then what? Peter thought. I'll return the loser and Zimri will sacrifice me. If the Heretic wins, then what? Thousands will flock to him—the victor over the Cornathians. What other revolutions will that start?

And one thought froze deeper than any heresy.

"Balor," Peter whispered softly.

Peter turned and ran down the deck of the ship, Conneachson following. Reaching the stern, Peter looked back through the showers of ice and spray kicked up by the ship.

"If we continue, I think we can shake our way free!" Conneachson shouted.

Peter ignored him.

"There they go again!" Another series of rockets rose from the schooner riding astern, and within seconds a series of answering rockets rose up from the starboard fleet.

"The rockets are command signals," Peter said.

"Yes, I would think so. Such heresy, though."

"To hell with that for now!" Peter shouted, and his arm swung out pointing to the heavy schooner a league astern.

"That is where the Heretic is!" Peter shouted. "And that is where we should be!"

"But Peter, he's beaten us. We should regroup, and then try the next passage. With a swift move we could—"

"There won't be another chance. Is there any way we can signal our ram pilots?"

"You ordered them launched," Conneachson said coldly. "They're gone now."

"Then we'll have to go in ourselves."

"What? Are you mad?"

"I want the Heretic," Peter said icily. "I want him dead."

"We're lucky we aren't dead ourselves."

"We will be anyhow, even if we escape," Peter shouted. "What do you think will happen to you and me when we return? But if we get him, perhaps we can still turn it around."

Conneachson looked at Peter as if he were mad.

"Damn you, can't you see?" Peter shouted. "He's fighting with a new set of rules. But if we kill him, most likely his followers will run away. We might still win. It's our only hope. We win or we die here! Because if not, we'll be dead anyhow."

Conneachson looked at Peter. The archdeacon stood off to one side, and Peter made a subtle gesture with his hand. If Conneachson defied him, he would be dead in five seconds. She was a Morian ship and Peter could at least control her.

Conneachson looked over Peter's shoulder to the enemy command ship. Another series of rockets leaped skyward.

"Prepare to come about, all ships to come about!" he shouted.

"Signal men, order our fleet to make for the enemy schooner with the rockets."

"But there are no signal flags for that," the signal officer protested.

"Saints damn it," Conneachson shouted. "Then spell it out to them. Put our ship around, the others will follow."

"Deck ho!" came the cry from above. "The enemy cruiser and frigates are coming up from the south by southeast."

"To hell with them now," Conneachson shouted.

"Helm a lee!"

"Helm a lee," came the response, and the cruiser heeled over as she ran into the eye of the wind and then came about onto her new tack.

"They're coming straight on," Seth said evenly. "Michael, we should come about."

"And run?" Michael said, turning on Seth. "Didn't you see them back there? Didn't you see them die shouting my name? No, I'll not run."

"But Michael, we're the command vessel. Lose this and the fleet comes apart. The battle is still not won."

"I hold to my course. We go in with the gold rams. Signalman, order general attack."

The rockets flew and Michael watched in grim fascination as the two sides of the trap swung in on a collision course.

The bowchasers popped off, their shot hummed overhead and bounded across the ice with little effect. The range closed. A gust of wind pushed the closing speed of the fleets to a hundred miles an hour.

The rams were pushing far ahead of the *Fire Wind*. One of the enemy frigates turned broadside to avoid a ram, but almost immediately two others, crews aboard, buried themselves in her side. The ship's powder magazine touched off.

The battle seemed to happen with a speed that defied the power of men to observe. Only brief snatches would be held by the mind—a ram tumbling across the ice, her crew trapped in the rigging; a bit of sail fluttering past; a headless corpse pumping great gouts of blood; shouts, yells, curses, and the screams of the dying.

The fleet closed. The golden rams of Daniel disappeared in a thundering roar of battle, while the two flanks of the enemy were stoved in by the attack of almost a hundred rams pressing in with every inch of canvas.

Michael didn't even see that as the fury of battle swept over him. He shouted with fierce and savage joy as one of the light frigates of the enemy swept through his forward rams and skirted before the bow of his schooner. A thundering volley echoed out, and with a shattering crack the foretopmast above Michael snapped clean off from an eighteen-pound shot. The stays snapped from the strain, cutting men down like a sickle. The frigate shot past, her men shouting curses and raining down a volley of arrows and bolts that slammed into the deck around Michael's feet. From behind the frigate came the image of death.

It was the command battle cruiser of the Cornathian fleet—the largest vessel Michael had ever seen—and it was bearing straight down upon him from less than a half-mile away. In front of the cruiser rode three rams, while a half-dozen of Michael's rams swung in from either side to attempt a kill.

Several crews released, and Michael watched as their sleds
dropped astern. Two enemy rams, riding in front of the cruiser,
decided for its defense and swung before Michael's attack. In
an instant the four rams collided at a hundred and fifty miles
an hour. Tons of wood, steel, sail, and human bodies were
telescoped into one convulsive wreck. Four Mathinian rams
pressed on. The enemy cruiser jinked and weaved. The rams
followed doggedly, then in a blinding instant they were past.
Three had missed completely, the fourth struck a glancing blow
off the starboard outrigger—which didn't catch. The ram slid
past the runner, lost control, and flipped.

Death was racing down on Michael Ormson. Seth held the
helm and Michael let him be the judge of their fate.

Two hundred yards. A hundred yards. The cruiser was not
turning!

Seth spun the wheel hard over, and the *Fire Wind* rose up
upon her larboard outriggers as she turned violently, the men
not having time to trim the sails in response to the wheel.

The cruiser roared past them, her guns trying to bear their
shots. For the most part the shots went wide. The great craft
edged in, ramming the port outriggers with her own damaged
starboard bracings.

The *Fire Wind* rose up and tottered as men and gear flew
across the deck. With a crack like a thunderbolt the mizzenmast
split from the force of the impact and tumbled down across the
deck and the larboard bulkheads. Seth grimly fought the tiller
to hold the ship on its course.

Michael closed his eyes and waited, but he wasn't prepared
for the bone-smashing impact that came. After riding for a
quarter mile on her starboard runners, the *Fire Wind* smashed
back down upon the ice. She had survived the glancing blow
of the cruiser, but had been destroyed nevertheless. The vio-
lence of the impact upon her rightening was so severe that the
runners and outriggers collapsed under the stress.

A howl filled the air as the disintegrating wood ground
against the Frozen Sea. Mass, sails, and rigging tumbled down,
crushing the crew below.

Explosions rent the air as hundreds of signal rockets went

up, tearing off the stern of the schooner. A cheer went up from the Cornathians and the battle wavered.

He crawled from under the outer jib. The deck was a nightmare of confusion, yet within seconds several dozen forms were climbing from the wreckage. The *Fire Wind* was still making some headway under her own momentum, leaving a wake of wreckage behind.

Seth crawled from beneath the smashed wheel, a trickle of blood flowing from his swollen mouth where he had hit his face against the wheel.

"Any rockets left?" Michael shouted, as he made his way over the sprawling wreckage.

Though the stern was in flames, a Companion ran into the fire and retrieved a box of rockets. As he jumped from the fire several others threw a sail over him to smother his flaming parka.

"They're whites," Rafe shouted.

"I don't care! Just send three up, and then three more. I think the fleet will understand."

The rockets climbed heavenward and burst, and a cheer rose from a thousand throats. He was alive.

The rockets set in motion the final act of the drama. The collision of the fleets had been deadly. For several miles around, Michael could see the flaming wreckage of dozens of craft. Not a half-mile away the enemy flagship had fallen victim to two rams, which struck broadside after a head-on blow had jammed her steering. The transports had taken a terrible beating, and the cries of thousands of men could be heard as they lay scattered over the ice or trapped in flaming hulls. Ten thousand tragedies were unfolding across five hundred square miles of ice, but for the moment Michael did not see it as he busied himself with those around him. Almost half of his surviving crew had been killed or wounded in the last attack. One man, old enough to be his grandfather, had been crushed beneath the shattered mainmast, and Michael held his hand as he softly cried away the last minutes of his life.

"Michael."

Michael turned to find Seth and the few surviving Companions behind him. Michael looked, and then he turned back to the old man.

"You better come."

Michael didn't turn from the old man.

"Go Michael," he groaned, "ye can't help me now."

"Go to sleep, Father. Go to sleep and free yourself."

The old man trembled, and was gone.

Michael rose and looked over the shattered rail of his command ship.

"They're coming back," Seth said, and his handless arm pointed to the southeast.

From out of the smoke of battle the ghostlike image of another cruiser loomed. In a minute it would be upon them. From over the wrecked side of the Cornathian command ship dozens of armed men swarmed out and charged across the ice, waving battleaxes and scimitars, a blue-clad priest in the lead.

"Michael, we can still get clear of the ship."

Michael turned to Seth. "We couldn't get a hundred yards, they would see us and run us down. No, Seth, I think it's over this time — the Cornathians know what they want. If I am to die, it will be here, defending this ship. Go, Seth. And take the others with you."

"No, Michael. I think I'll stay!"

On the cruiser came in its grim fury, her blackened sails like winged messengers of death. This time he would not be afraid. "This time I'll stand upon the shattered forecastle and wait for its coming." He watched with a terrible calm, and his men watched with him.

A half-mile. A quarter mile. Then, surprisingly, the bow-chasers opened up, their shot winging overhead and to the right. Puzzled, Michael turned to follow their trajectory.

"Ishmael!" he shouted.

The *Black Revenge* roared past the crippled *Fire Wind*, not a dozen feet clearing her starboard outriggers. Michael could clearly see Ishmael at the tiller. Except for a handful of men standing behind the helmsman, her decks were ominously empty. Alone, unseeing, stood Ishmael, looking straight ahead, his personal guards and warriors behind him, axes drawn, grim and silent.

The ship roared past, and not a hundred yards away the drama ended. The two mighty cruisers, the aging ship of Mathin and the last cruiser of the enemy, met head on. The impact lifted the vessels clear of the ice. The oaken bow of the Cornathian vessel sliced through the decaying wood of the Mathinian. The *Black Revenge* started to lean onto its side, and the two merged into one as they tumbled and rolled across the ice. The debris showering down crushed most of the Cornathians running on the ice. The two ships were ripped by explosions. And with the roar of battle in the distance, Michael watched as fragments fell around him. He experienced a blind numbness as the two ships burst into flames — the pyre of half a thousand men. He watched in awed silence as the sound of battle slowly drifted away.

CHAPTER 20

HE AWOKE WITH A TERRIFYING SCREAM: "ISHMAEL!"
The memory flooded back and a tremor swept through him.
Locked in his mind was the horror of the two fleets as they
clashed during the last moments of combat—the wreckage of
the two ice cruisers burning fiercely, the roar of battle that
surrounded them, and the pitiful screams of the few who had
survived their brief engagement.

After the destruction of the last Cornathian ice cruiser, resistance soon crumbled. A Cornathian light frigate and several
schooners managed to escape, but the transports and remaining
merchantmen struck their colors. In numbed shock Michael
watched as the battle died. But the screams, the screams of the
dying tore at him, and even in his sleep he could not escape.

He rose stiffly and walked out of his small cabin in the stern
of Zardok's ship. A Companion guarded the door, his uniform
scorched and bloodied.

"Rafe?"

"No, Michael, it's Balthwin. Rafe is dead. Don't you remember?"

"Yes," Michael said absently, and he made his way topside.

It was almost dawn. The eastern sky was showing its colors, but the ice around the *Wind Sweeper* was ablaze in light. A great circle of fires had been built around the ship from the wreckage of the frigate that had crushed Ormath's fort. Michael looked out and saw that many were already awake, and as they recognized him a great cheer rose. From the ships that were parked in a great circle around the *Wind Sweeper*, the cheer was picked up, and within seconds men were swinging off the sides of the ships to slip and slide across the ice.

They came and formed up beneath him and cheered wildly. "Michael, Michael," the chant started on a slow, primitive tempo that seemed to touch his soul. He looked out over their upturned faces, and from them to the Arch overhead. He somehow knew it would happen—and it did. Another Saint fell from the sky, a great light swept from the south to the north and all looked up at it and fell silent. They looked back from it to him, and then the cheering swelled. He was the Leader, the Promised One, and they knew it. They knew it, and now so did he.

"It was a terrible price," Michael said slowly, "but it had to be paid. A hundred and thirty-one rams lost, sixty-three crews, ninety-five pilots, seven command ships, two merchantmen, a frigate, and of course the *Black Revenge*. Almost six hundred men dead or dying, and again that many wounded. Seth, it was a terrible price."

"It would have been far worse, Michael, if *they* had won."

It *was* necessary, Michael thought, and every man had volunteered, but still . . . He looked at the personnel roster and his gaze swept over the names.

Ishmael, Ormath; Olin dead from a ram; Rafe, young Andrew, two other nephews of Zardok, and twenty-five Companions.

"What did we take?" Michael asked evenly, as he turned to Zardok.

His old friend's eyes were hollow and red, from lack of sleep and the terrible mourning that had swept over him with the death of three nephews in one day.

"We've captured nine transport merchantmen, a frigate, two cutters, and half a dozen schooners. Two other frigates can perhaps be salvaged, along with a cruiser."

"How many prisoners, Daniel?"

"Close to three thousand."

Daniel's adventures had, for once, been enough to satisfy him completely. His squadron had taken out the command cruiser, damaged a second, and had shared a kill in a third. He had fought and cursed his way from one end of the battle to the next. Half his crew had been swept away, but as usual the big berserker had come away unscratched.

"Well, I would assume that all is ready then."

"The ships have been stocked, Michael, and all is ready."

"Then let's take care of it."

They were drawn up on the Ice, the three thousand prisoners, and around them stood a ring of guards armed with axes and crossbows. Michael climbed to the bowsprit of his new command ship and looked out over the vanquished in the tradition as old as war—the defeated awaiting the decision of the victors. For several long minutes his gaze swept them, and he pulled back his hood and removed his goggles so that all might see him clearly.

"Men of Cornath," he shouted. And except for some muffled comments, they fell silent. "Men of Cornath, yesterday upon this Ice you were defeated. A defeat unlike any since the loss of the Garden. As the vanquished, you know the fate that tradition demands. For the priest, death; for you, exile and slavery. I now make an offer to you. You may choose this fate or you may swear allegiance to me."

He was greeted with silence.

"You have but to step forward and swear an oath unto me, and you will be free, to serve as the guards of those who refuse."

A low murmur arose, and after several minutes fifteen or twenty men stepped forward, to the jeers and threats of their comrades.

Michael looked at them coldly. "If I now order you to kill the men behind you, would you carry out that command?"

"We would!" shouted a gangly man with a hawklike visage.

Michael turned and motioned to Daniel. "Take them," he shouted, "and bind them. They are to be handed over to their own people, to let them decide the fate of traitors."

Several of the men broke and ran, but arrows brought them down, and the rest were led away to what would be almost certain death.

"Men of Cornath, remember what you saw here today. I too was a Cornathian. It is true that I have led this war, but not at my choosing. Rather, by the attack of your priests. I wish no traitors to join me, for in their way they would betray me and my cause as well.

"Men of Cornath, yesterday a New Age was born upon the Ice. Free men, without priests or church, threw over the tyranny of Mor and all the other brotherhoods. You call me the Heretic, and yet always remember the heretic, a nonbeliever, today set you free."

A murmur arose from the crowd. They had expected death or torture, and he was telling them they might live.

"Those of you who oppose me still, I command that you be fifty leagues north of here by this time tomorrow. We have stocked and provided enough transports to see all of you home if need be, and will give you a frigate as well, for protection. Those who wish to stay as friends and those who desire nothing from either me or Cornath are free to stay. Those of you who leave may return with your families or friends at any time to Mathin, where you will be welcome."

Michael looked out over them and saw the confusion. He waited for several minutes, until they had fallen silent, and then he continued.

"Some have said that I am the Messenger of God. I have never laid such claims—those are the words of others, not mine. I only claim that all men can work together to return the Garden by their own hands. We can explore the world, unlock the secrets of the past, and bring about a rebirth of thought by allowing a man the freedom to think and believe as he wishes. Look into your hearts, men of Cornath, and you'll see this to be true. Yesterday we defied all holy law and shattered your fleet in three hours. If what your priests said were true, we should have been stricken dead.

"Many have called me the Prophet, the Promised One, and perhaps it is true that I am the fulfillment of prophecies. For I say that the time of darkness has passed. With me you shall see the falling of the churches, and from that the new light that shall sweep the world. Men of Cornath, I give you your freedom to live as you choose."

He turned and went below deck, and to his surprise he heard a scattering of cheers.

He walked down the length of the torn ship to his cabin, contemplating what would come next. Daniel stood by the door and Michael came up to him.

"Did he say anything?" Michael asked.

"He said he would speak only to you. Pleasant enough fellow, but such hatred in his eyes—enough to freeze one to death."

Michael pushed the door open and stepped in.

Peter was looking from the stern window and turned to the sound of the door.

"You?" he said.

Michael stopped and looked closely for several seconds. Peter of Dulyn? He remembered Rifton's description of him.

"So," Peter said softly, "Michael Ormson is the Prophet. Won't Rifton be surprised." Michael's deadly look of icy scorn told Peter he was on dangerous ground.

"Zimri's secretary, I must assume? And religious protector of the attacking fleet?"

Peter nodded.

"I must compliment you on the handling of your fleet. You gave us quite a run there for a while, it could have been a near thing. Tell me, why did you order your fleet back in?"

"To kill you," Peter said without a hint of emotion.

"I see. Of course, I believe I would have done the same."

"We'll be back," Peter said. "We'll be back in the thousands, until either you are dead or we are dead. The two of us cannot exist side by side."

"I know," Michael said sadly.

"So why did you release those men out there? Most of them are true Churchmen, or are you so idealistic that you think they'll all come to you? Michael, in their superstition they think you are the Devil plotting."

"I know," Michael answered. "I'll let the priests go too; in fact, I'm even letting you go."

Peter didn't betray any reaction. Until the door opened he believed himself a dead man.

"Why?"

"Because every one of those men who returns will tell another of what happened here. The fact that the Church can be beaten. That alone is worth the sacrifice of a few transports and a frigate. Your priests will be the same—how many of them are doubting now? Besides, I don't need to kill you. I think Zimri will arrange that easily enough."

Peter looked into Michael's eyes. He could read cold satisfaction there. He knows I'll denounce Zimri upon my return, Peter thought.

"Anyhow," Michael said, "I'm telling all the men of your little betrayal of them before they sail. The fact that Zimri sent a message to us to warn of your approach."

"Very well planned," Peter said coldly. "Of course, if you do that I'll have to inform them of your relationship to a certain archbishop of the Church."

"Then I guess we'll destroy both sides in the process, won't we?" Michael responded as he turned from Peter and walked over to the stern window. "It would leak out anyhow," Michael said.

"I'm not sure of that. So far I'm the only one who knows for sure. It might be another year before it was confirmed, and in that time your uncle would get the Throne and you could strike a deal with him."

"Why are you telling me this?"

"Zimri left me hanging out here, and he'll try to stick me with the blame when I get back."

"Then why don't you come over to me?"

"I have my reasons for that, also," Peter said in a chilling voice. Michael knew in his heart why Rifton had turned. He had turned because he still loved Michael, but his love of the Church was stronger. If he struck at Michael then for some reason Michael must be dangerously close to the very underpinnings of the Church. Perhaps Rifton could be reached if he held the Holy Chair.

"Do you realize what you've started, Michael Ormson?"

"A revolution of thought, that many would say was preordained," Michael replied.

"You know that you've shattered every preconceived concept of war upon the Ice."

"Your master set me a problem that I couldn't win conventionally; therefore, I had to create a new set of rules. I thank Zimri for that—it was the key to unlocking all that is now going to happen."

"What is that?" Peter said, trying to control his voice.

"What you've seen is the beginning. The ice cruiser, the symbol of power of the Church, has been replaced. Why not other things as well? What of the Dead Lands, for instance. Or the Flowing Seas—we could go there. With Mathin the people will be free to choose their beliefs, and their thoughts, as well."

"Michael, it will destroy you."

"Perhaps, but it will also destroy the churches."

"Have we really been all that evil?"

"Yes."

"Michael, you are the true evil of the world. You can destroy us all. You could be the Bringer of Darkness, for you are the first in generations to defy the Prime Choosing."

"The what?"

"Michael, what do we believe of the Arch?"

As if by rote, Michael repeated what he had been taught when still a child at his mother's side. "The Sacred Arch is the symbol that God set over us when he removed the Light of Night. The Father set this over us as His Sign in the Heaven that would forever show man his sin."

"Very nice, Michael, I'm glad you still remember."

"What are you driving at?"

"The Church has known all along what the answer is—the

head of each brotherhood, and the fifty sacred ones. The Chosen Few."

Peter walked up to Michael and placed his hand on Michael's shoulder.

"Man created the Arch. Man destroyed the Garden. Man created the Ice. The rest is fable."

"What are you saying?" Michael asked, as if he hadn't really heard Peter's words.

"The heads of all three churches and Inys Gloi know that God had nothing to do with this nightmare world that we live in. Quite simply, man created it himself."

Michael looked into Peter's eyes and slowly read his thoughts and feelings. With a terrifying shock he realized that Peter was speaking the truth.

"Explain," Michael said numbly.

"We aren't sure. Somehow there was a light, an object in the sky. Man reached this light and there tested some device, a machine of great power, to take us even farther. The device exploded and destroyed this sun of the night—from that came the Arch. It was a machine to take men to the lights of the Saints and would travel at unimagined speeds.

"I believe that the hand of God intervened and prevented this. This action had its effects upon the world. Great storms were unleashed, and cities, in fact entire countries, were destroyed. From the records it must have been a terrible thing to behold. Then from the sky came the great storm of fires that the Bible speaks of. Parts of this destroyed world rained down upon the Earth and shattered entire nations, so that all mankind thought it would perish. Finally man in his madness unleashed terrible weapons of unknown power, believed by some to be not unlike the power of the great machine. It is said that within the space of thirty days not one man in a thousand still lived. The shape of the world was changed forever.

"Great changes occurred. The world moved from its path and grew colder, men wrote of not seeing the sun for a thirty-day period at a time. Then came the great cold, and millions more died, and the great seas froze. That was the Before Time. Among the seventy of us who know in the Cornathian Church and the thirty or so in the Ezrian and Sol churches, the debate is strong. Some argue that it was man alone who did this. Zimri for one. Others, like your Rifton, believe that God did act in this, but it was started by the hands of men. All the rest, though, is legend created by the Church.

"The three churches hold many manuscripts from this time, and it is rumored that the fortress of Inys Gloi is a vast storehouse of hidden knowledge."

A thousand questions reeled through Michael's mind.

"The Ezrians?"

"Yes, of course. Both sides know; in fact the two churches have cooperated on this since the beginning."

"Has anyone ever tried to talk?"

"Yes," Peter said thoughtfully. "They don't last long. Why do you think we have the Black Brothers? In fact, I heard you had a visit from one yourself."

Michael looked at him. "How do you know that?"

"I have my ways. Rifton did it because he knew you were on the point of breaking the Prime Choosing."

"And that is what?"

"It is the reason why you will fail eventually. It is the reason for the existence of the churches. At the end of the thousand years of darkness, mankind started to make its first tentative steps out of the night. The old church from the Before Time had survived and had gathered some information, somewhat as it did during a similar period three thousand years ago. Under one Church, now the Cornathian and Inys Gloi, came the few vestiges from the former time. Not much had survived, of course, because the destruction had been almost complete, but it was enough for the high authorities of the Church to gradually piece together the complete story. And from that came the Prime Choosing, which has ruled us for the last thousand years."

Peter turned away from Michael, walked across the room, and reached for a decanter. He poured himself a drink.

"The Church found that man, through his own folly, came to the very edge of extinction. In fact, man had defied all the odds by surviving in this hell-hole of a frozen nightmare. The Church decided never to let it happen again. We decided to make the legends fact, to teach the fact as doctrine, and to bury the truth so deeply that it would never be known. All progress was to stop for a thousand years, ten thousand if need be, until man matured, until he reached the point where he could handle the power that had once almost destroyed him.

"The Church would become the custodian of knowledge, and the knowledge would be held only by the Inner Council of the Church. That position would be conferred upon those who reached the archbishopric. All knowledge would be held by fewer than a hundred souls, until all had one day agreed that man could hold the power safely."

Peter drained his glass with a single gulp, then refilled it.

"The Church split over some petty doctrinal points after five hundred years of united rule. It was a split led mainly by the middle level, who knew nothing of the inner secret. In fact, some soon realized that this was all for the good because the petty wars would keep the people occupied. A few thousand dead a year, an enemy to fear—as long as the Prime Choosing was never violated.

"All areas in which knowledge could be advanced fell under the control of the churches. Your own order, for charts, navigation, and star-watching was a particularly difficult one to control. Observation of the night skies would counter Church doctrine on occasion. My order, of course, was even harder; Mor was originally metalworking and alchemy. The secret of powder and guns was slipped out, and before it could be stopped, it was too late.

"So, for the last thousand years we have faced this. The churches have controlled, men have died, but we have adapted more and more to our Ice world. The Garden can return when the day comes for the Church to share its secrets with a new Man, capable of using the information wisely. Michael, this is why you must turn back—that, or you'll be crushed. What is more, you will in the end kill hundreds of thousands. And one day, perhaps, destroy man as well. Michael, you are not the Bringer of Life. In fact, you are the Bringer of Death."

"How does Inys Gloi fit into this?"

"Ah, now that is an interesting question, Michael. During

the Council of the First Choosing, the Brotherhood of Inys Gloi severed itself from the Church and retreated to their island stronghold. We know they have agents in our ranks, and we believe that for the last thousand years they have plotted either to break the First Choice or to seize control of our brotherhoods. We pay them tribute when necessary, in order to prevent assassination, but beyond that I know nothing."

"How do you know all of this," Michael asked, "if the information is such a secret?"

Peter looked at Michael and poured himself another drink.

"I was told," he said wearily, "by Balor, head of the fifty scholars who keep the Records of the Ancients. He told me in the hour before I sailed, and he let it be known that if I ever told anyone but you, the Black Brothers would have me dead. The Black Brothers are the enforcers of the Prime Choosing."

"But why did he tell you?"

"He told me to show me the folly of letting you live, and what could happen if Zimri's plan was followed. Michael, you are too dangerous to the Church. You demonstrated that yesterday by destroying all tradition and ritual in battle. Michael, you are starting to knock the universe off the balance it has maintained for a thousand years. The Ice will be thrown into a convulsive war that will not end until we have totally destroyed ourselves.

"That is why Balor told me this, and I believe him. You have opened the book, and the Devil of Knowledge is even now springing forth to destroy us."

"What do you propose that I do, then?"

"Stop where you are. The changes that you've wrought have been seen by too many already—for that alone the Black Brothers will hunt you to the grave. The first one failed, but there will be others. Stop now, Michael. For the sake of mankind, don't let any more change occur."

They sat in a silence that seemed to stretch into eternity. From outside came the muffled shouts of the Cornathians as they made their decisions. The prediction of Peter was right on that point—the majority turned away from Michael's offer, as a trap of the Devil.

"No." Michael finally shattered the silence.

It was a voice of the deepest conviction, and Peter knew the decision was final, yet he tried once more. "Michael, you don't realize what you are doing."

"Damn you, I do!" Michael shouted.

"Answer me this: did Zimri truly think of the Prime Choosing when he came after me? Did he really think of the policy laid down a thousand years ago?"

Peter was silent.

"No, it was power that he desired. Perhaps man is doomed to make the same mistake again, but if so, let him make the decision himself. You've treated us as if we were mindless sheep, incapable of making our own decisions. You hand us the set formula and allow us no thought other than yours. Damn you, I won't do it!

"Perhaps the original fathers thought only of man, but like any power, the prime concern is now not the original purpose but merely the continuation of the power already held and the expansion of that power. Even after the need is gone, the power or persons who control it will continue to grasp and to hold— even if by so doing they destroy that which they once fought to preserve. No, Peter, I will not stop. I am giving back to man his right to question, the right to think, the right to be a man."

Peter pushed aside the glass that he had been holding and rose from the table. "I think I shall rejoin my brothers now," he said softly. "It shall soon be time for the evening prayers."

Bowing with a curt nod of his head, Peter started to make his way to the door. He stared at it for several seconds, and without turning he quietly asked, "Will you tell anyone of what was said here today?"

Peter turned and looked at him. He has Rifton's eyes, he thought. So much like his uncle. Poor Zimri. Had he never made an issue of Ormson, Michael eventually would have taken his uncle's chair, and perhaps one day the Holy See. Zimri would have held his power and died with honor in the brotherhood, and all would have been as planned. Such a strange twisting of fate. Peter smiled cynically, the word fate was almost on his lips.

Michael could almost read the thoughts flashing across Peter's mind.

"No, I won't tell them. At least nothing about you. You see, I need you to take care of Zimri. If your knowledge of this was known, the Black Brothers would hunt you, as well. Remember that, Peter."

"But will you tell anyone of it?"

Michael thought on this and smiled. "To what purpose?" he said softly. "The brothers would come on me with a vengeance, and besides, who would believe me?" He smiled bemusedly.

Peter smiled as well. He knew that to be true. The power of the Prophecies was the power of Michael with the common people. The Prophecies were rooted in Church legend as much as Peter's own power.

"Someday, Michael Ormson, the Heretic, this thing you have started will sweep you up in its power and destroy you. On that day remember my words. At that moment, my friend, I shall be there to watch your passing. Farewell, Michael of Mathin."

"Farewell, Peter of Mor."

And Peter was gone.

The shadows lengthened, and soon the Ice was a shimmering mirror of glowing red as the last light of day faded. In the distance he could hear Peter leading the evening prayers of the priests of Cornath. The rest of the Cornathians were gone, and already fifty leagues to the north. Tomorrow at sunset he would release the priests. Two thousand men would return to Cornath to tell of what had occurred and the might of this new Prophet of a New Age.

He listened as the prayers were chanted. The *Te Deum* rose up, the prayer of two thousand years, and in almost the same words from two thousand years before that.

He listened, and his lips moved to the words, "And deliver us out of darkness and guide us to the everlasting light. Amen."

CHAPTER 21

THE ICE WAS STARTING TO BREAK UP. FOR THE LAST WEEK
Mathin had echoed to the booming and roaring of the great
plain, as it shifted and moved. The battlements had been abandoned and the guns hauled into the warehouses, where they
were oiled and packed for next year. Spring had come early
that year, and many regarded it as a good sign, not only for
the crops, but for other things as well. Even Daniel had seemed
light of heart and acted in a rather unusual way that had puzzled
Michael until Janis confided that Daniel would soon be married.
The girl's father had even offered Daniel a partnership in his
business, which Daniel had refused since he knew that Michael
had need of him. He wondered what other arguments the father
had offered, but from the sight of the girl it seemed that she had
arguments enough of her own. If it was a boy, Janis said,
Daniel would name him after Michael. Michael had laughed
long and hard at the news. So there would be a wedding this
spring, one of many in Mathin, for the thousand men who
had come back with him, rather than return to Cornath, had
found the city to be to their liking. Michael hoped that the girl
could convince Daniel to bathe for the wedding.

Michael made his way along the path to the Grove. Here and there the ground was already bare, with grass and flowers springing up—their greens and bright yellows shining out boldly against the last snows of spring.

He walked through the Grove. Soon they would gather here again to talk and to dream, and he smiled at the thought. Perhaps it can be as it was, he wished. And yet he realized that it would never be the same again. The world had crowded in upon him at last, and that quiet happiness of the first days was gone forever.

The city had grown with the winter. Already over a hundred new cabins and huts had been built beyond the city wall, most of them rude shelters thrown up by the Cornathians but some belonging to men of the Southward Isles who had heard of this new master and had come to serve him.

From Cornath there had been little word. Rumor had it that Zimri had been denounced and that a rebellion of some monks had occurred. One report stated that Zimri had even resigned. Just before the break in the ice, a final word told of the death of the Holy See—by poison, it was said. Then all news had ceased.

Michael stood in the Grove and looked to the north; then, smiling softly, he turned away. Their problems were, for now at least, removed from him. The empires are collapsing, he thought, by their own dead weight of a thousand years, and we shall pick up the pieces. They will hold on for a while longer, yet they cannot face the New Age which I am bringing.

A dull boom rolled across the Ice. It grew in its intensity, and from the south Michael could see a great crack that ran across the Frozen Sea. Louder than any cannon shot, the boom echoed and thundered as the Ice finally broke. Michael stood in silence and watched. Before the week passed, the sea would be clear.

The plans of last winter were already in motion. Seth the missionary was alive with his crusade to spread the word of the New Day across the Southern Isles. With the first flow of spring a dozen ships would put out with Seth's followers.

"We were alone this time," Seth said with a fire in his eyes, "but give us five years, and every one of the Southern Isles shall throw off her old ways and join our side. The churches will collapse under the pressure we shall bring to bear. By Heaven's Master, we shall spread your word throughout the world."

He had stopped arguing with Seth over that one. At the very least it would create the needed alliances for the years to come. No matter what he said, Michael realized that they had created the aura around him. Right or wrong, he was the Promised One.

He never told anyone, save one, about the comments of Peter, for he knew that in some unexplainable way his prophecies were linked to the Church that was being replaced by him. It was a cold decision but it had to be done. Besides, as he had said to Peter, it was so incredible that only a handful would ever really understand.

He had told one person, a person who having seen the dream come true had finally gone to join his long dead daughter and the nephews who had died last fall. The night before Zardok died they had talked, and Michael had told him.

"Michael," Zardok said, "what Peter said has the ring of truth to it. You see, men live their lives in obscure drudgery, yet every now and again something fresh, something shattering, comes and sweeps them up with its power. Occasionally, it is something grand and powerful, like what has started here. More often, it is something terrible that brings desolation and ruin, like the Dark Times that Peter spoke of.

"To the generations that come afterward, our times will seem like something wonderful or terrible, with a power that can make men godlike. So, Michael, the story grows with the telling. As the years pass it becomes even more, until finally the deeds it tells become the work of a God. The Church found this to be true, and in their time chose to conceal it. Yes, Michael, such are the ways of men, to create these legends, and with you, to create the dream of a time to come. Such were the actions of our grandfathers, and of course, my dear Michael, such shall it be with your grandchildren." The old man had smiled.

In the morning Michael found him alone, forever asleep.

He looked out across the Ice, remembering and wondering. He wondered if one day they would even find the answer to the Ice, and set about the task of pushing it back, to return the world to the Garden that was.

Perhaps they will succeed, he thought, and perhaps they would make the mistake of their fathers before them, as Peter said, and destroy what they had. But at least they would have the opportunity to try. No angry god with his legion of saints would stand over them to chastise and punish.

And so his dreams took him far that day, until finally a gentle rustle made him return. He could feel her presence behind him, and turning, he looked into her eyes.

"I knew I would find you here," she said softly.

"Janis, you shouldn't have. The climb—" and he stood up with concern in his eyes.

"Michael, my father didn't raise a fine court lady, to sit and be pampered. I felt like a walk, and pregnant or not, I am taking one."

Michael smiled. "How I wish he could be here to see his grandchild."

Janis nodded her head slowly. It had been a hard winter, and often she had looked at Michael and wondered.

"His time was at an end, love," she said. "He knew it as well as we do now. He died as he wished, upon the Ice, with the last ship of its kind in his hand. It was a good end for him."

"Somehow I feel as if I killed him myself."

Janis shook her head.

"No, Michael, no. Don't ever say that. He died for you, Michael, as he would have died for any of his city if he felt that in so doing they would continue to protect what he loved. Give thanks, Michael, that he passed as he wished."

She embraced him and held him close. He was different now, no longer the young, hurt man standing alone and so much in need of protection. He was the Master. In many ways she had lost him forever; never again would they be alone here, without a fear or a care. The world had thrust itself upon him, and she was no longer all of it, but merely a part of it. For their child it would be even more so, as one day he took the world that his father was now molding for him.

"Come, love," she said softly. "It's getting late. Seth is talking about some meeting to plan for the Companions' going forth, and Daniel said he wants to talk to you—I think, love, it's his wedding, and promise you won't laugh when he tells you."

He looked at her and kissed her; then, together, they made their way down across the fields, which were still lightly covered with the last snows of winter. The city gates were open. From them came the sounds of a town preparing for the coming of spring, preparing for the coming of the light—the new renaissance of man.

About the Author

William R. Forstchen, who makes his home in Maine, was born in 1950. Educated by Benedictine monks, he considered the calling of the priesthood, but decided instead to pursue a career in history. Completing his B.A. in education at Rider College, he went on to do graduate work in the field of counseling psychology.

In 1978 he moved to Maine where he is currently an Instructor of Ancient and Medieval History at Maine Central Institute, Pittsfield, Maine. He also coordinates activities as Director of the Medieval Club, Live Dungeons, and Catapult Team Competitions. Forstchen lives with his wife, Marilyn, and their dog, Ilya Murometz, just outside the town of Waterville, Maine.

His interests include iceboating, Hobie Cat racing, sailing, skiing, pinball machines, Zen philosophy, and Civil War Battle Reinactments as a private in the 20th Maine Volunteer Inf.